THE
RESURRECTION
MURDER CASE

THE RESURRECTION MURDER CASE

Stanley Hart Page

COACHWHIP PUBLICATIONS
GREENVILLE, OHIO

To Grant Williams who inspired this tale by his remarkable achievements as organizer and former head of the Bureau of Missing Persons, Department of Police, New York City, I respectfully dedicate this book.

S. H. P.

The Resurrection Murder Case, by Stanley Hart Page
© 2025 Coachwhip Publications edition
Introduction © 2025 Curtis Evans

First published 1932
Stanley Hart Page, 1902-1979
CoachwhipBooks.com

ISBN 1-61646-622-7
ISBN-13 978-1-61646-622-0

ANOTHER ONE FOR THE PHILO BRIGADE

STANLEY HART PAGE AND THE CHRISTOPHER HAND MYSTERIES

CURTIS EVANS

In 1929 the prestigious firm of Alfred A. Knopf published Dashiell Hammett's tough and violent crime novels *Red Harvest* and *The Dain Curse* (*The Maltese Falcon* would follow the next year), forever altering the face of crime fiction with what reviewers dubbed the "hard-boiled" style. Yet at the very same time that Hammett commenced his great crime sweep, traditionalist American mystery writer S. S. Van Dine (Willard Huntington Wright), whose best-selling Philo Vance detective novels were published by Knopf's rival Scribner's, stood resplendent at the height of his popularity, having also in 1929 produced *The Bishop Murder Case,* the book which proved the most popular and enduring of his mysteries. Although the future of American crime writing might lie with the tough guys, what Hammett's Sam Spade or the Continental Op might have termed the "pantywaist" genteel amateur detectives were hardly down for the count. Indeed, that very same year Frederic Dannay and Manfred Lee, the two New York cousins who wrote as Ellery Queen, introduced, in *The Roman Hat Mystery,* a monocled amateur detective named, appropriately enough, Ellery Queen, a gentleman who in his studied affectations shared considerable affinity with Philo Vance, particularly in his early years in print. Five years later, Rex Stout's obese, orchid-loving eccentric genius,

Nero Wolfe, would make his first of many fictional appearances in the detective novel *Fer de Lance*. In between those epochal events in American mystery genre history, myriad Philo Vance wannabes made brief their own brief struts on the crime fiction stage. One member of this troop of toff tecs was Christopher Hand, who between 1932 and 1935 appeared in a quintet of novels by forgotten American mystery writer Stanley Hart Page.

Stanley Hart Page, who, ironically enough likely was distantly related to native Marylander Samuel Dashiell Hammett through mutual Dashiell ancestors of French Huguenot lineage, was born in prosperous circumstances in Chatham, New Jersey, on March 10, 1902, to Laurence Stanley Page and his wife Emma F. Jowett. Stanley's colorful entrepreneurial paternal grandfather was self-made millionaire coal tar king George Shephard Page (1838-1892), originally of Reading, Maine, and Chelsea, Massachusetts. Upon his death at the age of fifty-four George Page, the renowned "millionaire chemist" who was then an inmate of the New Jersey State Insane Asylum ("his mind was broken down by the worry introduced by a severe attack of the grippe" according to the newspapers), bequeathed to his four sons and one daughter the substantial fortune (about thirty-five million dollars in modern worth) which he had accumulated through his various business ventures, the best known of which today is the Vapo-Cresolene Company. This profitable enterprise with great success marketed Vapo-Cresolene, a therapeutic vaporizer used in the United States during the late nineteenth and early twentieth centuries in the hope of providing lasting relief to sufferers from such ailments as asthma, bronchitis, croup, whooping cough and diphtheria, despite the fact that the American Medical Association reported with dry derision in 1908 that "Vapo-Cresolene is a member of that

Stanley Hart Page

class of proprietaries in which an ordinary product is endowed, by the manufacturer, with extraordinary virtues."

Perhaps to salve his moral conscience George before his breakdown became a great advocate of both alcohol temperance, founding the New Jersey Temperance Association, and of universal free public-school education. He also founded Chatham's Stanley Congregational Church. After his death, Page's own rather more fortunate offspring inherited from the family patriarch his highly profitable, if arguably somewhat dubious, patent medicine business, over which they maintained firm control, with Stanley's uncle Albion Lambert Page serving as president, his uncle Henry de Bacon Page serving as vice president, and his own father, the aforementioned Laurence Stanley Page, serving as secretary. All three men additionally served as directors of the company, the remaining two of whom were Stanley's youngest uncle, Raymond Page, and his aunt, Florence Page.[1]

With a family fortune behind him, Stanley Hart Page might simply have lived a dilettante life, like the fictional Philo Vance, Albert Campion and Lord Peter Wimsey, taking a sinecure job from the firm; yet he went to work, rather, as the manager of the Montclair bureau of the *Newark Evening News* (then New Jersey's newspaper of record), after attending the Pawling and Peddie prep schools and Brown University and taking a token vagabond year out west employed as a cowboy and farm-hand. Yet in 1930, as he approached the age of thirty, he was still single and living under his parents' spacious roof in Chatham, New Jersey, the 64th wealthiest inhabitation in the United States in 2018, according to *Bloomberg News*. However, the next year he got himself an apartment in nearby Short Hills, where he found time—having been "[s]ince his boyhood . . . absorbed with mysteries and fictional detectives"—to write a pair of detective novels, *Sinister Cargo* and *The*

Resurrection Murder Case, which he successfully placed with none other than Alfred A. Knopf's Borzoi Books imprint.

Knopf evidently was on the hunt for another Philo Vance, judging from the back flap blurb description of Page's book, which boldly, if perhaps a bit precipitately, proclaimed that the author's sophisticated dilettante sculptor and amateur criminologist, Christopher Hand, already belonged in the pantheon of Great Detectives:

> We nominate Mr. Christopher Hand for a place in that distinguished company of detectives whose work has thrilled so many readers of crime fiction in both England and America. His ability as a forger, his utter disregard of such ordinary necessities as food and sleep, the fact that he is a dilettante of the arts and sciences, and his uncompromising persistence, make him worthy in every way to stand behind those masters—Sherlock Holmes, Philo Vance, Lord Peter Wimsey, Father Brown, Hanaud, Poirot, Dr. Thorndyke, Charlie Chan, Reggie Fortune and [Knopf's own] Sam Spade.

Certainly Knopf was no wallflower when it came to boosting its detective fiction to the American mystery-reading public. Beginning in 1919, the publishing firm had launched a hugely successful effort to boost the middling mainstream English novelist J. S. Fletcher as the greatest British mystery writer since Arthur Conan Doyle. In this aggressive commercial campaign Knopf made great use of the fact that President Woodrow Wilson had read Fletcher's detective novel *The Middle Temple Murder* (1919) and expressed his enjoyment of the tale.

"PRESIDENT WILSON HAS BEEN READING THE
MIDDLE TEMPLE MURDER A Fine Detective Story by
J. S. Fletcher," boasted Knopf's advertising in the November 22, 1919, issue of *The Publishers' Weekly*. Knopf made
a similar effort with Stanley Page's Christopher Hand mysteries, though nothing was said on their part about the admitted detective fiction predilections of President Herbert
Hoover, who was highly unpopular as the nation staggered
through its third year of crushing economic depression.

Knopf, which published Page's first three Christopher
Hand mysteries (*Sinister Cargo*, 1932, *The Resurrection
Murder Case*, 1932, and *Fool's Gold*, 1933), excelled itself
in the production design of the books, with each volume
in the series having a striking dust jacket and an appealing
uniform board design of serpentine lines. *Cargo* had dark
green lines on a lighter green background, *Resurrection*
blue lines on an orange-brown background and *Gold*, the
fanciest of all, red lines on a faux gold leaf background.
The jacket to *The Resurrection Murder Case* in particular is
memorably ghoulish, but all three jackets are fine indeed.

Sinister Cargo, about endangered New York financier
Robert Garrison and his retired stage musical actress
spouse, begins with a miraculous country house murder
and goes to some very queer corners indeed, was praised
by Isaac Anderson in the *New York Times Book Review*, who
in his notice avowed: "This story offers a continuous succession of thrills . . . . Christopher Hand has methods of
his own. Sometimes they are more than a bit high-handed,
and sometimes they are without the law, but they get results. This is Mr. Page's first detective story, but we gather that he intends to give us more stories of the exploits
of Christopher Hand. We'll be waiting." In the *Saturday
Review* William C. Weber was equally enthusiastic, writing,
in a notice which made the book sound more like a Doyle

Sherlock Holmes or Hammett Continental Op novel: ". . . the story does stand up. . . . There are two picturesque villains named Spitz and Spawn, a variety of successful and unsuccessful attempts to kill a wealthy New Yorker and his friends, and a pitched battle finale on a little island off the Maine coast. . . ."

Sinister Cargo's weird and colorful climax on a "haunted" Maine island at times seems like an anticipation of John Carpenter's classic ghostly fright film *The Fog* (1980). For this final section of the tale the author drew on the "many summers he had spent with his family on the coast of Maine." The narrative is punctuated by a series of wild criminal episodes which sometimes savor of pulp fiction, with Christopher Hand's slavishly loyal chronicler, Ralph Clark, getting more pieces of the action, as it were, than Philo Vance's poor pale shadow Van ever did. As in Doyle's *The Hound of the Baskervilles,* Hand is absent from a substantial chunk of the narrative but returns to the scene to elucidate all of the remaining mysteries. Despite their social standing Christopher Hand and Clark prove something more of men of action than the cerebral Philo

Cover courtesy Curtis Evans

Vance and Van, at least until the late Van Dine's late Vance detective tale *The Kidnap Murder Case* (1936). The body count in the novel ends up rather high indeed.

Upon the appearance of Page's follow-up, *The Resurrection Murder Case,* the reviewer in the *Boston Transcript* huzzahed: "The many friends of Christopher Hand will rejoice to meet him again . . .The devious paths followed until the crime is brought home are sufficiently interesting to hold the attention and to make it difficult to lay down the book. . . . One reads many pages half expecting the crack of a bludgeon on one's own head." For his part A. P. Bryan in the *Lexington Herald-Leader* wrote: "Mr. Page takes the most complicated plot that has come to the attention of this reviewer in many months and weaves it into a logical and interesting, yet baffling story of mystery and adventure. . . . [Christoper Hand] eventually solves the entire mystery by one of the most ingenious devices yet introduced to detective fiction." In the *Philadelphia Inquirer,* E. W. P. raved of the novel: "Hand the investigator is brilliant, and the dénouement is breath-taking."

Page dedicated *The Resurrection Murder Case* to retired New York police captain Grant Williams, a pioneering specialist in reconstructing faces from the skulls of murder victims (Dominick La Rosa and Lillian White were two of his most noted cases) whom the press in the Twenties dubbed a "modern Sherlock Holmes."[2] The so-called "sculptor-sleuth" headed New York City's Bureau of Missing Persons, between its organization in 1914 and his retirement in 1928. Read the novel to see wherefore the dedication. It is set in and around Mill Ridge, New Jersey, "a fashionable community of larges estates" located on a ridge above the Great Swamp, which sounds a lot like places where the author himself had lived, like Chatham and Millburn.

Page's third mystery, *Fool's Gold,* which he penned in 1932 and published with Knopf in the Spring of 1933, reads rather like a Sherlock Holmes pastiche, allowing for the fact that it is set in Depression-era America rather than Victorian/Edwardian England. In the novel it appears that some criminal fiend has murdered a pair of grizzled gold prospectors, who had traveled to New York to find investors in their Alaska mining concern, and purloined from them the bills and gold they had kept stashed in their money belts. Unhappily involved in the problem are the congregants of the Hendley Congregational Church, who contributed to the ill-fated venture the sum of $50,000 (over a million dollars today), constituting their life savings.

The presence of the Hendley Congregational Church recalls the real-life Stanley Congregational Church, which Stanley Hart Page's grandfather as mentioned had founded and which Stanley would attend all of his life. Along the way to the solution of the various crimes Hand confronts a locked room murder problem as well. The notice in the *Los Angeles Times* declared of the inventive novel: "[T]he reader will be caught and will hold on until the [culprits] are discovered. . . . [T]here is a trick in this tale that will almost fool an experienced student of mystery yarns." Almost! The reviewer for Kentucky's *Lexington Herald-Leader,* on the other hand, avowed that "there's no chance of [readers] beating the author to the solution," adding: "You'll be flabbergasted by the number of clues that appear and the amount of action that is jammed into a 24-hour period." On May 7, 1933, the *San Francisco Chronicle* listed the novel as the Bay Region's #6 fiction bestseller of the week.

Page's mysteries won praise as well in the United Kingdom, where the author did not even have a really prestigious publisher behind him. When the second Hand opus, *The Resurrection Murder Case,* was published by Stanley

Paul in England in 1933 (the author's name was abbreviated there, for some reason, to S. Hart Page) an anonymous reviewer for the *Manchester Evening News* roundly praised the mystery as "[a]n American thriller of the most intense kind." In the *Leicester Mercury,* the writer of the column "From My Library Table" reflected that "with the thousands of 'thrillers' that are turned out every year it is amazing that we can still be mystified over any plot. But

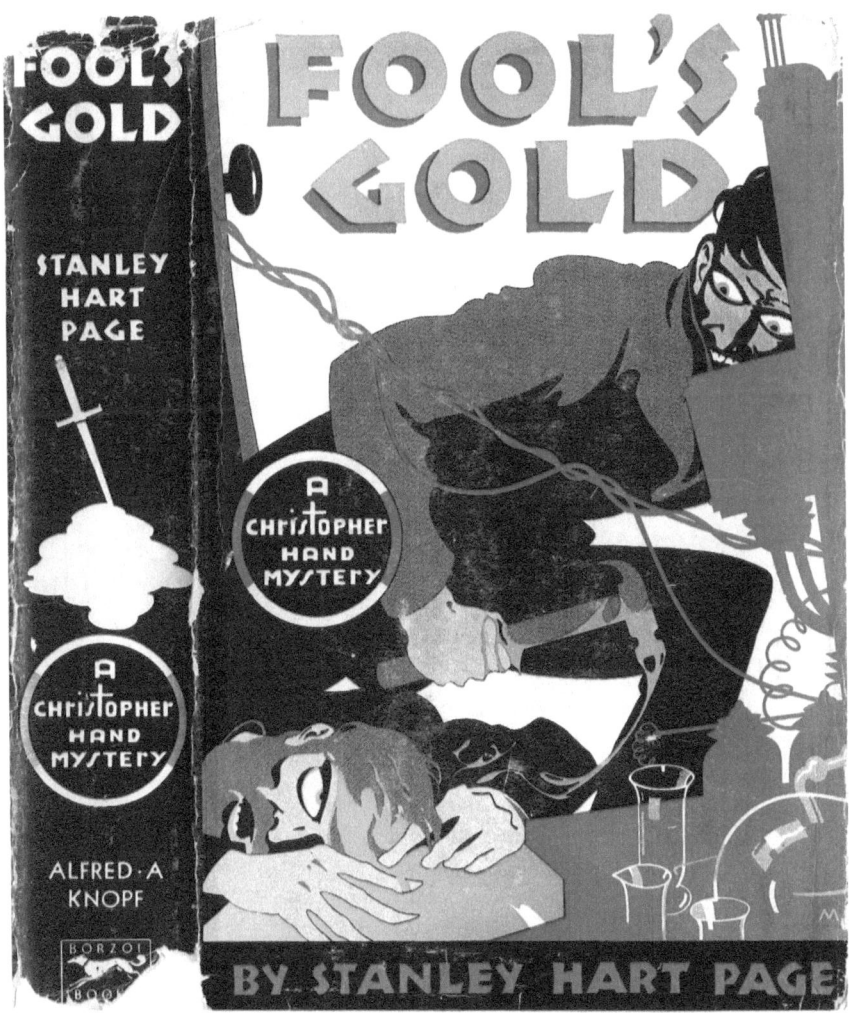

Cover courtesy Curtis Evans

S. Hart Page keeps us in suspense throughout and then gives us the necessary jolt at the end. . . . [*The Resurrection Murder Case*] stamps him as one those few writers who can be relied upon to give us breathless adventure and a mental puzzle."

No less a figure than British mystery writer Richard Keverne lauded *Fool's Gold,* when it was published in England the next year, humorously writing: "Quite early in the story I thought I had guessed the solution to the mystery of *"Fool's Gold"*. . . . but later on the idiot police detective tumbled to the same solution, and of course it was wrong. So it was left to the Sherlock Holmesian Christopher Hand to put us both right, and Mr. S. Hart Page makes him do it in a most agreeable manner." The *Leicester Mercury* pronounced the novel a "really gripping yarn" and the Daily Mirror found it "very readable."

As has been seen above Stanley Hart Page drew upon his own privileged background for his mysteries. His Grandfather George was a noted trout angler in the state of Maine, in 1867 founding, in the remote village of Oquossoc, an angling club on the shores of Mooselucmeguntic Lake. According to *The American Fly Fisher,* George Shephard Page's "reputation and fame as a fish culturist were international in scope." Christopher Hand's detecting companion and chronicler Clark is a devotee of trout fishing, declaring in *The Resurrection Murder Case:* "I had heard of the excellent fishing in the vicinity of Mill Ridge. . . . It was with a light heart that I fell asleep that night. I visualized myself wading in a trout stream." Recalling Philo Vance's enthusiasms in *The Kennel Murder Case* (1933), George Shephard Page was also a breeder of Scottish Deerhounds. With such a background it is perhaps not surprising that one of their scions ended up writing a detective fiction series headlined by a Philo-esque gentleman detective.

Stanley Hart Page grew up in privileged circumstances in Chatham, New Jersey, along with two elder brothers, George Shephard Page and Lawrence Stanely Page, Jr., an elder sister, Elizabeth, and one younger brother, Henry de Bacon Page. Despite their fortune, there was tragedy in the family's life. One Sunday morning in January 1919 Stanley's sister Betty died at the age of twenty-one from the Spanish flu then raging around the world. At her death Betty Page, whose obituary avowed had been "universally beloved" from childhood, was doing Red Cross work and taking a "special course in domestic science" at Centenary Collegiate Institute in preparation for her impending marriage. Less than a year earlier, Stanley's brother George Shephard Page, a professional aviator, had been killed in the Great War.

Described on his 1942 draft card as 5'11", 155 pounds, brown-haired (though balding) and blue-eyed, Stanley Hart Page in late 1931, not long before publishing his first detective novel, wed Beatrice Bayard, daughter of an affluent old-money New Jersey magazine publisher and descendant of Anne Stuyvesant Bayard, sister of Peter Stuyvesant, the ill-fated seventeenth-century Director General of the Dutch colony of New Netherland. Beatrice Bayard, a lovely, doe-eyed twenty-four-year-old actress who had graduated from the American Academy of Dramatic Arts, had acted in traveling company and played small parts in two Broadway plays, the hit 1929 Edward G. Robinson comedy *Kibitzer* (2nd neighbor) and the 1928 revival of John Colton's 1926 melodrama *The Shanghai Gesture* (apprentice mouse). She had spent the summer before her marriage traveling around Europe with an auntly chaperone. She and Page were married in a small private ceremony at the Episcopal Church of the Transfiguration in Manhattan, popularly known as "The Little Church around the Corner," which liberally catered to theater folk and other bohemian types.[3]

Page credited his imaginative wife with having helped inspire him to start writing mysteries and he dedicated his first novel to her. The couple dwelt at the roughly $500,000 (in modern value) Millburn, New Jersey, home of Beatrice's parents, along with her siblings Stuyvesant and Martha. The Bayards employed a single maid, a young black woman from South Carolina memorably named Ida May Neville.

In 1933 Stanley and Beatrice produced one daughter, Martha Pintard Page, and Stanley produced two more

Beatrice Bayard Page

Christoper Hand mysteries, the aforementioned *Fool's Gold* and *Murder Flies the Atlantic,* the latter of which innovatively is set on a zeppelin flying between London and New York. It was published by a rather less distinguished concern, Alfred H. King. Despite Knopf's vigorous pushing in the press and his supposed winning of "many friends," Christopher Hand sadly had not in fact become the Next Big Thing in the way of dilettante detectives. Two years

later there followed from Page's hand, as it were, Christopher Hand's finale *The Tragic Curtain,* which was published by The Dial Press. The author appears then to have laid down his pen, at least as it concerned crime writing.

Page continued to receive press praise for his last two detective novels, however, with, for example, the *Boston Globe* labeling *Atlantic* "a tense and thrilling story that is admirable written" and the *Houston Post* avowing of *Curtain:* "It is well-told, complicated and interesting." With *Curtain* Page provided a fitting end for the series. "There is a certain ingenuity in this work, one which makes it difficult to put it down," reflected the reviewer of the novel in the *Baltimore Evening Sun.* "Mr. Page . . . has thought up a solution to his crimes which pretty completely baffles the reader until the denouement is reached. Moreover, he plays fair and doesn't break the established rules of the game."

Although his detective thus vanished seemingly without a trace ninety years ago, Stanley Hart Page himself lived on for over four decades. For years he and Beatrice were actively involved in the Chatham Community Players, who in 1941 performed Stanley's play *A Welcome Stranger,* which the Chatham Press called a "lively, uproariously funny farce." Hardly in need of money, Page retired relatively young from the news business in 1952 and passed away after a lengthy illness at the age of seventy-seven on August 4, 1979. For nine decades now Page's sleuth Christopher Hand has waited to experience his own miraculous resurrection. While admittedly, despite all the puffing from his first publisher, no Philo Vance, Christopher Hand for a very short time was a name much bruited-about in mystery-loving circles. See for yourself what you think of this clever fella.

ENDNOTES:

[1] On Vapo-Cresolene and George Shephard Page and his children, see the online accounts provided by John Langlois, "On Beyond Holcombe: Vapo-Cresolene," *1898 Revenues: United States Revenue Stamps That Financed the Spanish American War*, 12 November 2012, and by Dan Edminster, "Lamps Designed for Medicinal Purposes: Vapo-Cresolene and Schering's Formalin Lamps," *The Lampworks: An On-Line Resource for Lighting Researchers and Collectors of Oil and Kerosene Lamps, Burners and Other Trimmings*, at http://www.thelampworks.com/lw_vapo_cresolene.htm. On the AMA's 1908 report on Vapo-Cresolene, see *Nostrums and Quackery* (Chicago: American Medical Association, 1912), 626. On the overall dubiousness of Vapo-Cresolene, see James Harvey Young, *The Toadstool Millionaires: A Social History of Patent Medicine in American before Federal Regulation* (Princeton, NJ: Princeton University Press, 1961), 215. George Shephard Page, bluntly notes William D. Eddy *in Stone Pond: A Personal History* (1982; rev. ed., White Plains, NY: Plain White Press, 1988), was "colorful, eccentric and ultimately mad. . . . In the quaint phrases of his obituary, he was 'deprived of his reason and removed to the State Insane Asylum at Morris Plains, NJ'" (p. 51. n. 4).

[2] A 1936 letter writer to *Time* detailed the Lillian White case:

> In April 1922, acting Captain Grant Williams of the New York City police department was imported to Rockland County, handed a skull and other bones found on Cheesecock Mountain and asked to solve the mystery of its presence there. Sterilizing the skull, he placed it on an artificial neck made out of a curtain pole shaved down to fit the opening of the spinal column. Inside the skull on either side of the pole, he wedged two radio tubes to hold the head steady. The other end of the pole he fitted in a stand made of a soap box.

Greasing his fingers, Williams then coated the skull with modeling clay. He spread it thinly, following the contour of the bone evenly. Gradually he applied other layers, feeling his own jowls & forehead for guidance. The length of the nose he determined by measuring the distance between the bridge and the roots of the upper teeth: its contour by following the curve of the nasal bone. To get the fullness of the cheeks he held a pencil from the cheekbone down to the jawbone and allowed a little for normal rounding. He used the same instrument to determine the set of the eyes, holding it slantwise from the eye socket to the cheekbone. . . . The brows he determined by beginning at the inside corner of the eye socket and following around the upper edge of the bone; the fullness of the lips by the protrusions and recessions of the upper and lower teeth. And so on. . . .

Until, 56 hours later, when he had dipped the flesh-colored clay in wax, inserted glass eyes and dressed the victim's original hair, which providentially had been recovered near the skull, he had before him the snub-nosed, sullen face of a temperamental Irish girl.

The rebuilt corpse was subsequently identified as Lillian White, an inmate of Letchworth [a New York residential institution]. The identification was upheld by Justice Arthur S. Tompkins of the New York Supreme Court; and her murderer, Joseph Blunt, was subsequently caught in Maine.

[3] The Church of the Transfiguration was built and consecrated in 1849. During the New York City draft riots of 1863, Rector George Hendric Houghto, gave shelter to African-Americans who were targets of a draft-protesting white mob. Houghton was said to have turned the rioters away, sternly admonishing: "You white devils, you! Do you know nothing of the spirit of

Christ?" The church's nickname came about thusly: In 1870 the rector of the Church of the Atonement refused to conduct funeral services for a deceased actor, airily telling his friend, famed thespian Jefferson Farjeon (grandfather of English mystery writer Jefferson Farjeon), "I believe there is a little church around the corner where they do that sort of thing." Farjeon allegedly responded: "If that be so, God bless the little church around the corner!"

I

THE CHINESE DAGGER

"Humph," said Christopher Hand, rattling the telegram that the messenger had just delivered at our rooms. He glanced at the yellow slip of paper again. His thin lips took on a faint smile. A softer light of reminiscence stole into his cold gray eyes.

"Personal?" I asked from the doorway to the bedrooms, where I had paused on my way to bed.

"Well, in a way," replied Hand, with a faint chuckle. "I hesitate to call an appeal to help out in a servant problem anything but a personal matter. You wouldn't call it a professional matter, would you, Clark? Unless we are to become domestic help experts."

"What are you talking about?" I impatiently demanded, going back into the living-room. "Do you mean to say someone has sent you a telegram at this hour of the night asking you to get him a servant?"

"No; to find his old one," he replied. "This wire is from Colonel Decker."

"Oh, yes, I've heard you speak of him. Friend of your father's, wasn't he?"

"He was my father's best friend," said Hand, sprawling angularly in his decrepit old morris-chair. "They were roommates at West Point and later served together in the army," he went on thoughtfully, as though talking to himself. "The colonel was at my father's side when he was killed in the Philippines. I see him once in a while at the Army Club. He purchased a large estate in Mill Ridge when he retired from the army a short while ago, you know. Although a bachelor, the colonel has something of a family—an adopted daughter and his brother, Joseph."

"But what's this about his servant?"

"Read this, Clark, and you'll know as much about it as I do," said my friend, passing the telegram over to me. It was addressed to Hand and read:

SERVANT DISAPPEARED. EXPECT YOU
IN THE MORNING.

I turned my puzzled face to Hand. Over his long nose he returned my perplexed glance with an amused one.

"It's just like the colonel," he said. "Of course he knows I have taken up criminology; so the minute his servant departs without permission, he sends for me. Anyone under him who acts without permission is a criminal in the eyes of the colonel. We will answer the call, Clark. The affair of the disappearing minister is closed, and I have a nice fat check for it from the trustees of his church. We will now turn to the glens and glades of New Jersey on the pretext of ferreting out a disappearing servant. At least it will enable us to partake of the colonel's excellent hospitality for a few days. What do you say?"

"Excellent!" I replied. "No one could be more footloose and fancy-free than your humble servant. When do we leave?"

"The colonel likes to be up and doing early," said Hand, rummaging through a drawer in the smoking-table at his side. He got out a time-table and glanced through it. "There's a train from Hoboken at six that will get us to

Mill Ridge shortly after seven thirty," he announced. "It means getting up at five, Clark."

"That's all right," I said. "I think I'll be getting to bed, though. Good-night."

The prospects of a few days in the country were cheerful. I would never have lived in New York at all had I been willing to part company with Hand. He could not be budged from the metropolis. I had heard of the excellent fishing in the vicinity of Mill Ridge. Before turning in I packed my dunnage, saving ample room for my fishing gear.

It was with a light heart that I fell asleep that night. I visualized myself wading a trout stream. Hand could dabble in the harmless mystery of the missing servant. All was well with the world.

We alighted from the colonel's machine, which he had sent to the station for us, promptly at a quarter of eight. I was paying my first visit to the colonel's house. It was a large, colonial structure standing in the center of a sweeping lawn. Its surroundings were wild. Mill Ridge was a fashionable community of large estates, located on a rugged, forest-grown ridge that extended like a finger out into the Great Swamp. Across the road from the colonel's house descended a steep hill overgrown with brush and tall grass. At its foot was the border of the swamp.

Hand walked up to the front door and energetically used the brass knocker. As we waited for someone to admit us, I gazed out over the flat, dismal swamp lands stretching off into the distance. Wooded hillocks rose from the morass like islands of a dead sea. Far in the distance was a large wooded space, completely surrounded by marshes. Hand touched my arm.

I turned quickly about to find a pale-faced servant holding the door open for us.

"I am Christopher Hand," announced my friend. "Colonel Decker is expecting me. This other gentleman is Mr. Clark."

"Yes, Mr. Hand," replied the servant in little more than a whisper. He stood rigidly aside as, followed by the chauffeur with our bags, we entered the house. The fellow seemed overawed. He strangely upset me.

"Right this way, sir," he directed us. We followed him across the hall and into a large room at the left.

I had entered the colonel's house that fine spring morning with buoyant spirits. The servant with his infernal solemnity had begun to dispel some of my light-heartedness. The spectacle that met our eyes as we marched into the living-room took away the last vestige of cheer that remained to me. Three men in solemn attitudes stood in the center of the room. A young girl clung to the tallest, an imposing, upstanding man with silvering hair. Her face was buried on his shoulder, and she was weeping copiously. One of the other two men was middle-aged. An expression of sorrow was on his sallow face. The third man was a good-looking young fellow, who held himself like an athlete. So absorbed were they that our presence was not noticed as we entered the room.

"Mr. Hand and Mr. Clark," announced the servant.

The three men glanced sharply around at us. The girl stepped back. She looked at us with tearful big brown eyes for an instant; then turned quickly away. She dabbed at her eyes with a handkerchief and commenced vigorously powdering her nose, but her sobbing continued. The tall man stepped quickly forward with a soldierly bearing. There was pain in his clear blue eyes, and his strong jaw was set. With grave aspect he took my friend's outstretched hand. What all this display of deep sorrow had to do with the disappearance of a servant I could not imagine.

"How do you do, Colonel?" said Hand, addressing the man. who had greeted him. "Pardon me, but I can't fail to be impressed by the sadness of your household. I hope nothing serious has happened."

"I made a mistake," replied the colonel gruffly. "I should have sent for you sooner, Christopher. Come."

He turned abruptly and led the way out into the front hall. Hand motioned for me to follow. We crossed the hall to the back where a flight of stairs ascended at the left and two doors were set in the back wall. Colonel Decker opened the one to the right and strode into a small room, quite evidently a den. My two companions stopped just inside the door. I walked up behind them and peered over their shoulders. Following their example, I directed my gaze to the floor. I was thankful the ominous atmosphere of the house had prepared me for a shock.

Stretched on the floor lay a man clad in a dressing-gown. Face upward, his glassy eyes were staring vacantly at the ceiling. His mouth hung open as if he were in the act of shouting. From his left breast there protruded the handle of a dagger!

"My brother," said Colonel Decker tersely.

"This is most unfortunate," murmured Hand. His tone was unkindly, preoccupied. His eyes were darting glances over the corpse and all about the room. His jaw had become set, and a sort of furtiveness had come over him that I easily recognized. "When did you make this discovery, Colonel?" he asked.

"Just before you arrived," replied the man, closing the door and quietly turning back to view the corpse of his brother. "I breakfasted early, as is my habit. I took a turn about the place and then came in here to do some work. That is the sight which greeted me."

"And the others?"

"They had just finished breakfast. I thought I had better tell them at once."

"Of course. Would you mind telling me who the others are? I recognized the young lady as your daughter."

"Yes, that was Patricia."

"How about those two men?"

"The older man is a friend of my brother's—visiting us the past few days. Name's Furness—Gerald Furness. He's lived in Paris a good many years. The other is Richard Fairfax. He and Patty say they're in love. Guess they are, too. They want to get married, and I've consented to it."

"And why shouldn't you? He looks worthy of her. By the way, this is Mr. Ralph Clark."

"Oh, yes, Mr. Clark," said the colonel, taking my hand in a grip of iron. "Christopher has told me about you. Live with him, don't you? Sorry I had to meet you like this."

Hand was kneeling beside the corpse. Colonel Decker and I stood silently by and watched him. Finally he got to his feet.

"Well, Colonel," he said, "do you suspect anybody of this?"

"No, I don't," replied the colonel gruffly. "I don't know what to think of it."

"Let me see," said Hand, squinting at the ceiling. "Pardon me if I'm a trifle blunt, Colonel, but as a matter of fact you don't know so much about your brother as you might, do you?"

"That is right," said Colonel Decker crisply. The effect of his military training was clearly manifesting itself. He was going through the harrowing experience like a Spartan. I imagined Hand was touching him on a tender spot into the bargain.

"Been away a good deal, hasn't he?" went on Hand.

"I'll tell you about him as clearly as I can," said the colonel, speaking with an effort. "He's been a rolling stone most of his life. Couldn't hold on to money. He's my younger brother as well as my only one, you know. I've always tried to keep my eye on him. But being in the army didn't give me much chance, I'm afraid. You're right, I don't know much about him, even though he was my own brother."

"How long has he made his home with you?"

"Ever since I've been here; a little over three months."

"How was he fixed financially?"

"Well, no use my covering it up. He was penniless."

"Never occurred to you that his life was threatened?"

"No; there can't be anything like that. This must be the work of a burglar."

"When did you last see him alive?"

"Last night about midnight."

"You retired before he did?"

"Yes, I did."

"I thought as much. Although he is wearing a dressing-gown, aside from his coat and vest he is fully clothed. Where was he?"

"In here."

"In here? That is significant. What was he doing?"

"Dr. Metz was giving him an examination."

"What for?"

"Joseph had been troubled by a nervous disorder. The doctor dropped in last night and chatted for a while. Finally he asked Joseph if he could see him in private, and they started off for the den. I happened to think of Joseph's nerves—he'd been a little more high-strung than usual yesterday. I suggested the doctor give him a looking over, and he said he would."

"You suggested that to him here in the den?"

"No; that was out in the living-room. I stopped in here on my way up to bed to see how they were making out. They hadn't begun the examination then, the doctor said."

"What were they doing?"

"Why, Joseph was seated at the desk there, and the doctor was sitting in that chair by the window. They appeared to be talking—nothing more."

"Was your brother wearing that dressing-gown then?"

"No; he was fully clothed."

"When you went to bed and left them, they were the only ones up in the house, then?"

"Well, with the exception of Maxwell—the servant who admitted you just now. He locks up after everyone has gone to bed."

"Who is this Dr. Metz?"

"He's from Barkersville—the next town down here at the beginning of the ridge. Seems to be a reputable doctor, but I don't know much about him. He got quite friendly with Joseph."

"I see. Now, what about this servant of yours? Your wire said one had disappeared."

"Yes. That's the real reason I sent for you. I can't see that it could have any bearing on this, but you might find a connection. It was mysterious enough. The fellow was here to my certain knowledge late the night before last. Yesterday morning he was missing. Soon after he was reported missing, Maxwell came to me and said he had found blood stains in the back hallway behind the kitchen. I went out and saw them for myself. We only have one police officer here. He came up and looked the situation over, but that's about as far as he got. I kept thinking about it all day, and finally decided to ask you to take a run up here."

"Who was this servant?"

"His name was Thomas Buckley. Been here ever since we moved in."

"What references did he have?"

"As a matter of fact, the only reference he had was Joseph's. Joseph knew him as a servant in a hotel he stayed at in London."

"Have you formed any theory concerning him?"

"None whatever. He was a good servant—seemed trust-worthy and steady. I don't know what to think of it."

"I'd like to talk to Maxwell, if you will summon him, Colonel," said Hand, walking over to the desk, which was set up against the side wall. My friend flung himself into a swivel chair in front of it. He looked thoughtfully down at the corpse, which sprawled on the rug in the center of the room. Colonel Decker pushed a button on the side of the desk.

"Have you notified your police of this?" asked Hand.

"No, I haven't," replied the colonel. "Guess I'd better do it." He picked up a telephone from the desk. From his conversation, he had no success in locating Mill Ridge's lone policeman.

"He's out patrolling the roads," announced the Colonel, putting the telephone down. "His wife will send him up as soon as he gets in."

In response to a timid rap on the door, Colonel Decker crossed quickly over to it and threw it open. Maxwell stood humbly at the threshold.

"You wished to see me in—in here, sir?" he asked.

"Yes; come in, Maxwell," said Hand. "Shut the door, Colonel. Now, Maxwell, what time did you go to bed last night?"

"It was quite late, sir," replied the fellow, keeping his white face studiously elevated and his eyes rigidly on the ceiling.

"What was the time?" insisted Hand.

"It was nearly one, sir. Mr. Decker called me in here and had me empty the ash-trays. Then he dismissed me and told me to go to bed."

"Was anyone in here with him?"

"Yes, sir. Dr. Metz was in here with him."

"What were they doing?"

"Just sitting here, sir."

"Was Mr. Decker sitting here where I am now?"

"Yes, sir. And Dr. Metz was in that chair by the window."

"Did they appear angry at each other?"

"Well, I—I couldn't say, sir."

"How's that? You couldn't say? Speak up, man! Did they appear angry?"

"Well, sir, Dr. Metz kept his face away from me the whole time I was in here—looking out the window. He was tapping with a pencil on the arm of his chair, and I got the idea he was a little—well, put out. Mr. Decker was kind of jumpy, but he was always like that, begging your pardon, sir."

"You didn't overhear them say anything?"

"No, sir. They didn't say a word while I was in here. Just sat there silent. Mr. Decker said: 'Empty the ash-trays, Maxwell.' Then when I got back with them, he said: 'That will be all, Maxwell. Don't sit up any longer. Go to bed.' I thanked him, sir, and went out and went to bed. It was about ten minutes of one when I turned out my light."

"How about this man Buckley? Can you tell us anything about him that might help to clear up the mystery of his disappearance?"

"I don't know, sir. He disappeared as clean as a whistle. He was a sort of a funny one, though. I'm not altogether surprised that he's gone."

"It would seem that you can tell us something, then. What is it?"

"Only what I told Colonel Decker and the policeman, Withers. Buckley used to prowl round at night. His room's right opposite mine, sir, and several times I heard him get up and go downstairs. I asked him about it in the morning, and he said he had insomnia so bad he had to get up and walk round. He used to sleep sound enough sometimes, though. I had to wake him up lots of times. He'd sleep right through his alarm-clock."

"Is that all that made you skeptical about him?"

"Well, he was a sort of a funny one, sir. Reluctant, he was, yes, sir. He was reluctant to talk about himself."

"That is a very good account, Maxwell," said Hand, leaning forward in his chair. "Now, there is just one more thing. When you saw Mr. Decker just before you went to bed, was he dressed exactly as he is now?"

The servant had been very careful not to look at the gruesome sight on the floor. He had entered the room with elevated eyes, and his gaze had remained fastened on the ceiling ever since. With a visible effort he rolled his eyeballs downward to the corpse. His breath hissed in through his teeth, and his eyelids fluttered closed. When he reopened them, he was again staring at the ceiling. "Yes, sir," he blurted in reply to the last question.

"What?" the colonel almost shouted. "When I went to bed, Joseph was wearing his coat and vest. Are you sure about that, Maxwell? Take a good look at him."

"I—I saw him, sir," declared Maxwell, his eyeballs moving no more than as if they were frozen in his head. "He was dressed just as he is now, sir, dressing-gown and all!"

Hand sat gazing thoughtfully at the floor for a moment. Then his eyes strayed to an outside door at the rear of the den.

"Maxwell," he said, "you lock all the doors at night, don't you?"

"Yes, sir."

"Was that outside door locked when you went to bed?"

"I—I don't know, sir. I didn't try it. With Mr. Joseph here—you see, sir."

Hand bounded out of the chair and crossed to the door. He carefully inspected the glass knob. Then he poured some powder from a small box into the palm of his hand. He sprinkled the powder over the door-knob; then carefully blew it off. He shook his head dubiously as he looked intently at the door-knob, squatting down to see the under part of it as well as the top and sides. Finally he gingerly turned the knob with his thumb and forefinger, and the door opened. The outside door-knob was subjected to the same treatment. Then he stepped out on the threshold and stood peering intently at the ground for several minutes. Finally he stepped back into the room and closed the door.

"No finger-prints on the door-knobs, and the door was not locked," he mused. He faced about and once more regarded the corpse. "Where did that dagger come from?" he demanded, indicating the handle of the blade, still fixed in the dead man's chest.

"It is mine," replied the colonel slowly. "It once belonged to a Chinese prince. I've had it ever since the Boxer Rebellion. Kept it on the desk there as a letter-opener. My God! I never thought it would deprive me of my brother!"

2

DR. METZ

The servant was told to leave the den, an order which he promptly carried out. Hand swung about, directly facing the corpse of Joseph Decker, and slumped down in his chair. Colonel Decker and I stood regarding him, somewhat uncomfortably. Hand's eyes seemed to bore straight into the body, as if to probe that pierced heart for its secret. Suddenly he hitched his shoulders and jerked up his head to meet the gaze of the dead man's brother.

"Colonel, your brother came to this room prepared to defend his own life or to take another," he announced.

"I can't believe that!" snapped the colonel.

"Very well, let me show you on what I base my deduction," said Hand. "In the right-hand pocket of your brother's dressing-gown there is a discharged automatic—thirty-two caliber, I'd say. I didn't remove it, of course; the police must see it first. But I felt the muzzle through a charred hole in the fabric of the pocket. Your brother fired the gun from his pocket. The bullet entered the wall over there—see the hole under the window? Whether he fired before or after he was stabbed, he missed his mark, and his life was forfeited. I think he fired before he was stabbed. I know something of anatomy, and I'm sure that blade penetrated his heart. If so, it is unlikely that he was able to fire afterwards. That, however, is immaterial. The regrettable thing is that he missed."

Hand bounded out of his chair and crossed to where the bullet-hole showed in the wall. "Hello!" he exclaimed, "perhaps my deduction was not so accurate, after all."

"Why?" I asked. The colonel and I carefully walked round the corpse to get closer to Hand, who was on his knees before the window.

"You are an authority on fire-arms and projectiles, Colonel," said Hand, looking up at the old soldier. "Wouldn't you say from the appearance of this bullet-hole that the bullet struck something before it hit the wall?"

"No doubt of it!" replied the colonel, a note of excitement creeping into his voice. "Either it was flattened, or it was deflected and went into the wall sidewise—partially so, anyway. But see here, how do we know where the bullet was fired from?"

"I think it's safe to say it was fired from where your brother's body now lies," replied Hand. "It makes very little difference, for this hole is too irregular to have been made by a bullet shot directly into the wall from any angle."

"We can make sure, by gad!" growled the colonel. "I'll get a hatchet and we'll have it out in no time. We can tell in a minute then."

"We really shouldn't disturb it until the police get here," said Hand.

"The police be hanged!" snorted the colonel. "I'm going to have a look at that bullet now!"

He turned to leave the room, but Hand grabbed him by the wrist. "Be careful how you cross the room," said my friend. "Go round by the walls."

The colonel regarded him in perplexity for a moment. Then he turned, skirted the walls, and left the room. Hand rose to his feet and glanced sharply about the floor once more.

"No blood stains anywhere except beside that corpse," he mused. "If that bullet struck anything, it must have been whoever was in this room with Decker."

The colonel returned carrying a hatchet and chisel. He carefully made his way round the border of the room and squatted resolutely before the little hole in the wall under the window. He went to work with the hatchet and soon had plaster and chips of lathing scattered over the floor at his feet. Suddenly he thrust the chisel into the hole he had made. He forced his fingers in beside it, and when he withdrew them, he held the plaster-covered bullet. He rubbed the plaster off and held the missile out on the palm of his hand.

"Struck something, all right," he grunted. "Something hard—like steel."

"No doubt of it," agreed Hand. "Could it have been anything in the wall?"

"No; it was embedded in wood. It didn't have a great deal of force left when it went into the wall."

"Hum-m. Whatever it struck, it struck it at an angle. It's flattened on one side near the nose. From the position of your brother's body, Colonel, and from the appearance of the bullet-hole in the wall, I'd say he fired the bullet from almost the exact center of the room. The person it struck was standing out a little in front of the desk. The bullet deflected toward the rear of the house and struck the wall."

"After it struck the other man?" growled the colonel. "Why in blazes didn't it finish him?"

"We can only guess at that," said Hand, "but I'd venture to say he wore a bullet-proof vest."

"Then he came here for mischief!" declared the colonel. "He murdered Joseph, and I don't think it was in self-defense, either."

"Perhaps not," said Hand slowly. "This much is plain, however: your brother fired at him before he was stabbed. The man would have had to be standing very near the desk for the bullet to be deflected from him to the position in the wall where we found it. Probably he had grabbed the dagger and was making for your brother when he shot him."

"That would be the way of it," said the colonel with a satisfied air. "He attacked Joseph with the dagger, and Joseph shot at him. That cursed bullet-proof vest decided the whole thing. How about that doctor? It certainly looks like him!"

"He's in a bad position, all right," agreed Hand. "We must determine when he got home."

"What difference does that make? He was here with Joseph until nearly one o'clock—we know that. He was the last one to be with my brother, and he must have killed him!"

"Your brother was killed long after one o'clock."

"What makes you think so?"

Hand indicated the ash-tray on the desk. In it were the stubs of two smoked cigars. "He smoked two cigars after one o'clock," he said simply. "Maxwell said he emptied the ash-trays shortly before one. Your brother smoked two cigars after that, Colonel, and his companion smoked one."

"How do you make that out? I see only two cigar-ends."

"There is another one on the floor over under the chair by the window. It fell there while it was lighted—you can see it has burned the nap of the rug. I think your brother was smoking it when he was stabbed. He smoked one of the two in the ashtray, also. You notice one of those in the ash-tray is all chewed up; the other hardly shows the marks of the smoker's teeth. They are different brands, too. The one under the chair is not only all chewed up, but it is the same brand as the chewed one in the ash-tray. Was your brother in the habit of chewing his cigars?"

"Well, yes, he was."

"I thought so. Now, there is only one more thing that I have been able to determine here, and it is quite possible I am wrong about that. I am not a medical man, but from the rigidity of the muscles of your brother's body I should say he met death about three o'clock. A medical examiner might contradict that."

From his pocket he took a small metal box. Into this he placed the unchewed cigar from the ash-tray. He closed the box and dropped it back into his pocket.

"I shall leave the matter of getting the county medical examiner here in your hands, Colonel," he said. "Don't wait for that policeman of yours. Call the authorities in Barkersville and have them notify the examiner."

"What are you going to do?" asked Colonel Decker.

"Going over to see that doctor," replied Hand. "I'll have to take your car. Your chauffeur knows where the doctor lives? Good. Come on, Clark. We'll be back shortly, Colonel."

Hand opened the door, and we strode out into the hall. The two men and the girl, still in the living-room, regarded us curiously as we passed the large door of the room. Outside we found the colonel's car waiting at the door with the chauffeur standing beside it. Although he was dressed in faultless livery and stood as straight as a ramrod, the man appeared unusually well along in years for such a job. His clear blue eyes, however, were as steady as one could wish. His sharp features were tanned and weather-beaten.

"What's your name?" Hand asked him.

"MacClintock, sirr," replied the chauffeur with a broad Scotch burr. "I thinks to m'sel', they'll be awantin' the carr; so I'll keep it herre."

"Good work, MacClintock," said Hand. "Drive us to Dr. Metz's in a hurry."

"Yes, sirr."

Within ten minutes we were at the doctor's door. Hand rang the bell. After a few moments the door was opened by a little old fellow, evidently a factotum, who regarded us inquiringly over the tops of steel-rimmed eyeglasses.

"Is the doctor in?" inquired Hand.

"The doctor's hours are from two to three in the afternoon," the old man primly informed us.

"We are rather concerned about him," said Hand with a worried expression. "He left quite late last night, and we were a little bit anxious. Did he get home all right?"

"Oh, yes," said the man, showing a little more deference. "He got home all right."

Hand affected an attempt to cover a smile. "What time did he get home?" he asked meaningly, with a twinkle in his eye.

"Oh, it was a party, was it? Heh, heh," said the old man with a cracked laugh. "He came in about three o'clock. I heard him. He stumbled on the top step, but he got home all right. Heh, heh."

"Three o'clock!" exclaimed Hand. "He certainly made good time. Are you sure he was in before three?"

"Well, mebby later. Not much, though. I heard the clock strikin' three before he came in. The doctor kin drive like Ol' Sam Hill when he gets agoin'. Heh, heh."

"Well, I'm glad he got home all right. I don't suppose he'll be back very soon. Not much sense of our waiting to see him."

"He won't be back 'fore noon. Leastwise he never is."

"All right," said Hand. "We won't wait."

He turned and descended the steps from the porch. We climbed back into the car, and MacClintock started up.

"Ye'll go back to the corronel's noo, sirr?" asked the chauffeur over his shoulder.

"MacClintock, do you know Dr. Metz's car when you see it?" asked Hand.

"I do, sirr."

"Drive round this town a little, and see whether you can find it. I'd like to see that doctor before he gets home."

We drove up and down the few streets in Barkersville, but MacClintock had no luck in sighting the doctor's car.

"I wooldna be surrprrised if we found him overr in Mill Ridge, sirr," said the man at last. "He's got patients overr therre."

"All right," growled Hand. "I hate to waste all this time, but I'd give a lot to find him."

We started along what MacClintock described as the Ridge Road—the only highway leading to Mill Ridge. Suddenly MacClintock straightened behind the wheel and peered intently through the wind-shield.

"By thunderr, that's him advancin' on ahead of us, I think, sirr," he said, pointing ahead to a car going in our direction.

"Overtake him!" ordered Hand. "By Heaven, this is a stroke of luck!"

Our car rolled forward with increasing speed. It took but a couple of minutes for us to come up alongside the other machine. It was a coupé with a single occupant, a man with a round, pudgy face adorned with a sandy mustache and goatee. His small eyes peered at us through heavy spectacles as we drew up alongside.

"Ask him to stop a minute, MacClintock," said Hand.

"Doctorr, would ye mind pullin' up to the side?" roared MacClintock.

The doctor's car slowed down and stopped at the side of the road. MacClintock brought our machine to a stop just ahead of it. Hand bounded out. I followed him as he walked back to the other car. Dr. Metz sat perfectly still and blandly regarded us as we walked up to him.

"Pardon me, sir, but you are Dr. Metz, are you not?" asked Hand.

"That's my name, yes," he replied in a reedy voice. "You have the advantage of me, I think."

"Yes, I have," admitted my friend good-naturedly. "Let me introduce myself. I am Mr. Hand. This other gentleman is Mr. Clark. We are friends of Colonel Decker's."

"Oh, is that so?" said the doctor, extending his hand through the window of the car. "I am acquainted with the colonel myself. I was over at his house no later than last night."

"So I understand," said Hand, affecting a sorrowful tone of voice. "I don't suppose you've heard of the tragedy there early this morning."

"Good gracious, no!" exclaimed the doctor. "What has happened?"

"This morning Colonel Decker discovered his brother dead on the floor of the den with a knife in his heart," replied Hand solemnly.

"Joseph?" cried the doctor. "Dead! Good Lord, man, is this the truth?"

"It is, unfortunately," said Hand, sorrowfully shaking his head. "It's terrible! I understand you were a friend of Joseph's."

"I was, indeed. My dear sir, this is shocking! Have you any idea who did it?"

"I'm afraid none. The colonel said you were with Joseph when the colonel went to bed. I thought perhaps you might shed some light on the matter. Not that we think for a minute that you—"

"Not that you believe I stabbed him, eh?" interrupted the doctor with a faint smile. "It does place me in rather an embarrassing position, doesn't it? However, I'm glad I was with Joseph last night. Perhaps I can give you some information that will help, but for the life of me I can't see how. You are Christopher Hand, the criminologist, aren't you?"

"I hardly expected to be recognized out here," replied Hand with a bow. "I have long been a friend of Colonel Decker's, however. If possible, I should like to clear up the mystery of his brother's death. I should be very greatly indebted to you if you could tell me anything that might aid me."

"I should be only too glad to do it!" exclaimed the doctor. "As I said before, I don't know how any information I can give you will be of any value, but you're welcome to it. Joseph appeared as usual when I left him. Of course, he was quite nervous, but that was directly due to a nervous trouble he has been suffering from."

"What time did you leave him, Doctor?"

"Let me see—it was a little after one. He had been giving me his symptoms—stomach wasn't functioning perfectly and that aggravated his nervous trouble. I gave him an examination. Nothing wrong with him really—a little indigestion. He'd always been high-strung. Nothing to worry about."

"You prescribed for him?"

"Yes; told him to take a little bicarbonate of soda when he didn't feel right. That's all he needed."

"You had quite a long conversation with him, didn't you?"

"Yes. We had been thinking of organizing a hunt. We discussed it at some length."

"You hadn't known Joseph very long, had you, Doctor?"

"No; I learned of Joseph's long-standing nervousness from Joseph himself," replied Dr. Metz with a smile.

"You were very friendly, were you not?"

"Very. Joseph was a sterling man. I admired him very much."

"Did you often visit with him late at night?"

"Not very often," replied the doctor shortly.

"Pardon me, I don't want to give the impression that I am grilling you," said Hand. "I just wondered whether he was in the habit of staying up late."

"On the contrary, I believe he was in the habit of retiring very early," said the doctor. "I have advised him to, at least."

"When you left, you saw no one about the grounds?"

"No, I didn't. Of course I didn't look round, though."

"Of course not. It appears, however, that Joseph was attacked by an intruder. If we could hear of any suspicious character being round the neighbourhood, it would be significant and might lead to his apprehension. I suppose you traveled over this road on your way home."

"Yes, I came right along this way."

"Didn't see anything that aroused your suspicions?"

"No."

"You live in Barkersville, don't you, Doctor?"

"Yes, I live there."

"It's not much more than a ten-minute drive from the colonel's house to Barkersville, is it?"

"No; you could drive it in that time without much trouble."

"At that rate you would have been home about one thirty, I suppose."

"About that time."

"Then I don't believe you can help us much. You see, we believe Joseph was murdered about three o'clock."

"I was home long before that," said the doctor, settling back in his seat. "Well, well. This is very sad. Poor Joseph! Still, if this thing had to happen, it's a relief to know it didn't happen right after I left. I'm glad you are on the job, Mr. Hand. We shall look for an early solution of the mystery with the matter in the hands of such an expert."

"Thank you," said Hand earnestly. "Do you smoke cigars, Doctor?"

"No, thanks," replied the physician quickly.

"Pardon me, I wasn't offering you one. But this is most interesting. It couldn't have been you, then, who smoked the cigar we found in the ash-tray this morning—the ash-tray on the desk in the den."

"No, I didn't smoke a cigar last night. I smoked a number of cigarettes. Perhaps Joseph smoked the cigar. Now that I think of it, I remember he did smoke a cigar. By Jove, I'm quite sure he smoked two of them."

"Those must have been the two we found in the ash-tray."

"Undoubtedly."

"Well, I won't take up any more of your time, Doctor. I'm sorry to have troubled you like this. You have been very patient with me."

Hand stepped back with a bow. Suddenly he sprang forward and wrenched the door of the doctor's car open. "Hi! Look out there!" he cried, grasping Dr. Metz by the arm and dragging him out of the car. He waved his hat round inside the car as the doctor and I stood in amazement and watched him.

"There he goes," cried Hand at last, pulling his head out of the car. "A wasp—did you see him? They make nasty company in an automobile. One nearly did for a friend of mine. Poor Harry paid more attention to the wasp than he did to his driving. The fearful little insect wasn't even frightened away when the car crashed into a telephone pole. Harry says he distinctly remembers being stung as he lay half-conscious among the wreckage. Well, Doctor, we'll say good-by. You may have helped us—who knows?"

3

THE COLONEL'S GUEST

The doctor's car pulled out to the center of the road and sped away as we climbed back into the colonel's machine.

"That was good work, MacClintock," commended Hand. "We'll go back to the colonel's now."

"It looks worse than ever for the doctor," I remarked in a guarded tone. "Don't you think we should inform the police?"

"That will be done as soon as we find the police," replied Hand.

"Pretty simple case," I said somewhat loftily. "Lucky thing you were right on the spot."

"It does appear that the doctor is fairly well enmeshed," assented Hand. "But we have hardly dug our toes in yet. The few facts we've skimmed off the surface have mostly pointed to the doctor's guilt, I'll admit."

"His statements were most damaging," I said heatedly. "He lied about the time he got home; that was plain enough. Why would he do that unless he had something sinister to conceal?"

"Was that the only discrepancy you noticed in his account?"

"Let me see—yes, that was all, wasn't it?"

"Don't tell me the cigar episode eluded you! The ashtrays were emptied shortly before one; the doctor says he left shortly after one. Yet he is sure Joseph Decker smoked the two cigars we found in the ash-tray today."

"By Jove! Then he couldn't have left shortly after one!"

"Perhaps he just made a mistake. He may have forgotten for the moment that the ash-trays were emptied. Still, the doctor is in no position to make inaccurate statements."

"I agree with you," I said. "See here, what was all that furor about the wasp? I didn't see any wasp in the doctor's car."

"There wasn't one, either," replied Hand. "I'm glad my friend Harry—if I have a friend Harry—has never had such an experience as I described. Nothing but a trick, Clark. I found out that the doctor is not in the habit of wearing a bullet-proof vest."

"Oh, I see. But he might have worn one last night, though."

"He certainly might have. And if he did, it would be unlikely that he would be wearing it today. I felt it wise to make sure, nevertheless."

The car turned off the road into the colonel's driveway. Two automobiles and a motor cycle were standing in front of the house.

"The policeman has been found," observed Hand. "I rather expect one of those cars belongs to the county medical examiner. When the colonel starts anything, it moves!"

As we walked through the door, we found the colonel in the center of the hall talking to a young policeman and two other men. One of them, an official-looking person with scarlet hair, was introduced by the colonel as Dr. Travers, the medical examiner. The other, a stalwart man in golf togs, we learned was Geering Middleton, president of the village of Mill Ridge. The policeman was Patrolman Withers.

"With you here, we have an advantage, Mr. Hand," said Dr. Travers. "I understand you have already made an investigation."

"A cursory one," replied Hand. "Withers, I think I should tell you immediately that we have gathered some rather significant information concerning Dr. Metz of Barkersville. He was with Joseph Decker just before one o'clock this morning. They were in the den, where the body was discovered later. I went at once to the doctor's house after learning of this. He was out, but I talked with his servant. The man said he was positive the doctor returned home after three o'clock. On the way back we were fortunate enough to meet Dr. Metz. He told us without the slightest hesitation that he got home about one thirty."

"He's your man, Withers," snapped Mr. Middleton, frowning importantly at the policeman. The village president, with his bushy eyebrows, coarse sandy hair, heavy features, and bold eyes, struck me as being a trifle overbearing and self-important.

"You won't need me, will you, Doctor?" asked Withers of the examiner.

"No, I don't think so," was the reply.

"I'll just get after Dr. Metz, then," said the policeman quite ominously. "Where'd you see him last, Mr. Hand?"

"He was on the Ridge Road, headed for Mill Ridge," replied Hand. "I shouldn't wonder if you found him right round here somewhere."

Withers clapped his cap on his head and strode out of the house. Dr. Metz was in for an embarrassing experience, I had no doubt.

"Have you viewed the body, Doctor?" asked Hand.

"No, I haven't," replied the examiner. "I just this minute arrived. You say your brother's body is in the den, Colonel?"

"He lies in the den," said Hand quickly. "I'll be glad to show the doctor, Colonel."

Colonel Decker, Mr. Middleton, and I remained in the hall as Hand guided the medical examiner over to the door of the den. When Hand had closed the door after them, the colonel turned to me.

"Is he sure Dr. Metz murdered Joseph?" he gruffly asked.

"He won't say," I replied. "You can't get Hand to make a snap judgment. Before he accuses a man of anything, he has exhausted all his resources to determine him guilty."

"A very good system," declared Mr. Middleton pompously. "A very good system indeed. This affair must be cleared up, Colonel. To think of it's happening in Mill Ridge! We never had any violence here before. Shocking! I shall give Mr. Hand the benefit of my assistance."

There he was—the amateur meddler! I had been expecting him to pop up.

"You haven't met my daughter and the others, Mr. Clark," said the colonel. "Come into the living-room; I want to introduce you. Come along, Geering. We'll have to wait for the doctor to complete his examination."

We marched into the living-room, still occupied by the two men and the girl. The older man sat in a chair beside a table. His tall, slim body was all hunched over, and his colorless eyes gazed absently off into space. The young fellow and the girl stood close together before a window on the far side of the room. They broke off their earnest conversation and turned toward us as we entered the room.

The girl was distinctly a Latin type. A warm flush colored her dark, creamy cheek, her big brown eyes regarded us frankly, and her full red lips parted in a sad little smile of greeting. The light from the window glinted upon her coal-black hair as she moved her head. The boy was fair-haired, with engaging blue eyes and a strength of character stamped on his good-looking face. Together they formed a striking, delightful contrast.

Although the man at the table sprang to his feet, the colonel seemed to pay no attention to him. Mr. Middleton gave him a perfunctory nod as the colonel led us straight up to his daughter and her fiancé.

I was introduced to Patricia Decker and the young man, who I learned was Richard Fairfax. The girl subjected me to a careful scrutiny. I felt rather flattered instead of uneasy because of it. The young man gripped my hand warmly. Mr. Middleton ponderously expressed his sorrow.

The other fellow had sauntered over to us. The colonel hastily introduced him to me as Mr. Furness. He returned my greeting in a grand, European fashion. I thought I detected a look of dislike creep into Miss Decker's brown eyes.

"Have you made any headway in solving the mystery of my friend's death?" Mr. Furness asked me. "We are all deeply shocked. Poor Joe!"

"I really couldn't say," I replied, some of the evident discomfort of the colonel and his daughter imparting itself to me. "You see, I am not a criminologist myself, and I'm afraid I display a woeful lack of aptitude in that direction. I follow in the footsteps of my friend, Christopher Hand. I flatter myself that I know more of the workings of his mind than anyone else. But even I come far from knowing all that goes on behind those penetrating eyes of his."

"I see," said Furness thoughtfully. "Well, I wish him all the success in the world. If there's anything I can do to help, please let me know. I'm not the man to sit by and see a friend murdered in cold blood!"

I could not help noticing that the man's manner did not fit in with his stout assertion. He seemed as nervous as the younger Decker was said to have been. His eyes were too unsteady, and the unhealthy pallor of his cheeks belied the red-blooded man of action. However, I thought, I might have misjudged him.

"You have lived a good deal abroad," I said conversationally.

"Yes; I'm an expatriate," he replied. "I've knocked about a lot. A rolling stone gathers no moss, but it does get a polish, y'know," he added with a tight-lipped smile.

The colonel seemed ill at ease. I began to notice a tension about the group, and it seemed to me that Furness was the disturbing element. He nervously lighted a cigar, experiencing considerable trouble in getting his patent lighter to work.

"Haven't a shot of rye handy, have you, Colonel?" he asked. "All this beastly tragedy gets a fellow a little on edge. I could do with a good old jolt or two."

"I'll see about it," said the colonel, none too civilly. He crossed over to a bell-cord and pulled it. Then he paced up and down with his hands clasped behind his back. Mr. Middleton went over and joined him.

"I suppose you're glad your father has retired from army life," I said, turning with a smile to Miss Decker.

"Oh, yes, I am," she hastily replied, evidently glad to turn to a more cheerful subject. "We used to be separated for such long stretches! I just finished school last year, and he wanted me to go on to college in the fall. I rebelled—open rebellion, he called it. I won out, anyway. That's why he left the army. I suppose I was awfully mean to him; he's such a dear! He bought this home for me and everything."

"And now, right off, you are going to leave it," I chided her, smiling knowingly at young Fairfax.

"Oh, no, I'm not," she corrected me with much concern. "This place is going to be a wedding present to Dick and me, and Dad's going to live with us. We wouldn't think of letting him do anything else, would we, Dick?"

"You bet we wouldn't," replied the youth, smiling into her eyes.

"Well, the colonel's a lucky man," I said with a sigh.

"Oh, and you and Mr. Hand must visit us often!" she cried. "Dad is awfully fond of Mr. Hand, and I'm sure he will become just as fond of you. Dad loves to hunt and fish, and he's—"

"Fishing!" I exclaimed. "By Jove! We're on common ground there. I'd rather fish than eat. About the only place I ever see a fish lately," I ruefully added, "is at the aquarium."

"There are lots of them round here," Miss Decker assured me. "Dad has such fun in the streams! I know he'd be delighted to take you with him. He likes company. Often I go along with him and sit on the bank."

"Don't you ever fish?" I asked incredulously.

"No," she replied, with a shake of her raven locks; "I hold the net and take them off the hook when he catches them. I'd rather watch."

"Get a decanter of rye whisky for Mr. Furness, Maxwell," broke in the colonel's voice. "He'll have it served in the library," he added, with a quick glance at Furness.

"Thanks, Colonel," said Furness, turning to leave the room. "Anybody like to join me?"

We all declined his invitation, and Furness, with a shrug of his shoulders, turned to leave the room. At the same time Hand and the medical examiner strode in from the hall. We all stood in rather rigid attitudes awaiting the examiner's verdict.

"Well, Colonel, it's murder all right," he said curtly. "Mr. Hand agrees. I'm sorry, but I'll have to order your brother's body removed to the morgue. My duty demands that I perform an autopsy in such cases."

"Oh, no!" cried Patty Decker piteously. The colonel crossed quickly over to her and put his arm around her shoulder.

"I'm sorry," said the examiner in confusion. "It was thoughtless of me. I shouldn't have spoken while the young lady was present."

"Quite all right, Doctor," said the colonel crisply. "Of course these things have to be done. By gad! I want to find out all I can about this!"

Patty clung to her father and gazed compassionately into his eyes. The manner in which the old soldier's face softened as he looked down at her was wonderful. Once again Patty's eyes filled with tears, and Dick Fairfax was plainly distressed at sight of them.

The examiner bowed and considerately took his departure. Furness followed him out of the room, and Hand walked over to the rest of us.

"Well, Christopher, you have established the guilt of Dr. Metz," said the colonel, holding out his hand to my friend. "It was very quick work. I wish to heaven I had got you down here yesterday; you would have prevented this just as readily as you have solved it, I have no doubt."

"You never change, Colonel," retorted Hand, departing from his usual chilliness to regard the colonel fondly for a moment. "You invariably calculate the abilities of an enemy with a fine degree of accuracy, but you are forever overestimating your friends. My investigation has only begun."

"But the doctor!" exclaimed the colonel fiercely. "You say he lied about the time he got home. Three o'clock or later, his servant said. What time did the medical examiner fix Joseph's death at? You said about three o'clock."

"And so did the examiner," said Hand. "At least I have been corroborated in that."

"Then where's the difficulty in pinning this on the doctor?" demanded Mr. Middleton. "Withers should have him in custody by this time. Lock the wretch up, I say, and let the law take its course!"

"Oh, I have no doubt he has been locked up already," said Hand. "You see, he is safe and sound. In a murder case you can trust the police to grab the first person they can lay their hands on. They are altogether right in that, too. They leap the moment the faintest finger of suspicion is directed at a person."

"I don't call that such a faint finger of suspicion!" declared the colonel explosively.

"Nor do I," agreed Hand. "There is more to implicate the doctor than the hour at which he got home. Trouble with the police is that they are too easily satisfied. Give them a logical reason for suspecting anyone, and they are content to let it go at that. They'll work like fiends to gather enough evidence to hang that person, but if their case falls down, they find they've wasted a great deal of time and effort and got nowhere.

"I work differently. I don't say that Dr. Metz is innocent. On the contrary, he looks convincingly guilty. But even if we knew, which we do not, that he was with Joseph Decker when he was murdered, Dr. Metz would be only one of several I should suspect of the crime. I go into a case suspecting everybody; I even suspect you, Colonel."

"Oh! and me too?" asked Patty, her eyes, once again dry, becoming bigger by the minute.

"I'm afraid so," smiled Hand. "I'll let you in on a secret, though—I don't think I can prove it on you."

"I hope you're not joking about this, Christopher," said the colonel with something more than an injured air.

"Not a bit of it!" Hand quickly assured him. "But I'll go at this case exactly as I've tackled all the others I've handled. I'll attempt to find the murderer by a process of elimination coupled with the discovery of evidence pointing to the guilty party. I repeat—I have just begun."

"You see, Colonel," said Mr. Middleton with a lofty smile, "that is the difference between the direct mind of a soldier and the subtle mind of a criminologist. Mr. Hand is right, of course. I am not altogether unversed in the art of detection. I'll admit it's nothing but a hobby with me, but I'd be glad to give you the benefit of my help, Mr. Hand."

"I should be delighted," replied my friend, with a bow. I could see, however, that he was anything but delighted. "Dr. Metz is taken care of," he went on quickly. "I have notified the Barkersville police to make out a search warrant to enable them to get into the doctor's house. By the way, Colonel, have you told them of me?"

"The Barkersville police?" asked the colonel in surprise. "Of course not. What made you think so?"

"Well, they seemed to know me and were anxious to cooperate. They are going to place a guard at the doctor's house and arrest the members of his household. They offered not to disturb anything until I should get there. That is being considerate for you."

"Humph, showing more sense than I gave them credit for, I'd call it," said the colonel. "You don't seem to realize people know of you outside your beloved New York."

"Let's get down to business," said Hand crisply. "What do you gentlemen know of the doctor's household?"

"He's a bachelor," said Mr. Middleton. "Has a housekeeper—rather youngish woman. He got hold of a queer old fellow to act as a sort of butler a few weeks ago. Can't imagine why he wanted a person like that for a servant."

"That's the fellow we talked to," said Hand. "He did seem rather out of place. Know anything about him?"

"I don't," replied Mr. Middleton, and the colonel and Dick both shook their heads in the negative.

"Then we'll leave the doctor and his servants for the present. How about your own household, Colonel? We have you, Patty, Mr. Fairfax, and Mr. Furness. Then we have Maxwell. What other servants are there?"

"There is the cook, Mrs. Dykes. There was Buckley—he's gone," replied the colonel.

"And Sergeant Tim and Sergeant Hughie," said Patty.

"Corporal Hugh MacClintock!" corrected the colonel. "MacClintock was demoted last week, Patty. I told you that."

"Just for forgetting to meet you at the railroad station," the colonel's daughter pouted at him. "I think it was mean!"

"Have you brought your regiment to Mill Ridge, Colonel?" asked Hand in astonishment.

"Just my two old orderlies," replied the colonel, a little crestfallen at his daughter's scolding. "They've been with me for years—O'Brine and MacClintock. They're a great pair," he said, a faint smile appearing around his stern lips. "Alternated as my orderly the past twenty-five years. I've promoted and demoted them so many times I couldn't begin to tell you. They were pensioned out—over the age limit. I retired from the service shortly after. Looked them up and brought them here. I—I guess I couldn't get along without O'Brine and MacClintock. MacClintock's my chauffeur; O'Brine's superintendent of grounds."

"MacClintock looks every inch a soldier," I remarked. "I haven't seen O'Brine."

"They are both soldiers to their finger-tips," said the colonel proudly. "They are peculiar men. You could trust them with your life—I've done it many a time. They profess to scorn each other; yet either would lay down his life for the other, and just about has more than once. Never have a civil word for each other. They both have their faults, though," he added with a shake of his head. "MacClintock has a wretched memory. O'Brine is a tenacious man, but he's sadly lacking in intelligence."

"They're both dears," said Patty impulsively. "They've been my nurse-maids ever since I can remember, almost."

"It's remarkable the way they worship the ground Pat walks on," observed the colonel.

"I don't see anything remarkable about that," said Dick Fairfax. The young fellow and the girl suddenly became lost in each other's eyes. The rest of us discreetly moved over to the other side of the room.

"I don't think we need bother to go into young Fairfax's business here," said Hand with a twinkle in his eye. "This fellow Furness, however, presents something of a different story. The mere fact that he was closely identified with your brother makes him a character of interest, Colonel. Do you know how Joseph met up with him?"

"They met on the boat from South Africa to London, so Joseph told me," replied the colonel. "I don't know much about him, though."

"How long had they been friends, do you know that?"

"No, I don't. Not long, I believe. Joseph came to me Wednesday and said this friend of his had turned up from Europe. Said he had told Furness, if he ever came home, to look him up, and it appears that Furness took him at his word. Joseph asked whether he could invite him out, and I told him to go right ahead."

"When did Furness arrive?"

"He got here Thursday afternoon. Been here two days."

"Your servant Buckley disappeared Thursday night. You see how suspicious I am? Furness arrives in the afternoon; Buckley disappears that night."

"Good heaven! There can be no connection between the two incidents."

"Perhaps not. I am overlooking nothing. What opinion have you formed of this fellow Furness?"

"I don't like to talk about a guest."

"Under ordinary conditions, no. But these are far from ordinary conditions. Come, Colonel, what do you make of him?"

"Well, he was a friend of Joseph's. I was prepared to like him, and I tried to do it. His personality doesn't appeal to me."

"I should judge it doesn't appeal to your daughter and her fiancé as well," I said. "I don't think I made a mistake about that."

"You didn't," said the colonel. "Patty took a distinct aversion to him the minute he arrived. I'm sorry she showed it. I'll have to speak to her about it. I didn't know Dick disliked him, though."

"Well, he certainly isn't very popular," said Mr. Middleton.

"By the way, where is he?" asked Hand.

"He's in the library," said the colonel shortly.

"Where is the library?"

"It's at the back of the house beside the den," explained the colonel. "Here, I believe I have a plan of the house in this desk," he added, turning to a small desk in the corner where we were standing. He opened it and commenced sorting over some papers. He extracted one and quickly ran his eye over it.

"Is that it?" asked Hand impatiently.

"Well, this is a sketch of the first floor," replied the colonel. We bent over it as he laid it out on the writing-board of the desk. In order for the reader to have a clear idea of the arrangement of the rooms I reproduce it below.

Hand scanned the drawing intently for a moment. "That back hall there," he said, placing his finger on the spot. "That is where you found the blood stains yesterday morning after the servant disappeared, is it not?"

"That's where it was," affirmed the colonel. "And here's where our friend Furness is having his whisky, since you ask," he added, indicating the room marked "library."

"Is Furness still in there?" whispered a voice over my shoulder. We all glanced up into the intent face of Dick Fairfax.

"I suppose he is, Dick," replied the colonel. "He seems to stick pretty close to my rye whisky whenever he gets the chance."

"I'd like to talk to you about him, Mr. Hand," said the young man earnestly.

"Go right ahead," invited Hand quickly. "Clark, keep your eye out for Furness. Now, what is it, my boy?"

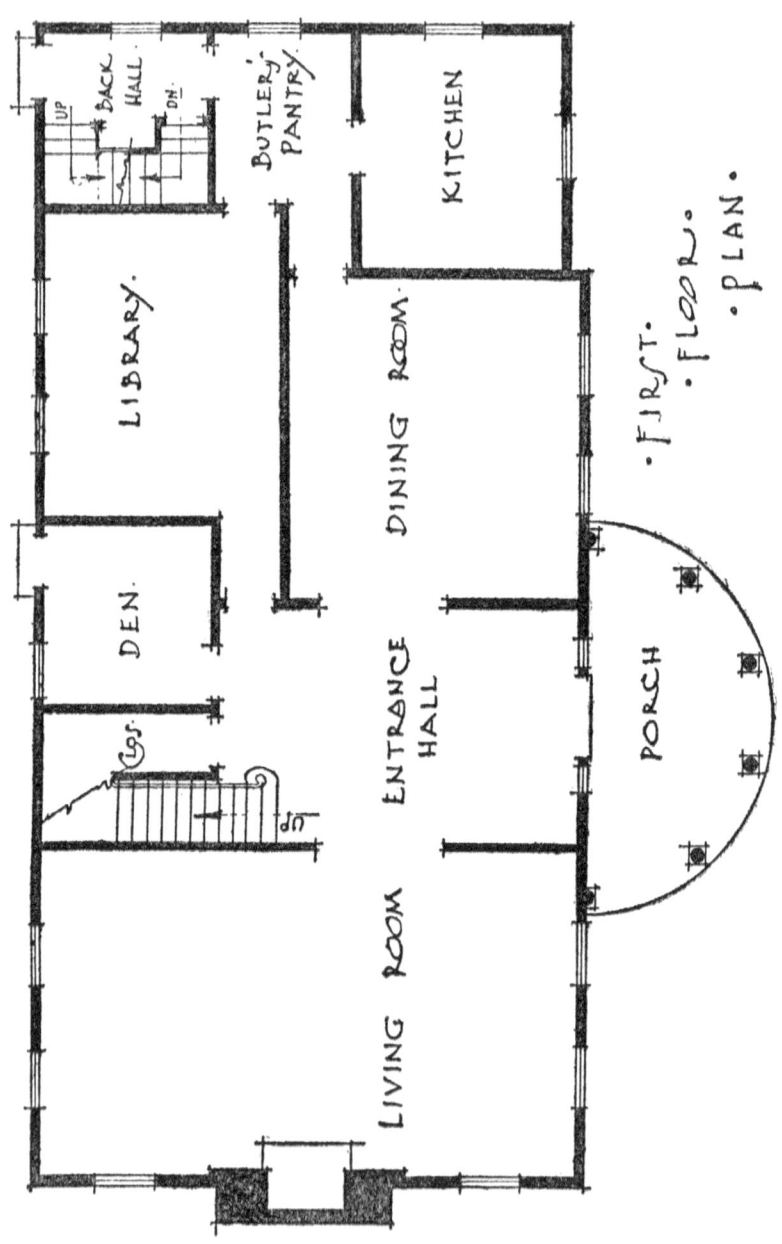

"It was last night, sir," began Dick, speaking very rapidly. "I didn't know whether to tell you or not, because I don't like to cast undue suspicion on anyone. I asked Patty just now, and she advised me to tell you right away. She's gone upstairs because she thought she'd be in the way. It's about this fellow Furness."

"Yes?"

"I don't know what to make of it. Last night about two o'clock I woke up. It seemed to me I had heard someone go by my door. I looked out into the hallway, but there didn't seem to be anyone there. I thought I must have been mistaken and went back to bed again. The room I'm occupying is at the back of the house near the end. I happened to glance out the window, and I thought I saw a light shining out on the ground from one of the windows on the first floor near the center of the house. I poked my head out, and sure enough, light was streaming out on the back lawn."

"Did you investigate it?" asked Hand intently.

"Yes, I did," replied Dick. "I got into my dressing-gown and slippers and stole downstairs. I didn't know whether someone had just forgotten to turn off the light, but more than ever I was convinced I had been awakened by a stealthy step passing my door. I was pretty sure the light had come from the den. I got to the foot of the stairs and started over toward it. The door was closed, but a faint light came from under it. I didn't know just what to do—I wasn't armed, you see. I stopped there in the hall for a moment; then I heard a voice from within the den."

"Did you recognize it?"

"I did, Mr. Hand. It was Uncle Joseph's voice."

"Could you tell what he said?"

"Not at first. I could just catch a word or two."

"If you could remember even one word, it might be very important."

"I just caught fragments of a couple of sentences. I'm quite sure he said: '. . . not here,' and '. . . you'll get nothing.'"

"Didn't you hear anyone else speak?"

"Yes, I did. Whoever it was spoke so low I couldn't make out what he said. Uncle Joseph interrupted him right away, too."

"Could you identify the other voice?"

"No, I couldn't. It was very low—just a mumble."

"As soon as you had determined it was the colonel's brother who was in the den, I suppose you went back to bed."

"Certainly. I didn't want to be an eavesdropper."

"But you didn't go right to bed, did you?"

"No; as I was going up the stairs, the door of the den opened. I was too far up the stairs to see it, but I could tell it had opened, because Uncle Joseph's voice became so distinct."

"What was he saying?"

"He was angry—almost shouting. I remember perfectly what he said. He said: 'You can do what you like about that, but you'll either give it to me or I'll go ahead on the other thing. Now get back to bed.' Then the door closed sharply."

"But somebody had left the den."

"Yes. I had an urge to run up the stairs to get out of the way, but I thought better of it. After all, there was nothing out of the way about my actions. I didn't fancy being thought a snoop, though, so perhaps I did quicken my steps. I was on the landing when I overheard the remarks I just told you of. I made my way back to my room as quickly as I could. When I got to my door, I looked back toward the center of the house. A man was just leaving the stairs from the first floor. There was a light burning in the center hall at the head of the stairs, but none down the hallway where I stood. He looked about, and apparently he didn't see me. Then he went down the hallway toward the other end of the house. It was Furness."

"Sure about that?"

"Positive. He stood right under the light; I had a good look at him."

"See here, Dick," broke in the colonel. "Why didn't you say the other person in the den with Joseph was Furness? You said you didn't know whose the other voice was."

"And I don't yet," replied Dick, leaning forward intently. "There was a third man in the den with them."

"What?" said the colonel. "How do you know?"

"Because when I got in my room again and turned out the light, I chanced to look out the window once more. The light was still burning in the den. Just as I looked, the outside door of the den opened and a man went out."

"Did you see who that one was?" asked Hand.

"No. All I saw was his shadow. Light streamed through the door for a moment; I saw the shadow cast by the man for a second as he went out; then the door closed again."

"Maybe it was Joseph himself," said Mr. Middleton.

"Maybe it was, sir," agreed Dick. "I looked out the window, but the night was so dark I couldn't see a thing. But if it was Uncle Joseph who went out, the other man stayed in the den. I could see the shadow of a man standing before the window inside the den all the time."

"What did you do next?" asked Hand.

"I decided it was none of my business and went to bed," replied Dick.

"Did you go right to sleep?"

"No; I tossed round for a while. Finally I dozed off."

"Didn't hear anything else during the night—later?"

"I don't know. I woke up later on. I felt as if something had wakened me. I hopped out of bed again and looked out the window once more. The light was still streaming out on the lawn from the window, but I didn't see any shadows. I went back to bed again—didn't sleep very well, though."

"Do you know what hour it was when you woke up the second time?"

"Yes, I do. I have an alarm-clock with a luminous dial on my dresser. It was ten minutes of three."

"Joseph Decker fired a pistol at his assailant," said Hand. "I have no doubt it was that which woke you the second time. Strange it didn't waken anyone else, Colonel."

"Rather strange," agreed the colonel. "Both Patty and I are heavy sleepers, though. The walls of this house are quite massive, besides. The report of the gun wouldn't go far. The servants are all on the third floor. It must have been that doctor, by gad! If Gerald Furness went upstairs about two o'clock and went to bed, it's not likely he stabbed Joseph."

"Let's just see whether he did go upstairs to bed," said Hand. "He went upstairs all right; we know that much. But didn't you say, Mr. Fairfax, that you heard him pass your door when he went downstairs?"

"Well, I assumed it was he," said Dick. "I'm sure I heard someone."

"Where is his room?" asked Hand quietly.

Dick's jaw suddenly dropped. "By Jove!" he exclaimed. "How stupid of me! His room is right across from mine!"

"And yet, when he returned to the second floor, he walked toward the other end of the house," said Hand. "He didn't go right to bed, you see."

4

EVIDENCE

"There you are, Colonel, we now have two persons who look equally guilty," said Hand after Dick Fairfax had unburdened himself concerning his experiences on the fatal night. "This is one of the times when I wish I could be in two places at once," he added quickly. "I'd like to inspect the belongings of both Furness and Dr. Metz. The doctor's house is under guard; therefore Furness will be the first one to command my attention."

"You mean you want to go through his effects?" asked the colonel rather apprehensively.

"Please forget the trepidations of a host, Colonel," said Hand with asperity. "This is serious business. You must get Furness out of the house for a while. The minute Withers hears of this, he'll arrest him, anyway."

"How are we to get him out?" demanded the colonel. "He hasn't stirred out of the house since he arrived here."

"I think I can arrange that somehow," said Hand. "Pardon me while I go to the library a moment."

He turned abruptly and strode from the room. The colonel turned to Dick and grasped him affectionately by the shoulders.

"I always knew you were on your toes, Dick," he said. "It's peculiar," he added thoughtfully; "I took Joseph to see you play last year. Joseph was pretty keen, you know.

He didn't know anything about football, but before the game had gone very far, he turned to me and said: 'Dick is the most alert man on the field. He's in every play. Some day that will count when he gets out of college.'"

"You played football?" I asked the young fellow.

"Some," he modestly replied.

"He was the best half-back Princeton ever had," said the colonel proudly. "You should have seen him get under a forward pass. And run with the ball! He was a streak."

"The colonel puts it a bit strongly," smiled Dick, shifting his feet.

"Not a bit of it, lad," protested Mr. Middleton. "You were a whiz! I've seen you play many a time."

"Oh, I say, Colonel," interrupted Furness's agitated voice.

"Yes," replied the colonel, turning toward his guest.

"May I borrow your car for a while?" asked Furness in a great hurry. "Something has come up."

"Why, certainly," said the colonel heartily.

"Matter of fact, it was that stupid fellow Hand!" sputtered Furness. "My last bottle! Medicine, you know. I'm not well, and the prescription's the only thing keeps me going. Supposed to take it after every meal. I forgot it after breakfast, with all the excitement going on, and I just had Maxwell go up to my room and get it. What does this fellow Hand do but trip over the rug and pitch head foremost into me just as I was pouring it out into the glass of water? Clumsy ass! The whole thing went on the floor, and then what does he do but bring his heel down on the bottle and smash it to bits! Beastly mess on the rug, too. You'd think he'd be a little careful after I'd just told him how important that medicine is to me!"

"That's a shame," said the colonel, trying to be sympathetic. Dick suddenly found trouble with his shoe-string.

"Nearest drug-store is Barkersville, so Maxwell says," said Furness disgustedly. "I didn't feel like going out this morning, dash it!"

"You may take Patty's roadster," the colonel hastened to offer. "MacClintock will give you the keys to it. Sorry I can't send you down in my own machine, but in the circumstances I'm afraid I may need it."

"All right, Colonel, thank you," said Furness. "Lucky I have that prescription with me," he muttered as he left the room.

Dick finally seemed able to adjust his shoe-string to his liking. He straightened and turned a crimson face to us. "Wow!" he exclaimed. "Mr. Hand does things with neatness and dispatch."

"Well, with dispatch if not with neatness," observed Mr. Middleton, repressing a smile. "I wonder where he's got to now."

"I'll take a look for him," I said, glad of the opportunity to rejoin my friend. I walked quickly over to the library. It was deserted, but Maxwell appeared behind me carrying a pail of steaming water and a cloth. At the end of a table in the center of the room I saw the shattered remains of a glass bottle, and a silver spoon lying on a wet spot on the rug.

"Too bad, Maxwell," I said.

"Yes, sir," replied the servant. "Makes a nasty mess."

"Don't cut yourself," I cautioned him as I turned to leave. At the door the sound of a starting motor caused me to pause and glance back. Through the large window at the rear of the library I could look out to the garage. A roadster pulled out into the driveway. At the wheel was Furness with anything but a cheerful expression on his face.

I concluded Hand would have gone to the second floor as soon as Furness had departed, but I bumped into him coming out of the den.

"Looking for me, Clark?" he asked. "Let's go up and see what we can find. The coast is clear."

As we walked over to the stairs, Dick came out of the living-room. "He's gone," he informed us with a grin.

"Yes," said Hand quickly. "By the way, where is this fellow's room?"

"Go to the head of the stairs and turn to your left," directed Dick. "His room is the last one at the front. Mine is across the hallway."

"Where is Joseph's room?"

"Down the other way. Uncle Joseph's is the second from the stairs at the back. The colonel's is the last at the front down that way, and Patty's is across the hallway from it. Won't need any help, will you?"

"No, thanks," replied Hand, to Dick's evident disappointment. "Come on, Clark."

The door of Furness's room was not locked. I did not feel at all uncomfortable about entering it as we did; I had invaded other people's rooms on just such a mission before.

"Looks innocent enough, doesn't it?" said Hand. "Look through that closet, will you, Clark? Examine everything in the pockets of the clothing. I don't think you'll find anything, but don't let that make you careless."

I went assiduously to work. I took down the suits I found hanging there and went through them like a pickpocket. Finding nothing out of the ordinary in them, I carefully put them back again. A dressing-gown yielded nothing of interest. There remained only three pairs of shoes. I made sure there was nothing concealed in them and then stepped back into the room. Hand was closing the bottom drawer of the dresser. He glanced at me, and I shrugged my shoulders.

"So much for the closet and dresser," he said. "Did you see his bag?"

"Er—no," I replied, reopening the closet door. The bag was on the shelf. It felt empty as I brought it out into the room. Hand opened it and ran his hand around inside.

"It's empty," he said, picking the thing up and giving it a shake. "Bags are interesting things," he went on as he ran his sensitive fingers over and all about the leather object. "Remember the bag of the Chinese merchant? That was a clever thing. I have it among my keepsakes. Mr. Wu made it himself, I'm sure, although he wouldn't admit it. This is a well-made bag. British manufacture, by the trade-mark stamped on the bottom here. By Jove, Clark, this is not unlike the bag you just bought."

"I've been noticing it," I said. "Who made it?"

"Kentham," he replied, holding the bag upside down and peering at the trade-mark.

"Mine is a Kentham," I said. "This one has been knocked round a good deal, but I think it's the same bag as mine. That's a—"

"Ah!" suddenly exclaimed Hand. He quickly placed the bag on the floor bottom side up and commenced pressing the bottom surface up and down with his thumb. It seemed to yield as readily as the stiff leather would permit.

"What is it?" I asked excitedly.

"Do you hear that crackling sound as I press on this?" he asked. I listened intently, lowering my head to hear better. Distinctly I heard a faint crackling sound.

"What do you suspect?" I asked, looking at him.

"Clark, I have a feeling your bag is going to suffer for this," he said, picking up Furness's bag and starting abruptly for the door.

"What do you mean?" I demanded, running after him. "Do you think there's something in that bag—concealed in it?"

"I intend to make sure," he replied, walking down the hallway. "This is my room, next to Dick's. Yours is next to mine, nearest the stairs. I saw our bags in them as we passed by."

He walked into his room; then turned to me. "Did you close Furness's door?" he asked. "No? Go do it, Clark. Then look up Maxwell and get him to find a file for you—any kind of file. Hurry up."

I left the room, closed Furness's door, and scooted downstairs. Maxwell was just finishing cleaning up the mess in the library.

"Do you know where there's a file?" I asked him.

"A file, sir?"

"Yes, a file. You know, for scratching things."

"I'll look round, sir."

"Well, look round in a hurry. I want that file as quickly as you can get it."

Maxwell left the room. I paced impatiently up and down while I waited. It had long since dawned on me that the file was going to figure in the defacement of my bag. I failed to get much comfort from the thought. Maxwell returned in short order with a broad implement with large serrations.

"Will this do, sir?" he asked, holding it up dubiously.

"It's just the thing," I said, snatching it from him. Up the stairs I raced. Hand was not in his room, but I found him in mine. My effects were tumbled in a heap on the bed. My open bag lay on the floor. Hand sat on the edge of the bed with Furness's bag upside down on his lap. He was digging at it with a knife.

"Quick work, Clark," he commended as I entered the room. "We're in luck; your bag is almost exactly like this one. It's a little later model—the lock is slightly different. It will never be noticed on the shelf. This is a most fortunate coincidence."

As I handed him the file, I was thinking the coincidence was not so fortunate for me. Just as I expected, he tossed Furness's bag on the floor and grabbed mine.

"Now to touch your bag up to look like this one," he said, never thinking to ask my permission. With the hand of a surgeon, he duplicated the scratches and worn places on my bag that he saw on Furness's. At last he stood up and held my bag out at arm's length, regarding it with the proud eye of an artist. I was no longer proud of it.

"There you are!" he exclaimed. "Perfect! Just take it and put it on the shelf in Furness's closet."

When I returned, he was again sawing away at the bottom of Furness's bag with his knife. It was tough leather, of the same sort that had induced me to buy my bag. He had a hard time of it, but at last he had a cut long enough to enable him to see under the leather covering.

"There's a paper in there, Clark," he informed me, squinting into the slit he had made. "Can't get at it yet," he announced, picking up the knife and vigorously starting to lengthen the slit.

He kept at it until he had cut the leather almost the entire length of the bag. Then he inserted his fingers into the opening. Carefully he withdrew them and pulled into view the edge of a white paper. Taking hold of it with the thumb and forefinger of each hand, he extracted a piece of paper about a foot square. The side which we looked down upon was blank, but when he turned it over and laid it on the bed, I saw that the other side bore some sort of message in handwriting. Both of us bent intently over it.

I read: "I, Joseph Decker, do hereby confess that while posing as one John Day, I obtained employment in the banking house of Littleton & Meeks, Southampton, England, and that on the third day of October 1928 I absconded with £5,000 belonging to that institution. In recognition of services rendered I will pay to the holder of this document, who shall remain unnamed, the sum of $10,000 not later than the third day of October 1929, at which time this document is to be surrendered to me." It was signed: "Joseph Decker."

"He was in a pretty hole when he wrote that," said Hand.

"But this almost proves Furness innocent," I cried. "Why should he kill Joseph Decker when by doing so he removed all chance of collecting on this thing? If Decker killed Furness, it would be more logical."

"On the face of it, yes," said Hand. "But Joseph had his back to the wall when he wrote this. Nothing else would have induced him to leave such damaging statements in the hands of anyone. It gives a terrific advantage to the holder. That ten-thousand-dollar limit for the price of it means nothing. The possessor of this thing could set his own price for it."

"Well?"

"Don't you see, it was quite possible that Joseph and Furness have been involved in other crimes? Perhaps Joseph had just as much on Furness as Furness had on Joseph. Of course Furness, having this written statement in his possession, had an advantage. There is little doubt that he came here for the purpose of coercion. Joseph, however, has no money. Faced with such a desperate situation, he may have threatened Furness just as greatly as Furness threatened him. Perhaps he was able to prove a more recent crime Furness had committed in this country. I'll admit that is nothing but conjecture, but the skeleton of our assumption is not without some body. Let me repeat for you what Dick Fairfax overheard Joseph say to Furness last night: 'You can do what you like about that, but you'll either give it to me or I'll go ahead on the other thing.'"

"That fits in, I must admit."

"Witness that this document was redeemable some time ago. Furness has not been very prompt to claim his ten thousand. Perhaps he was afraid to."

"Well, I'll admit you have shaken my first opinion, but I can't see how it proves him guilty of the murder."

"It doesn't," admitted Hand, folding the paper and putting it into his pocket. "But it may lead to it. We must get rid of this bag. Put it on the shelf in your closet for the present. Hurry up and put your things away; we want everything to look perfectly innocent. When you get through, join me in Joseph's room. It's the second door on your right beyond the stairs."

He turned and left me alone in the room. I put my fishing gear away a trifle ruefully. It did not look as if I should get a chance to use it, after all. My task was soon finished.

When I entered Joseph's room, Hand was crouching before a fireplace.

"Find anything?" I asked, closing the door after me.

"Clark, do you like the name Clara?" he asked incongruously.

"Hum-m, well, it's fair enough, I guess. Why?"

"What sort of person do you picture having the name Clara?"

"Well, a woman, for one thing. Almost any kind of woman could be named Clara. What's that got to do with it?"

"Maybe a great deal. A person by the name of Clara threatened to kill Joseph Decker, I should say."

"Good heaven! How do you know?"

"Come here and look at this," he said, pointing to the ashes and burned logs that littered the floor of the fireplace. "See that burned piece of paper. Someone—Joseph, no doubt—destroyed it. But ink is impervious to flame. A portion of that letter can still be read if you shine an electric torch on it. The dull, charred paper doesn't reflect the light, but the ink marks do to some extent. One must be in just the right position to see them, even so. I don't think you want to read it, Clark. I went through some pretty maneuvers to do it. I can tell you what it says—in part, that is."

"What?"

"Only the last line is legible. It is part of the last sentence, and I must say it's ominous enough. The words I read were: '. . . killed you, and I may do it yet.' It was signed 'Clara' very plainly."

"Good heaven, that's another one! The more we uncover, the more complicated this problem gets!"

"Yes, doesn't it? Quite interesting," he said, getting to his feet and rubbing his hands with satisfaction. "Your fly-box, Clark!" he suddenly exclaimed. "The very thing!"

"How's that? My fly-box?"

"Yes; go and get it."

"You mean the tin box I keep my trout-flies in?"

"Yes, of course. Hurry along."

I went dubiously down the hallway after the box. I was beginning to wish I had brought nothing with me but the clothes on my back. I was sure my flies would all get lost, and what he wanted with the box was beyond my imagination. I returned with it, and he snatched it from me.

Kneeling once more before the fireplace, he opened the box and grasped the ash shovel standing in the rack with the tongs and poker. He got the burned letter on it and with the greatest of care slid it into the box.

"That was a delicate piece of work," sighed Hand, closing the lid. "We'll leave this in my room. It may yet play an important part in the lives of several. Odd, isn't it? The letter is destroyed by flames, and the man who burned it is dead—both leave a problem for us to solve."

After Hand had secreted the box in his room, we returned to the first floor. The colonel spied us from the living-room and joined us in the hall.

"How have you made out?" he asked anxiously, in a lowered tone.

"We've made some rather important discoveries," replied Hand. "Have you a minute? I'd like to talk to you in the library."

"I've all the time you want," declared the colonel gruffly.

As we were making for the library, Mr. Middleton burst out of the den. Puffing excitedly on a cigar, he caught sight of Hand and bounded over to him.

"By the Lord Harry, I've made an important discovery!" he exclaimed. "Footprints, Mr. Hand, footprints! Right under the window of the den. They're fresh, too. Come see them!"

Mr. Middleton dashed back into the den. With a shrug of his shoulders, Hand followed. The colonel and I trailed along. The corpse on the floor of the den had been covered with a sheet. Mr. Middleton gave it a wide berth. He glanced back nervously at it as he stepped through the outside door. As a consequence he missed the step and went careening down the path, barely saving himself from a tumble. Disregarding the mishap, he skipped over to the wall of the house. Directly under the den window was a lilac bush. Mr. Middleton pulled the branches back and dramatically pointed to the soil under the bush. In the soft earth were the prints of a man's feet.

"I asked O'Brine," began Mr. Middleton excitedly, "I asked O'Brine about this bush. He said he loosened the earth up around it yesterday—yesterday, do you understand? Those footprints were made last night, Mr. Hand—no question about it! You can see, the fellow stood here for some time. Notice how he shifted his feet. This is important!"

"It surely is," said Hand gravely. "Very interesting."

"I'll have more evidence for you before long," promised Mr. Middleton. "You take care of the inside of the house, Mr. Hand. I'll clean up every clue to be found out here!"

"That's fine," said Hand. "Well, Colonel, can I see you a minute?"

We paraded solemnly through the den and into the library. I closed the door after us. Hand turned to the colonel and regarded him intently for a moment. "I don't have to handle you with kid gloves, Colonel," he said. "How friendly did you think your brother and Furness were?"

"Well, I assumed they were quite friendly," replied the colonel. "There were a few times, though, when they acted rather strangely toward each other. Now that you speak of their relations, I remember quite clearly that I was puzzled at them once or twice. Most of the time they were very cordial, however."

"Could that have been a little forced?"

"It could have been very easily. Sometimes I was as much surprised by their excessive cordiality as I was by catching one of them regarding the other with dislike."

"You should have been a criminologist," declared Hand. "How to see and how to notice is one of the first requisites. Colonel, your brother and Gerald Furness were not friends. They may have been once, but they weren't yesterday."

"Well, I'm not greatly surprised. What does it all lead to?"

"I hate to show you this, Colonel," said Hand, taking the paper from his inside coat pocket. "No use beating about the bush—you've got to see it sooner or later, anyhow."

He handed the colonel the paper we had found in the bottom of Furness's bag. The colonel eyed Hand narrowly as he unfolded it. Then he held it up to read. As his eyes traveled over the paper, his face became white.

"Where did you get this?" he asked huskily at length.

"It was cleverly hidden in the bottom of Furness's bag," replied Hand. "It wasn't a very new trick, however. The bottom of the bag had two thicknesses of leather instead of one. That paper was between them."

"I was afraid of this—I was afraid of this," repeated the colonel in a strained, far-away voice. "Well," he said, shaking his broad shoulders, "what do you read between these lines, Christopher?"

"That your brother and Gerald Furness were engaged in other nefarious schemes besides this one," replied Hand, brutally frank. "I think they were deadlocked in their threats against each other. Perhaps Joseph had more deadly information concerning Furness than Furness had concerning your brother. That might have led Furness to murder him, you see."

"By gad! And the wretch is harbored under my roof as a guest!" thundered the colonel. "What do you advise my doing?"

"Nothing, for the present," said Hand. "Withers may arrest him—you can't tell. Perhaps he's arrested now for driving an automobile while drunk."

"Don't joke, Christopher."

"My dear Colonel, I should say not! I was never more serious. In fact, I'm quite sure that Furness is already locked up in Barkersville on two charges: driving without a license and driving while under the influence of liquor."

"My word!" I said.

"You see," went on Hand, "when I had the misfortune to smash his bottle of medicine, I suggested he take Patty's car and get his prescription filled in Barkersville. He objected because he had no driver's license, but I laughed at his fears. After he left, my conscience began to trouble me, Colonel. I knew he'd been drinking, you see."

"You called the Barkersville police," I accused him.

"I had to do my duty as a law-abiding citizen," said Hand righteously. "I told the sergeant, Colonel, that I didn't think you'd mind if the doctor examined Furness

and found him intoxicated. He had two or three drinks—
maybe he was drunk. At any rate, Mr. Furness will stay
where we want him for a few days, and we shan't have to
show the police that confession of your brother's. Having
helped the police to take a drunken driver off the road, my
conscience has taken a holiday."

"By gad! Christopher, how can I thank you?" asked the
colonel, keeping a stern grip on his emotions. The muscles of the old soldier's jaw were working under his tanned
skin.

"By continuing to give me the benefit of that alert
mind of yours," replied Hand. "We'll leave Furness for the
moment. Colonel, do you know a woman by the name of
Clara who was acquainted with your brother?"

The colonel gave a start. He regarded Hand almost
balefully for a moment. "There is such a woman," he said,
harshness in his voice. "By gad! You go deep. What the
devil is this now?"

"A woman named Clara suggested she might kill your
brother," explained Hand simply. "I think the threat was
made within the last two or three days."

"How much do you know of her?" demanded the colonel. He had regained his self-control, but a tenseness still
remained about him.

"I don't know anything about her," said Hand, "except
that she wrote to your brother that she might kill him yet."

"Oh, you found a letter she sent him?"

"The charred remains of one. Your brother had burned
it. I found it in his fireplace. What was she to your brother, Colonel?"

"His enemy—deadly enemy," growled the colonel. "Gad!
Well, I suppose there's no help for it. I had hoped I'd never have to mention it again, but with her right here in the
neighborhood . . ." The colonel's voice trailed off, and he
seemed wrapped in meditation. He brought himself back

with a jerk of his shoulders. "The Clara you speak about, Christopher," he said with an effort, "is Clara Compstock. She's the widow of Beverly Compstock and lives on the other side of the ridge from here. Shortly after I was graduated from West Point, I was engaged to be married to her."

"You were!"

"I was. She was Clara Southington then—a beauty if one ever lived. Came from Georgia. She was a divorcee, which in those days was not what it is now. I fell in love with her, nevertheless," continued the colonel gruffly. "Joseph tried to dissuade me. He went to your father, and between the two of them they tried to convince me she was not the type of woman I wanted for my wife. Like a fool, I would not listen to them. We became engaged; I thought she returned my love, you see, Christopher. Your father and Joseph would not stand by and see me marry her. Your father and I were stationed in New York, and Clara lived there—alone. Joseph and your father watched her carefully. Clara was not rich, and she had a craving for money. I won't go into the rest of it—our engagement was broken."

"Through the efforts of Joseph and my father?"

"Yes. She hated them both as only a passionate woman can hate. Your father and I were ordered to the Philippines soon after. Joseph wrote that Clara had instituted breach-of-promise proceedings against me, but he had taken care of that, too. I don't know what he did; he'd never tell me, but she did try to kill him afterwards."

"And now, you say, she is living in Mill Ridge?"

"She is. She married Beverly Compstock, a wealthy wastrel. He lost all his money, and she left him, I believe. Beverly's brother owned the place Clara now lives in. He died last year and left the house and grounds, but not much else, to his brother, who, unknown to him, had died a week or so before. Clara turned up and got the place.

She's there, anyhow, hanging on by the skin of her teeth. All that is nothing but gossip; I pay no attention to it. She's there, nevertheless."

"Didn't you know she was living here when you bought this place?"

"No, I didn't," growled the colonel. "Neither did Joseph, I'm sure. He picked this place out for me. I don't know why, but he was crazy to have me buy it."

"Pardon me, Colonel, I hate to dwell on this painful subject," said Hand, "but what have been your relations with Clara Compstock since coming here?"

"Agreeable enough," grunted the colonel. "I was for avoiding her at first, but you can't do that here. Seemed to run into her every place I went. Finally she was riding over here, either on horseback or in her car—she has a small one. She makes a brave attempt to keep up appearances. I—I'm rather sorry for her, in a way."

"Colonel, what are your feelings toward her? You must understand I am not prying into your personal affairs out of idle curiosity. This may all be very important. I hope you realize that and answer honestly."

"All right. I've—well—in a way I've forgiven her, Christopher."

"How old is she? Is she still attractive?"

"She's still a striking-looking woman. She's really not so old."

"I see. Have you seen her lately—in the past two or three days?"

"No. She was coming over here to dinner Tuesday night. We had a rather large dinner-party. She was ill, though, and couldn't come."

"Colonel Decker—the phone, sir," announced Maxwell, cautiously entering the room.

"Who is it?" demanded the colonel quickly.

"Mr. Furness, sir," replied the servant. "He's terribly excited. I told him you were busy, but he insisted on talking with you at once."

"They have him!" exclaimed Hand with satisfaction. "Better tell him you'll get him out, Colonel. It won't do a bit of harm to tell him that."

5

THE DOCTOR'S HOUSE

I looked thoughtfully back at the colonel's mansion as MacClintock drove us out over the driveway. At last we were on our way to inspect Dr. Metz's house.

"The colonel must have made quite a good go of it in the army," I observed. "He must have paid handsomely for that place."

"That place wasn't bought with Uncle Sam's money," said Hand, with a smile. "The colonel had lots of it before he ever got out of West Point. His father was Frank W. Decker, one of the biggest financiers in the country during the latter part of the last century and the first of this. He left both the colonel and Joseph money to burn."

"And Joseph burned it, eh?" I said.

"He did. That's just the word for it. He burned it up and down Broadway first, and then all over the world. Poor Joseph ended without a cent, but with a reputation that was not too savory. All the while, his brother was carving out an enviable reputation in the army. They weren't very much alike. But Joseph, with his flair for the bright lights, was able to save his brother from an unfortunate marriage. We can say that for him."

"Yes, in that respect the colonel can be glad his brother knew the ins and outs of the free-and-easy," I agreed. "But perhaps by saving his brother from conjugal Hades, Joseph sealed his own fate."

"If that's the case, he saved him twice."

"How's that?"

"It appears to me Joseph has stepped in just recently to ward off this designing female from charming the colonel again. She was ill Tuesday night, and I am just beginning to imagine the cause of her illness. The colonel has never married. Neither have I, but I think that when a man begins to feel sorry for a woman, he's on the brink. I think Joseph felt the same way about that."

"You mean she had hoped a second time to ensnare the colonel?"

"She was making nice headway, if that was her scheme. She needs money now more than ever before. I have no doubt that she faces disaster, since it has become common knowledge. If Joseph did step in again, it's easy to reconcile her failing to show up at the dinner-party Tuesday night. But the most significant thing is that if he did interfere, it would not be surprising that she sent him a letter threatening his life. More than that, judging the lady from what we know of her, she would be quite likely to carry out her threat. You see, we can build up a rather strong case against her."

"Yes," I agreed, "that's the trouble, you can build up a rather strong case against all three of them. I can't understand it, unless all three of them had a hand in it."

"There's nothing to indicate that all three or even two of them acted in concert. The only connection between any of them is that Dr. Metz and Furness are occupying the same jail, but not by their own design—not quite."

"There goes the morgue wagon," I said, as the depressing thing flashed by us. Thereafter we rode in silence.

A few minutes later we arrived at the doctor's house. A lanky policeman leaned nonchalantly against the front door, placidly chewing tobacco. When our car stopped, he straightened smartly. Under his suspicious scrutiny, Hand and I mounted the steps to the porch.

"Everything's all right, eh, officer?" asked Hand.

"Yeah, everythin's okay, an' it's goin' t' stay okay," replied the arm of the law truculently. "Who might you be?"

"I'm Christopher Hand," announced my friend.

"Yeah, an' I'm Christopher Columbus," said the policeman derisively. "See anythin' green about me? You changed awful quick, Mr. Hand."

"See here," demanded Hand quickly, "what's happened?"

"Why, I'm jest goin' t' look you fellas up a little bit," replied the policeman, pulling a whistle out of his pocket and blowing lustily upon it. "So Mr. Hand has come t' call on us," he said mockingly. "I'll jest have Kelly call up headquarters an' we'll look you over pretty thorough, Mr. Hand. Don't move! I got you covered!"

Another policeman came hot-footing it round the corner of the house. Breathlessly he joined us on the porch. "Who ya got here, Sam?" he demanded.

"This here's Mr. Hand," replied the first policeman, bowing elaborately to my friend. "Ain't that nice, Joe? Here we was all het up t' see th' big detective, an' along comes two o' him in the same mornin'."

"Let's straighten this out without any more foolishness," said Hand angrily. "Here, take a look at this."

He displayed his gold badge of honorary membership in the New York Police Department. His name was inscribed on the emblem, which was given him by the commissioner out of regard for his aid in solving the College Hill murder. The policeman absently lowered his pistol as he bent over to look at the gleaming badge. Then he looked apprehensively at his brother officer. The two exchanged an uneasy glance.

"MacClintock," shouted Hand. "Come up here, will you?"

MacClintock hopped out of the car and hastened to the porch. "Do you know this man?" asked Hand of the policemen, indicating MacClintock. They both grunted an uneasy affirmative.

"MacClintock, just tell me who I am," directed Hand.

"You'rre Misterr Chrristopherr Hand," complied Mac-Clintock mechanically. "You'rre a frriend of Corronel Deckerr's, stayin' at his hoose."

Hand turned to the policemen. "Are you men satisfied now?" he demanded. "Quite evidently someone has been here impersonating me. You let him in, I suppose."

"Well, he said he was Mr. Hand," retorted Sam, his lean face reddening. "He acted like Mr. Hand, too. I—I guess we kinda made a mistake."

"I guess you did," agreed Hand grimly. "Well, the doctor has forestalled me. You can mark this one up against me, Clark."

"You couldn't be in two places at once," I stoutly protested. "You had to stay at the colonel's in order to—"

"Yes, yes," Hand interrupted me before I had thoughtlessly said too much. "Did Withers arrest Dr. Metz in Mill Ridge?" he asked the policemen.

"No, sir," Sam quickly replied, all his self-importance gone. "We arrested him right here in this house."

"I thought so," said Hand. "This door open?"

"Yes, sir," affirmed Sam. "Kin I help ya in there? Glad t' take orders from ya, Mr. Hand. Anything ya want—anything at all."

"Yes, you may come in if you want to," assented Hand. "Let's see," he mused as we entered the hall, "yes, there's his office. Front of the house, you see, Clark. He was in his office when you arrested him?"

"Yes, sir, he was."

Hand led us into the office. "Hum-m, yes, phone right here on his desk," he said half aloud. He picked up the instrument and removed the receiver. "Hello," he said into the mouthpiece. "Divisional traffic manager, please, and hurry it along." Then, turning to the policeman, "What time did you arrest Dr. Metz?" he asked.

"Let's see," replied Sam, concentrating deeply. "I'm on nights, an' they got me up. This is a pretty big case, Mr. Hand. We got th' whole force out. I suppose you're used t' these big cases, but—"

"Yes, I am," interrupted Hand. "What time did you say you arrested him?"

"Oh. Well, they got me up at fifteen past ten. Called me on the phone an' th' wife woke me up. I knew it was somethin' big. This here's th' biggest thing we've had— leastwise since I been on th' force, goin' on four years. I sez t' the wife—"

"What time did you say you arrested Dr. Metz?" repeated Hand patiently.

"Oh. Well, I got down t' headquarters—" began Sam.

"Hello, hello," said Hand into the mouthpiece. "Divisional traffic manager? Just a second, please. Now, what time did you arrest Dr. Metz!" he snapped at Sam.

"Huh? Oh, 'bout quarter to eleven," was the startled reply.

"Hello, traffic manager," said Hand, speaking once again into the telephone. "I'm talking from the residence of Dr. Henry W. Metz in Barkersville. The number is Barkersville 654. I believe there was a call made from this phone about fifteen minutes to eleven this morning—yes, fifteen minutes to eleven. I think it was the last call made from here. Dr. Metz has been arrested as a murder suspect. The police are interested in learning where that call was made to. Trace it, will you? It's rather important. . . . All right, I'll hold on."

"How did he know th' doctor's name?" asked Sam in a mystified whisper.

"I suppose he saw it on the name-plate by the front door," I replied acidly.

"Gee whilikers, how'd he know th' doc made a phone call?" was the next query whispered into my ear.

"You've got me there," I replied resignedly.

"Hello," said Hand sharply into the telephone. "Yes . . . good! I'll be very much obliged to you. When you get it, notify Barkersville police headquarters. Thank you."

"Success?" I asked.

"Well, they've got the number he called. It's in Forest Town. They're checking up now to see whose number it is."

"How'd you know the doc made a call?" asked Sam eagerly.

"Because of your experience with that other self of mine," replied Hand with a twinkle in his eye. "The doctor must have smelled a mouse, Clark. When did this other Christopher Hand arrive here, officer?"

"He hadn't left more'n fifteen minutes before you got here."

Hand looked at his watch. "It's twelve ten now," he announced. "We've been here four or five minutes. Let's say he left here at eleven forty-five. That's an hour after the phone call, approximately. How far is it to Forest Town from here?"

"It's a good fifty miles," replied Sam. "I took the mileage on—"

"How long did he stay here?"

"Only a minute. I was kinda surprised at that. You see—"

"About five minutes?"

"Not any more'n that. I got t' thinkin' after he'd—"

"Did he take anything with him?"

"Jest a bag. You know, it seemed t' me—"

"He didn't have the bag when he arrived, but he did when he left? In other words, he got the bag here and took it away. Is that it?"

"That's eexakly right. By golly, Mr. Hand, you sure—"

"Well, he could have come from Forest Town," mused Hand. "Fifty miles in an hour isn't impossible. The phone call might have been made quite a while before a quarter of eleven, too. Where's that other policeman?"

"He's gone back behind th' house," said Sam.

"Get him," ordered Hand. "We'll give the house a going over, anyway. I don't imagine we'll find anything now, but we'll look."

"Ya ain't goin't' hold us t' blame fer lettin' that feller in here, are ya?" asked Sam with much concern. "We had orders t' let ya right in th' minute ya got here. We was jest bein' agreeable."

"I should say you were," said Hand vigorously. "Don't worry about it. This is a very big case, you know. I sometimes get mixed up myself."

"Well, if you do I guess we kin once in a while," said Sam in a relieved voice. "Ya know, I'm trainin' myself t' be a detective too. I—I'm takin' a correspondent course. I ain't told nobody about it outside o' you. If ya could give me a few pointers, it'd be great!"

"Just give me a little time," pleaded Hand. "With such material there's no telling what we could make of you. Run along now and get that other man."

"Thank you, Mr. Hand!" exclaimed Sam delightedly. He turned briskly, caught his toe on the leg of the desk, and crashed heavily to the floor. His pistol, still gripped in his right hand, discharged with a terrific roar. The bullet sped through the door of the office and demolished a mirror set in a hat-rack hanging on the wall across the hall.

"Seven years o' bad luck!" said Sam dismally as he got to his feet. "Did ya ever see such punk luck, Mr. Hand?"

"Good Lord! I never saw such good luck!" exclaimed Hand, peering intently out into the hall. "Sam, you're great!"

He darted out of the office. I followed him, leaving Sam to stare after us in amazement. Hand stepped briskly up to the hat-rack. It was a thick, diamond-shaped board with hooks in the corners. The glass had been set in the center. Its shattered pieces lay scattered about on the floor. Behind where it had been set in was revealed a shallow receptacle about a foot square. Several small packages of white paper remained in it. Others exactly like them had fallen to the floor with the glass.

"What are they?" I asked Hand, who had picked up one of the little white papers. He opened it and sniffed cautiously at some white powder done up in it.

"Cocaine," he said. "Several thousand dollars' worth of it here."

"Good heaven!" I exclaimed. "Then the doctor is a—"

"Dope-peddler," finished Hand. "We're running into things, Clark. We may be instrumental in breaking up a dope ring here. I must call the chief. Hurry up, Sam; get that pal of yours. You've redeemed yourself."

Hand called police headquarters and told the chief to expect a call from the telephone company. He asked the official to take whatever information the telephone people had and hold it for him. As he was replacing the receiver, a shriek of agony, followed by the sound of a falling body, caused me to whirl about in alarm.

"Sam!" I heard someone cry in dismay. "I beaned him! I beaned him!" the voice wailed.

"Sounds as if the police have made another mistake," said Hand, cautiously peering through the door of the office. "Yes, it's another case of mistaken identity, I'd say. Joe has felled our friend Sam."

The hall extended from the front door to the rear of the house. Near the back, three steps descended to a small square hallway at the back door. On the floor of this hallway lay Sam, moving his arms and legs feebly. Standing over him, black-jack in hand, was his friend Joe, gazing dolefully down upon him. Hand leaped down beside the fallen policeman and helped him to his feet. Although very groggy, Sam appeared to be coming round all right. He stared vacantly at Joe, and his lips moved over sound-less words.

"He's all right," announced Hand. "Who did you think he was?"

"Gee hosaphat!" exclaimed Joe. "I heard a shot and sneaked in here. I was hidin' in those cellar stairs when Sam sticks his head round th' corner. I let him have it be-fore I seen who it was. He ducked, an' I only soaked him on th' side o' th' head."

"That was fortunate," observed Hand. "We'll just let him sit in the parlor for a while. He's getting quite a lump on his head, but aside from that he's as good as ever."

We helped the dazed policeman into the parlor and left him lying back in an easy chair mumbling incoherently. Then commenced the search of the house. We pried into everything, but in the end Hand was satisfied there was nothing else of importance to be found. Unless it was hid-den within the walls, there was no bullet-proof vest in the doctor's house. Our visit to the place, however, had been far from fruitless.

As we descended the stairs, Sam came out of the parlor tenderly feeling of his head.

"How do you feel?" asked Hand.

"Who hit me?" demanded Sam indignantly. "Did you get him?"

Joe shifted nervously from one foot to the other.

"Don't you remember?" asked Hand. "You tripped on the top step and fell."

"What, again!" demanded Sam. "I don't remember fal-lin' down after that time in th' doctor's office."

"It's not surprising," said Hand expertly. "You had a slight frontal concussion. Your magnesium plates were jammed together, causing forgetfulness of the highest degree."

"Gosh! I better get to a hospital!" exclaimed Sam in alarm. "I'm hurt bad. Call th' ambulance, Joe; don't stand there like a fool!"

"You're all right, Sam," said Hand reassuringly. "I can see from here that your head is as good as ever. You don't remember what happened during the past few minutes, but your intellect is just as good as it always was. Now that your memory has returned, you're completely over it."

"I don't feel just right yet," said Sam skeptically. "Do ya suppose me an' Joe got t' stay here any longer?"

"I've no authority to change your orders," replied Hand. "Clark and I are leaving for police headquarters, however, and I'll suggest to the chief that there's no sense in keeping you here longer."

"Tell him t' let us off soon as possible," said Sam earnestly. "I don't like this frontal concoction stuff. I want t' get home an' let th' wife fix me up somethin'."

Hand gathered all the cocaine together and put the papers into his pocket. MacClintock was still waiting patiently in the car. He soon had us before the Barkersville police station.

A small brick building housed the headquarters. A large plate-glass window in the front afforded us a view of the interior. A policeman, whose uniform bore much gold braid, strode up and down puffing lustily on a huge black cigar. Another officer, with sergeant's chevrons on his sleeves, sat behind a long desk staring vacantly out into the street.

Once again we asked MacClintock to wait. Hand and I entered. The man who had been pacing up and down whirled about and regarded us intently through the dense cloud of cigar smoke. The fellow at the desk continued to stare at the window.

"Are you Chief Huddy?" asked Hand of the one with all the gold braid.

"That's me," he replied. "You Christopher Hand?"

"Yes," said Hand, shaking hands with the chief. "This is my friend Mr. Clark."

"Glad to know you—glad to know you both," said the chief heartily. "Well, Mr. Hand, it's a lucky thing you were right on the spot. This is a pretty big case. We got our man in no time, thanks to your tip."

"The Barkersville police are certainly to be commended," said Hand. "You arrested Dr. Metz promptly, and I hope you have that fellow Furness also under lock and key."

"Yes, he's here, all right," the chief dubiously assured us. "Say, that feller wasn't soused. He put up an awful holler when Doc Graham told him he was drunk. I put the doc up to it, just like you said. I don't know about that—I don't want to get in Dutch with Colonel Decker."

"You won't, I assure you," said Hand. "This case is broadening out. It's far from inconceivable that Furness committed that murder himself."

"Not on your life!" retorted the chief. "Metz did it, and we'll give him the works. That old guy he had workin' for him finally opened up and told us Metz didn't get home until after three, just like you said he told you. Metz still claims he got home at one thirty. Now why would he lie like that if he didn't do it?"

"He allowed himself to be trapped there," admitted Hand.

"We have uncovered one or two other things besides that make his position even less secure. By the way, did the telephone people get in touch with you yet?"

"They did," replied the chief. "Hey, Tom, where's that name?"

"Name?" asked the man at the desk, rolling his eyes wonderingly in the direction of his superior. "What name?"

"The name the telephone people gave us," explained the chief testily. "I had it a minute ago; where is it?"

The sergeant's eyes commenced slowly roving over the desk. The chief stamped over to him. "There it is, right in front of your face," he said, glaring at the sergeant. "Frank Boscombe, 343 Chestnut Street, Forest Town," he read. "What's this guy got to do with this?"

"I'll tell you in a minute, Chief," promised Hand. "Tell me, first, what sort of man is this Dr. Metz?"

"I dunno," replied the chief, removing his cap and thoughtfully scratching his head. "He had lots of business."

"How long had he been here?"

"About three years—yes, just about three years."

"Know where he came from?"

"Came from Brooklyn, so I'm told. I never got to know him well. None of the boys did. Used to see him round, that's all."

"Did you ever see him round late at night?"

"I ain't round late at night. Tom, you was on nights until three months ago. Ever see Doc Metz round late? The Township Committee promoted Tom three months ago, for why God only knows!" explained the chief.

"What'd ya say, Chief?" asked Tom thickly.

"I say did you ever see Doc Metz travelin' round late at night?" thundered the chief.

"I kin hear ya," complained Tom, regarding the chief reproachfully. "Sure, he was out late lots o' times. Busy man. Doctors is very busy men."

"He was busy, for a fact," said the chief. "Used to be cars from all over stoppin' at his house nights. Guess he was pretty well known."

"I guess he was," agreed Hand. "Chief, I have every reason to believe Dr. Metz was selling drugs."

"Dope!" exclaimed the chief. "What makes you think so?"

Hand pulled several of the white papers from his pocket. "This is cocaine," he said. "We found it hidden in a hatrack in the doctor's house. Of course, it's not unusual for a doctor to have cocaine in his possession, but there's enough right there to supply several hospitals."

"Phew!" said the chief, picking up one of the little packages Hand had deposited on the desk. He opened it and sniffed at the powder. "It's dope, all right," he said. "You think he was peddling it, eh?"

"I think he was peddling cocaine, and I think he was peddling other drugs as well," declared Hand. "Before I got to his house this morning, another man went there and impersonated me. He left with a bag that he didn't have when he arrived. I think he carried a quantity of drugs away."

"Did Kelly and Phelps let that guy in?" demanded the chief pugnaciously.

"Yes," admitted Hand, "but it may have been a stroke of luck that they did. Besides, it was through Phelps, if that's Sam's name, that I was able to find the cocaine. They're all right, Chief."

"How'd you find out that this guy Boscombe carried dope away with him?"

"I think the doctor knew he was in for some kind of grilling in connection with this murder. The sensible thing for him to do was to get rid of the evidence of his drug activities until the storm blew over. When he saw your men coming to his house, he had to act quickly. Since this man Boscombe knew enough to impersonate me, Dr. Metz must have been in touch with him. The inference was that he used the phone."

"By golly! I'll call the Forest Town police right away and get 'em to pick up Boscombe," declared the chief, starting for the telephone.

"Perhaps it would be better not to go too fast," cautioned Hand. "Why not have the Forest Town police put a man on Boscombe to watch him for a few days? You might catch other fish."

"Sure enough!" exclaimed the chief. "I'll do it. By golly! I'll do just that."

He soon had the Forest Town police on the wire and explained the situation to them. He set the telephone down and turned to Hand.

"This is a mighty big case," he said. "Look at that!" he exclaimed disgustedly, catching sight of the sergeant, who had resumed his doleful inspection of the street. "The biggest thing that's happened in Barkersville since the Town Hall burned, and he acts like he's settin' on a bank fishin'! Lordy, Tom, you got as much life as a dead woodpecker!"

Just to show that the chief was wrong, the sergeant slowly opened his mouth, but he closed it again without having said anything.

"Well," said the chief, "that's another thing against Doc Metz. Pretty important, too."

"It is rather important," agreed Hand. "It proves a theory I had formed that Dr. Metz had been selling cocaine to Joseph Decker."

"How's that?" asked the chief excitedly. "He sold it to Mr. Decker?"

"Somebody did, and it's pretty safe to say he was the one," replied Hand. "I found papers of cocaine in the pocket of Joseph Decker's dressing-gown."

"Then they got into a row over dope!" asserted the chief, banging his fist on the desk. "He's the guy, all right!"

"But Furness is in this too," warned Hand. He told the chief what Dick Fairfax had witnessed the night before.

"Well, we'll keep him locked up too," said the chief. "On this fake charge, eh? We don't want to charge 'em both with murder."

"The drunken-driving charge will do," assented Hand. "We'll just play along with him for a while. You can keep him here for arraignment."

"Sure, we can keep him here," agreed the chief. "But Doc Metz will have to be arranged. We can hold him until tomorrow night, maybe, but then we'll have to turn him over to the prosecutor. The only thing the judge can do is turn him over to the prosecutor. Murder, you know. That's mantitary. Ain't nothin' else we can do, Mr. Hand."

"There's no reason why you shouldn't carry out the law," replied Hand. "Turn Metz over to the prosecutor as soon as possible, by all means. There is just one more thing concerning him: out of deference for my friend Colonel Decker, I feel I should request you to keep the possibility of his brother's having been a drug addict confidential."

"Oh, sure," complied the chief willingly. "You can trust me, Mr. Hand. And if Tom says anything about it, I'll break every bone in his body!" he added, glaring venomously at his sergeant.

"What's that ya say, Chief?" inquired the sergeant sleepily.

"Aw, nothin'," growled the head of the Barkersville police force. "He ain't heard a word we said, Mr. Hand. Don't worry about him."

"My request won't embarrass you, Chief," Hand assured him. "It's very important that nothing be given out concerning the drug angle of the case. If it gets round, the little scheme under way in Forest Town will come to nothing."

"By golly! That's right," said the chief soberly. "We'll have to keep it under our hats. Well, what do you want to do now, Mr. Hand?"

"I'll just have a little talk with Dr. Metz, if you don't mind," replied Hand. "He's pretty astute, I think. We caught him off his guard once before, however; maybe we can do it again."

6
THE MAN IN THE WOOD

Chief Huddy went behind the desk. He picked up a large ring on which were two huge keys; then he led us to a door at the back of the headquarters. We entered a large room situated at the rear of the building.

"Hi!" called a voice immediately. "By the gods, I thought you'd never get here! Here, you cops, let me out of this infernal place!"

It was Furness, peering indignantly through the bars of a cell against the back wall. Beside the cell in which Furness was caged was another one. On a cot in this sat Dr. Metz. He showed no such agitation as his neighbor was manifesting; merely regarded us almost humorously as we stepped into the room. His old servant and a woman sat uncomfortably at a table in the center of the room. Standing guard over them were Withers and another policeman.

Hand strode angrily up to Furness's cell. "Can't tell you how sorry I am about this, old man," he said to the colonel's guest. "Colonel Decker is wild. I wouldn't let him come over here for fear he'd lose his temper."

"Have you been all this time persuading him not to come?" demanded Furness acidly. "This is outrageous! You got me into this!"

"The horrible part of it is, I can't get you out," said Hand sadly.

"What!" exploded Furness. "You can't get me out? By heaven, I won't stay in this place another minute—not another minute! Here, unlock this door! Unlock it, I say! I'll have the law on you—the whole lot of you! Let me out of here, I tell you!"

"Don't get excited, I beg of you," pleaded Hand. "We are doing all we can. You won't have to stay here long, I assure you."

"I don't want to stay here at all," howled Furness. "The very idea! Colonel Decker is supposed to be a gentleman, and yet he lets one of his guests be arrested and locked up—locked up, mind you! It's preposterous!"

"It's unfortunate that we have so much else on our minds," murmured Hand, slowly shaking his head. "Nevertheless, we won't forget you, I give you my word. I'm sorry, but there's nothing we can do for the moment. How do you do, Doctor? It's a relief to see you so philosophical in the midst of all these distressing circumstances."

"Mistakes will happen," said the doctor epigrammatically. "I won't hold this against Chief Huddy or his men. Simply doing their duty. Matter of fact, as a citizen of Barkersville I'm proud of them. They can't be blamed for taking me in. My unfortunate visit to Joseph Decker last night could only place me under suspicion."

"I have no doubt you will be able to prove an alibi, Doctor," said Hand. "I should be glad to help you do it, if you could accept my poor services. For that purpose I've asked the chief to let us talk in private."

"That is very kind of you," murmured the doctor, a little uncertainty overshadowing his bland attitude.

"Well, Chief," said Hand, stepping aside, "it's all right, isn't it?"

"Sure," assented Chief Huddy. "We can go into my office." He stepped importantly up to the door of the doctor's cell and inserted one of the ponderous keys in the lock. The bolt yielded with a protesting, metallic screech, attesting to its unaccustomed use. Dr. Metz emerged rather uncertainly from his confinement.

He tried not to look at Hand. Nevertheless, his eyes, straying to my friend, bestowed a suspicious glance upon him.

"That's the door, over there to the right," directed the chief, pointing to a door beside the one through which we had entered the cell-room. He kept his eyes focused on the stocky figure of the doctor as he followed him toward the door. Dr. Metz, looking neither to right nor to left, walked into the chief's office. Chief Huddy closed the door after us.

"Hey! Hey! Aren't you going to let me out too?" came Furness's raised voice from the cell-room.

"Take it easy," was the muffled reply of one of the policemen. "Relax."

"Sit down, gents," invited the chief, lowering himself into a rickety swivel chair at his desk as he bit off the end of another black cigar. Since there were only two other chairs in the office, Hand, the doctor, and I regarded each other blankly for a moment.

"Sit there, Doctor," said Hand, indicating one of the chairs. "You sit over there, Clark. I hardly ever sit," he explained, turning to the chief, who seemed unconcerned about that. Hand turned smartly back to face the doctor. "You have acquired quite a large practice since coming to Barkersville, haven't you, Doctor?" he asked.

"Fairly large," replied Dr. Metz, shifting in his chair. "Not so large as one could wish for. I like the country, though, and I'm willing to be a small-town practitioner."

"But you didn't have to rely altogether on Barkersville and Mill Ridge even so," said Hand. "I understand you had a number of out-of-town patients, attracted here, no doubt, by your growing reputation."

"You're very flattering, Mr. Hand. I have one or two, yes."

"Your modesty is too much, Doctor. I have it on good authority that you have quite a number of out-of-town patients. Came to your office at night, mostly—that being about the only time a busy doctor can be found at his office. As if it weren't enough to put in a hard evening treating patients at your office, your profession has required you to get out your car and visit others far into the night on frequent occasions. The life of a doctor is surely a strenuous one!"

"No more so than that of a criminologist, I fancy. What do you say?"

"I have found little time to sleep on several occasions. But I think my time was spent less profitably than yours, Doctor."

"I don't know. Some of the fees you get must be tremendous."

"But people don't require me as urgently as they do you. Joseph Decker for instance. In a way, we might say I have taken up where you left off."

"You are not very consistent, Mr. Hand. A moment ago you said you felt sure I could establish my innocence. Now you accuse me of murder."

"Not at all. I merely inferred that Joseph Decker needed your services a great deal more than he needs mine."

"Well?"

"All he is to me is someone who has lost his life and by so doing left a problem for me to solve. He is not concerned with my success. On the other hand, when you dealt with him, he was very much interested in what you were able to supply him."

"I'm afraid you have got a bit over my head."

"Perhaps we can straighten it out for you. You told me during our last interview, if I remember correctly, that you and Joseph discussed the plans for a hunt you were arranging. You also considered his physical condition. Did you dwell most on Joseph's health and matters pertaining to it, or on the proposed hunt?"

"Why, we talked mostly of the hunt. We had his health settled in a moment."

"Yeah, with a knife," growled the chief. Dr. Metz flushed angrily.

"Had you been giving Joseph anything for his health?" asked Hand

"Why, no. I prescribed the bicarbonate of soda; that's all."

"From what I've been told of Joseph Decker," said Hand casually, "he had the characteristics of a drug addict. Did you ever notice anything of the sort about him, Doctor?"

"No indeed," replied Dr. Metz with warmth. "I'm sure you're wrong there. Joseph Decker was too fine a man for that!"

"If he had been a drug addict, you would have been able to detect it—unquestionably?" asked Hand.

"Not unquestionably," admitted the doctor.

"But, being a medical man, you could be reasonably sure whether he was addicted to drugs—say cocaine, for instance?"

"I'm not so sure of that. Frequently it's impossible to tell, unless it's pretty far along."

"Would it surprise you, Doctor, if I told you I have absolute proof that Joseph Decker was addicted to cocaine?" asked Hand.

"I'd think you were crazy," said the doctor with a short laugh. "I'd be more than surprised—I'd be greatly astonished."

"Oh, no, you wouldn't," snapped Hand. "Let's come right out in the open, Doctor. You wouldn't be surprised to know Joseph Decker used cocaine, because you provided him with it!"

"What do you mean, sir!" cried the doctor, rising angrily to his feet. "Here, Chief Huddy, take me back to that cell. I don't mind a mistake being made by a lot of simpleton, small-town cops, but I'll not be insulted into the bargain. I was good enough to submit to your questioning, Mr. Hand. I hoped I might aid you, but if you're going to be just as stupid as these policemen, I refuse to answer another question. By heaven, sir, you owe me an apology."

"I don't think so," replied Hand easily. "I may as well be frank with you, Dr. Metz. Your game is up. Your friend Frank Boscombe has spilled your beans all over the place. We have the whole gang."

If Dr. Metz was guilty of Hand's charges, he did not show it. He remained standing in the same angry attitude in which he had been regarding my friend when he started to speak. At the conclusion of Hand's remarks he threw himself back into the chair with a short, nasty laugh.

"Are you trying to flimflam me, Mr. Hand?" he asked amusedly.

"You know better than that, Doctor," reproved Hand sternly. "I advise you to pay strict attention to what I have to say. It may be the means of saving your life."

"You don't say so," remarked Dr. Metz mockingly.

"You may stall for time all you like. I haven't much regard for your scruples, but I have for your intelligence. I'm sure that if you will take time to think over what I am about to say, you will see things just as I do."

"Well, what is it?" demanded the doctor with a grin.

"Besides being proved a dope-peddler, you are under a serious cloud regarding this murder. In fact, Chief Huddy refuses to believe you didn't kill Joseph Decker. My own mind remains open. Perhaps by uncovering your drug activities we have opened the way to prove you innocent of the murder."

"Not on your life!" exploded the chief. "A couple o' snowbirds in a argument. One pulls a knife, and the other a gun. Clear as ice!"

"There you are, you see," said Hand to the doctor. "You are in a desperate situation, Dr. Metz. But I am not quite as willing to believe you guilty as is the chief. Our investigation has led us to suspect others besides yourself. If you are innocent of the murder, the quicker I find it out, the quicker will my attention be focused upon the guilty person. I can tell you quite frankly that you might as well admit you are a purveyor of drugs. Did you go out on that business after you left Joseph Decker last night?"

"I refuse to make any statements until after I have conferred with my lawyer," declared the doctor, all at once becoming sullen.

"I don't blame you for being cautious," said Hand, "but this is an urgent matter. If you delay too long, you may find your alibi dissolved into thin air. If you have an alibi, you had better announce it."

"You carry things with a pretty high hand," sneered the doctor. "You can't wring a confession of any sort out of me. Better give it up."

"You have an advantage that you are not aware of," said Hand. "It would be a pity for you to renounce it without knowing you were doing it."

"What do you mean?"

"I told you a moment ago that Boscombe and the rest of the gang had been apprehended. One of them has established an alibi for you. Are you going to corroborate it? It will save your life if you do."

"Someone said I visited him last night—at the time of the murder?" asked the doctor cautiously.

"Since that is the only way he could establish an alibi for you, why ask?"

"Who was it? What is his name?"

"It was—. No; I'm sorry, I can't tell you. I must keep a card or two up my sleeve. If I should tell you which one it was, your corroboration would have no force. If, on the other hand, you give us the right name, there can be no doubt that you are both telling the truth."

"Why are you so anxious to establish my innocence, Mr. Hand?"

"Because I am not fond of chasing a red herring," replied Hand testily. "Come, Doctor, you must see your position. Unless you can work yourself out of this murder charge at once, you will become deeper and deeper entangled in it. The authorities will spare nothing to convict you. If you have an alibi, the quicker you present it, the more it will count. You don't have to dwell upon your drug activities to do it. I don't believe your lawyer could give you better advice than that."

"Just the same, I want the advice of a lawyer," declared the doctor, wetting his dry lips and shifting nervously in his chair.

"Very well," said Hand, with an indifferent shrug of his shoulders. "But if you confer with anyone before you attempt to prove your alibi, I, for one, won't give a penny for it. The natural inference will be that the alibi was arranged."

"He ain't got no alibi," growled the chief. "If he tries to cook one up, we'll shoot it full o' holes."

"Very well, Chief," said Hand, turning to leave the office, "take him back to his cell."

"Just a minute," said Dr. Metz, clearing his throat nervously. "I— As a matter of fact, I did visit someone last night after I left Colonel Decker's house."

"Oh, you're changin' your story now, are you?" said the chief, cocking an eye at the doctor. "When we picked you up, you went right home from the colonel's house. Now it's different, eh?"

"Mr. Hand, I've decided to take your advice," said the doctor, ignoring the chief. "If you care to hear where I went last night, I'll tell you."

"Let me commend your wisdom," said Hand quickly. "Before you tell me, however, let me remind you that I already know where you were supposed to have gone. If you give the same place, your alibi is established."

Dr. Metz drew a deep breath. Then he turned resolutely to Hand. "I went to the home of Patrick Delano in Elmwood," he said in a strained voice.

"Delano," said Hand sadly. "Too bad! I'm sorry, Doctor; Delano is not the one who said you visited him last night."

"I say I did visit him!" flashed the doctor. "If Delano isn't the man, then it was Carrigan in Lincolnville. I visited them both."

"Ah, now you have it!" cried Hand delightedly. "Carrigan it was! Just tell me where those men live and it's complete."

"Howard Carrigan, 49 Spruce Street, Lincolnville," replied Dr. Metz hastily. "Delano lives at 16 Gates Avenue, Elmwood. I was at both of those addresses last night after I left Joseph Decker."

"Good!" said Hand. "It will be simple to get Delano to corroborate your story in just that same convincing fashion. Both have been arrested, of course. Carrigan told us the purpose of your visit. Do you wish to strengthen your story by confirming what he told us?"

"Well, I saw him on business," replied the doctor cautiously.

"Very well. I told you that you need not dwell upon your connection with those men. You have acted very wisely, Doctor. Your statement was made in the presence of three reliable witnesses. I will be glad to take the witness-stand on your behalf to substantiate your alibi—if you ever do go to trial for the murder. As far as I'm concerned, you are no longer under suspicion for the murder."

"But that ain't as far as I'm concerned," Chief Huddy assured the doctor. "Back into that cell you go, and there you stay till we pack you off to the county prosecutor. He can do what he likes about you."

The chief opened the door, and Dr. Metz, with lowered eyelids and bowed head, strode out of the office. He returned to his cell and sat down on his cot with something of relief in his bearing.

"Back again?" asked Furness in surprise as he regarded the doctor through the bars. "I thought you were out. See here, Mr. Hand, have you arranged to get me out of here yet?" he called to us as we stood waiting for the chief to finish locking the doctor's cell.

"Have patience, Mr. Furness," pleaded Hand. "We'll be back again. I hope we'll have a surprise for you when we do."

"Mean to say I've got to stay here?" demanded Furness.

"For a little while," replied Hand as we followed the chief out into the front room. The door closed upon us, partially cutting off Furness's bitter objections. Hand crossed over to the desk. He picked up a paper pad from under the sergeant's nose, but that worthy seemed not to realize that once again he had company. Hand took a pencil from his pocket and commenced to write on the pad.

"Say, you didn't tell me those other dope artists have been nabbed," complained the chief. "Why didn't you let me in on that? Gosh, I thought we was goin' to grab off all the credit."

"So you are, Chief," said Hand, passing the paper he had been writing on over to the official. "There are the names of two more members of our dope ring, together with their addresses. Better get working on it right away. Lincolnville and Elmwood are small places, aren't they?"

"They ain't so small," replied the chief. "About five thousand inhabitation in each. Say—you mean to say you cooked all that up? Ain't those fellas been arrested?"

"Not yet," smiled Hand. "Lincolnville and Elmwood are not so far away from here, are they, chief?"

"About fifteen mile."

"How far apart are they?"

"Oh, about four or five mile apart."

"Hum-m, something funny about this. Of course, the doctor could have got to both places and back between the time he says he left Colonel Decker's house last night and the time his servant says he got home. But why would he call Boscombe in Forest Town, fifty miles away, if he wanted to get hold of one of his gang in a hurry this morning?"

"Yeah, that's right," mused the chief. "Somethin' funny about that."

"Well, we'll clear that up in due course," said Hand briskly. "Better get hold of the police of Lincolnville and Elmwood right away, Chief. I'd suggest they merely keep their eyes on those two fellows for a while, too. The police of all four towns can keep in touch with each other, and when the time comes, the hauls can all be made at once."

"Right; and in the mean time we'll just keep Doc Metz and Mr. Furness cooped up here," agreed the chief. "How about that fella and girl we took in up at the doc's house?"

"I don't think the old fellow is in on this," replied Hand. "I didn't just understand him at first, but I think I do now. The doctor thought he had an old fool who could easily have the wool pulled over his eyes. Funny, it was the old servant who got him into trouble. The young woman we don't know about. Better hang on to them both."

"But we ain't got no place to keep womin," protested the chief.

"Well, I think the best thing you can do is to arraign the doctor and the girl as soon as possible," said Hand. "Hold them both on an open charge and remand them to jail. Then you can pack them both off to the county penitentiary. Lock the old servant up in the cell the doctor's occupying now and hold him as a material witness for a day or so before turning him over to the prosecutor. How soon can you get your judge here?"

"Frank Hogg's our justice," replied the chief, squinting through the front window. "That's him over in that barbershop across the street. He's shavin' the chairman of the Township Committee now—there's a meetin' tonight. Soon's he gets through, we can arrange Doc Metz an' the girl."

"Good," said Hand. "I'd get them off to the county jail as soon as possible. We won't need Dr. Metz any more, or so it appears."

"You don't think he murdered him, eh?"

"On the contrary, I still suspect him almost as much as ever. But he'll be safe and sound in the county jail, you see. Besides, we may need that other cell of yours."

"Oh Lord! You gonna bring some more in?"

"It's possible. Oh, that reminds me!"

"What?"

"Your sergeant there."

"Tom? He ain't said nothin'."

"No; it's the way he looks. You still have two men on guard up at the doctor's house, Chief."

"Sure, I know it. And I've got one more man left here besides Tom."

"I told Sam I'd tell you he needs to go home. He hurt his head."

"How in blazes did he do that?"

"He tripped and fell downstairs. He has a nasty bump on his head."

"He's the clumsiest chump I ever saw! If you was to drop a match on the floor here, he'd trip over it the next time he come in. If it wasn't that most of his weight's in his feet, he'd kill himself. Do you suppose it would be safe to let him leave the doctor's house?"

"I think so," Hand averred. "Let the other fellow stay there for a while."

"All right," said the chief, "I'll call them up at the doc's house right away and send him home. What a time for that galoot to get hurt!"

"We'll say good-by to you for the present, Chief," said Hand, starting for the door. "Get Dr. Metz and the girl off to the county jail as soon as possible. We'll probably see you later on."

Chief Huddy picked up the telephone. "By heck, I'd rather see you than anybody else," he declared warmly. "No! No! No! I ain't talkin' to you, operator. Give me— er—what's Doc Metz's number, Tom? Hurry up, ya lummox! Get the book! Get the telephone book!"

"Don't forget to call the Elmwood and Lincolnville police, Chief," cautioned Hand, pausing in the doorway.

"By gosh! That's right!" exclaimed the chief, excitedly jiggling the hook of the telephone. "Hey, operator! Operator! Tom—look up the Elmwood police. Hurry up, ya dead-head! No! No!—not you, operator. Have ya got it, Tom? For the lova Pete, get a move on!"

We closed the door on the frenzied scene going on in the police headquarters. Hand started across the sidewalk to the colonel's car. MacClintock sat stiffly behind the steering wheel. Evidently he hadn't budged since we left him.

"Where are we going now?" I asked.

"We are going to pay our respects to Mrs. Compstock," replied Hand.

"But, look here," I protested, "aren't we going to eat today? We had breakfast at five o'clock this morning and now it's nearly two. I'm starved."

"Have you had any lunch, MacClintock?" asked Hand.

"No, sirr," replied the old driver. "Don't ye let that worrry ye, sirr. I've gone wi'oot me rrations many's the time. I'm takin' m' orrderrs frrom you, sirr."

"Then go get a bite to eat," said Hand. "There's a restaurant down below police headquarters, Clark," he said resignedly to me. "Come on, we'll get a snack and then be on our way."

MacClintock disappeared into a lunch wagon, and Hand and I entered the little restaurant. As usual, my friend consumed his food in the twinkling of an eye. Then he sat and impatiently watched each mouthful I took. I had got used to the practice and was able to enjoy my meals. I took as little time as possible, however, and in a few minutes we were back on the sidewalk. MacClintock was already behind the steering wheel.

"We'll go to Mrs. Compstock's, MacClintock," ordered Hand as we got into the machine. MacClintock nodded and we started. Back over the Ridge Road we went into Mill Ridge. It was a comfortable feeling to lie back against the soft cushions and watch the landscape rush by. The Ridge Road was lined with deep forests on both sides. Idly I wondered what the adventuress whom we were about to meet would be like. All at once I noticed MacClintock stiffen and peer intently ahead.

"Who was that, MacClintock?" demanded Hand abruptly.

"Did ye see him, sirr?" inquired MacClintock. "He's a funny one. I've seen him herreaboots thrree orr fourr times, and he always ducks into the bushes like that."

"Stop the car," ordered Hand. "This is about where he went in. Come on, we'll have a look for that fellow."

I had seen nothing of the man they spoke of. However, as MacClintock brought the car to a halt, I jumped out with the others. All three of us entered the wood. The tall trees grew close together. On the ground was a mattress of dried leaves. The thick bushes that grew at the side of the road extended only about ten feet back from it. Even so we could see but a short distance ahead as we stood peering intently from side to side among the trees. Not a sound broke the stillness of the forest. The only movement about us was the gentle swaying of the branches far above our heads.

"We could deploy, sirr," whispered MacClintock.

"Are you armed?" asked Hand.

"I am," replied MacClintock grimly. He produced a huge service automatic from a holster under his tunic.

"All right, we'll spread out," said Hand. "If you don't see anything in five minutes, return here."

Careful to keep my bearings, I started off to the right of my companions. Although I moved as cautiously as possible, the leaves underfoot set up a great crackling as I trod upon them. Dried twigs snapped under my feet with what sounded to me like pistol-shots. I held my pistol in my hand as I slunk from tree to tree. Although the day was bright and clear, under the trees, not yet even in full bloom, no sunlight reached me. I stepped over the rotten trunk of a fallen tree. As I put my foot down, it descended upon a sharp rock hidden under the carpet of leaves. My foot slipped from under me, and I barely saved myself from a tumble. In catching my balance I swung round and was just in time to see a dark form disappear behind the trunk of one of the largest trees. Quickly I stepped behind another tree. After a minute or two had passed and I had seen nothing, I decided to investigate. As I stepped forth, the crackling leaves betrayed me. A man darted from behind the tree and sped away.

"Stop!" I cried as I started in pursuit, "stop or I'll fire!"

The fellow paid no attention to me. I raised my pistol and fired over his head. If anything, the shot helped him gain speed. He was darting in and out among the trees so rapidly that I doubt whether I could have hit him if I had tried. Again I fired over his head, not wishing to chance wounding him for no particular reason.

Whoever he was, the man I pursued was fleet of foot. He soon outdistanced me and I lost all but an occasional glimpse of him through the trees. At last I stopped exhausted and leaned against a tree. Behind me I heard someone running toward me. It was Hand, who spied me leaning weakly against the tree, gasping for breath.

"Where did he go?" demanded my friend, rushing up to me.

"Right down that way," I gasped. "Heaven knows where he is now."

Hand turned and ran off in the direction the mysterious man had taken. I followed, but the best I could do was to walk feebly after my friend. I was suddenly startled out of my wits by MacClintock, who stepped from behind a tree ahead of me.

"Oh, it's you, Misterr Clarrk," he said. "Who did the shootin'?"

"I did," I replied, breathing heavily. "Where did you come from? I thought you were behind me."

"I was, sirr," he affirmed. "When I heard the shots, I rreconnoiterred arroond this way on the dooble. Wherre's Misterr Hand?"

"He's gone on after him," I said. "I don't think there's a chance of catching that fellow—he was sprinting when last I saw him! It's a shame either you or Hand didn't see him instead of me. I'm afraid I bungled it."

"Ye did the best ye coold, sirr," said MacClintock soothingly. "I'm used to gettin' arroond in the forrests, smokin' out men. We did it plenty in the Arrgonne and Belleau Wood, too. The Philippines was full of 'em. Let's get on afterr Misterr Hand. We'll sprread oot—you go that way, and I'll go this. Maybe that fellow will dooble back."

MacClintock left me, and once again I commenced stalking through the wood. After a while I was hailed by Hand.

"No use looking for that chap any longer," he said after he had joined me. "Have you seen MacClintock?"

"He's around here somewhere," I replied. "He pounced upon me once. Then we parted again and set off after you. This is a fine mess if we've got to go poking round after him—everybody armed and ready to shoot on sight!"

"Herre ye arre, sirr," suddenly called MacClintock. He had been standing behind a tree not twenty feet from us.

"We'll get back to the car, MacClintock," said Hand. "You didn't see anything of that fellow, did you?"

"No, sirr, he went like a hoot in a gale of wind. I see Misterr Clarrk thrree times, but I didn't see you at all, sirr."

"So you've seen that chap several times before, Mac-Clintock?" asked Hand as we started back through the wood to the car.

"I see him twice rright nearr herre, sirr," replied Mac-Clintock. "And then I see him once doon nearr the corronel's hoose. Every time I see him, he ducked into the bushes."

"Did you ever follow him before?"

"I did, sirr. When I see him doon by the corronel's hoose, I went after him. He's quick as a fox, I tell ye. He was gone."

"Did you ever get a good look at him? He seemed rather young to me."

"He's a young one, sirr. Aboot twenty-five, I'd say. Darrk, he is."

"What do you say, Clark? Did you see him plainly?"

"I saw him plainly enough," I said, "but I didn't see his face. He was going away from me for all he was worth. He seemed to be a young man, though. He had dark hair and wore a dark suit, tan shoes, and a light cap."

"Hum-m. Well, we'll keep our eyes open for him," said Hand. 'There's the car. At last we'll get on up to see Mrs. Compstock."

7

A LADY AT BAY

Once again we proceeded along the Ridge Road. A short distance on we passed the road that branched off to the colonel's. A quarter of a mile farther on, MacClintock turned into a narrow road leading up to a knoll.

"Is this the road to Mrs. Compstock's?" asked Hand.

"Yes, sirr," replied MacClintock. "Herr hoose is at the top of the rrise. 'Tis a grrand view she gets frrom therre."

"Hold on, MacClintock," said Hand suddenly. "Whose car is that coming from her place?"

The other car had come round a turn in the road. The roadway itself was so narrow there was barely room for both machines to pass. MacClintock and the other driver both slowed down.

"I think it's the taxi frrom Barrkerrsville, sirr," said MacClintock. "Yes, sirr, that's what it is."

"Stay out in the road and make him stop," ordered Hand. "Can you see who is in that taxi?"

"It looks like Mrs. Compstock's maid to me, sirr," replied the driver, applying his brakes.

"By Jove, here's a bit of luck," said Hand with satisfaction.

MacClintock stopped the car so far out in the center of the road that the taxi was also forced to halt. The taxi-driver, a fierce-looking old fellow, stuck his head out and demanded a clear road. The two cars were almost side by side.

Hand got out and walked up to the rear door of the taxi.

"Are you Mrs. Compstock's maid?" he asked a pert-looking girl, speaking through the open window of the door.

"No; I was," she replied with a toss of her head.

"Oh, you're leaving, then," said Hand. "Mrs. Compstock is unfortunate."

"She's more than that!" sniffed the girl.

"Ah, I perceive you've had trouble with your erstwhile mistress."

"Yeah, plenty! All's I've had is trouble ever since I came here. I showed her where she could get off, though!"

"There you are, Clark, that just proves it," said Hand, turning to the colonel's car and addressing me through the window.

"Proves what?" asked the girl.

"What we have just been arguing about," replied Hand. "I was just telling my friend that feminine beauty inspires growing admiration in the hearts of men and growing hatred in the hearts of other women. I don't wonder that your mistress was unkind to you."

"Oh, yeah?" simpered the girl. "You got a hot line, mister."

"It's the truth," declared Hand, surprisingly showing attributes of a flirt. "So you left the lady flat."

"Yes, I did," affirmed the girl, suddenly becoming a little annoyed. "What business is it of yours, mister?"

"I am after information concerning Mrs. Compstock. She owes our firm quite a sum of money. I thought I'd stop in and see her."

"Owes you money!" exclaimed the girl with a raucous laugh. "Say, that's rich! Do you know how much chance you got of collectin' it?"

"No, I don't. I hope a good chance."

"Well, you haven't. What do you think I'm leavin' for, a change of scenery?"

"Why, I thought you just said your mistress treated you badly."

"She did, too. She's a devil! But that's not all—I haven't had a cent of wages for two months!"

"Hum-m, that's interesting."

"Yeah—that's a dirty gyp, that's what that is!"

"I should say so. Well, it looks as if we have a problem on our hands. I don't suppose you'd mind giving us as much information concerning the lady as you can. I might be able to collect your wages along with the rest."

"You got a Chinaman's chance, but you're welcome to go to it. What can I tell you, though? All's I know is she won't pay her bills."

"Well, that's a starter. Have you any idea how much she owes?"

"She owes me two months' wages, for one thing. Then she owes Patou for a lot of dresses and things. She hasn't paid the coal bill—I know that. We changed butchers just the other day—no more credit. Grocery man's gettin' hot under the collar, too. If I hadn't left when I did, I guess I'd of been starved out anyway."

"How long have you been with Mrs. Compstock?"

"Nine months. I don't know how I stood it!"

"Now, I wonder—did you notice a change come over her about three months ago—anything at all?"

"I hope to tell you I did. That's when all the fun started."

"What was the change?"

"Well, she started in puttin' on the dog. Went right out and bought the fanciest, highest-priced clothes you ever saw. Got a couple of housemaids besides the one she had. Got a butler, too. They've all left long ago. She never did pay them. That's when I started dyein' her hair in real earnest, too."

"Say!" interrupted the taxi-driver. "Think I got nothin' t' do but stand here in the middle o' this here road while you gabber about the neighbors? This is just costin' you twenty-five cents every fifteen minutes, miss!"

"Get out of the way, mister!" said the girl excitedly. "Let him get me to town. I haven't got too many of those quarters he's talkin' about."

"I'll be glad to make it right with him," Hand assured her. "Not only that, but your information is fast becoming worth ten dollars to me."

"Fire away, then," said the girl, her good nature completely restored.

"What else did she do about three months ago?"

"Well, she started goin' to the beauty specialist in New York. René Lavier, too—just about the most expensive there is. I know all about René. He's singin' the blues now along with the rest."

"Do you know what caused her to do all this?"

"Makin' a splurge, that's sure. She was quiet enough up to then. But when she stepped out, she stepped out!"

"Did it appear to you that she was trying to impress anyone in particular? Was she fond of a man?"

"Well, I always thought she had her eye cocked for that old Colonel Decker. I hope she don't get him; he's too good for her."

"What made you think she was after him?"

"It's a cinch she was. Whenever she heard he was goin' to call on somebody, off she'd go to be there too. Then she was always tryin' to get him to go horseback-ridin', you know. I'll hand it to her—she's not so bad on a horse, and she's no spring chicken. Thinks it keeps her figure down, I suppose. You wouldn't ketch me on one of those things, fat or no fat!"

"I see. Anything else?"

"Well, she was all steamed up over a dinner-party she's goin' to give for the colonel on his birthday next month. Where she's goin' to get the groceries is a mystery to me."

"One more thing—did Mrs. Compstock go out last night?"

"I can't tell you that, mister. She had me workin' yesterday, believe me. I was all tired out, and I went to bed right after I got through. Maybe she went out after that, and maybe she didn't. I don't know."

"You've been very helpful," said Hand. "Here are your ten dollars—justly earned, I assure you. And here's a dollar for your wait," he said, holding out a bill that was quickly snatched by the taxi-driver.

"Say, mister, you haven't got my name and address," protested the girl, tucking the ten dollars away in her pocket-book. "How're you goin' to get my money for me if you don't know that?"

"How did I ever forget that!" exclaimed Hand. "Here, write it out on this card. That's it. If I have any luck, I'll let you know at once."

He got back into the colonel's machine, and MacClintock backed out of the way of the taxi. The cab started up with a jerk, spoiling the nonchalant flourish of farewell given us by the girl in the back seat.

"Continue on up to Mrs. Compstock's," Hand ordered MacClintock. Then, turning to me; "The lady had her cap set for the colonel, you see, Clark. There's a motive for you."

"It appears so," I agreed. "But somehow I can't feature a woman wearing a bullet-proof vest. It's unlikely, too, that a man would shoot at her. He'd just take the knife away from her."

"Yes," replied Hand absently, "you're right about that. We can't get much further until we've seen Mrs. Compstock and had a chance to size her up. Now, it's up to you to get us into her house, Clark."

"My word, how am I to do that?"

"Well, you can understand if I told her who I was right off, she'd more than likely refuse us. No doubt she has a stinging recollection of my father, and she might make the connection. All you need do is announce who you are and say you have a message from Colonel Decker. She'll recognize his machine, which will give you countenance. Once inside we will not be dislodged. Here we are; get ready."

As MacClintock brought the car to a halt before the entrance of the house, Hand leaned forward and whispered something into the driver's ear. MacClintock seemed puzzled, but he nodded in the affirmative.

The Compstock house was rather less imposing than the others we had seen in Mill Ridge. The grounds had not been kept up, and the house itself was badly in need of a coat of paint. It was a large residence, however, and could easily have been made a handsome one. Hand and I quickly alighted and strode up to the door. My friend hung back as I pushed the bell-button. We had quite a wait, but at length the door-knob suddenly turned.

"So sorry to have kept you waiting!" exclaimed a cheery feminine voice as the door swung inward. "My maid— Oh, whom did you gentlemen wish to see?" she concluded, her voice cooling by degrees.

"Permit me to introduce myself," I said, doffing my hat. "I am Mr. Clark, and I have a message for Mrs. Compstock from Colonel Decker."

I was sure the woman who stood before us was not Clara Compstock. A mass of golden hair surmounted her head. She had brilliant blue eyes, and her cheeks and lips were bright with the bloom of youth. The light was rather subdued in the hall, where she stood regarding us, but even so I could see that she was beautiful. She peered beyond us to the colonel's automobile.

"Colonel Decker sent you with a message for me?" she asked, her tone somewhat mollified.

"He did," I replied. "May we come in?"

"Oh, yes, pardon me," she murmured. "Step right in, won't you please? My maid has just left me. Sorry to have kept you waiting."

We followed her tall, willowy figure as she led us through the hall into a living-room. She motioned for us to take chairs and stood quite aloof beside a rich mahogany table in the center of the room.

Hand stepped forward. "My friend is very remiss," he said. "I am Mr. Hand. I presume you are Mrs. Compstock."

"Mr. Hand?" she inquired, her eyes darting to my friend. She had taken a position with her back to the windows. Hand had guided me over so that we stood almost behind her. When she turned to look at Hand, the light from the window fell upon her face. I saw then that the soft light of the hall had been far kinder to her than the bright light of the living-room. What I had mistaken for the bloom of youth was nothing more than any woman can acquire in a beauty-shop. Her hair was still beautiful, but the maid had explained that. Even so, I should not have taken her for more than forty.

"Mr. Hand?" she repeated to herself. Suddenly her eyes fixed me with an oddly disturbing glance. "What is the message that Colonel Decker entrusted to you?" she demanded.

"He wished me to—I was about to say . . ." I stammered.

"It is rather a sad message," broke in Hand, coming to my rescue.

"Oh, poor Joseph, of course!" exclaimed Mrs. Compstock. "I should have realized. It was sweet of the colonel to think of me at this time. I have heard of it, of course. It is horrible!"

"Quite horrible," said Hand. "It was murder, you know."

"Yes, so Mrs. Middleton said. That frightful Dr. Metz! They have arrested him, she told me. It makes my blood run cold to think he was here just last week! I had a sick headache," explained Mrs. Compstock.

"The police are quite certain he did it," said Hand. "There is little doubt of it, to be sure. Of course the colonel is thankful his brother's murderer has been apprehended so quickly."

"Why, of course; we all are," Mrs. Compstock assured us. "We are drawn very close together in this little community. We are like one big family here. Everyone is deeply shocked. I should have gone over to see the colonel, but I thought he would rather not be bothered at a time like this. Of course he got the message I asked Maxwell to give him?"

"Oh, yes," replied Hand blandly. "It was thoughtful of you. Colonel Decker asked me to thank you and to give you his best regards. He would have come himself, but there is so much to be done that he couldn't get away."

"The colonel is a dear," smiled Mrs. Compstock, preening her hair. "I really should have gone down, I suppose. Perhaps I could have helped him."

"Perhaps you can yet," said Hand quietly.

"What do you mean?" demanded Mrs. Compstock sharply. Her eyes flashed to Hand's face; then the delicate lids fell over them. "If there is any way I can possibly be of service," she said in a low, sad voice, "I would thank you a thousand times for telling me."

"Joseph Decker had been in an excited state of mind for several days, or so it is believed," began Hand glibly. "The colonel rather believes his brother was expecting an attack. As he was here Tuesday—"

"No," interrupted Mrs. Compstock with a slow smile, "Joseph Decker was not here Tuesday."

"Oh, I beg your pardon!" exclaimed Hand. "It was Monday, wasn't it, Clark? I remember perfectly now—the colonel said Monday, to be sure."

"Yes, he said Monday," I felt called upon to say.

"Why, yes, he was here Monday," said Mrs. Compstock, walking gracefully across the floor and seating herself facing us. "He dropped in for a little call. He seemed perfectly all right then."

"Of course it is not my intention to pry into personal affairs," said Hand, "but are you perfectly sure he didn't appear nervous—high-strung? Perhaps you just didn't notice it."

"Perhaps not," agreed Mrs. Compstock. "He stayed here and chatted for a while. I assure you he didn't seem nervous."

For the first time in my life I saw Christopher Hand embarrassed. He stammered unintelligibly, gulped once or twice, and finally ended by having a fit of coughing.

Mrs. Compstock regarded him curiously. "Why, what is the matter with you?" she asked my friend.

"Th-the letter, madam!" blurted Hand.

"Letter?" asked Mrs. Compstock nervously, half rising from her chair.

"Yes, yes," replied Hand quickly. "The letter which you wrote Joseph."

Mrs. Compstock swayed and then collapsed in the chair. The rouge on her cheeks and lips stood out in tragic relief as she fought to regain control of herself. Despite his fidgety bearing, Hand was observing her narrowly.

"Mrs. Compstock! Are you ill?" he cried, rushing over to her. "Ring for a servant, Clark. Get some water. Ah! Is that smelling-salts I see on the desk?" he said excitedly, running over to an antique affair across the room.

"No! No!" cried the woman, getting shakily to her feet. "I am all right, do you hear me!" she almost screamed at Hand, who was rummaging about the desk.

"Oh, I'm sorry to have caused you such a shock," said Hand, straightening from the desk and approaching the lady. "Believe me, had I known the effect it would have on you, I wouldn't have mentioned that letter."

"What letter?" demanded Mrs. Compstock. "Really, I don't know what you are talking about. I have not been well lately. I am subject to fainting spells; one almost overcame me then."

"Then you didn't understand me to mention a letter?" asked Hand.

"I'm sorry; I didn't," replied the woman, seating herself once again. Although she appeared calm enough, I noticed that her knuckles stood out whitely as she gripped the arm of her chair. I thought I detected something of defiance in her demeanor as she looked unwaveringly at my friend.

"I mean the letter which you sent to Joseph Decker," said Hand almost timidly. "It—it was a little strange, we thought."

Mrs. Compstock dropped her eyes to the floor. When she raised them again, she was smiling. "Did he keep that silly thing?" she asked.

"Unfortunately, he did," replied Hand. "I found it among his effects."

"Has the colonel seen it?" she almost blurted.

"No, he has not," Hand truthfully replied.

"Then you didn't come here to deliver a message for the colonel at all," accused Mrs. Compstock. "Did you come here to interrogate me? If that is the case, I shall feel highly insulted!"

"I hope you won't," said Hand. "It was really the only thing we could do. You must see that yourself. I feel sure you can give me a satisfactory explanation for the letter in no time. The colonel hasn't seen it, you know. That should be evidence of my good faith."

"Your good faith—I wonder," she said, regarding my friend intently. "Well, if that foolish message has come to light, I suppose you are entitled to an explanation for it. It is really nothing, I assure you." Suddenly she leaned forward and smiled at Hand. "Do you think that I killed him—that I could kill him?" she asked softly.

"Why, of course not!" he stoutly asserted. "You didn't hesitate to say that you might kill him yet, but I didn't take that seriously."

"You are a wise man," she said, settling back in the chair. "I didn't kill Joseph Decker. I won't dissemble, though. He and I were not the best of friends. He got the silly notion somewhere that the colonel and I were becoming interested in each other. Joseph Decker was not exactly an admirable character, Mr. Hand. He realized that if his brother married, his own position would become rather difficult. He gave no thought to his brother's happiness; rather he had an eye on his fortune. He came here Monday morning to cause trouble between the colonel and me. He tried to arrange matters so that I would give the colonel an affront."

"He didn't succeed?"

"How can you ask such a question, sir! Naturally he failed. I saw through his contemptible plot immediately. He tried to make me believe the colonel had maligned me. Such a thing is inconceivable!"

"I should say so! He didn't attempt to threaten you in any way?"

"Indeed, no! What ever put such a notion into your head?"

"The tone of your note, madam."

"Oh, I was distraught when I wrote that. How could I have been else? It was not the first time he had attempted to interfere with me in such a base manner."

"Recently?"

"I think I have gone into my private affairs quite enough!" said Mrs. Compstock, rising indignantly to her feet. "I should never have penned that foolish note. Since this tragedy has brought it to light, magnified its importance, and distorted its meaning, I agreed with you that an explanation was in order. I have given it. Now I can rely upon you as a gentleman to return the note to me at once."

"I would gladly do it," replied Hand, "but I haven't it with me. Stupid of me to leave it behind! It is up in my room, where I left it this morning. Clark, where did I put that letter?"

"I think you put it in the top drawer of your dresser," I replied, playing up to him. "I remember now, you meant to get it."

Mrs. Compstock tapped her foot in exasperation. "When may I have it?" she demanded. Her face had become flushed, and her eyes flashed with anger.

"I can have it for you very shortly," announced Hand, glancing at his watch. "Please don't worry about it, madam. By the way, what an interesting collection of coral!" he suddenly exclaimed, crossing over to a large glass case in a corner of the room. On shelves were displayed several dozen pieces of the calcareous formation.

"My husband's brother collected it," explained Mrs. Compstock, rather impatiently. "I've been meaning to have it thrown out."

"Not a magnificent collection such as this!" protested Hand. "I am a collector of these specimens myself. I assure you this collection is quite valuable."

I knew he was up to something, for he had never collected a piece of coral in his life. Nevertheless, he took a great deal of interest in the collection of Mrs. Compstock's late brother-in-law. The lady showed a momentary interest herself when she heard the collection termed valuable.

Her interest, it was soon evident, was dissipated by her impatience at our postponed departure. Hand continued to move about the case, exclaiming over each new piece he inspected. All at once there was a prodigious yell from outside at the front of the house.

"My goodness! What's that?" cried Hand, whirling about from the show-case. Mrs. Compstock gasped and turned in the direction of the front door. Hand bounded by us and, crossing the hall, pulled the door open.

"Get out o' therre!" I heard MacClintock roaring at the top of his voice. "Police! Constables! The hoose is bein' rrobbed!"

"What is it, MacClintock?" shouted Hand.

"Quick with ye, Misterr Hand!" howled MacClintock. "A mon has joost clumb up the side o' the hoose. He's gone into one o' yon windows!"

"An intruder!" shouted Hand as he sped across the hall to a flight of stairs. "Stay with Mrs. Compstock, Clark. I'll look after this fellow!"

"What does this mean!" cried the woman, glancing wildly about. "Where did he go? This is outrageous!"

She turned and rushed for the stairs as fast as her legs would carry her. I started after her, calling for her to stop, but she paid no attention to me.

"Please don't go up there!" I entreated. "Something has happened. There may be danger!"

The speed with which she rushed up the stairs amazed me. At the second floor we both halted. My companion gazed frantically about, but Hand was nowhere in sight.

"Please come downstairs," I said in a hoarse whisper. "Someone is up here. You may be in danger!"

"If there is someone up here, I intend to find it out," she coldly replied. "You stay where you are. I can take care of myself. If I want help I'll ask for it."

I was thoroughly cowed by her cold, overbearing manner. She disappeared into a room, returning a moment later with a small automatic in her hand. I glanced at Mrs. Compstock's face and was glad I was not the object of her quest.

"Won't you let me accompany you—I am armed?" I asked her.

"You stay where you are!" she commanded me.

I felt quite sheepish standing there at the head of the stairs while she inspected the rooms on the second floor. Finally she reappeared.

"There's no one here," she announced. "What has become of your friend, Mr. Hand, do you suppose?"

"Perhaps he has gone to the third floor," I said quickly. "Show me the way up there, and I'll go see."

"If he has gone to the third floor, he will have to stay there," she replied decisively. "There is only a small space above this portion of the house. I have locked the door to it. Come, we will go down."

As we turned to descend the stairs, I heard a great puffing, and one of the most rotund women I had ever seen came struggling up them.

"Th' saints save us!" she gasped. "Mrs. Compstock! Oh, Mrs. Compstock! Th' divil is chasin' his brother through th' house!"

"Did you see a man, Margaret?" demanded Mrs. Compstock. "Where was he? Where was he going? Quick! Don't stare at me; answer my question!"

"I seen wan—two ov thim!" gasped the woman. "Out in me kitchen. They come tumblin' down th' shtairs. I was like t' faint, I was!"

"Get out of my way," ordered Mrs. Compstock, angrily pushing the woman aside. She rushed down the stairs, with me after her. The fat woman collapsed on the stairs and began to wail loudly.

As we reached the hall, Hand walked into the house through the front door. Mrs. Compstock stopped short in her headlong rush. She took a deep breath as she regarded Hand for a moment. "Will you please tell me what has been going on?" she demanded icily.

"By Jove! There was a fellow got into your house, Mrs. Compstock," replied Hand. "I surprised him on the second floor. He escaped down the back stairs into the kitchen and rushed out the back way. MacClintock and I chased him through the wood, but he got away from us."

"The same man we met before!" I cried excitedly. "What do you suppose he is up to?"

"I don't understand this yet," said Mrs. Compstock irritably. "Will you please explain why a man would break into my house in broad daylight?"

"But how can I?" protested Hand. "The only opinion I can venture is that he is a desperate character. As Clark says, we came upon him down the road on our way up here. When he saw us, he dived into the wood, and we followed him. Clark saw him and fired two shots over his head. He paid no attention to them. We lost him. Have you a man on the place? I don't think it right for you to stay here alone after this."

"Really? I'll look after my own affairs, Mr. Hand!"

"But, madam, this man might return, and if—"

"I said that I would take care of my own affairs!"

"Oh, very well. Should you like, I'll ask the colonel to send one of his servants up here to afford you protection. I know he'd be only too glad to do it. He would not be comfortable otherwise."

"Is it impossible to persuade you that I wish to take care of myself?" said Mrs. Compstock, drawing herself up. "Good-day, gentlemen. I shall look to hear from you on that other matter before evening."

Put entirely out of countenance, we departed abashed. Mrs. Compstock was certainly an unusual woman.

Hand ordered MacClintock to take us back to the colonel's. As the car rounded the drive and began the descent of the knoll, I turned to my companion, who sat utterly absorbed beside me.

"You may not agree with me, Hand," I said, "but I am more than ever convinced that Mrs. Compstock did not kill Joseph Decker."

"But I do agree with you, Clark," he replied. "Quite a woman, isn't she? She can turn from the softest of kittens to the most ferocious of tigresses. She is very interesting."

"Nevertheless, I don't think it right for her to stay there alone with that fat old Irish woman," I declared. "If there is a desperate character roaming these woods, someone should be sent there to guard her."

"That reminds me!" Hand suddenly exclaimed. "That was very good work, MacClintock. I shall commend you to the colonel."

"Thank ye, sirr," said the driver over his shoulder. "I come nearr forrgettin' ye, sirr. I was five minutes late. I hope it didn't rruin yerr plans forr ye," he added anxiously.

"Not a bit," replied Hand quickly. "You merely provided me with an opportunity to look over Mrs. Compstock's coral."

"Yes, sirr," said MacClintock dubiously.

"There's something between you two that you didn't let me in on," I accused Hand with an injured air.

He turned quickly to me with one of his rare, impulsive smiles. "I am genuinely sorry, Clark," he said, placing his hand on my shoulder. "The idea occurred to me so late that I didn't have time, really, to tell you of it. I don't think I should have in any case. I enlisted the aid of your delightful qualification to be surprised and to show it. That always makes a deception so much more successful."

"Do you mean to say there was no intruder in Mrs. Compstock's house?" I demanded.

"None—except ourselves, perhaps."

"But the cook said she saw two men rush through her kitchen. One was you, but who was the other?"

"The power of suggestion, Clark. She was so flabbergasted she was incapable of knowing exactly what she had seen. I told her I had chased a man through the kitchen; immediately she was convinced she had seen him. I left her collapsed in the sink, gulping great mouthfuls of air, and believing two strange men had invaded her kitchen."

"Under any conditions, I don't think it was right to terrify those two women," I said severely.

"That is where we differ," sniffed Hand. "The ruse worked perfectly, and through it I was able to gather a good deal of valuable information."

"What?"

"Well, in the first place I was interested in determining whether Mrs. Compstock could be induced to leave her home. You see, she will not budge from it. More than that, she will not stand for having anyone on the place."

"What does that lead to?"

"As you say, Clark, it's not very probable that Mrs. Compstock murdered Joseph Decker. If she wanted to remove him, however, it's quite possible that she arranged to have it done. Professional murderers are not hard to get.

Red Mike, you remember, was willing to dispatch anybody you could think of for the modest sum of two hundred dollars—one hundred before and one hundred after."

"Yes, that's so."

"Now, then, Mrs. Compstock may or may not have a hired murderer calling upon her tonight to collect his satisfactorily earned sum of money. If one should call there, however, he will get himself and the lady into trouble. That house is going to be watched."

"Oh, I see, Mrs. Compstock is fated to be watched over regardless. Who is going to do it?" I asked a little apprehensively.

"I haven't just made up my mind yet," replied Hand negligently. "Now, you see, Clark, we have part of the picture complete. Let us assume that Mrs. Compstock hired an assassin to do away with Joseph Decker. We have the motive—no question about that, and it appears rather strong. Then we have determined that she gave someone a check for a rather large sum of money—a thousand dollars. I think it was made out last night. Now all—"

"Hold on," I interrupted. "How the deuce do you know that she gave someone a check for a large sum of money?"

"I have the reverse of it in my pocket. A desk can always be relied upon to yield something of interest, especially a lady's desk. Mrs. Compstock's desk furnished me with a blotter—used, once, to blot a check made out for a thousand dollars."

"Oh, so that's what you got when you were after the smelling-salts."

"Nothing of the kind. I saw it then, but I had no opportunity to purloin it. When you and she followed me upstairs I rushed down the back stairs and out into the living-room. I had plenty of time to get the blotter and then get out of the house. Here it is—only been used once, you see. No trouble to see the amount of the check, but the signature is not so distinct. I have no doubt it can be read quite easily by reflecting the blotter in a mirror. The date should become decipherable too. Ha! Here we are at the colonel's."

Hand placed the piece of white blotting-paper in the leather folder he carries for just such a purpose. He put it into his inside coat pocket as MacClintock brought the car to a halt before the colonel's door. We went quickly into the house. Colonel Decker suddenly appeared from the den. In spite of his schooled nature, he seemed quite excited. Catching sight of us, he hurried across the hall.

"By gad! I thought you'd never get back!" he exclaimed. "We have made a discovery—an important discovery, I'll be bound!"

"What is it?" asked Hand quickly.

"Sergeant O'Brine called our attention to it," said the colonel rapidly. "Christopher, this house has been practically torn to pieces!"

I looked about me in astonishment. The building, as much as I could see of it, appeared as substantial as ever.

"In what way?" asked Hand.

"The walls—the walls," cried the colonel, swinging his arms about and glaring at the inoffensive partitions. "The walls have been honeycombed! Look here."

He led us into the dining-room and pulled a picture out from its place on the wall. Behind it was a badly patched hole, uncovered by wall-paper. A heavy sideboard had been pulled out from the wall. Behind it I could plainly see where the boards of the wainscot had been ripped out and put back.

"It's the same behind all these pictures," growled the colonel indignantly. "In the library, too. The wainscoting has been removed there, but put back more carefully. No doubt of it!"

Hand walked slowly round the dining-room and carefully inspected the wainscot. Finally he stopped and turned to us. "Every third or fourth board has been removed and replaced again," he announced. "Have you noticed this anywhere except in here and the library, Colonel?"

"Everywhere!" sputtered the colonel. "Someone has probed every wall on the first floor. Up the back stairs as well. Dick is inspecting the second floor now. The cellar walls have been tampered with, too. That is where O'Brine first noticed it this afternoon."

"Humph," mused Hand, thoughtfully pulling his lip. "Funny what things turn up when a man gets murdered! Find any tools that might have been used to do this, Colonel?"

"I didn't think of that!" exclaimed the colonel, bringing his fist into the palm of his hand. "No, I haven't found any. Perhaps Sergeant O'Brine found some in the cellar. We'll ask him."

Colonel Decker turned and walked briskly across the dining-room. Hand and I followed him out to the kitchen.

"Mary," said the colonel to a woman busy at the stove, "where is Sergeant O'Brine? Have you seen him?"

"He's in the cellar, Colonel," replied the woman. "He's excited. He bounced up here a minute ago and said he's found another one. I don't know what he was talking about, I'm sure."

The colonel crossed over to a door and opened it. "Sergeant!" he called. "Ho! Sergeant O'Brine, where are you?"

"Right here, Colonel darlint," answered a voice from below. "I hov found another ov thim holes. Thot I hov, sor."

"Come up here, Sergeant," called the colonel. "No, wait a minute—we'll come down," he added hastily, beckoning for Hand and me to follow him.

We descended to the gloom of the cellar. A white-haired, stocky man in overalls came out of a coal-bin carrying a lantern. He peered at us with merry blue eyes. His features, though unmarked by intelligence, suggested an infallible good humor.

"By gollies, 'tis anoother hole in th' cellar wall thot I'm just afther findin', sor," he said. "That'll make five ov thim. It looks t' me like there are siveral ithers where th' shtones is loose, too, Colonel, fer th' love ov me owld father dead an' gone these many years in Ireland, it looks t' me like somewan has bin shtealin' th' cellar right out from under yez!"

"Where's this new hole, Sergeant?" demanded the colonel.

"Right over behint th' furnace, sor," replied O'Brine, eying Hand and me curiously.

"Let's see the first one you found," said Hand.

O'Brine turned and led us into the coal-bunker from which he had just emerged. We climbed over the coal after him to the wall at the back of the house.

"There it is, sor," he said, raising the lantern. "I was shovelin' th' coal out t' th' front ov th' bin whin me shovel goes shmack up against th' wall. Like t' shook me brand-new teeth out, that shlip. But th' worst ov it was, me shovel knocks wan ov th' bricks right shmack through th' wall— kerplunk down inside. Thin I see the job was bad. I hov bin afther noticin' siveral places in th' cellar walls where th' bricks was put in bad, sor. Whin I come near knockin' th' intire house down on me head wid me coal-shovel I goes off t' report t' th' colonel."

The coal-shovel was still resting up against the wall where O'Brine had left it. Hand grasped it and struck it sharply against the wall where the brick was missing. The bricks around the hole shifted as he struck them. In a moment they broke away and fell in. Hand got out his electric torch and flashed it into the hole.

"Funny these walls are hollow," he muttered. "Foundations like this are usually solid."

He thrust his head into the hole and squeezed in his hand with the torch. After a few moments he withdrew his head and brushed the mortar off his shoulders.

"Nothing in there," he said. "This work must have been done at night. Shouldn't wonder if this explains Buckley's insomnia. Did you ever hear any pounding at night, Colonel?"

"No," growled Colonel Decker. "I'd have looked into it if I had."

"As a matter of fact, I guess there wasn't any pounding," said Hand, holding the light close to the hole and inspecting the edges. "Those bricks were originally removed with the greatest of care. Some sharp instrument was used to loosen the mortar first." He turned and started climbing back over the coal. "Let's look at the others you found, Sergeant," he said. "I think we'll find there's one in every room."

"Sure an' there does seem t' be wan in ivery room, sor," said Sergeant O'Brine, following Hand. He ceremoniously displayed all the holes he had found, five in all.

"The wall in the room where you store your tools seems to have suffered more than the others," observed Hand. "Come in here," he added, leading the way to the tool-room. "Do you see, these bricks have all been removed and then replaced," he said, indicating a rectangular space about two feet high and four feet across. "By the way, Sergeant, have you come across any strange tools down here—tools that might have been used to tear these holes in the walls?"

"Thot I have not, sor," replied O'Brine. "All th' tools on th' place are right here in this room, 'ceptin' those thot

Corporal MacClintock's got t' kape the ingines ov th' auty-
mobiles arunnin'. Sure, he's foriver layvin' thim all over
th' place fer me t' pick up, but they ain't in here, sor."

An electric bulb in the ceiling shed a good light in
the room. Even so, Hand used his electric torch to look
in and about the piles of rakes, shovels, picks, and other
gardening implements with which the room was cluttered.
Suddenly he thrust his hand in among the tools piled in a
corner and withdrew a trowel. It was rough with hardened
mortar. He pulled the tools aside and revealed a bag of
cement.

"That's what was used to seal up the walls with, anyway," said Hand. "Here's the bucket the cement was mixed
in. O'Brine hand me that crow-bar."

Armed with the bar, Hand advanced to the wall. He
struck the center of the space where the bricks appeared
to have been tampered with. "They're loose, Colonel," he
said. "Shall we take them out?"

"We might as well," said the colonel. "I won't have the
wall left in that condition, anyway. Go ahead, Christopher, take them out."

Hand swung the bar lustily against the wall. The bricks
began to loosen after he had struck them two or three
times.

"There they go!" shouted O'Brine, stepping back as the
bricks suddenly became dislodged and tumbled outward
to the floor. "Hey, lookit! Holy St. Patrick, there's a dead
man in th' wall!"

We stood in horrified amazement and gazed at a gruesome face that grinned at us through the opening. Just
the head and shoulders were visible through the aperture
Hand had made.

"Good Lord!" I gasped. "A body was sealed up in the
wall!"

"It's Buckley!" cried the colonel. "By gad! Another murder!" Hand took out his light and, walking up close to the wall, flashed it on the head of the corpse. "Struck over the head," he muttered. "One blow killed him outright. Hit him from behind, too. I think we'd better leave this body right where it is for the present. We'll have to get our friend the medical examiner here again, Colonel. Did you say something about this case becoming more and more complicated, Clark? Now what do you think of it?"

"It's hopeless!" I said. "This upsets whatever theories I had formed."

"What do you think of it, Christopher?" asked the colonel anxiously.

"We shall see," replied Hand absently. "One thing is sure, however. This fellow and Joseph didn't lose their lives at the same time. This man's been dead long over twenty-four hours."

"He must have been killed the night before last," said the colonel. "He's probably been in that wall ever since we missed him yesterday morning."

"No doubt," agreed Hand, turning to the door. "We'll just lock this room up until the examiner gets here."

"I ain't had such a experience since I woke up in a dug-out and found meself shleepin' wid a dead Heinie," remarked Sergeant O'Brine.

We left the room and Hand closed the door. There was no key in the lock, but one of his master-keys secured the door.

"I wonder whether Dick has found any more holes in the walls?" said the colonel. "What do you suppose these holes mean, Christopher? There can't be a corpse hidden behind every one of them!"

"Not behind one of them, at least," replied Hand grimly.

"Holy shmoke, Colonel, sor, don't yez be thinkin' they've turned the house into no mozolium," said Sergeant

O'Brine soothingly as we walked to the stairs. "That feller Buckley was no good nohow. Sure an' it was only th' ither day th' shpalpeen was near gettin' killt by meself. Thryin't' poison me goat, he was! Throwin' broken bottles t' th' pore baste what had no better sinse th'n t' thry an' ate thim! Near died ov th' intistinal cumbustion, he did. I'd hov give Misther Buckley th' batin' ov his life right then an' there but fer the buttin' in ov Corporal MacClintock! An' me his sooperior officer, into the bargain! A private's what he should be, sor. I sez . . ."

"Yes, yes, O'Brine," cut in the colonel. "Are you going to follow us into the dining-room?"

"Yes, sor—er—no, sor," stammered the sergeant. "Are yez through wid me, sor? I'll be lookin' afther me goat if yez—"

"We won't need you, Sergeant," broke in Hand. "That was good work."

"Thank yez, sor," said Sergeant O'Brine, giving my friend a snappy military salute. With his chest fairly bursting the buttons from his overalls, he strode through the kitchen, no doubt on his way to harass the ears of Corporal MacClintock with a long-winded account of his commendable activities. The rest of us proceeded on to the front hall. As we entered it, Dick Fairfax and Patty Decker were descending the stairs.

"Did you find any more, Dick?" called the colonel.

"No, I didn't," replied the young man. "I looked in all the rooms."

"Isn't this a shame!" exclaimed Patty. "Who do you suppose did it, Buckley?"

"Perhaps," replied the colonel awkwardly. Hand disappeared into the den and closed the door.

"When is Mr. Furness going to bring my car back?" asked Patty. "He wasn't here for luncheon, and he's not back yet. Do you suppose he's had an accident or something?"

"It was something," said Dick, trying not to smile. "Mr. Furness has been locked up in Barkersville. Your father told me."

"Locked up!" gasped Patty. "Put in jail? Oh, what for?"

"For driving your car while under the influence of intoxicating liquor," announced Dick solemnly. "My goodness, the company you keep!"

"Dick, are you kidding me?" asked Patty, looking after her father, who had wandered off into the living-room. "Honestly, I don't want him to have my car. I wish he'd bring it back!"

"Well, he won't," said Dick. "You can ask Mr. Clark. I'll tell you what let's do. I'll get MacClintock to drive me over; then I'll drive your car back. I don't suppose the cops would object, would they, Mr. Clark? After all, it is Patty's car."

"I'm sure they'd give it to you," I replied.

"Why don't you come with me, Pat?" asked Dick. "You've been cooped up in the house all day. We'll just have time for a little spin before dinner."

"Oh, but Father might need me," protested Patty. "Poor dear! Isn't he brave, Mr. Clark? Just think—his only brother."

"The colonel has my admiration," I replied, glancing into the living-room to where the old soldier was pacing back and forth. "I really think it would do you good to get a little air, however. Hand and I will be here until you get back, I assure you. I think you should go."

"All right, Dick," she said. "I'll just ask Dad whether he minds. I'll be with you in a jiffy."

As Patty walked into the living-room, Dick Fairfax turned to me. "What do you think of all these mysterious holes in the walls?" he asked. "I never heard of anything like this before."

"Did you see those in the cellar walls?"

"Yes; they're peculiar too. What do you suppose they were made for?"

"Well, one of them was made to hide the body of the colonel's servant, Buckley," I replied in a low voice.

"What!" gasped Dick. "Mean to say—"

"We found Buckley's body between the walls in the cellar," I said. "It was in the room where the tools are kept. He was murdered!"

"Ye gods!" exclaimed Dick, slapping his thigh. "That makes it nice, doesn't it? Gee whiz! What do you know about that?"

"Considering the circumstances, I thought it would be a good idea if you got Patty out of the house for a while," I said. "Hand is summoning the medical examiner again, and that morgue wagon will have to make another trip too, I suppose."

"Oh, gosh, yes!" said Dick. "Pat is a brick, but I don't want her to go through that again. Here she comes—how about it, Pat?"

"I'll just get my things," she replied. "Dad implored me to go, the old dear! Be right down, darling."

"Who do you suppose cooked Buckley's goose?" demanded Dick when Patty had run upstairs. "I can't imagine who could have done that."

"I'm as much at sea as anyone," I told him. "Just about the time I come to a conclusion about this case, something else turns up to ruin it."

Patty came running down the stairs getting into her coat. She and Dick quickly left. I started into the living-room to join the colonel just as Hand came out of the den. He took my arm, and together we went into the living-room. The colonel stopped his pacing and confronted us. "Did you get the examiner?" he asked.

"He's hurrying over here now," replied Hand. "Colonel, have you inspected Buckley's room at all?"

"Withers and I looked it over," said the colonel. "Joseph was there too. He didn't have anything that afforded a clue."

"Well, I think I'll just look over his belongings, anyhow," said Hand. "Mind showing me where it is?"

The colonel turned and led us out of the room. We went back to the kitchen. Near the back door we found a flight of stairs which took us up to the third floor at the end of the house. Colonel Decker guided us into a room near the head of the stairs.

"This was his room," he gruffly announced. "Everything is just as he left it. Withers wanted to tear things up, but I stopped him."

"The bed hasn't been made up since?"

"No. It wasn't slept in, as you can see. His body was fully clothed, wasn't it? Guess he hadn't been to bed at all."

"No, I guess not. Was Joseph in the habit of moving round late at night?"

"He used to go to bed very early. As far as I know, he never got up until morning. He was a very sound sleeper."

"Did he ever seem tired during the day?"

"Used to nap quite frequently. He wasn't very well."

"Yes; I know. Let's see what there is here."

Hand commenced a systematic search of the room. After he had inspected everything to be found belonging to the unfortunate servant, he stepped back to the center of the room. The colonel and I watched him as his eyes darted over the walls, ceiling, and floor. A slow smile came to his lips, and he turned to the colonel. "Seemed to like pictures, didn't he?" he said meaningly.

Colonel Decker reached over to the nearest picture and pulled it away from the wall. Behind it in the bare plaster wall was a spot about four inches in diameter where fresh plaster had been set in.

"He tapped the wall, all right," said Hand. "He had a number of pictures, didn't he? I shouldn't wonder if you found the same sort of evidence behind every one."

It did not take the colonel long to determine that Hand was right. He let the last picture swing back to its position on the wall. "Now that beats me!" he growled. "Why do you suppose anybody'd be digging holes in the walls all over the house?"

"You're sure those patches weren't in the walls when you moved in?"

"Positive! I looked the place over when the walls were all bare."

"Another indication that Buckley was the mysterious workman. Who sold you this house?"

"Middleton. This was his home. He's the founder of Middleton's, the big jewelry house in New York, you know."

"Why, it's just failed!" I exclaimed.

"Yes," replied the colonel, with a smile, "but Geering was out. He sold it and retired about a year ago. He's a smart chap. He told me he could see business was precarious for the firm."

"Did he buy this house or build it?" asked Hand.

"He bought it," replied the colonel. "He lived in it seven or eight years. He assured me it was very well built."

"I dare say it is. Do you know what induced him to sell it?"

"Why, yes. He told me his wife always regretted that they hadn't built on the location where they finally built the house they now live in. It's the last one out on the ridge—stands on a prominence. They get a view in all directions. It really is a much better location."

"Well, it's fortunate we have the former owner of the place collaborating with us," remarked Hand dryly. "He'll be only too eager to supply us with information concerning the house."

"I hope you're not offended by the interest he is taking," said the colonel earnestly. "He's been very agreeable to us; I'm rather fond of him."

"And he of you, I'll wager. He will give us all the help he can, that seems sure. Don't worry, Colonel, I don't take exception to him. He has already been of value, but I must say I had seen those footprints before. I wonder whether he sold you more than he realized when you purchased this house from him?"

"How's that?"

"It seems certain that something of value is secreted in the house somewhere. People don't bore holes in walls for the fun of it."

"I—I wonder—do you suppose Joseph could have hidden something here?" asked the colonel, with an effort.

"I didn't like to mention it," replied Hand, "but it seems logical. We know by his own confession that he had his hands on five thousand pounds once—that's over twenty thousand dollars considerably."

"And Furness knew he had it!" I exclaimed.

"Yes, but it was some time ago," Hand reminded me. "It's an indication, however, that he might have got hold of some more. Let's stop conjecturing and get down to practical matters. I think we should open one of these patched-up places just to see what lies behind it. One will be enough—we can take it for granted if there's nothing behind the first there'll be nothing behind any of them."

"I'll get you a chisel or something," offered the colonel, turning to go.

"Never mind," replied Hand. "I have something here that will answer."

He produced his leather case filled with the odd collection of tempered steel instruments. From it he extracted a small bar sharpened at one end. He pulled one of the pictures out and commenced digging at the plaster. Soon he had the new plaster entirely removed.

"This is peculiar," he remarked, flashing his light into the small opening. "That hole isn't big enough to afford much of a view of the space between the walls. The lathing has been carefully sawed away, but only two pieces of it. I can touch the ones above and below the hole."

"By gad! I hate mystery!" growled the colonel. "I'd give a lot to know what those holes were made for."

"They must have been made by someone who wanted to look into these wall-spaces," said Hand. "Trouble is that they're so small he couldn't see much. Hold on a minute— yes, that might be it!"

"What?"

"He could have used a periscope arrangement. With that and an electric torch he would have been able to inspect the wall-space without much trouble. Would have enabled him to make a small hole instead of a large, conspicuous one."

"Well, periscope or no periscope, he couldn't have seen much, anyway," declared the colonel; "there's only a narrow space between the wall-beams."

"I've been thinking of that," said Hand. "Colonel, there must be something hidden in the walls of this house— something valuable. Whoever dug these holes all over the house must have known it was here, somewhere."

"Do you suppose he found it?" I asked.

"That's more guess-work than ever," replied Hand with a smile. "I'd say, however, that Buckley was the man. It's hardly to be supposed that anybody else tore his room up like this. Let's see whether there are any holes in the other servants' rooms."

Hand started for the door. All of a sudden he stopped, and I bumped squarely into him as I was following him out. The colonel and I stepped back as Hand began to teeter back and forth on his right foot.

"What's the matter, Christopher?" asked the colonel. "Got a cramp?"

Hand was, I knew by the expression on his face, beyond paying any attention to us. Bounding to one side, he leaned over and grasped the edge of the rug, giving it a yank that nearly capsized the colonel and me. He tossed the rug aside and dropped to his knees. Pressing his fingers against two or three of the floor-boards, he finally selected one. Once again he took out the leather case, from which he got a flat bar. This he inserted into the crack between the floor-boards, and, with the greatest of ease, he pried one of them up. He lifted it away, and we looked down upon an incongruous assortment of tools.

"There's his periscope," said Hand, picking up a tubular affair about a foot long. "Not bad, eh? See, he's attached a small electric torch to this end, pointing in the same direction as the lens of the periscope. He could thrust this thing through the wall and, by turning it, look in any direction he chose. Let's see what else we have—a square trowel for replacing the plaster, this little rip-saw, chisel, and this putty knife, which he used to mix plaster, you see. The only thing missing is the plaster, but I saw that down in the tool-room."

"Then it was Buckley," I breathed.

"No doubt of it," replied Hand, getting to his feet. "Let's have a look at these other servants' rooms. How many are there up here, Colonel?"

"Just Maxwell and the cook. O'Brine and MacClintock have quarters over the garage."

"Haven't you a maid?"

"Not yet. I'm getting one for Patty. I didn't realize she was grown up until she and Dick wanted to get married. But I don't like women servants! I've always been used to men."

We inspected the rooms of Maxwell and the cook. Both servants were busy downstairs preparing dinner. They did not suffer by our prying; the walls of their rooms were intact. There was another room in the servants' quarters. Its blank walls yielded nothing of interest.

We returned to Buckley's room, where Hand gathered up the contrivances he had taken from under the floor.

"Buckley was the man," he said. "I wonder whether his search led him to his death. Perhaps he made his own sepulcher."

9

TRAPS

The medical examiner and the morgue wagon arrived simultaneously. The doctor, for a man in his position, was quite excited as he walked into the living-room.

"What's this, another murder, Mr. Hand?" he asked.

"So it appears," replied my friend. "Perhaps I had better give you the details of this latest discovery before we view the body."

Colonel Decker and I listened to Hand briefly outline for the examiner the manner in which we had found Buckley's corpse sealed up in the wall. He exhibited the dead man's tools and explained their significance.

"Humph, didn't find any dope around him too, did you?" asked the doctor. "Joseph Decker—"

"Yes, yes, Doctor," broke in Hand. "Let us go to the cellar at once. Right this way."

"What's that?" asked the colonel quickly.

"Right this way, Doctor," repeated Hand, taking the examiner by the arm and literally dragging him toward the door.

"Just a minute!" barked the colonel. The examiner swung about, and Hand resignedly dropped his arm. The official looked in perplexity first at the anxious face of Colonel Decker and then at the disgruntled features of my friend. Hand regarded him reproachfully.

"Did I put my foot in it?" asked the examiner.

"Rather," said Hand. "Still, Colonel, you would have known of it anyway, I suppose. Your brother had the drug habit. At least, circumstances certainly indicate that he did."

"I didn't know I was giving away a secret," declared the doctor, still mystified.

"I had hoped we shouldn't have to give the colonel the pain of telling him," explained Hand, glancing at the bowed head of his father's old friend.

"Oh, I'm sorry, Colonel," blurted the examiner. "I thought of course—"

"That's all right, Doctor," said the colonel gruffly, straightening his shoulders. "My brother's whole life seems to have been marked by his weaknesses. I blame myself for a good deal of it; it's not a pleasant thought. I should have looked after him better. What a pity!"

"It can do no good to let this information leak out," said Hand earnestly to the examiner. "Out of regard for the colonel—"

"I give you my word I'll say nothing about it except to the proper authorities," interrupted the examiner quickly. "I'm sure we can keep it confidential, unless subsequent events force it out, of course."

"Of course," agreed Hand. "Come, let's attend to this other matter."

We found two men from the morgue waiting in the front hall with their ominous basket. The doctor motioned for them to follow us as we passed through the dining-room into the kitchen. The cook and Maxwell regarded us whitely as we solemnly proceeded down the cellar stairs. The colonel and I remained in the furnace-room while Hand and the men crowded into the room where the dead face of Buckley peered blankly through the wall.

"I'm glad Pat isn't here," said the colonel suddenly. "That was clever of Dick to get her out. By gad! I'll be glad when this is all over!"

The colonel paced back and forth before me as we waited. About five minutes later the two undertakers, straining under the weight of their basket, came out of the room.

"Here, take it out this way," commanded Colonel Decker, hastening over to the cellar door and throwing it open. The two men disappeared with their burden, and the colonel closed the door after them. Hand and the medical examiner joined us from the tool-room.

"Murder, eh, Doctor?" inquired the colonel.

"Oh, unquestionably," replied the examiner. "Struck over the head from behind with some blunt instrument. Killed him instantly. Been dead between thirty and forty hours, I should say."

"I don't feel safe in my own house," growled the colonel, glancing about the gloomy cellar. "Let's go upstairs."

We returned to the first floor, and Hand turned the periscope and other implements of Buckley's over to the examiner. The official said good-night to us and started for the door. Colonel Decker followed him out to the porch, where they stood talking.

"My word, Clark, don't tell me you're getting hungry again!" exclaimed Hand, noticing that I was taking a great interest in Maxwell, who was preparing the dining-room table for dinner.

"I won't be sorry when it's dinner-time," I replied, with a smile.

"I'm going up to my room for a minute," said Hand. "Tell the colonel I'll be right down."

Shortly after Hand went upstairs, Colonel Decker came into the house. "What have you been doing all day?" he demanded. "I haven't seen anything of you since this morning. Have they still got Dr. Metz under lock and key?"

"I should imagine he's been taken to the county penitentiary by this time," I said. "If he gets out of the murder
charge, he's still head and foot in a charge of selling dope."

"What!" exclaimed the colonel.

I told him of our experiences with the doctor, and also
those with Furness. I was careful to refrain from any mention of Mrs. Compstock.

"Then Dr. Metz must have provided Joseph with drugs!"
snapped the colonel. "They must have got into a fight over
it and gone at each other! Of all the pernicious hounds!
Confound him!"

"That's exactly the attitude the police have taken,"
I said. "But Dr. Metz may be able to establish an alibi
through these confederates of his. There's little doubt,
however, that he supplied your brother with cocaine. Hand
found some of it in your brother's pocket this morning."

"That's pretty conclusive," admitted the colonel sadly. "Well, I'm going to hold the funeral tomorrow. The
medical examiner said he'd authorize a burial permit to
be issued. I'm going to have Joseph buried in our family
plot out in Ohio. I'll accompany the body. I've asked one
of my old junior officers, Captain Bartlett, to come out to
look after Patty while I'm gone. He's applied for leave, and
I'm sure he'll get it. I thought I'd do that so that you and
Christopher could be free to do what you pleased. By the
way, where is Christopher?"

"He asked me to tell you he'd gone upstairs," I replied.
"Hello, what's the row out back?"

"Sounds like O'Brine and MacClintock at it again!"
muttered the colonel, starting across the hall for the den.
I followed him out the back door. Dusk had fallen rapidly.
I could make out the shadowy figure of a tall man standing
in the center of the driveway at the corner of the house.
From his voice I knew it was MacClintock. O'Brine was
answering him spiritedly from the direction of the garage.

"Th' viry ideer talkin' t' yer sooperior officer like thot!" he was howling. "See here, Corporal MacClintock, yez'll look afther yer kyars yer ownsilf widout no help from me. Come orderin' th' shuperintindint ov grounds around like thot! An me a sergint t' boot! Go long wid yez."

"Vera weel," said MacClintock with dignity. "I'll go back alone, which is just what I'd be if ye went with me, anyhoo!"

"So!" was the shocked reply of Sergeant O'Brine. "If yez do go alone wid yersilf, yez'll be in bad company, I kin tell yez thot!"

"What's going on here?" demanded the colonel. Sergeant O'Brine and Corporal MacClintock wilted from their haughty attitudes. Stony silence ensued.

"What are you two scrapping about now?" asked Colonel Decker in his best military voice. "What is it, Sergeant?"

"Sure, Colonel darlint, 'tis no more than what yez're afther tellin' me time and time agin'," replied O'Brine, walking smartly over to the colonel. "Kape away from each ither's work was yer orders, sor. What does Corporal MacClintock do but come shneakin' around here thryin't' git me t' do his work fer him."

"'Tis a lie, sirr," objected MacClintock, running over to the colonel. "I'm doon the rroad wi' two flat tirres. One sparre is all I've got, as ye know, sirr. What wi' walkin' all the way back herre, and wi' mess call aboot t' soond, I asked this sawed-off boy scoot—"

"Owoo!" howled O'Brine.

"Silence!" roared the colonel. "How did you get two flat tires, MacClintock?"

"Yes, sirr," gulped MacClintock. "Two of them went oot, sirr. They were non so gude, as ye know, Corronel; I was aboot to change them, anyhoo. The sparre I've put on the frront, but the rright flat one is as rrearr as a pancake—ah—the flat rrearr one is—ah—"

"The right rear one?" asked the colonel sternly.

"Yes, sir," replied MacClintock, with a sigh of relief.

"Well, you could have given him a hand, O'Brine," said the colonel sourly. "Go on now, both of you. Fix that tire and get the car back."

With a "Yes, sorr" and a "Yes, sirr" accompanied by the smartest of salutes, the two old soldiers executed an about-face and marched off into the gloom, keeping perfect step.

The colonel and I turned to re-enter the house. Immediately we both bumped into the figure of Christopher Hand.

"My word!" gasped the colonel. "Where did you come from, Christopher?"

"Heard you talking," murmured Hand. "I want to talk to Clark a minute, Colonel."

"Er—ah—yes," said the colonel, taking his departure almost guiltily. Framed in the back door, he glanced quizzically back at us; then he stepped inside and closed the door.

Hand turned to me.

"Where are Patty and Dick?" he snapped.

"MacClintock drove them over to Barkersville to get Patty's car," I replied. "They were going to take a little ride."

"Very well. MacClintock left the car down by the Ridge Road, I suppose. Let's go down and look it over."

"Look it over? Surely you don't suspect anything mysterious about a car getting a couple of flat tires."

"I suspect something mysterious in everything that goes on around here. Come on."

Together we set off down the lane in the darkness. Enough light remained, however, for us to see our way. But with the trees on the one side and the tall bushes lining the road at the top of the hill on the other, the lane would soon be as dark as a pocket. We walked quite a distance before we saw the parking lights of the stalled car.

"Take it easy," whispered Hand. "I want to approach that car quietly."

We took to the side of the road. Hand's tall figure before me was almost blotted out now by the gloom. We skulked up near the car, stopped to listen, and then approached it warily. The right rear wheel was jacked up, and the tire was removed from the rim. Otherwise the car had nothing unusual about it.

"Well," I breathed, "let's go back."

Hand did not answer me. Instead, he flashed his light on the ground and commenced moving off behind the car. Perhaps thirty feet back, as I followed after him, he stopped. His light swung back and forth. From the brown surface of the road bright flashes of light greeted the beam of his torch.

"Glass," he muttered. "That's what brought MacClintock to grief."

He quickly stooped and picked up a piece of paper with fragments of glass sticking to it. He flipped it out flat on his hand, and I bent over it. It was an obvious counterfeit label of a time-honored brand of whisky.

"Score another for the Anti-saloon League," I grinned. "The Demon Rum. Even his container is destructive."

"Certainly looks like nothing but a minor accident," grumbled Hand. "Since we are here, however, I am going to make sure it was nothing but this broken bottle that gave MacClintock trouble."

Once more we set off along the lane behind the car. Hand swept the road with his torch, but no other agency that might have punctured a tire came into view. All at once he snapped out his light and threw his arm across my chest.

"Quick! Get in among the trees," he hissed.

With outstretched hands, we stumbled in among the trees at the roadside. We both stood side by side behind a big one.

"What is it?" I whispered.

"Car coming round the bend," he replied. "I saw its headlights through the trees."

I must confess that I was a little out of patience with him. Here he had dragged me off almost at the dinner-hour to make a great fuss over two flat tires. Now we were skulking about like a pair of thieves at the approach of an innocent car. No doubt we should miss a lift back to the colonel's house. I had no doubt the approaching car held Patty and Dick.

Presently the lights of the car shone down the lane. It came on, then slowed down, and stopped almost in front of us. I could see that it was a small roadster and waited for Hand to step out and declare ourselves to our friends. He did nothing of the kind. There we waited, and there stood the roadster, motionless, impassive. At length it drove on, but the driver proceeded in low gear. When it arrived alongside the colonel's stalled car, the roadster stopped. Someone got out of it.

I could plainly see that it was a woman who stood in the road beside the roadster. Her figure was outlined by the headlights beyond it. The woman was not Patty Deck-er, of that I was sure. She was too tall for Patty. But I felt quite certain who she was.

The woman crossed over to the colonel's car and in-spected it carefully. After a few moments she got back into her car. To my astonishment, she put it into reverse and backed up until she was nearly abreast of us once more. Then she got out again.

By this time I was thoroughly intrigued by her actions. Hand scarcely breathed at my side. Dimly I could make out the figure of the woman as she left the car and walked quickly down the road behind it. Hand pressed my arm, a signal that he wished me to stay where I was. Then, like a shadow in the air, he left me.

I had not long to wait before the next action took place. The woman quickly returned to the car, got into it, and drove swiftly away in the direction of the colonel's house. When the lights of the roadster had disappeared, Hand stepped up beside me.

"Could you see where she stepped off the road?" he asked.

"I didn't even know she stepped off the road."

"Well, she did. And I know just where she left it. If possible, we'll see what she did it for."

Not until we had gone back along the road for twenty-five feet or so did Hand flash his light. When he did, it was to step quickly into the bushes at the top of the hill.

"She went in but a few feet," he mumbled, as if to himself. "I'd say it was about here. Seemed as if she stooped over. Help me look over the ground here, will—never mind, I have it!"

From a cavity in a small stump, he pulled forth a folded bit of paper. He handed me the light, which I held for him on the paper as he unfolded it. He scanned it rapidly; then he held it for me to see. This is what I read:

> "We are positive now that they and you are to be in the same old funny-looking house. If we don't see you, look for us. Yet don't think I do not want this thing to happen. You see it, don't you?"

"Well," I said, "as usual, I don't understand."

"Hold this for me, Clark," ordered Hand, handing me the note. "Keep the light on it; I want to copy it."

After he had copied it, he put the note back into the stump just as he had found it. A moment later we were back on the road. Once again my companion started scanning the road-bed with his light.

"What now?" I asked. "The roadster didn't run over any bottles."

"Who do you think that woman was, Clark?"

"I didn't see her face, but I'll bet it was Mrs. Compstock."

"You win. Although I didn't get a good view of her face, from her figure I judged it was Mrs. Compstock. What I see in the road here confirms my opinion."

"Well, what do you see in the road?"

"You have eyes, Clark, but you simply will not see. Can't you see the marks left by the tread of the tires on that roadster?"

"Yes. What about them?"

"I'm not an expert on automobiles, but my penchant is the evidence that anything leaves behind it. In that manner I have gleaned quite a knowledge of automobile tires. Those marks on the road tell me that the roadster was equipped with a cheap grade of mail-order tire. I noticed a good many of the same sort of tracks in the drive at Mrs. Compstock's house, particularly near the garage. I'll wager there is not another such set of cheap tires in this fashionable community."

"Yes, that seems to clinch it; it was Mrs. Compstock. But I was sure of it when I saw her standing against the light. What do we do now?"

"We go back to the house, and I hope this expedition has your appetite. Quite valuable flat tires, weren't they, Clark?"

As we neared the colonel's house, a car came down the drive. Hand once more pulled me off the road. We stood in the blackness under the trees as the same roadster that we had seen before went by us, this time going in the opposite direction. When we got to the house, we received further verification that we had rightly identified the occupant of the roadster.

"Where have you been, Christopher?" demanded the colonel. "I've just received a call from Mrs. Compstock. She wanted to see you, fancy that. I didn't know she was aware of your presence here."

"Yes; I met her this afternoon," murmured Hand.

"Another thing," said the colonel, anxiously. "Patty and Dick have not arrived yet. It's past dinner-time. By thunder, I'm beginning to worry about them."

"Don't be foolish, Colonel," laughed Hand. "Time means nothing when you're in love, you know. Have Maxwell tell the cook to hold dinner. Neither Clark nor I feel the least bit hungry. I want to speak to MacClintock a minute. Clark and I will be with you shortly."

Out we went again. As we rounded the corner of the house, O'Brine and MacClintock came down the drive carrying the spare tire, one in front of the other. O'Brine was grumbling; MacClintock was haughtily silent. Hand hailed them, whereupon MacClintock stopped so suddenly that O'Brine, in the rear, rammed the tire into the small of his back.

"Keep yerr eye on the frront rrank, ye rrooky!" he snapped.

"He he," snickered Sergeant O'Brine. "Haltin' wid—"

"MacClintock, where does this lane go?" demanded Hand, pointing in the direction away from Barkersville.

"It winds back to the Rridge Rroad, sirr," replied Mac-Clintock. "Therre's nothing brranching off it but the Bak-errs' drriveway."

"Good," said Hand. "Now, then, you fellows go back and fix that car as soon as you can. O'Brine, you go up to that end of the lane and keep your eye out for Miss Patty's

car. If it comes along, you get on it and ride back to the
house with them. If it's stopped when you see it, reconnoiter. Are you both armed?"

"We arre, sirr," replied MacClintock.

"All right. MacClintock, Mr. Clark and I are going
along the lane in the opposite direction. When you get the
car fixed, drive along after us to pick us up. Keep your eye
out for us. Come on, Clark."

Cautioned not to use my light, I stumbled along in the
darkness beside Hand. Soon we passed the Bakers' house,
all aglow with cheerful lights. Beyond, the trees and
bushes pressed closer to the road. We felt our way along
fully a quarter of a mile. Suddenly Hand clutched my arm.

"Look!" he whispered.

"Where?" I tensely replied.

"Off to the right—through the trees."

Then I saw what had caused him to stop. Through the
trees came a glow of light, diffused and soft. It was a
powerful beam to penetrate the thick wood at all. I had
no doubt it came from the headlights of an automobile on
a turn of the road ahead.

Hand broke into a run. I followed him, expecting to
rush headlong off the road and crash into a tree at any
moment. Soon, however, the light ahead, although coming
through the wood, was strong enough for us to see our
way. We quickened our pace.

The road made an S turn, following the contour of the
hilltop, to the left. As we rounded the first turn, we could
see the light flooding the road from round the next. Looking off through the underbrush, we could see the lights
themselves.

The car was standing still!

We approached the bend at a dead run. Then my companion laid a cautioning hand on my shoulder.

"Not too fast, Clark," he said. "Hold on, what's that?"

We came to a halt and stood listening. Down the hill-side I heard voices and the dry crackle of moving bodies in the underbrush. Faintly I made out a light moving through the bushes.

"No use for caution now," said Hand. "Let's see what's doing."

Once again we broke into a run. As we rounded the turn, the powerful lights of the automobile blinded us. Even so, upon approaching it I could see that there was another car parked behind the first one. The first one was Patty Decker's roadster. It was empty!

"Nobody in either car," growled Hand. "Hello!" he called. "Who's down on the hill-side?"

The voices below us stopped. Then someone called: "Who's that?"

"Is Dick Fairfax there?" shouted Hand.

"Yes, I am," came Dick's voice. "Who is that, Mr. Hand?"

"Yes," shouted Hand. "Where's Patty, Dick?"

"She's back at the Bakers'," replied Dick. "Wait a minute, I'll come up."

We stood motionless beside the two cars. Presently Dick, panting from the exertion of climbing the hill, burst out of the bushes.

"Hello," he said. "I told Patty not to tell her father about this."

"Well, at any rate, her father hasn't told us about it," said Hand. "What's going on here, Dick?"

Dick grinned. "You're the greatest fellow I ever saw," he said. "You don't know what's going on, but here you are, just the same. You must have a sixth sense, I swear!"

"What's it all about, Dick?"

"I'll tell you. Patty and I took a little drive. We were coming home, right along here, when all of a sudden I heard somebody shout: 'Help! Help!' I stopped the car, and Patty and I both heard the cry repeated. It was getting dark. Boy! That gave me a funny feeling!"

"What did you do?"

"Patty wanted me to jump out and rush to the rescue. I don't know, Mr. Hand, maybe it was a cowardly thing to do, but I didn't go. I couldn't see leaving Pat alone in the car with a murderer somewhere in the neighborhood, like as not. I drove on as fast as I could go."

"Good boy! What did you do then?"

"I was going back for you, but Pat stopped me. She said her father had enough trouble without this. We stopped at the Bakers', and I got Mr. Baker and his son, Gene. Mr. Middleton and his wife were there for dinner, and Mr. Middleton came along with us. We drove by here, listening, but we didn't hear anything. Then we turned round and came back and stopped. I think this is where we heard the shout."

"What's this other car?"

"It's Mr. Middleton's. They're all down there looking round now. We can't find a thing. Looks as if somebody fell into the swamp. That's nice, eh? I suppose I'm to blame for this, but I—I couldn't help it! By thunder! I couldn't leave Pat alone on this road, that's all there is to it!"

"You did perfectly right," said Hand. "It might have been even wiser had you taken Patty right home; her father is worried about her. We'll do it now. Here, you drive," he added, opening the door of the roadster.

"What?" said Dick, his jaw dropping. "Say, I can't go off and leave the others like this. I brought them over here, you know."

"Clark will fix that up. You stay here and flag MacClintock, Clark. Then both of you go down and help out in the search. I'm willing to wager you won't find anything. Undoubtedly the fellow who shouted was the same man we chased through the wood this afternoon. He doesn't like company; probably a mile away by now. Tell the Bakers and Mr. Middleton, Clark, that the colonel was worried and Dick and I took Patty home."

Dick got into the car and started it. They drove off, leaving me to stand in the road to stop MacClintock. I was so relieved to know that nothing had happened to the colonel's sweet little daughter that I hardly gave a thought to the mysterious business that was keeping me there. It was not long before MacClintock came streaking round the turn in the road. I waved my arms to attract his attention, and he brought the car to a halt with a screech of brakes. Dust swirled about it as I walked over to speak to him.

"You got here in a hurry, MacClintock," I said. "Just park the car in front of this one and come with me."

The old soldier asked no questions. When he had parked the car, he got out and followed me down the hill. At the edge of the swamp we found the three men. Mr. Middleton held a long pole with which he was probing the slimy surface. The two others held electric torches to aid him. All three had valiantly waded into the mud and were standing in it up to their ankles. As MacClintock and I approached, Mr. Middleton gave up poking the pole into the mire and turned inquisitively toward us. The two men flashed their lights on us.

"Oh, Mr. Clark," said Mr. Middleton in surprise. "Where is Dick?"

"Hand wanted to take him somewhere," I said, rather lamely.

"Did Mr. Hand know that I was here?" asked Mr. Middleton.

"Yes; Dick told him," I replied.

"Oh, that explains it," said Mr. Middleton pompously. "He realized I could handle this. By the way, this is Mr. Baker and his son, Gene, Mr. Clark. They are neighbors of the colonel's, and formerly lived next door to me—rather, I lived next door to them," he amended with a laugh. "We have a mysterious bit of business here, sir. I suppose Dick has told you about it."

"Yes, he did," I said. "What do you make of it?"

"Looks like a joke," grumbled Mr. Middleton. "A nice mess we're in, too! You won't get to see your girl in those clothes, Gene, my boy. You see, Mr. Clark, this is the only place where there are any footprints. They didn't seem to go right into the swamp, but we decided to investigate anyhow. Nothing more to be done here; we might as well go back. I'll notify Withers of this."

We made our way back up the hill. Mr. Middleton drew me aside from the others and inquired about the Decker case. I told him about Dr. Metz, and he was astounded. Furness he was not so surprised at, although I failed to mention the confession we had found in the bottom of the bag. Finally he confided to me that he was working on a theory which he expected to solve the case. I told him Hand would be much interested to hear it, and MacClintock and I set out for the colonel's.

As we turned into the driveway, I saw Patty's car standing in front of the porch. The others were just getting out of it. The colonel came out on the porch through the front door. Patty rushed up to him, and they embraced. Hand hopped out of the roadster and trotted over to us.

"We'll go right up and get O'Brine," he said to MacClintock as he climbed in with me. "How did the search turn out?"

"They were just about giving it up when we got down there," I told him. "Mr. Middleton thinks it was a joke. If it was, he failed to see the point."

When MacClintock stopped the car at the Ridge Road, no sign was to be seen of Sergeant O'Brine.

"Good heaven, where do you suppose he is?" I asked in some alarm.

"He's arroond herre, sirr," said MacClintock unconcernedly. "Ye can bet yerr boots he's watchin' us rright noo."

As if in answer, the next instant Sergeant O'Brine stepped up from behind the car. He was stowing his automatic away as he opened the door. "Not wan t'ing did I see, sor," he said.

"All right, Sergeant, get in," said Hand. "Take us back to the colonel's, MacClintock, Mr. Clark is hungry. By the way, I have a job for you two. Have you ever kept watch over a house all night?"

"Sure, an' we've kep' watch over most iveryt'ing many's th' all night,' replied O'Brine.

"Fine! I want you to conceal yourself in the wood near Mrs. Compstock's house tonight, and every night from now on until I give you further orders. Choose a position where you can see anyone who might pay the lady a nocturnal visit."

"Beggin' yer pardon, sor; a what visit?"

"A night visit. If it is a very late visit, nab the visitor and bring him back to the colonel's. Be careful, however, not to let Mrs. Compstock know you have taken her visitor away with you. Your vigil starts as soon as it gets dark; it ends with the rising sun. When you leave us at the colonel's door, put the car away and go right up there. I'd suggest that you take a couple of blankets with you; one of you can sleep while the other keeps watch."

Rather than becoming glum over the prospects of losing their beds, the two old soldiers perked up and seemed highly pleased with their orders. O'Brine edged over nearer MacClintock. For once they forgot to squabble as they commenced making plans for the night.

"Clark, you and I are going to spend the night in the colonel's library," announced Hand. "If anyone enters that house tonight, it will be to get a surprise. Thus we have three traps set, you see: the police watching Dr. Metz's confreres, MacClintock and O'Brine watching Mrs. Compstock, and ourselves watching the colonel's house. Perhaps we shall catch some game."

10

THE RIDGE ROAD

The events up until the following evening were of no special interest. Hand and I spent a miserable, uneventful night in the library. I slept fitfully in a large leather armchair that had my back all out of joint by morning. MacClintock and O'Brine reported a quiet night at Mrs. Compstock's house.

Captain Bartlett arrived in the morning. He was a jolly, good-looking chap whose spirits were so buoyant that they were even impervious to the funeral. All of Mill Ridge turned out for the solemn function. Immediately after the service Colonel Decker departed with his brother's remains. To my astonishment, Hand left with him to drive as far as New York, where the colonel was to entrain for the West. My friend mentioned that he had some affairs to attend to in New York that would very likely detain him until the following day. He cautioned me to keep the vigil in the library that night, an admonition that left me rather depressed.

Just before dusk Captain Bartlett and I were taking a stroll about the house. What he had to say to me perhaps explained the excellent manner in which he had borne up during the funeral service.

"Not such a bad break for the good old colonel as you might think," he said in reply to a condoling remark of mine concerning the colonel's late brother. "Joe Decker was bad from the ground up. It may sound pretty steep, my talking about the dead and all that, but the fact remains, Joe Decker was pretty poor stuff."

"You knew him?" I asked, a little startled at him.

"Sure I knew him. He was always turning up like a bad penny around R.H.Q. He could get into more jams per day than an old lady's white cat with a fondness for the coal-bin. Nasty ones, too. As soon as he got into a fix, he'd beat it for the colonel. If he couldn't get to him, he'd wire or cable. The old man'd raise plain hell, but he always got him out of 'em. It wasn't the money—the colonel's got two dollars for every whisker in Russia—but he worried the old man half to death. He'd have got them all into some kind of mess before long. I only hope the way he made his finish won't do it. The colonel's foolish if he tries to pry into that affair. Better to let sleeping dogs lie!"

I was wondering whether I did not agree with him. Nothing we had uncovered so far concerning Joseph Decker's affairs had been the least bit consoling to his brother. Coupled with that had come the mysterious affairs in the lane the night before. I seemed to smell menace in the dank air that was blowing in off the swamp. Perhaps it was better to let sleeping dogs lie.

We turned a corner of the house and came upon Sergeant O'Brine. The old fellow was emerging from the kitchen door with a pan filled with beet-greens in his hand. He nearly dropped it in his haste to salute the captain.

"There yez are, Capting darlint!" he exclaimed. "Sure an' I've bin maynin't' show yez me goat, sor. As fine a little baste as yez iver seen. Come wid me, now, an' jist tell me what yez t'ink ov him."

"You don't mean you've acquired a goat at last, Sergeant!" exclaimed the captain, giving me a sly wink. "The critter'll give you hoof and mouth disease as sure as you're standing there. It's a wonder to me that MacClintock stands for it."

"Corporal MacClintock—" began O'Brine, bridling.

"Corporal!"

"Yes, sor, 'tis busted he is. An' wid good reason, too. Layvin' th' poor colonel shtranded in Barkersville in th' middle ov th' night!"

"Oh, MacClintock can still forget his orders, eh? So, now that he's nothing but a corporal, he must perforce stand exposed to hoof and mouth disease from this goat of yours."

"Thot he must, by th' saints! Ah, yez're a great lad, sor. There ain't a man in th' army wid half the monkey-shines. Sure an' I got rid ov th' only goat th' colonel would iver let me have jist on account ov thot hoof an' mouth disase yez were afther gittin' me all worked up about. 'Twas Mac-Clintock himsilf showed me th' foolishness ov it. Sure an' I can't get me foot widin two fate ov me mouth!"

"That's three feet," said the captain quickly. "Suppose you got two feet within four feet of your mouth, how many feet would that be, quick!"

"Four fate widin—two fate widin—would yez mind sayin' it over agin, sor?"

"Never mind," said the captain. "I guess you won't get hoof and mouth disease after all. Where's the goat? Let's see it."

O'Brine led us proudly round the garage to the rear. Inside a board-fence enclosure stood a billy-goat, eying us suspiciously. O'Brine threw the beet-greens to it, and the greedy little animal immediately forgot its interest in us.

"All me life I've wanted a goat," said O'Brine, leaning over the fence and gazing fondly upon his pet. "Me owld father in Ireland had one. Sure an' 'twas near th' death ov 'im too, sor. Th' baste went t' atin' me mother's bustle jist as she was layvin' fer a wake. Both th' owld man an' his goat was a turrible sight fer days afther that!"

"See, they mean nothing but trouble," sniffed the captain.

"Oh, go long wid yez, sor," replied O'Brine with a grin. "This goat is a gintleman. Sure, he was brought up wid a family ov rich kids. This is no place fer 'im a tall! Thot owld fool, Hughie! Bawlin' himsilf black in th' face whin I brought me goat t' me quarters!"

"Didn't MacClintock mention something to me about that goat butting his bureau over?" asked Captain Bartlett accusingly. "Broke his mirror, he said, continuing his bad luck another seven years."

"He's nothin' but bad luck, anyhow!" snorted O'Brine. "As fer th' mirror, sor, 'tis a blessin't' himsilf thot he don't hov t' look at himsilf in it!"

"Well, I don't see why the colonel lets you keep such an omen of bad luck on the post," said the captain, turning to go.

"Sure an' he was glad t' hov him, sor!" declared O'Brine, tagging along with us as we started back to the house. "Afther me retiremint I was night-watchman at a powder works. Wan night me an' me goat was makin' our rounds whin there come a turrible knockin' on wan ov th' doors. T'gither we wint up t' th' door, an' I opens it. There shtands th' colonel, natural as yez plase. 'O'Brine,' sez he, 'this is no work fer yez. Sure, I'm mustered out mesilf,' sez he. 'Yez're me orderly an' yez must come wid me.' 'How about me goat, sor?' sez I. 'Bring th' baste along,' sez he. 'If yez kape it around here, he'll go an' chew somethin' up an' blow th' whole works t' smithereens!'"

"As easy as that!" exclaimed Captain Bartlett.

"Aysier, sor, aysier. We lift right away at wance, we did. Out t' th' kyar we wint, me and me goat an' th' colonel. What do I see but Hughie MacClintock adrivin' th' colonel's kyar. Th' colonel opens th' back door, an' thot little sinner ov a goat pops in all by hissilf. Th' saints preserve us, yez should ov heard Hughie holler! 'Sure, 'tis all right, MacClintock,' sez th' colonel. 'Th' goat belongs t' O'Brine, an' he's takin' it wid him.' Hughie sez nothin', but th' back ov his neck begins t' shwell up like a balloon. There we was, me an' me goat in th' back, an' th' colonel an' Hughie in front. Off we goes, layvin' th' powder works, wid me A.W.O.L."

"Well, all joking aside, it's a fine goat, Sergeant," said the captain. "You're a lucky man to have it."

"Thank yez, sor!" exclaimed O'Brine, his face beaming. "Sure, I'll let yez fade him tomorrow. I knew yez liked him th' minute yez laid eyes on him. He goes fer thim he don't take a notion to."

"All right, Sergeant," laughed the captain as he entered the back door to the den. I hung back to speak to O'Brine. MacClintock had driven Hand and the colonel to New York, and I wanted to see what arrangements they had made for keeping watch on Mrs. Compstock's house.

"Are you going to wait for MacClintock to get back before going up to Mrs. Compstock's?" I asked O'Brine in a low voice.

"Thot I am not, sor," he replied. "As soon as it gits good an' dark, I'm takin' mesilf up there alone. Hughie'll come along afther."

"Good work," I said as I entered the den. Captain Bartlett was standing in the center of the room looking around.

"So this is where the dirty work was done," he said. "Suppose it messed up the rug; I see it's gone."

"Yes," I affirmed, a little nettled at his indifference to the tragedy. In fact, no one but the colonel seemed to mourn his brother's passing. The neighbors quite obviously had attended the funeral out of respect for the colonel.

Even Patty seemed less touched by Joseph Decker's tragic end than she was by the effect it had upon her father. Poor indeed the man who never knew the warmth of true friendship!

Suddenly the telephone bell rang insistently.

"I'll answer it," offered the captain. He picked up the instrument, said: "Hello," and then turned to me. "Someone wants your friend Hand," he said. "Seems all excited."

"Let me take it," I said quickly, taking the telephone from him. "Hello, did you want to speak to Christopher Hand?" I asked.

"Yes," replied a voice. "This is Chief Huddy over in Barkersville. Where is Mr. Hand? Somethin' awful has happened!"

"This is Mr. Clark," I said hastily. "What's the matter?"

"That feller Furness has busted out o' jail!"

"Good heaven! When did he get out?"

"Tom just went in to give 'em their grub, an' Furness was gone!"

"Start looking for him," I ordered. "Hand has gone to New York. I'll be right over."

"Heck!" ejaculated Chief Huddy disgustedly, and hung up. I felt rather aggrieved that the offer of my own services had not aroused any enthusiasm. I decided, however, that the thing for me to do was to investigate this latest turn of events.

"What's doing?" asked the captain.

"A man has broken out of the Barkersville police jail," I explained hurriedly. "I'll have to run over there for a while. I think you had better stay here and look after things."

"Them's my orders, and I'll stick to 'em," replied Captain Bartlett, striking a heroic pose. "Far be it from me to be inquisitive, but it's passing strange that a guest of Colonel Decker's should get all hot and bothered over a jail break in Barkersville. Why not let the hobo go his weary way?"

"Listen," I said, dropping my voice; "that fellow who escaped from Barkersville may be Joseph Decker's murderer! I've got to see about it."

"Oh, ho! So that's it. And you think he might come back here with more murderous intent?"

"I don't know what to think. But keep your eyes open, Captain. There's more to this than one sees on the surface."

"Go your way in peace, and let your soul be not troubled," said Captain Bartlett. Although his words were light, the voice with which he uttered them was grim. "Dick Fairfax is here. He and I with Sergeant O'Brine can stand off a regiment. How are you going?"

"I'll take Patty's car," I said. "By Jove, I wonder whether the keys are in it. Where is Patty?"

I rushed out into the hall. Patty and Dick were in the living-room.

"May I borrow your car for a while?" I asked her as matter-of-factly as possible. "I should like to run over to Barkersville."

"Why certainly, Mr. Clark," she replied. "But can't you wait until after dinner? It's about to be served."

"I'm afraid not. This is very urgent. Are the keys in the car? I hate to trouble you like this, but—"

"Oh, it's no trouble at all! The keys are up in my bag. I'll just go up and get them. Be back in a j iffy."

As she ran out of the room, Dick turned inquiringly to me. "Now what's happened?" he asked anxiously.

"Furness broke out of jail, Dick," I told him. "I don't know what's going on around here, but we've got to be careful after what happened last night."

"Don't worry, Mr. Clark," said Dick grimly. "I have my eyes open!"

"That's the boy!" exclaimed the captain, who had joined us. "If they want war, let it begin here."

Patty ran into the room holding out the keys to me. I thanked her and hastily left through the den. A low-hanging pall of clouds was making a premature end of daylight. Already objects were becoming indistinguishable in the dusk. At the garage I met O'Brine, who was just emerging from the entrance to his quarters. He had a blanket-roll slung over his shoulders, and a huge automatic swung fearsomely from a web belt around his waist.

"Is the garage unlocked, O'Brine?" I asked quickly.

"It is, sor," he replied, regarding me with astonishment. "Yez aren't layvin', are yez?"

"I've got to go to Barkersville," I replied. "I'll give you a lift as far as the Ridge Road. Keep your eyes peeled tonight, O'Brine, there may be something brewing."

We opened the garage doors and started out. I noticed a thin mist collecting on the wind-shield.

"It's going to be a nasty night, O'Brine," I said. "It's a pity you have to be out in it."

"Whiniver yez shmell th' shwamp, yez kin bet there's a shtorm cornin' up," he said. "East wind, thot's why. But don't yez go faylin' sorry fer Hughie an' me, Mr. Clark. I've got me poncho an' Hughie's shilter-half as well as me own. I'll put up th' pup-tint, an' wan ov us kin shlape in it while th' ither kapes watch. Whin yez've bin carryin' yer atin', shlaypin', an' fightin' implyments around on yer back wid yez over half th' earth, yez don't mind a wet night no more."

"I suppose that's true," I said. "I admire you, O'Brine."

"It's jist wan way ov livin', sor," said Sergeant O'Brine simply. "Beggin' yer pardon, Mr. Clark, I ain't niver asked quistions whin I got me orders, but what makes yez say somethin's abrewin', sor?"

I glanced sharply at him. "I think I can tell you, O'Brine," I said. "Gerald Furness, who was a guest at the colonel's, you know, is suspected of having murdered Joseph Decker. He was locked up in the Barkersville jail. He escaped a little while ago. You may tell MacClintock, but neither of you breathe a word of it to anyone else."

"No, sor!" said O'Brine emphatically.

"Here you are, O'Brine," I said as we came up on the Ridge Road. "I hope it doesn't get down to a real rain to-night. Good luck."

"Good luck t' you, sor," replied O'Brine as he moved off in the dark.

I proceeded on to Barkersville, keeping a watch out for our mysterious stranger who had such a liking for the tall timbers. I drove into the town, however, without even having passed another car.

The police headquarters appeared tranquil enough as I stopped before it. The sergeant whose acquaintance we had made the day before sat as immobile as the desk before him. From all appearances he had not shifted his gaze from the street since he had come on duty that morning. I stepped briskly in upon him, but I made no impression on the stony fellow.

"Where's Chief Huddy?" I demanded.

"Where—what—who?" replied the sergeant, slowly turning to look at me.

"Where's the chief?" I repeated.

"Out," replied the sergeant laconically.

"Has he instituted a search for Furness?"

"Well, he's lookin' fer him."

"Who's back in the cell-room?"

"Jest that old guy. Furness got away."

Without bothering to ask his permission, I strode back into the cell-room. The doleful old man in the cell was the only occupant of the room. I walked back to inspect the cell from which Furness had made his escape. The old fellow in the other cell regarded me without much interest from over his eyeglasses.

I saw without trouble how Furness had managed his escape. The lock on the cell door was covered with rust. On the inner side around the keyhole were numerous bright scratches. It would not have taken a very accomplished picklock to unfasten the ancient bolt. A window at one side of the room was wide open. I walked over to it and stuck my head out. The ground was no more than six or seven feet below.

"That's the way he left me," announced the old man in the cell.

"Why didn't you give the alarm?" I demanded, turning about.

"There you go! There you go!" whined the old man plaintively in his high, cracked voice. "Jumpin' on me! Jest like all the rest. D'ye think I wanted to git shot? That feller was dangerous!"

"How could he shoot you?" I asked disgustedly. "He didn't have a gun. How could he have one when he was locked up in jail?"

"Well, I didn't know that! He said he'd shoot me, that's all I know."

"How long ago did he make his get-away?"

"'Bout a half-hour ago. He picked the lock with somethin' he got out of his pocket, and hopped out the winder. I can't do nothin' with this lock, though. Looka here, what's your name?"

"My name is Clark. What is yours, by the way?"

"Mine's Carley. Looka here, Mr. Clark, I wanta git outa here. I wanta go back to my daughter's in New York. She gives me a good home."

"I'll see what I can do about it, Carley. They'll have to keep you here a little while as a witness. That employer of yours is in hot water. Don't pick the lock, though. That will only get you into trouble."

"All right, I won't, Mr. Clark."

"See here, did Furness say anything to you?"

"Only that if I hollered he'd—what was it—he'd blow me so full of holes I'd look like a bay winder."

"When did he start to pick the lock?"

"Right after that friend of yourn took his picture."

"Hand? Was Hand here?"

"Hand, yeah, that's what they called him. He come in here and gummed this feller Furness's fingers all up with ink. Then, by gorry, he had two cops hold him up against the wall. He put a camera on the table there and then set off a lot of gunpowder. Filled the room right up with smoke! That feller Furness kicked up some. He raised Holy Ned around here!"

"When did all this take place?"

"This afternoon. Right after your friend and the cops went out, Furness started to pick the lock. Took him quite a while, but he did it, by gorry!"

"Well, you just take it easy and don't worry," I said reassuringly. "We'll have you out of here and send you back to your daughter's before you know it. Leave that lock alone, now."

"All right, Mr. Clark. I can't get it open with my belt-buckle, anyhow. Wisht I had a knife! It's lonesome here. Say, you ain't goin'!"

I was going, and presently I was back in the street. Just what to do was a matter I was having difficulty to decide. I could not see much sense in driving aimlessly round the countryside looking for the fugitive. It occurred to me that if I were fleeing the spot, I should strike out for

Markstown. It was a good-sized place on the main line of
the railroad, about eight miles from Barkersville. I got
back into the roadster and set out along the Markstown
road. I came upon three pedestrians before I arrived there.
I drew up beside each one, saw that it was not my man,
and, to their astonishment, pulled away. I did not leave a
very good impression of myself with them. Each one took
it that I was about to give him a lift. I reached Markstown
with their bitter imprecations ringing in my ears.

First I went to the railroad station. Furness was not
there. I then cruised about the town scanning the faces of
the people on the sidewalks. That also was in vain. Suddenly I thought of the police and whether Chief Huddy
had sent out an alarm. I found the police station and inquired. They had not heard of Furness's escape. I supplied
them with a description of the man and was assured he
would be picked up if he entered Markstown.

There seemed nothing more to be done in that direction, and I turned the car toward Mill Ridge. I had been
gone some time. A little nervously, I wondered whether
anything had happened during my absence. My foot on
the accelerator mirrored my anxiety, and soon I was skim-
ming along at a rapid clip. The mist had turned into a
drizzle that was rapidly becoming worse, but the road was
straight, and I was in no mood for caution, anyhow.

On my way by I stopped at the Barkersville police station. The sergeant was still in charge, and nothing new
had developed.

After I had gone about a mile along the Ridge Road, my
motor began to cough. I frantically pulled the choke, but
with a final sputter the motor died altogether. I glanced
at the gasoline gauge on the instrument-board. The indi-
cator, in spite of my tapping, refused to register anything
but zero. To make matters worse, a steady downpour had
set in!

Gloomily I sat in the stalled car and endeavored to ascertain my position. It seemed to me there was a house not far up the road ahead of me. Resignedly I pulled up my coat-collar and got out into the wet.

"I hope that bounder Furness is out in this too!" I grumbled to myself as I started sloshing up the road. My thoughts turned to the philosophical O'Brine as the water started trickling down my neck. Being forced out of the dry recess of an automobile into the pouring rain was enough to utterly ruin my disposition. But on a fishing trip I would stand contentedly in the rain for hours, getting soaked to the skin with the greatest of pleasure. Strange are the fancies of civilized man.

On I trudged, with no heaven-sent glimmer of light to guide me. The road was fast turning into a river. The seething splash of the rain-drops grew steadily in volume, and I became wetter just as steadily. Here was I, who a few short hours before had been dreaming of living in just such a place, wondering now what ever drove people to settle down in such wilds.

My discordant thoughts were suddenly interrupted. I stopped so suddenly that I slipped and slid in the mud. Was that a voice I had heard above the murmur of the rain? I drew back into the bushes at the side of the road. Standing there tensely still, I heard the splash, splash of someone walking in the muddy road. My unsuspecting company on the Ridge Road must have numbered more than one. Distinctly I heard voices; it sounded as if two men were approaching me. What they were saying I could not make out until they were nearly abreast of me. Their conversation, when I finally was able to comprehend it, was not reassuring.

"Snap right into it, I say," one of the men was saying. "That guy Hand will be back on the job before you know it. I could get along without him!"

"Keep your ideas to yourself!" snapped the other. "I'm runnin' this. When I get ready, we'll go to work—not before! Do you get it?"

The first man mumbled an unintelligible reply as they passed by me. Who they were I had no idea, but I meant to find out. I drew my pistol and my electric torch from my pockets and stepped out into the road.

"Halt! I have you covered!" I cried, flashing the light on them in such a way that they could see the pistol held in my hand.

What happened next will never be clearly fixed in my mind. With a savage cry one of the men whirled about. I dimly remember firing my pistol as something came flying at me through the air. The next instant the world was full of brilliant, shooting lights; then utter darkness.

A great peaceful silence was broken by some villain who would not let me alone. He was attempting to drown me. Above my upturned face was a huge waterfall. Beside it stood a man whose power over that waterfall was amazing. He would raise his arm and the onrushing water would pause in mid air; then with the dropping of his arm the cataract would plunge on again to smite me in the face. Occasionally the man would leave his waterfall in a state of suspension while he placed me in a sort of popcorn popper and shook me up. I cried out in protest, and the man answered me as if from afar. Gradually the voice came nearer, until at length I began to comprehend what the man said.

"Ye'rre cornin' arroond fine, noo," said the voice. "That's it—open yerr eyes. Carreful noo—that's it, sirr. Don't trry to get up yet. Ye'll be as good as everr in a few minutes."

"MacClintock!" I weakly exclaimed. "What on earth has happened?"

"Weell, ye've got the prrettiest lump on the side of yerr head that I everr see, ferr one thing, sirr," replied Mac-Clintock. "Firrst I see Miss Patty's carr standin' all alone in the rroad, and then I come acrross ye lyin' herre in the rroad like a sack o' oatmeal. Was ye rrobbed, sirr?"

"I don't know," I groaned, struggling to a sitting posture. I was convinced one more move like that would split my head asunder.

"I see Miss Patty's carr was oot o' gas, an' I wonderrs what to do aboot it," continued MacClintock glibly. "I decides whoeverr was drrivin' it was up this way, because I hadna met anyone frrom Barrkerrsville, herre, d'ye see, sirr? The firrst thing I knew, I come nearr rroonin' overr ye lyin' in the rroad herre; I was just able to stop."

"That was nice," I said.

"I gets oot and starrts sloshin' waterr in yerr face, sirr," went on MacClintock. "I'm sorrry I got ye all overr mud-dy water, but honest, sirr, ye was half drrownt when I got herre."

"Quite all right, MacClintock. Here, give me a hand; I think I can get up now. What a beastly mess I'm in! I'll never be able to get into the colonel's car—I'd ruin the upholstering."

"Ye can sit on a rrobe, sirr. I'll drrive ye rright home. Then I'll get some gasoline and brring Misterr Rrichard back wi' me to get Miss Patty's carr. Therre ye go, sirr, sit rright doon."

"Just a minute, MacClintock," I said as I settled back against the cushions. "You didn't happen to find a brick or anything lying near me, did you? I was struck by something."

"I didn't, sirr," he replied. "I'll go rright back and have a look wi' me flashlight."

He was gone a few minutes and then returned with a stick in his hand. Without a word he passed it back to me.

The stick was of heavy oak, freshly cut with a knife. One end tapered off, and on the other was a heavy, gnarled knot. The thing was about three feet long. Someone had provided himself with a formidable cudgel, and I had been his victim. I would have given much to learn his identity.

MacClintock started up, and soon he was helping me into the colonel's house. The others were just leaving the dining-room. They were filled with dismay at sight of me.

"Mr. Clark!" cried Patty, running over to me. "What has happened?"

"Have an accident, old man?" asked the captain, taking my arm.

"Yes, yes, an accident," I said. "I ran out of gas, and as I was walking to get some, I slipped and fell. MacClintock fortunately came along on his way home from New York and brought me in."

"Oh, what a terrible bump on your head!" cried Patty in dismay. "I'll get some arnica. Take him into the living-room, Dick. I'll be right down."

"I'm covered with mud," I protested. "I'll get it all over everything. I really don't need anything, Patty. I'm still a little dizzy, but I'll be over that soon. Please don't bother about me."

"You're not all right, and I'm going to attend to you," she said firmly. "Sit right down until I get back!"

With such a determined little nurse in charge of me, I had nothing to do but comply. Patty whisked out of the room.

"See here," said Captain Bartlett distrustfully; "mean to say you got that bump from falling down?"

"No, I didn't," I quickly replied. "That was for Patty's benefit."

I told them all about my encounter on the Ridge Road with the mysterious pair. Dick became more and more concerned. Captain Bartlett was astounded. He grabbed the stick that MacClintock was holding.

"Soaked you with this, eh?" he said, inspecting the club. "It's a wonder it didn't fracture your skull. Do you suppose you hit him when you shot at him?"

"I don't know," I replied. "They were gone when Mac-Clintock got there, at any rate."

"Well, you want to get to bed right away," cautioned Dick. "I'll fix you up a drink so that you won't take cold. Can you imagine this happening in Mill Ridge!"

"Easily!" I replied with feeling. "That was the loneliest spot I've ever seen. I can't go to bed, though, Dick."

"Why not?"

"I promised Hand I'd stay up in the library and keep watch."

"What for?" demanded the captain.

"I don't know," I replied. "It was one of Hand's orders. From my experience tonight, I'd say it was well merited."

"I'll take the duty for you," offered the captain quickly. "MacClintock and O'Brine can spell me."

"They won't be able to," I said. "Here, quick, before Patty gets back I want to tell you two a few things."

MacClintock moved discreetly out into the hall. I told Dick and the captain everything concerning the case that I could in the brief moment I had at my disposal, not even sparing the episode of Mrs. Compstock.

"Score one for Joe Decker," said the captain. "I'm not surprised at his connection with Gerald Furness, or the doctor either. But I didn't think he had it in him to pro-tect anybody—not even his own brother."

"By thunder! this is getting serious," said Dick. "Where's that fly-cop they have around here, anyway? He should be on the job. There have been two murders in this house already."

"Two!" exclaimed the captain.

"We found the body of one of the servants stuffed in the cellar wall," explained Dick gloomily. "Somebody broke his head the night before Uncle Joseph was done in."

"We'll all take turns standing guard tonight," I said. "I'll be fit enough after I've had a couple of hours' sleep. You take the first, Captain, Dick next, and then call me. Here comes Patty—not a word of this to her!"

"There, now, I'll just bathe that bump and tie it up," said Patty, approaching me with bottles and bandages. She set to work on me, and I must confess her ministrations were most welcome.

"He looks like the Spirit of Seventy-six," grinned the captain.

"Oh, Dick," I said, suddenly recalling, "MacClintock wants you to go with him to get Patty's car. Watch yourself, boy!" I whispered in his ear as I got up. He patted a bulge under his coat to indicate that he was armed.

"Come along, now," said Patty, taking my arm; "I'll fix your room for you. If you can get a quiet night's sleep, you will be all right."

"Nothing would suit me better than a quiet night," I assured her.

Captain Bartlett grinned.

11

A BIRD WITH A BROKEN WING

When I next awoke, it was broad daylight. Dick and the captain had perfidiously allowed me to sleep the whole night through. My head, though still quite tender, once again was clear.

The new day was as beautiful as one could wish, although the earth was still drenched from the rain of the night before. The first thing I did was to call the Barkersville police. Furness had not been found.

As we all left the breakfast table, Dick turned to me. "What's to be done now?" he asked. "Nobody walked into our traps last night."

"I may be exaggerating my own importance," I said, "but I think it more or less essential for us to investigate my experience last night. The road was very muddy; there should be footprints to be found."

"That's right!" said Dick quickly. "MacClintock is back; let's get him to drive us over there."

"You'd better stay with Patty," I said. "Captain Bartlett and I will go over and see what's to be found. I think it should be done."

As soon as Patty had left us, I suggested to the captain that we go over to the spot where I had come to grief the night before. He readily agreed, and, pressing MacClintock into service, we set out.

"This is the place," I suddenly called, peering out of the car window. "It's still very muddy; be careful how you walk round."

The vestiges of my disastrous encounter with the two strangers were plain in the road. The tracks of the two men were off to one side of the ruts made by the passing cars, as were my own. The imprint of my recumbent body, however, was athwart the road and partially obliterated by automobile tracks, providing a nasty suggestion.

"Here's where they came along," I said, leading the captain along the automobile ruts. "They walked abreast. Here's where I stepped off the road to allow them to pass and then stepped back again to accost them. You see, I didn't move before I was struck. By Jove! Those fellows didn't even come back to see whether they had killed me. Although they stopped when I hailed them, their tracks go right on from there. They ran, too; see how the deep imprint of the front part of their feet is all that is visible?"

"Perhaps it's a good thing for you they didn't come back to investigate your remains," said the captain. "They weren't very anxious about your good health in the first instance. It's hardly to be supposed they have had a change of heart even yet."

"I guess you're right," I agreed. "Here's where Mac-Clintock came over to me. Just look at the water he was throwing on me!" I exclaimed, indicating a muddy pool at the side of the road. Evidently MacClintock's hand had splashed a generous quantity of mud along with the water. His scooping fingers had dug quite a trench at the edge of the puddle.

"You looked like a mud pie when you got home," snickered the captain.

"Well," I said a little stiffly, "let's see whether we can tell where those fellows got to. MacClintock," I called to the driver, who had stopped the car on the other side of the road, "just drive along slowly ahead of us. We'll see whether we can follow these tracks."

The men had run quite a distance. Suddenly the captain gave evidence that he was not altogether unversed in tracking.

"By Jove! Clark, you hit one of those men!" he exclaimed.

"How do— Oh, I see! That staggering track, to be sure! See, they stopped here!"

"If there was any blood, it has all been washed away," mused the captain, closely inspecting the ground. "They went on again, more slowly, you see. They left the road right up there."

"Yes," I said, running ahead to where the footprints veered off the road. "I think it was right round that bend up there that I parked Patty's car, or rather where it ran out of gas. They probably saw its lights and took to the wood. It would be hard to track them in there."

"Practically impossible," replied the captain, who had leaped the ditch and was making his way back from the road. I followed him. We were able to follow the trail for a short distance, but then we lost it altogether. The humus under the trees was hard. A thick covering of dead leaves made anything but an ideal surface to retain the evidence of a man passing over it.

"It seems to me they would have inspected the car," I said.

"On the other hand, I don't think they would," disagreed the captain as we halted. "They were steering clear of it. Otherwise, why would they have entered the wood back there?"

"To reconnoiter," I explained. "Those fellows would stop at nothing. They would—"

"Ah!" exclaimed the captain suddenly. "Move over, Clark, you're standing right on the first real bit of detective work I've ever done."

"What is it?" I asked quickly, jumping to one side. Captain Bartlett stooped over and fumbled among the leaves. Finally he withdrew his fingers. On them was a faint crimson stain, and between his thumb and forefinger he held several white threads.

"Blood," he announced. "They stopped here, all right. They bandaged up that fellow's wound. Ripped a shirt up to do it, I'd say. The blood has been washed off the top leaves, but there is a little underneath that the rain didn't get at. It's congealed, you see, but the damp leaves have diluted it somewhat and kept it rather liquid."

"He must have been bleeding quite badly," I surmised. "Perhaps he couldn't go much farther. Maybe he's still here!"

"I'd say you winged him, either in the arm or in the leg. Blood doesn't get away from a body wound so much. Most likely it was the arm. At any rate, you didn't put his legs out of commission."

We looked all about through the wood, but no further evidence of the pair could we find. We worked along in the direction in which I had left the car. I saw MacClintock walking through the trees toward us.

"What's the matter?" I called.

"Therre's footprrints crrossin' the rroad doon herre, sirr," he said. "They come oot o' the woods on this side and go overr."

"Let's see them," I said hastily. We followed the old fellow back to the road, where he displayed the tracks.

"I left the car back there," I said. "Evidently they went round it through the wood."

"Those fellows just couldn't stay on the road," declared the captain. "Let's see whether we can find anything on the other side."

Our search of the hill-side was unavailing. We went down the road toward Barkersville to determine whether they had returned to the road again in that direction, but no more footprints did we see in the mud.

"Let's go back and see where they came on the road in the first place," suggested the captain. "Perhaps we can track them to where they started from, even though we can't tell where they went."

MacClintock turned the car round in a lane, and we started back. When we came to the spot where I had encountered the men, MacClintock slowed the car down to a walking pace. Captain Bartlett and I hung out the windows, keeping our eyes on the footprints. About two hundred yards from where I had met the men, their tracks crossed the road and disappeared into the underbrush.

"That's the same side of the road that they finally left it on," I said. "There's nothing at the foot of that hill but the Great Swamp. They couldn't have come from there, and by the same token they couldn't have returned to it."

"You've got me," said the captain, with a shrug of his shoulders. "They did come from the hill-side, and they did return to it. They walked along this road in the direction of Barkersville about two hundred yards. Then they met you and had a little fracas, in which one of them got shot, probably in the arm, and you got beaned. Then they left the road, went through the wood a way, and then crossed over the road again. That's about all we found out about them, and I'm hanged if I can see that it did us much good."

"Just the same, I'm glad we did it," I retorted. "Let's see whether we can find out anything about them on the hill-side here."

"All right," agreed the captain, getting out of the car with a rueful grin. "I'm about as wet as I can get already. It won't make much difference my knocking a little more water off these bushes."

We had no more luck, however. The hill-side where the men had left it was as barren of evidence concerning them as it was where they had returned to it. We got disconsolately back into the car, and MacClintock drove us home.

"Where have you been!" exclaimed Patty as we walked into the hall. "You're both soaking wet!"

"I am," I agreed, "and the worst of it is I've got nothing else to wear except my fishing togs."

"Oh, did you bring them with you?" asked Patty. "Put them on, then, and we'll go fishing while your clothes dry. I'll have Maxwell press that suit along with your other one."

"I should certainly enjoy a little fishing, and it's a perfect day for it," I said. "But isn't it—wouldn't it be a trifle—er—disrespectful if we—" I stammered.

"Oh, yes," interrupted Patty, hanging her head, "I hadn't thought."

"Nonsense!" exclaimed Dick. "The colonel wouldn't mind at all. We'll all go fishing. We don't have to make a display of ourselves. There's a peach of a stream right behind the house. It's on the colonel's property; nobody will see us. What do you say, Captain?"

"I'm a pretty poor fisherman, but I'll bet I can catch more fish than any of you," asserted Captain Bartlett. "I haven't any fishing tackle, though."

"We can give you all you want," said Patty. "I'll get you some clothes to wear, too. I've been wondering whether you'd be as handsome without that snappy uniform, and now I'll find out."

"Look out, Dick," cautioned the captain, with a laugh; "I'm a bachelor, you know."

"Yes; so is Mr. Clark," grinned Dick. "We'll get you out of those brass buttons, though, and then I'll breathe easier."

To Dick's feigned disgust, the captain was by common agreement as handsome in fishing togs as he was in his uniform. My spirits rose as we set out for the wood behind the house. We were rather a curious fishing party. With the exception of Patty, each had a pistol concealed about him.

"You're in the right place if you like trout-fishing, Mr. Clark," declared Dick. "There are a number of little streams that gurgle through the woods around here. They empty into the swamp."

"What would happen to one of those poor little trout if he left his nice, clear pool and got out into the Great Swamp?" asked Patty.

"He'd be in exactly the same fix I'm in when I get to New York," replied Captain Bartlett. "I'm from the great open spaces, I am. New York beats me. The police are always holding up traffic while they get me out from under a trolley car or something. A trout in the Great Swamp would be worse off than I am in New York, Patty. When Forty-second Street gets lost, I can ask a cop where it is."

"But the trout could ask a bullfrog," said Patty. "Wouldn't that be cute? Anyway, if the fish only knew three such determined fishermen were descending upon them, they'd all flee to the swamp."

Patty carried a net in place of a fishing-rod. She wore riding-breeches and looked like a supple young boy as she bent low to pass under branches and skipped over fallen logs with the agility of a young Indian. The outing was doing her good. She gayly chided the captain and me for lagging behind where the underbrush grew the thickest. It was rough going in the wood behind the colonel's house. There was a gentle up-grade, and the ground was generously sprinkled with rugged bowlders. Here the trees did not grow so close together, but heavy vines and brambles were luxuriant.

"We'll fish fairly close together, don't you think?" I said, glancing significantly at Dick and the captain. "Then Patty can keep track of the number of fish each catches."

"Good idea," cried Dick. "The one who catches the least fish has got to make a speech on why he wasn't born a trout."

It was in quite a gay mood that we arrived at the stream. We seemed to have left the tragic atmosphere of the past two days completely behind us. Only the tender swelling on the side of my head served to remind me that a cloud still hung over us. I dismissed the thought, resolved to get as much enjoyment out of the sport as it could provide.

The setting could not have been better. The clear brook wound among the trees and bowlders, its rippling surface spangled by the glinting rays of the sun. Here and there the water gushed over rapids, murmuring a tuneful melody in keeping with our mood. Poor Joseph Decker—at last he was out of my thoughts too.

We were soon ready with our rods. We pulled our boots up and stepped into the stream. Captain Bartlett was above me, and Dick fished below. Patty picked a spot, not far from me, at a bend in the stream where she could watch us all. In a very few minutes the captain had his line all tangled in a branch. While he was freeing it, Dick and I each landed a beautiful fish, giving Patty a good deal of excited work with the net. Before the disgruntled captain was back in the running, I had captured two more, and Dick was having a time of it with his second. I never saw anyone get so thoroughly excited over fishing as Patty Decker. I waded over and sat on the bank to enjoy her delightful antics as Dick was playing the trout. Her eyes sparkled, and her lips were parted as she danced up and down, giving Dick breathless instructions. At last they had the speckled prize in the net.

"Oh, the poor little thing!" exclaimed Patty, echoing the remark she had made after each of our catches. "Let's let him go, Dick."

"Not on your life!" replied Dick emphatically. "That's the prize trout this spring. Look at him, will you—isn't he a beauty! Did you ever see such a person as Patty, Mr. Clark?" he called to me. "She gets all bubbling over the minute you hook a fish, but after you've landed him, she wants you to toss him back. What a way to fish!"

"Well, it's fun to catch them," said Patty, with a becoming pout. "It would be just as much fun if you threw them back; don't you think so, Mr. Clark?"

"It's a theory I've never dwelt upon," I replied with a laugh. "I suppose it would be just as much fun to catch them, but you would never get to have a fried trout. Don't you think—"

I was interrupted by a prodigious yell from up-stream. I glanced quickly behind me and beheld Captain Bartlett hobbling out of the water. He yanked off one of his boots and emptied what were seemingly gallons of water from it. Then he stood perched on one foot, holding the boot out at arm's length, and peered dejectedly down the stream at us.

"Say, you need a submarine to get around this river!" he shouted. "Why doesn't the Bureau of Navigation set up a few buoys to warn storm-tossed mariners like me away from these sink-holes? I thought I was going clear down out of sight that time!"

"The captain is not having a successful fishing trip," I remarked.

"The captain is not having a fishing trip at all," corrected Captain Bartlett, overhearing me. "I'm through tempting fate. No watery grave for yours truly. How you fellows stay afloat is a mystery to me! I've got to be a national hero before I can go to my eternal rest; therefore I shall go back in the sun and dry off."

He replaced the boot, which emitted a squashy sound. Then with a wry face he set off for a barren knoll that rose back from the stream a short distance. With an unsympathetic laugh we resumed our fishing.

Dick and Patty worked down-stream quite a distance from me. I did not realize it until I heard someone making his way through a thicket beside the stream. I had been absorbed and had not noticed the distance widening between us. I breathed a sigh of relief, however, when Captain Bartlett stepped out of the bushes on to the bank. For a wonder, his face bore a solemn expression.

"See here, Clark," he accosted me, "I've just stumbled into something."

"Not a nest of hornets!" I exclaimed in mock horror.

"No; this is something serious," he replied.

I was impressed by his solemnity. "What is it?" I asked.

"Come along and I'll show you. It's back here a way."

"How about Dick and Patty? I'd like to keep them in sight, you know."

"They have lungs, and they can shout. We can get to them in a minute if anything happens. But nothing's going to happen in broad daylight. Come on."

"All right," I agreed, wading over to the bank. I reeled in my line, and set the rod against a tree. "Where is this discovery you've made?" I demanded.

With a last anxious glance at Patty and Dick, I followed the captain into the thicket. We emerged into a clearing overgrown with wild blackberry bushes. I was glad I was clad in heavy duck, for the brambles tugged tenaciously as we forced our way through them.

"You don't mean to say you walked deliberately through this infernal tangle!" I growled.

"Clark, do you believe in transmigration of the soul?" he astonished me by asking. He had stopped and turned toward me, an utterly bland expression of innocence upon his features. I regarded him quizzically before replying. I was afraid the captain was exercising his favorite tendency to take his companions for a short stroll through the realms of hoax.

"I don't know," I replied at length. "What's that got to do with my being lured to the center of this bramble patch?"

"That's just it," he said. "I was lured to the center of it by a bird with a broken wing."

"I thought you said you came from the great open spaces!" I exclaimed disgustedly. "Here you've been completely taken in by a trick put over on you by a bird! It was a grouse, my dear fellow—a hen which was enticing you away from stumbling upon her nest. She makes believe she has a broken wing and flutters along the ground so that you will chase her. This is a good one on you, Captain; it's a pity I had to share in it!"

"Just a minute!" said the captain as I turned to retrace my steps to the stream. "I haven't showed you what I came after you for yet."

Resignedly I followed him once more. He stopped at length, and as I came up abreast of him, he stretched out a booted leg and swept aside the thorny branches of a thick bush. Grinning up at me from the rank earth was a gleaming skull!

"This is where I followed the bird," announced the captain. "Now what do you think? Perhaps that bird was the spirit of this fellow come back to show us where his last earthly remains lay hidden."

"Why, it's a whole skeleton!" I exclaimed, thrusting the bushes aside.

"It is," said the captain, "and as curious a skeleton as I ever laid my eyes on—at least the way in which it is garbed is quite beyond me. He must have come to grief while walking in his sleep."

"By Jove! That's so!" I exclaimed. "The bones appear to be in a bathrobe."

"And pyjamas," added the captain. "I looked it over pretty carefully. The feet are encased in bedroom slippers, as well. Now what do you think of my discovery? Worth coming through these brambles for, isn't it?"

I did not reply. All the tragic atmosphere that had been growing about me since coming to Mill Ridge returned a thousandfold. I seemed fated to run into tragedy at every turn.

"What do you think of it?" insisted the captain.

"This must have taken place in Mill Ridge," I said. "If the body were fully clothed, we might assume that he was slain somewhere else and brought here afterwards for concealment."

"Did the colonel tell me he was retiring to the nice, quiet life of a country gentleman?" said Captain Bartlett with a grin. "I haven't heard of so many bodies lying round since the war!"

"It's awful!" I exclaimed. "I don't know what to expect next. There's one thing certain, however. This fellow lost his life long before the colonel came out here to live. His death can have no connection with the present murder case."

"I guess not," agreed the captain. "Question is, what are we going to do about this? I don't think we should let Patty know about it."

"By all means, no," I said. "I don't see any objection to letting this fellow lie right where he is for the present. I'd like to get Hand out here to look him over. The authorities can wait that long, I should think. Perhaps I can reach Hand at our rooms in New York."

"It's all right with me," complied Captain Bartlett, with a shrug. "This chap's been here so long now that a few hours won't make a bit of difference. Let's go back and find Patty and Dick."

Each occupied with his own thoughts, we made our way silently back to the stream. I got my rod, and we started out to overtake the other two. We walked down to the bend where I had last seen them. Round it there was an extended view of the little stream, but neither Patty nor Dick was in sight. I began to feel a little uneasy.

Suddenly the captain caught my arm. "How do you cough discreetly?" he asked in a stage whisper. "Turn round, now, and we'll both try it."

I glanced quickly about to see what he was driving at. Patty and Dick were standing under a tree about ten feet back from the opposite bank. The young man's arms were about Patty, and he was smiling down into her beautiful eyes. Dick's fishing-rod and Patty's net were abandoned on the bank. So absorbed were they in each other that they had failed to notice our approach.

My companion and I both placed our backs to the stream. With a side glance at me, Captain Bartlett set up a hectic coughing, and I joined in. Patty gave a little shriek, and an instant later I heard Dick's throaty laugh. "Where did you two come from?" he demanded, rather embarrassed. "I thought we'd lost you for keeps."

"How many fish did you get, Dick?" I laughed.

"Only two," grinned Dick. "They got away; Patty dropped the creel," he added, with an injured air.

"Yes; wasn't that too bad!" said Patty. "Those two nice fish got right back into the brook. Now poor little Dickie won't have his trout for lunch. I'm so sorry I could sit right down and cry."

"Yes, you could!" said Dick, trying to appear stern.

"Speaking of lunch, I think we should be getting back," I said, choosing that as a pretext to return to the house. "We all have to get dressed, you know. Besides, the captain is all wet."

"Who's all wet?" demanded Captain Bartlett, drawing himself up and pretending to be indignant.

"Perhaps you're not now," said Patty mischievously, "but you're on the wrong side of the brook, you know. You've got to wade across to get home. Come on, I'll fish you out with my net as soon as you sink out of sight."

Captain Bartlett, grinning broadly, stepped into the stream. He pretended to slip and lose his balance on the way over, for Patty's benefit, but he gained the other side without mishap. Soon we were back at the colonel's house. I slipped away from the others and closeted myself in the den. In response to my call to our rooms I got our landlady on the telephone. Mrs. Flemming said Hand had left early that morning for Mill Ridge. As it was then nearly noon, I could not imagine what had prevented his arrival hours before.

After luncheon Captain Bartlett proposed a game of bridge. Patty and Dick forthwith proceeded to give us a fearful trimming. Our defeat was thoroughly enjoyed by Captain Bartlett, who continually recalled that I had announced I was rather good at the game. I decided to be less boastful thereafter. A jester is sometimes a valuable companion.

"If Mr. Clark had made that slam bid of his, we'd have crawled up over a hundred on that rubber," declared Captain Bartlett, tossing our few tricks out on the table. "You only went down five on that hand, didn't you, Clark? But how could you know that would happen when you redoubled!"

"Let poor Mr. Clark alone," commanded Patty. "What could you expect? The way you bid is a scream, and you paid utterly no attention to his discards! Don't mind him, Mr. Clark, he's forever poking fun at somebody. Daddy recommended him for his War Cross, but he always said Captain Jack probably kidded those poor Germans into surrendering."

The game went on until late in the afternoon, when I saw through the living-room window the very same taxi-cab that we had encountered in Mrs. Compstock's lane. Maxwell crossed to the door, and the next moment Hand strode into the living-room. Everybody jumped up to greet him. The captain and I finally managed to get Hand by the arm, and, excusing ourselves, we went to the den.

"That was very promptly done," said Hand when I had closed the door. "I wanted a report from you, Clark. Anything develop since I left?"

"The world has just about tumbled from its orbit," declared Captain Bartlett. "Really, I hadn't bargained for such excitement."

"In the first place, Gerald Furness has escaped," I said.

"Yes, I know," said Hand. "I had a chat with Chief Huddy before I came out here. Anything else?"

"A band of cut-throats nearly polished Clark off last night," replied the captain nonchalantly. I explained the details of that episode while my friend slouched in a chair, keeping his eyes on the floor, and an inscrutable countenance presented to us.

"But today," I added excitedly, "Captain Bartlett stumbled upon the most gruesome, incongruous object imaginable. Hand, out in the wood behind this house there lies the skeleton of a man clad in night-clothes!"

12

THE RESURRECTOR

I can hardly say that Christopher Hand showed excitement when I told him there was a skeleton lying in the wood. But his eyelids flew up, and he fixed me with a knife-like glance. He said nothing. I knew, however, that I was expected to elucidate the incident without further delay.

"Extraordinary," he murmured when I, ably assisted by the captain, had finished my recital of the discovery of the body. Then he shot a piercing glance at Captain Bartlett. "What were you doing in the wood?" he demanded.

"There I go on the mat," grinned the captain. "My proceedings in the wood were innocent enough, although I went there for the avowed purpose of murdering fish. I'm no worse than Clark, however. He didn't say so before, but he was with me and was a prime instigator of the expedition."

"What did you leave the house unguarded for, Clark?" demanded Hand. "Didn't you promise me you'd keep your eyes on things here?"

"But Patty and Dick were with us," I hastened to explain. "We were all armed, and we stuck together."

"Just the same, it was foolish," growled Hand. "However, you are to be congratulated upon discovering that body, Captain. Can you fellows take me to it?"

"Can we!" I exclaimed. "I can't be satisfied until you've seen it."

"If we're going out to view that body, we'd better get started," said Hand. "It will soon be dark. You'll come along, won't you, Captain?"

"Rather!" replied Captain Bartlett heartily. "I haven't had an opportunity to see you work, you know. I wouldn't miss it for anything."

"Very well, we can go right out through this door," said Hand pulling open the back door of the den. "Where are MacClintock and O'Brine?"

"Out in their quarters, I guess," replied the captain.

We found O'Brine feeding his goat, and MacClintock fussing with the engine of the colonel's car. Hand called them together in the garage.

"We are going to be away for a short while," he told them. "I want you to keep your eyes on things. Get hold of Mr. Fairfax and tell him I don't want him or Miss Patty to leave the house. Now, have you a tarpaulin?"

"No, sor," replied O'Brine, "but we have two shilter-halves. Yez can have thim; they'll be jist as good."

"Fine," said Hand. "Get them, O'Brine. We'll return them shortly."

"We should have some kind of ax," said Captain Bartlett. "It was all very well pushing your way through the bramble patch in fishing togs, but these clothes would be ripped to shreds."

"Ye'd like to cut a swath thrrough the booshes, sirr?" asked MacClintock. "I've got the verra thing—a machete I picked up in the Philippines. One of them heathens trried to chop my head off with it."

"Get it, MacClintock, it's the very thing, to be sure," said Captain Bartlett. "Wonderful how those two fellows can get you what you want," he added when O'Brine and MacClintock had departed on their missions.

"Well, there's something else we need that I can get," I said.

"What's that?" asked the captain.

"Boots," I replied. "We've got to wade that stream, you know. If I have Maxwell dry one more suit for me, he'll quit the colonel flat."

At length we were ready to go. The boots, being brown, did not present such a striking contrast to the captain's uniform. Hand and I, however, were incongruous objects as we set out. Captain Bartlett carried MacClintock's evil-looking machete, and I carried the shelter-halves. Hand followed us.

As soon as we had waded the stream and approached the bramble patch, the captain went to work with the machete. His good nature all but deserted him as the wiry, prickly branches seemed to strike back at him when he severed them. I discovered the captain was possessed of quite an army vocabulary. Slowly we advanced into the heart of the bramble patch. Finally the captain ceased swinging the machete and glanced back at us over his shoulder.

"Here it is," he announced. "Can you get up beside me?"

"Clear the bushes away from the body a bit, Captain," requested Hand. "Be careful not to disturb the bones."

When he had complied, the captain lowered the machete and stood aside. My friend and I stepped up beside the gruesome object that lay among the stubble. Hand knelt beside the skeleton, leaning first one way and then the other to inspect it.

"Well, what are your deductions, Mr. Hand?" grinned the captain.

Hand looked up at him with a half-smile. "He was struck in the back of the head with a hatchet," he said. "The hatchet has a broken handle."

"You're not kidding me, are you?" asked the captain, his grin fading.

"No indeed," Hand assured him. "There lies the hatchet under that bush where the murderer threw it. There is no doubt its blade made the cleft in the skull, right here, you see. Both the hatchet and the body were thrown in here by the murderer for concealment."

Hand next turned his attention to the clothing. It was still possible to determine, as the captain and I had already done, that the clothing consisted of a bathrobe and pyjamas.

"There's something in the pocket of this bathrobe," said Hand. "I can see the bulge of it, and besides, it is sticking through the fabric. Looks like a pistol."

Hand carefully inserted his hand into the pocket, but, careful as he was, the rotten fabric parted. Then he laid caution aside and ripped the pocket open. Lying on the faded cloth over the hip-bone of the skeleton was a curious object. It was of metal, heavily encrusted with rust, and appeared to be a wide, two-pronged fork. The most curious part of it was that the tips of the prongs were connected by a thin bar which passed through the center of a small spike. The heavy end of the spike extended down between the prongs, and the pointed end projected out beyond them.

"What on earth do you call that?" I demanded.

"I don't know," replied Hand. "Let's look this fellow over a little more. Pyjamas have pockets too."

He commenced to fold the bathrobe back from the body. The fragile cloth crumbled and tore. The pyjamas, being of a lighter texture, were not so well preserved as the bathrobe. Hand got out his little instrument kit. With a metal bar he commenced probing about the remnants of the pyjamas.

"This undoubtedly was the breast pocket," he announced, touching the moldy cloth near the left shoulder of the skeleton. "There is something in it," he added, thrusting the cloth aside with his instrument.

"I'm hanged if I can see anything in it," said the captain, bending over.

"Nevertheless, he carried a paper in that pocket, and the remains of it are still there," retorted Hand. "The action of moisture has just about disintegrated it, but we may yet salvage a portion."

I could see then that what he said was true. But the paper was reduced to a mere pulp, hardly to be distinguished from the cloth around it. Hand took a pair of small tweezers and, exercising the greatest of care, took hold of the soggy paper. The portion that he grasped with the tweezers pulled away from the rest. His second attempt was more successful, but as he lifted the paper, part of it crumbled away.

"Its consistency is about gone," he muttered. "Part of it stuck out of the pocket and is beyond redemption. There seems to be a little stiffness left in the center of the wad, however. The inner folds may have been protected sufficiently to keep them preserved. It's to be hoped, anyway."

He held his leather case in his left hand. The thing was divided into sections by isinglass partitions. Into one of these he placed the remains of the paper. In another section of the case I saw Mrs. Compstock's blotter. My attention was too much occupied for me to inquire about it.

Hand placed the case in his inside coat pocket. Still kneeling, he thoughtfully regarded the skeleton. The captain seemed not to understand this meditation. He regarded my friend quizzically, but he remained silent.

Finally Hand nodded his head in that purposeful manner that told me he had weighed a matter and come to a conclusion. He reached out and picked up the skull. Holding the gruesome object in his hands, he regarded it intently.

"Alas, poor Yorick," declaimed the captain, grinning at Hand.

Hand paid no attention to him. He quickly picked up one of the shelter-halves and proceeded to wrap up the skull in it.

"Ye gods! What do you want with the skull?" demanded the captain.

"You never can tell," replied Hand enigmatically. He picked up the peculiar object he had taken from the bathrobe pocket, and the hatchet.

"Going to take all that stuff with you?" asked the captain. "The only thing that seems valuable to me is the paper."

"Perhaps it is," replied Hand as he turned to leave. "It pays to overlook nothing if you care to find out as much as possible, though."

"Well, it's a mighty strange assortment," declared Captain Bartlett. "Clark and I decided not to notify the authorities of our find until we had seen you. We should do it now, don't you think?"

"I'm grateful to you for having waited until I got here," said Hand. "I'm about to be more grateful to you than ever, for we are not going to notify the authorities of this at all—at least not for a while. I can't see why the medical examiner should mind—we've kept him busy enough as it is."

Dusk was gathering as we crossed the lawn to the house. We left the unused shelter-half and the machete outside, and the captain and I followed Hand into the den. Hand laid the ominous object wrapped in the shelter-half on the desk.

"Let's have a look at that paper," suggested the captain excitedly.

"Not yet," replied Hand with a shake of his head. "It must be dried first. If we tried to unfold it now, it would just pull apart. It will be extremely fortunate if it doesn't after it is dry. I'll just take it up to my room."

He placed the rust-covered forked object and the hatchet on the desk and departed. Hardly had he gone when, to my consternation, Patty and Dick walked into the den. Although the skull was completely covered by the shelter-half, I quickly stepped in front of the desk so that they could not see it.

"What have you been up to?" asked Patty, shaking her finger at me. "I saw you sneaking up into the wood. Mr. Hand just scurried upstairs in hip boots, and you two are all booted and spurred as well. You act as if you had discovered a goldmine. Have you any of the nuggets with you?"

"Well, yes, four," grinned the captain, his gruesome irony lost to the others. "Children should be seen and not heard, you know."

"I'm no child!" protested Patty. "Come on, give the little girl a chance. Won't you tell me what you've found?"

"Patty, didn't I—" began Dick.

"Never mind," she laughed. "I had my orders before Dad left. 'Do what Mr. Hand and the others tell you, and don't ask questions,' he said. I just wanted to tell you it's getting time for dinner. I hope you're not planning to come to the table in hip boots, Captain Jack."

"I shall be immaculate, fair lady," replied the captain, bowing low.

"I'm going up to dress—see you later," called Patty as she left the den.

"What are you so carefully concealing behind your back, Mr. Clark?" asked Dick, crossing over to the desk. "What have you got here in this canvas? Holy smokes! A skull!"

"Hand likes it," grinned the captain. "If you'd like a souvenir too, there's lots more of that chap out behind the house. Clark and I don't go in for that sort of thing."

"Neither do I!" declared Dick with a shudder. "Say, where did you get this?"

We quickly told him of finding the skeleton, and Dick looked at us reproachfully. "It's a wonder you wouldn't tell a fellow before this!" he said.

"A fat chance we had," sniffed the captain, "with you sticking closer to Patty all afternoon than the skin on an egg!"

Dick picked up the incongruous object we had found in the bathrobe pocket. "What do you call this?" he asked.

"If you can tell us," replied the captain, "you're a better man than I am, Gunga Din. We found it on the skeleton."

Just then Hand returned to the den. Dick turned quickly to him.

"What do you think of this skeleton?" he demanded. "Do you suppose we're in for more trouble because of it?"

"Impossible!" I exclaimed. "That man we found out in the wood was dead long before Colonel Decker came to Mill Ridge. He may have been dead for years."

"He was dead long before the colonel came here," agreed Hand. "But I don't think he's been dead for years, Clark. It's practically impossible to estimate how long he has lain there, but from the condition of the bathrobe and pyjamas it seems improbable that it was more than two years."

"It makes small difference, anyway," said the captain. "Come on, let's get ready for dinner; I've got an aching void."

A circumspect rap on the door arrested us. Before Dick opened the door, Hand carefully covered the skull. The opened door revealed Maxwell.

"Mrs. Compstock," he announced, "asking for Mr. Hand."

My friend gave me a sharp glance. "Come on, Clark," he said.

We found Mrs. Compstock seated in the living-room. She looked stiffish and out of sorts. The situation was going to demand tact, I could plainly see. Hand strode over before her and bowed.

"There is no need," began Mrs. Compstock, without preamble, "for me to state the nature of my call. I was of the opinion that you gave me your word as a gentleman to return that letter."

My friend, with a slow smile, placed his hand in his inside coat pocket. Mrs. Compstock leaned expectantly forward, her rouged lips parted. But then she leaned back with a glitter in her eyes. Hand had withdrawn his cigarette-case, which he opened and offered to the lady. She took a cigarette—snatched it, rather—and allowed Hand to hold a match for her.

"Why are you so anxious about that letter?" asked Hand, abruptly.

Mrs. Compstock sneered.

"I thought so," she said. "When you said you were a friend of Colonel Decker's, naturally I assumed that I was dealing with a gentleman. When you so unconcernedly broke your word, I began to wonder. Now I see that I was wrong. Well, my friend, what is your price? I want that letter!"

"Madam, the letter is priceless."

"You mean that I may not have it?"

"I assure you that I could not produce it at any price."

"Then what is your game, if it isn't blackmail?"

"I think you know."

"That you are a detective? Yes, I know. Such a famous criminologist! But—I wonder how you make your money. Do you find just such mean little letters as I wrote Joseph Decker? I should think so. It's not hard, is it, to terrify people into paying well for them. Particularly women.

Well, you're not dealing with a fool now, Mr. Hand. You may try to prepare me for the slaughter all you like, but you'll find in me a woman not easily put to fright. You are right, my letter is priceless. It is priceless for the simple reason that I won't pay you a single, solitary cent for it! I shall speak to Colonel Decker, and then we shall see what comes of your precious scheme!"

"Might I ask why you have not done so already?"

"Naturally I wished to avoid it. But I promise you that I will. If you have an ounce of regard for Colonel Decker, you had better give me the letter and have done with this business. If not, I assure you I will tell him a great deal about his excellent brother that will not be pleasant to him."

She had risen to her feet. Her lips were drawn in a straight, red line, and a malice that I thought no woman capable of gleamed from her bright eyes. Hand smiled and shook his head.

"I don't think you can tell the colonel anything about his brother that he doesn't already know," he said. "It wouldn't do any good to speak to the colonel, madam, because—I have the letter."

"We'll see about that!" she snapped.

She turned and walked majestically out into the hall. Hand slowly followed her. As I had lingered near the entrance to the living-room I could see her as she stalked up to the front entrance. Maxwell had appeared from nowhere, and now he was holding the door open for her. As she was passing out to the porch, she turned swiftly back to Hand.

"You beast!" she cried, and her voice was hard and rasping.

Then, in uncontrolled fury, she grasped the door-knob, pulled the door from Maxwell's polite hand, and yanked it to with a prodigious slam.

Maxwell raised shocked hands. As for me, I heaved a sigh of relief. Hand, with a shrug, turned toward the den, and I followed him. Dick and the captain had remained on guard over the skull.

"I need a car," announced Hand. "Do you suppose the keys are in Patty's car, Dick?"

"Yes, they are," replied the young man. "But dinner will be ready in a few minutes. Mr. Clark beat it off just before dinner last night, and look what happened to him."

"I'll chance it," replied Hand, making for the outside door.

"Now where do you suppose he's going?" demanded Dick.

The captain and I shrugged our shoulders. In response to a timid rap on the outside door, I stepped quickly over and flung it open. Sergeant O'Brine, hat in hand, stood on the step.

"Are yez t'rough wid our shilter-half, sor?" he whispered.

"Why, yes, O'Brine," I doubtfully replied. "I'm terribly sorry, but I'm afraid you won't want it. You see, we—"

"Ye gods, O'Brine doesn't care!" interrupted the captain, seizing the canvas and tumbling the skull out of it.

"Th' saints save us, where did yez get thot, sor!" exclaimed O'Brine.

"Found it," replied the captain laconically. "Here you are, O'Brine, pleasant dreams."

"Thank yez, sor," replied the sergeant as I closed the door.

Christopher Hand did not return until dinner had been over for some time. He marched into the house with a package under his arm. The rest of us were in the living-room. Hand stalked across the hall and disappeared into the den. I quickly excused myself and followed him. My abrupt departure evidently served as a hint that I wished to speak to my friend alone. Hand had placed his package on the desk and was untying it.

"What have you got there?" I demanded.

Hand looked up at me with a twinkle in his eyes. "Modeling clay, several shades of human hair, an assortment of glass eyes, and a box of water-color paints," he said.

"Good heaven! What are you going to do?"

"Reconstruct the face on that skull."

"What! How on earth—"

"Hold on, Clark. I know precisely what you are going to ask next. How do I know what this fellow's face was like—that right? Well, I haven't any more idea than you have, except that he had high cheek-bones, a low forehead, and a receding chin."

"But a good many people have those very characteristics!"

"Your objections are entirely in order, Clark. I was rather too serene about announcing I would reconstruct this man's face—I admit it. Just another of my theories, Clark, that's all. Are you sufficiently interested to hear me expound it?"

"You know very well that I can hardly contain myself!"

"All right. In the first place I must confess that my idea was induced by the operations of Professor Ericson at the museum. The professor, as you know, is an archaeologist. He has from time to time got possession of prehistoric skulls. In an effort to determine racial characteristics, he builds faces on the skulls with clay. Of course, he has no possible way of determining just how nearly he duplicates the features of his subjects, but that is not what he is after. He is more particularly interested in the forehead and jaw. He pays no attention to the hair, eyes, and nose. The cheek-bones do attract him, though. You would be surprised at the characteristics he is able to produce."

"But aren't they nothing but a concoction of his own imagination?"

"Not at all. Take the tips of your fingers, Clark, and run them over your face. You have a depression just above the bridge of your nose—feel it? The flesh follows the contour of the bone, you see. Another outstanding example on your face is that cleft chin of yours. That's it, feel of it. I'll wager your chin-bone is cleft, too. Didn't I tell you? Now, notice the thickness of the flesh over your forehead—pretty thin, isn't it? Now run your hand down past your ear to your jaw-bone and out to the end of your chin. The flesh is not very thick over that portion of your face, either, you notice. Now touch your cheek-bones— there is a very thin covering there as well. Now, the space between your cheek-bones and your jaw-bone has a thick covering of flesh. Here, look at this skull. You notice how the contour slopes inward from the cheek-bone to the teeth, and then from the teeth outward again to the jaw-bone? If that were leveled off, the contour of the cheek would be the result."

"Hold on!" I exclaimed, breaking into his rapid discourse. "How about fat? How do you know whether this fellow had a lean face or a pudgy one?"

"My theory only pertains to bodies that have lived less than forty years. After the forty-year mark, changes take place. Lines form in the face, the flesh sags, there is apt to be puffiness and distortion due to fat. You might find those characteristics in a younger face, but there is a great deal less chance of it."

"Sounds grotesque, but interesting. Here's a point, though. How do you know the man whose skull lies there was not over forty?"

"Look at those teeth, Clark! It doesn't take a dentist to tell that he was a young man. They're almost perfect."

"Just the same, there are a lot of things that I don't see how you are going to determine."

"What are they?"

"This fellow might have been fat, even though he was young. I don't see how you are going to tell the color eyes to use, and how about hair?"

"Fat men are in the minority, I think. I shall make my face that of a man of medium weight. That will strike an average. The rest, Clark, we shall leave in the hands of the future."

"All right; assuming that you do construct a likeness, how are you going to employ it to identify the man?"

"In the first place, I'll have the colonel invite every man in Mill Ridge to come here and view it. If none identifies him, we'll resort to the newspapers. I'll take a picture of him, have cuts made, and publish them with a notice of reward for information concerning him. If my theory is right, something should come of it."

"Well, anyway, it's a very interesting piece of work," I said dubiously. "But at this time, when we're already up to our necks trying to solve one important murder mystery, why take the time for it? It can wait."

"Clark, I continually try to impress you with my methods, and you continually forget them. The immediate circumstances concerning a crime are of scarcely more interest to me than the chain of events which preceded it for some time back. Of course, if a witness can be found, if finger-prints or other clues immediately identify the criminal, or if circumstances point an irrevocable finger of guilt at one person, then the case can hardly be termed a mystery; and whatever history there is to the case is superfluous. But we have none of those features here. The knife used in the murder, I can tell you, had no finger-prints on it. Either it was wiped off, or, as is more likely, the murderer wore gloves. If there was a witness, we have been unable to find him. Circumstances of guilt, rather than being absent, are so prolific that they only heighten the mystery. Among the immediate circumstances of the murder there is little to guide us to the solution. We must go back, Clark. Every insignificant bit of evidence must be trailed to its source. When enough of them have been cleared up, a starting-point soon becomes evident. To the lay mind, such as yours, my boy, it appears exactly the same as if you were watching a motion-picture reel run through backward, starting with the conclusion and ending with the beginning. It is all the more confusing because much of it is missing. The important thing is to find the beginning. Then the reel can be run through in the proper direction, each event can be slipped into its proper place, and its true significance clarified. The further we go from the beginning, the less complex what follows becomes."

"I think I follow you," I said; "but how far back do you intend to go? This fellow was dead months before Joseph Decker was murdered."

"I have been busy, Clark," said Hand, a trace of weariness coming into his voice. "We came here Saturday morning; this is Monday night, and I have not slept since we took up the case. While you slept in the chair in the den Saturday night, I was wide awake, indexing in my mind the material we had uncovered. I have arrived at the starting-point of which I spoke a moment ago; now I am working toward the conclusion. However, my ideas are not set."

This last was, I knew, to serve notice that he was not ready to divulge what he was about to anyone—not even to me. Still, my curiosity had been pricked. I was intensely eager for more information. I violated my self-imposed agreement to contain myself until he should be ready to enlighten me on his findings.

"I know you took Furness's picture and got his finger-prints," I said. "Have you discovered anything about him? Is he your starting-point?"

"I have learned a good deal about Furness," replied Hand, with a slow smile. "I set up a rogue's gallery manufacturing plant in the Barkersville police headquarters while the colonel waited impatiently outside in his automobile. A cheap camera procured at the neighboring drug-store and some gunpowder served as an identiscope. I got his finger-prints through the medium of India ink from the same drug-store. The New York police easily matched his finger-prints from among their own collection, and his picture had its place in the sun of their rogues' gallery. Furness has an unenviable record of crime, ranging from bucketeering in Wall Street to using the mails to defraud. The last heard of him by the police, he was in Europe. I don't think, Clark, that he is our man."

"You don't!"

"No. The police say he is particularly cowardly—had a marked aversion to violence, and the sight of blood once caused him to faint in a New York police station. Still, those things can be overcome by a determined man. I never did think Furness murdered Joseph, though."

"Why not?"

"You remember, don't you, that Dick Fairfax said he saw Furness go upstairs, but that he didn't go to his room? On the contrary, he went toward the opposite end of the house, where Joseph's room was located. He went to Joseph's room, Clark, and he stayed there until he heard the shot. Then he made tracks for his own room, where he shivered and shook in an agony of fear all the rest of the night."

"My word! How do you know that?"

"Furness told me."

"You don't mean to say you took his word for it!"

"Not altogether. In the first place, where we found the remains of Mrs. Compstock's letter, there were a number of cigarette stubs. They were of a peculiar brand—French. I had noticed the same sort of cigarettes in Furness's bureau drawer when we searched his room just previously. Yesterday he told me he had got the habit of smoking them while in France and preferred them to the American brands. He was able to buy them in New York at a certain tobacco-shop and continued using them after returning to this country. Maxwell told me he had cleaned out Joseph's fireplace the evening before the murder; so the stubs must have come there during the night. They partially substantiated Furness's story."

"But what could he have been doing in Joseph's room?"

"He was waiting for its occupant to return. I confronted Furness with the confession we found in the bottom of his bag. He didn't admit he was attempting to coerce Joseph, nor did he admit that Joseph came right back at him in his own coin. It's pretty evident, however, after what I found out about him in the city, that such was the case. Furness did admit that he sought out Joseph in the den to speak to him, and that Joseph put him out. He said Joseph told him he had an appointment, although there was no one else in the den at the time. He went up to Joseph's room determined to wait until he should return."

"Then, if he's telling the truth, Dr. Metz had left."

"Yes, the stories of the two men dovetail. Dr. Metz has established his alibi. Yesterday afternoon I told Chief Huddy to pass the word along to make the hauls in the dope case as soon as they felt ready. Last night the police of Lincolnville, Elmwood, and Forest Town, acting at an appointed hour, nabbed five members of the dope ring. They have all admitted their guilt— they had no choice since they were caught red-handed. Carrigan and Delano have established Dr. Metz's alibi. They have also cleared up the little question as to why Dr. Metz didn't phone them instead of Boscombe, away off in Forest Town. Both Carrigan and Delano were carrying out the doctor's orders to be on the road delivering dope that morning. Now, what Metz's alibi would be worth before a jury, I don't know. I don't know either how Furness would make out with his story of sojourning in Joseph's room while the murder took place. I do know, however, that their stories fit in with my deductions."

"But how could they?" I protested. "Dick said he saw someone leave the den by the back door just after Furness left it through the hall. Yet Furness says there was no one in the den with Joseph."

"Dick merely saw a shadow," said Hand. "He thought it was the shadow of a man going out, but it could just as easily have been the shadow of a man going in. The lateness of the hour would have induced him to think as he did. At that time of night one naturally expects callers to be leaving instead of arriving. Perhaps Joseph did have an appointment—a fatal one."

Hand turned back to his package on the desk.

"By the way, where the deuce did you get that stuff?" I demanded.

Hand turned his head slightly toward me and chuckled. "Not long ago I met a man," he said. "He came to the rooms when you were out. He had a petty theft problem on his hands that the police weren't having much luck in stopping. I wasn't able to spare him the time to look into it, but I gave him a few suggestions. He wrote me in a few days; said he had followed my advice and caught the thief. That man is in the business of manufacturing dummies for store-window displays. His factory is in Markstown."

13

A FACE OF MYSTERY

There remained no one for me to fasten my expectations upon but Mrs. Compstock. That Hand had not given me all his reasons for ceasing to suspect Gerald Furness and Dr. Metz I was well aware, but the mere fact that he had thus made up his mind was enough for me. I presumed that he expected to pin the murder upon the lady.

Hand turned from the desk. To my astonishment I saw that, after having unfastened it, he had once again tied up the package.

"Going to give up the idea of reconstructing the face on that skull?" I asked. "Or are you going to wait for morning? I should think you'd turn in early and get some sleep tonight."

"I haven't any time for sleep!" he said impatiently. "No; I've decided to make the hall closet my workshop. It's a good big closet and has a light in it. I can be working in there while you fellows keep watch over the house from the library. You and Dick and the captain can arrange your watches to suit yourselves. Before I do anything else, I've got to boil this skull. I fancy the jaw-bone will drop off it when I do, but I have some wire here to fasten it back on. There's a small gas stove in the laundry that I'll use."

He put the skull under his arm and marched out into the hall. I glanced anxiously into the living-room. Fortunately,

Patty had her back to the hall and did not see what my friend was carrying. Dick and the captain, however, saw him at once and watched with much interest his progress through the dining-room to the kitchen. Coincident with Hand's disappearance into the kitchen there came a shrill scream from that part of the house. Patty's hands flew to her breast.

"My goodness! What was that?" she exclaimed.

"I think Hand has frightened the cook," I explained.

"Oh," said Patty wonderingly. "What do you suppose he did?"

"I don't know," I replied untruthfully. "He went into the kitchen rather abruptly. He just can't help moving silently. It's no wonder she screamed."

Patty invited me to join their circle. "You and Mr. Hand are awfully mysterious," she said. "Has he formed any conclusions?"

"Yes," I admitted, "but what they are he won't say. He keeps them to himself until he's positive about them. Hand gets credit for always being right, but as a matter of fact he's often on the wrong track. I think he gets on the wrong track more often than anyone else, to tell the truth. But that is because he follows more tracks."

"I know I'm being kept in the dark something shame-fully," pouted the colonel's daughter. "But you can't keep everything from me," she added with a smile, shaking her finger at us. "I know you've been keeping a watch down-stairs all night, and I know Sergeant Hughie and Sergeant Tim have been going off every night as if they were on the march."

At this news Dick was dismayed. "How did you find that out?" he demanded. "You've been—"

"Sleuthing," laughed Patty. "Well, why shouldn't I? Everybody else around here is doing it—poking round into everything. I know more about it than any of you—except

Mr. Hand and Mr. Clark. Mr. Middleton showed me all about detective work. He's always doing it. He told me everything."

"What an education!" grinned Dick. "Say, what else do you know?"

"I know that Buckley was killed as well as Uncle Joseph," said Patty.

Dick's jaw dropped. "Say, how did you find that out?" he asked.

"From the newspapers, silly," replied Patty.

"What are your theories, Miss Gum-shoe Nell?" asked the captain.

Patty leaned forward, an earnest expression on her face. "I know you won't tell Dad what I think, it would only hurt him," she said. "I think Uncle Joseph and Buckley had a fight, and Joseph killed Buckley. Then I think Uncle Joseph killed himself with the knife!"

Captain Bartlett broke out laughing, and Dick smiled a little skeptically at his fiancée. Patty tossed her head and settled back petulantly in her chair. The captain, seeing that his laughter was unkind, hastened to make amends.

"I know that you didn't have any great love for your Uncle Joseph, Pat," he said, "but I think you're doing him an injustice. I didn't have any use for him at all, as you know, but I don't think he was capable of murder. As for taking his own life—he didn't have the courage!"

"Let's talk about something else," Dick hastened to say. "Let's ask the captain when he's going to give up his life of wickedness and get married."

"Never!" asserted Captain Bartlett. "The only one who could induce me to relinquish my single blessedness is Miss Patricia Decker. See what you've done to me, Dick?"

Although he spoke banteringly, I had an idea the captain meant what he said. At any rate, he had left himself open to a good deal of good-natured raillery from his two

friends. I sat back and enjoyed the fun. It was a relief to
get my mind off the case.

While we were still talking, Hand returned from the
cellar. He carried the skull rather less ostentatiously than
when he had made off to the kitchen with it. He also carried a kitchen chair and had a board under his arm. He
deposited them in the hall closet, got his package from
the den, and then disappeared into the closet and shut the
door. Patty, with her back still to the hall, was unaware of
his actions. I stayed with the others in the living-room until Patty announced she was going to bed. The captain gave
me a sly wink and propelled me out to the dining-room.

"You don't know when to bow out," he complained
when he had me in the dining-room. "Didn't you realize
you were in the presence of two lovers who wanted to say
good-night? Now then, having no one to cherish and keep
us, we'll turn to the demon rum for solace. Name your
poison—the colonel has just about everything illegal here
that there is."

It took Dick a considerable length of time to say farewell to Patty for the stupendous period of one night. Fortunately, he got back in time to save me from Captain
Bartlett's avowed intention to "fix me up."

"By Jove! The lost has been found!" he exclaimed as
Dick strode into the dining-room. "Have a drink, Dick?
Just to get you back to earth, you know."

"Just a small one," grinned Dick. "By the way, what's
Mr. Hand doing?"

"He's reconstructing the face of the chap we found out
in the berry-patch," I said, as if my statement were the
most usual in the world. My two companions immediately
began plying me with excited questions. The upshot of it
was that we set our glasses down and crossed the hall to
the closet. I opened the door, and we crowded inside.

Hand sat on the kitchen chair with his back to the door. Across the back of the closet he had made a bench of the board I had seen him carrying. Resting on this was the skull and the material he had acquired in Markstown. My friend was diligently applying clay to the facial bones of the skull. He paid no attention to our entrance, and for a moment we stood and watched him. The irrepressible captain finally broke the silence.

"How long do you suppose it'll take?" he asked.

"Don't know," grunted Hand. "I've never tried it before. I'm hoping to have it completed by morning. It's important to finish it quickly."

"I hope you do," said Dick; "I'd like to see it, and since the colonel will be home tomorrow, I should be getting back to work. I've stayed away from the office rather longer than I should already."

"Have you fellows decided upon your watches yet?" asked Hand.

"I'm a bit fond of my watch, but I'll swap it for yours, Dick," said the captain with a grin.

"I mean the hours you are going to keep watch in the library," said Hand testily, never leaving off his work on the skull, however.

"I had a good night's sleep last night," I said. "These fellows never called me at all. I'll take the whole night tonight if you want."

"Nothing doing!" replied Dick. "If there's a chance for fireworks, I want to be in a front seat."

We finally decided that I should take the first watch, from eleven to two, Dick the second, from two to five, and the captain the third, from five on. We turned to say good-night to Hand.

"There's one thing I want to ask of you," he said, turning to face us for the first time. "This is an experiment I

am conducting here—nothing more. After I have finished
the face, I am going to invite people in to view it. If someone recognizes it, the experiment is a success. But in order
for the identification to be positive it must be made immediately. For such an identification to have its greatest
force there must be the element of surprise. Perhaps someone is missing from this neighborhood. If we tell these
people the purpose of their visit, subconsciously they will
be prepared to identify the face as that of the missing person. On the other hand, if they identify the face without
first having heard about it, the identification, in my opinion, would be complete. Therefore I request all of you to
say nothing of this experiment to anybody."

We each agreed to keep the matter confidential. Then
we backed out of the closet, closing the door on him.

"Phew! It's stuffy in there," said Dick. "I'd never be
able to keep awake in that atmosphere."

"And Hand hasn't had a wink of sleep for two nights,
either," I said.

Dick and the captain went off to bed. I drew a chair
over near the wall by the door of the library, situating myself so that I could not be seen from the hall. There I sat as
the clock in the hall chimed off the quarter-hours. To help
me keep awake I employed myself with attempting to ap-
ply the methods Hand was forever trying to impress upon
me. We had Dr. Metz, Gerald Furness, and Mrs. Compstock as possible murderers of Joseph Decker. Who murdered Buckley I could not imagine, nor could I conceive
of a reason for his death. There was plenty of background
for Decker's murder, but Hand had discarded most of it by
announcing he no longer suspected the doctor or Furness.
Mrs. Compstock, I thought, was not likely to have taken
such drastic measures to remove her enemy in the colonel's
house. We had the weakest case left to us, I was sure.

I could not seem to arrive at an adducible conclusion of the case. When I had about given it up, my wonderings were rudely interrupted by a shadowy form that suddenly materialized in the doorway.

"Hisst, Mr. Clark?" it said.

"Is that you, Dick?" I whispered.

"Yes," he replied, moving over toward me with out-stretched hands.

"It's not time for you yet," I said, looking at the luminous dial of my wrist watch. "I've ten minutes to go."

"That's all right," he whispered. "How's Mr. Hand making out?"

"I haven't been in," I replied. "I'll look in on him on my way upstairs. You'd better stay out here so that somebody's on the job. You can look over his handiwork when the captain relieves you."

I pressed Dick's arm and left the library. Opening the door of the closet, I bobbed in and quickly closed it again. Hand was bent over the improvised bench. His tall figure, even in a sitting position, completely obscured my view of what he was at.

"That you, Clark?" he muttered without moving his head.

"Yes," I said. "How is it coming?"

"Not much to show for it yet," he replied, getting to his feet and stretching his muscles. "Pretty slow work."

The face of the skull was covered with rough plaster with the exception of the teeth, nose, and eye-sockets. The clay over the forehead had been smoothed down, but the remainder was just as it had been applied.

"It doesn't look very natural to me yet," I said.

"No reason why it should," he growled. "All you see there are the beginnings. From now on I should make better progress."

"Dick just relieved me," I said. "Guess I'll turn in."

"Yes; I heard him come down the stairs and cross the hall."

"Sure there's nothing further you want me to do?"

"No; better get to bed. No reason for your staying up, Clark."

Somewhat reluctantly I left him in the closet and mounted the stairs. I went into my room and commenced to undress in the dark. Pausing in the act of hanging my coat over a chair, I struck an attitude of listening. Was that the sound of a commotion below stairs I had heard? I hastily donned my coat and moved quickly over to the bedroom door. Opening it, I thrust my head out into the hallway. Distinctly now I heard low, gruff voices. Although they all seemed pitched in anger, one stood out as if in wrathful protest.

I drew my pistol and made off toward the stairs. As I reached them, I was conscious of another presence in the hallway with me. I stopped and backed up against the wall. All at once a faint light from below diffused through the hallway. I found myself standing very close to Captain Bartlett. We each held a pistol directed at the other. The captain wore slippers and was without his tunic; otherwise he was fully clothed.

"What's up?" he whispered, lowering his gun.

"I don't know," I replied. "Let's go down and see."

"Easy," breathed Captain Bartlett, laying a restraining hand on my shoulder as I started to descend the stairs. "We'll go down the back stairs and come out through the dining-room. No sense of making a target of ourselves on those stairs," he added, leading the way along the corridor.

We tiptoed down the back stairs, through the kitchen and butler's pantry, and out into the front hall through the dining-room. Light poured through the library door. I could hear only one voice. I was sure it was Hand's and that he was talking in a very calm, persuasive tone. The captain and I quickly crossed the hall and peered into the library. What I saw filled me with astonishment.

Mr. Middleton stood in the center of the room. His face was choleric, but he held himself with great dignity. Behind, in attitudes of extreme uneasiness, stood O'Brine and MacClintock. Christopher Hand faced Mr. Middleton.

"So you see, it was all my fault," he was explaining. "O'Brine and MacClintock merely carried out the orders I gave them. The mere fact that they brought you here at all is proof of their integrity. I am delighted with them, and infernally sorry for myself."

"And with excellent cause!" sputtered Mr. Middleton.

"You demanded an explanation, and you are certainly entitled to one," said Hand, trying to placate the indignant gentleman. "Let me remind you that we are engaged in a serious business here, Mr. Middleton. We are attempting to solve the mystery of Joseph Decker's death, and you can aid us."

"You go about it in an astonishing manner, sir!" snapped Mr. Middleton. "Setting a secret watch on a lady's house and carrying off her respectable guests by force! Where is Colonel Decker? I'll have an explanation for this from him, not from you!"

"The colonel has not returned yet," replied Hand. "He knows utterly nothing of this, anyway."

"I should hope not!" snorted Mr. Middleton.

"Mr. Middleton, you are as anxious as anyone to have this murder solved, are you not?" asked Hand.

"Certainly!" declared the man. "Don't try to leave the subject, sir! You had these men bring me here by force, and I want to know why!"

"Because by visiting Mrs. Compstock you walked into one of my traps," replied Hand simply. "Mrs. Compstock is suspected of having had something to do with Joseph Decker's death."

For a moment Mr. Middleton's eyes blazed, and the expression of anger deepened upon his face. He uttered a short laugh of disgust and shrugged his shoulders. "Of all the fool nonsense!" he said resignedly.

"I don't wonder that you think so," said Hand. "However, we have evidence to show that Mrs. Compstock bore Joseph Decker an ill will and, furthermore, made a threat against his life."

Mr. Middleton regarded my friend intently. Gradually the expression of anger faded from his face. Walking over to a chair, he flung himself into it. For several minutes he sat gazing at the floor, apparently weighing a knotty problem. Finally he raised serious eyes to my friend.

"Mr. Hand," he said, "you can't blame me for having lost my temper just now. Such actions, in my opinion, were unjustifiable. But let that go. I was about to pay you a call tomorrow morning, anyhow."

"I'm glad to see you taking this so fairly, Mr. Middleton," said Hand, with relief. "I was counting upon you long since to supply me with some information that may help to clear up this business. I believe you formerly owned this house and sold it to Colonel Decker."

"I did," affirmed Mr. Middleton. "The colonel took possession of it three months ago. That is not what I wished to talk to you about, however."

"Ah, you said you were going to pay me a call tomorrow," prompted Hand.

"I was. Mr. Hand, you are terrifying a lady! She has appealed to me in her distress, and as a gentleman I intend to see that she is protected. You must forgive me if I haven't much use for you, sir!" blazed Mr. Middleton suddenly, his face once more turning scarlet. "The manner in which you have dealt with that poor unprotected woman is nothing short of contemptible to anyone with a sense of honor!"

"I felt that it was necessary," said Hand stiffly.

"Mrs. Compstock called me on the phone," went on Mr. Middleton, ignoring Hand. "She saw those two fellows skulking about in the wood. Unable to get hold of Withers, hang him! I wanted to bring my chauffeur with me and have him spend the night there, but she wouldn't hear of it. I rushed right over myself, though."

"Doesn't it strike you as a bit odd that Mrs. Compstock refuses to allow anyone to lend her a manservant for protection?" asked Hand. "I offered her the services of one of the colonel's men, but she refused."

"I suppose it does seem odd to you, but it wouldn't if you knew her," asserted Mr. Middleton. "She is very self-willed. She takes a pride in handling her own affairs, too, but you have driven her to seek my aid. She shall have it! She told me of the note she sent Joseph Decker. It is unthinkable that you should pay any attention to it. Mrs. Compstock is an impetuous, high-strung woman. I can well understand her writing that note, but as to any serious intention of harming anyone—preposterous!"

"Do you know her reasons for writing that note?"

"I do not. She didn't seem inclined to tell me, and of course I didn't press the point. Some trivial difference of opinion, that's all."

"I happen to know the reason, and it's not so trivial as you think."

"I suppose it wouldn't be in your eyes. It's a shame that defenseless woman is exposed to your suspicious nature. I'll speak to the colonel about it as soon as he returns, I warn you. I'll have him remove this insidious vigilance you are keeping over her. By the way, I'll just call Mrs. Compstock and tell her there is no further need to worry about the fellow she saw lurking about her place."

He strode into the den and put in his call. We heard him telling the lady he had cleared up the mystery of the man she had seen, that there was nothing to worry about, and to rest assured he would "attend to that other matter." Captain Bartlett removed the grin from his face as Mr. Middleton walked truculently back into the library. Hand ceased his pacing to and fro.

"I'm glad you did that," he said to Mr. Middleton. "I really don't want to persecute Mrs. Compstock."

"Well, that's what you're doing," said Mr. Middleton severely. "I stayed with her tonight as long as I felt I decently could. It's a shame! Now then, what is this help you intimated I could give you? Have you heard that I am working on a new theory?"

"No, I hadn't heard," replied Hand dryly. "There is a peculiarity about this house that I think you could explain. It has a double foundation with a space between. That's rather unusual, you know."

"Yes, I saw in the newspapers that Buckley's body was found in the foundation," said Mr. Middleton reflectively. "I happen to know why it was built that way, too. When I bought this house, it was in bad repair. Just by chance I got hold of the same fellow who built it and had him renovate it for me. He told me about the foundation. The plans don't call for a double affair; it was his own idea, he said. I don't think it was worth while, although this chap said it insulated the cellar. When I built my new house, I didn't have it done. Just one of those peculiar wrinkles those building fellows get."

"Who owned the house before you did?"

"An old fellow by the name of Stark. He was a recluse and let the place run down horribly. I added to it a good deal, besides."

"Was this man Stark wealthy?"

"He was reputed to be immensely wealthy. Gossip had him a sort of miserly old villain. I really don't know anything about him, though. He died, and I purchased this place from his estate."

"When you were in this house, did you ever have any trouble with your servants, Mr. Middleton?" asked Hand.

The man regarded my friend curiously for a moment. "How in blazes—" he began, half to himself. "Say, maybe you're a deeper one than I gave you credit for," he said with a smile. "If I answer your question, will you tell me how you came to ask it?"

"With pleasure," laughed Hand.

"All right, it's a bargain. We had a servant—called himself a Spaniard, but I always thought he was an Italian. I don't know whether the man was actually dishonest or not, but he certainly had peculiar habits. I thought I heard a burglar in the house one night. I investigated and found this chap Gonzalos prowling round downstairs—came upon him right in here, in fact. Said he couldn't sleep."

"By heaven, that's a remarkable coincidence!" I exclaimed.

"How's that?" asked Mr. Middleton, a little startled by my abrupt interruption.

"Go on, sir," said Hand. "I'll explain my friend's remark later."

"Well," continued Mr. Middleton, "his explanation didn't satisfy me. I reprimanded him and told him if he couldn't sleep to stay in his room anyway. He was a good servant, and I didn't want to dismiss him without just cause. Everything went along all right for a week or so, but then my wife said she thought she had heard someone prowling round at night again. I took Gonzalos to task, but he denied that he had been down here again at night. I couldn't prove it, of course; so I let the matter rest. I

decided, however, to keep my eye on him. One night soon
after, my wife woke me and said she was sure someone was
downstairs. I crept down here, and, would you believe it,
there was Gonzalos in the library again! I gave him notice
at once."

"What happened then?"

"He was a most peculiar chap. The next day he came
to me, very penitent, and implored me to reconsider his
case. He offered to take a reduction in wages if I wouldn't
discharge him. As he didn't seem to have taken anything
in his nightly rambles through the house, I gave him another chance. Then one day my wife caught him asleep in
the den. Mrs. Middleton was rather sick of him. She woke
him up and told him he might win my sympathy, but she
wouldn't stand for him any longer. She gave him a week's
notice. Gentlemen, the very next night that fellow disappeared! I found out from the other servants that he went
to his room as usual. Nobody heard him go, but in the
morning he had vanished!"

"Did he take his belongings with him?"

"That's the odd part of it. I looked about his room, and
everything he owned seemed to be there. He apparently
left everything behind him that he didn't take away on his
back."

"Do you know what clothes he had on his back?"

"Well, really, I wasn't familiar with his wardrobe. He
left two suits and his uniforms behind him, I know that.
I put his stuff in a box and kept it in the attic, thinking
he'd return for it, but he never did."

"Did he steal anything when he disappeared?"

"Apparently not. We made a careful inspection of the
house, but nothing was missing. It was very peculiar."

"Did you report this disappearance?"

"I told Withers about it. As a matter of fact, Gonzalos's
disappearance didn't cut much of a figure with us. After

all, he was merely a servant, and if he wanted to leave in that fashion, I suppose he had a right to."

"How long ago was that?"

"Last July, I think. Yes, it was just before we started to build the new house."

"This is certainly very interesting," said Hand.

"Gonzalos hasn't turned up, has he?" asked Mr. Middleton.

"No, but there appears to be a connection between your man Gonzalos and the colonel's servant Buckley. You see, Buckley had a habit of prowling round the house late at night, too."

"You don't mean it!" exclaimed Mr. Middleton excitedly. "See here, this is deeper than perhaps you suppose, Mr. Hand. Maybe my wife was not so silly after all. The disappearance of Gonzalos was followed by an episode which had a very definite influence upon our deciding to leave this house."

"How was that?"

"I'll take up the account where I left off. Gonzalos disappeared, and I thought that would be an end to the mysterious business. It was not long after, however, that my wife became concerned afresh. She told me she was positive she had heard someone moving about the lower floors at night. As there continued to be nothing missing, nor any signs of an intruder, I put her alarms down to the nervousness that Gonzalos and his peculiar actions had roused. But a few nights later I thought I heard someone downstairs myself. I got my pistol and investigated. There appeared to be no one on this floor, and I was about to go to bed, convinced that I had been mistaken. Then I heard a faint sound in the cellar—a sort of knocking."

"Ha! In the cellar was it? Did you go down there?"

"I did. As soon as I opened the door at the head of the cellar stairs, I heard the sound quite distinctly. It sounded as if someone were digging at the cellar walls. I crept silently down the stairs. At the foot there is a light-switch controlling the light in the furnace-room. I switched it on and looked quickly about. The sounds stopped, but there was nobody in sight. I called to whoever was there to come out and give himself up. There was no answer. Then I cautiously walked over to have a look in the laundry and the other basement rooms. A scraping sound behind me caused me to whirl about. A man was scurrying across the furnace-room toward the basement door at the back of the house. He passed out of my sight round the corner of the laundry, and when I had rushed back into the furnace-room, he was opening the outside door. He had his back to me, of course, and I called upon him to halt."

"Did you get a look at his face?"

"Yes, I certainly did. I wish to heaven I hadn't! I was prepared to shoot the scoundrel if he didn't heed my command, for I was thoroughly vexed at the liberties that had been taken in my house. When I called to him, the fellow turned toward me, at the same time flinging the door open. Good heaven! Gentlemen, you never saw such a face! Had it not been for the blazing orbs that were turned upon me, I should have been certain I was gazing at a death's-head! There appeared to be no nose, and the teeth were exposed to the gums! The whole face was horribly blanched—as white as that shirt-cuff! Ugh! It makes me shudder to think of it."

"He got away from you?"

"By heaven, I was struck with such horror at sight of that monstrosity that I couldn't move! I stood there like a graven image, with the pistol forgotten in my hand. I thought the creature laughed at me, but it may have been just the devilish mirth stamped on his features, exactly the same as those on a skull! Anyhow, when I had collected my wits, he had whisked out the door and was gone."

"Did you follow after him?"

"I did not! It may be shameful to confess it, but I was trembling like a leaf. I returned to my bedroom, and my wife immediately saw the condition I was in. She had always lamented the fact that we had not built on the prominence at the end of the ridge. After this harrowing experience she renewed her pleas that we build a new home on that location, and I finally consented."

"But you remained in this house for some time after that."

"Yes; while they were building the new house. We moved out of this one just before Colonel Decker moved into it."

"Did this mysterious prowler return again before you left here?"

"Not to my knowledge. I employed a private detective to keep watch over the house at night. He stayed on the job until we moved out, but nothing ever occurred. I had evidently frightened the intruder as badly as he frightened me, and he never returned."

"Not while you remained here with a detective on the job," said Hand in a guarded tone. "But after the colonel moved in, it is quite evident he returned. Fact of the matter is, he is making another visit here at this very minute. Don't anyone move to betray that we know he is there, but just such a hideous face as you describe, Mr. Middleton, is peering in at us through the window at the back."

I felt the hair bristle at the back of my head, and the room suddenly became insufferably hot. In our efforts to appear innocent of the awful presence at the window, I am afraid we took on the aspect of a group of wooden Indians. I, for one, scarcely breathed.

Hand had been standing with the window directly at his left. Now he swung about with his back squarely to it. He raised his head and gazed at the ceiling.

"O'Brine and MacClintock," he said, almost in a whisper, "I'm about to send you out of here. Circle around the house from the front door and capture that fellow. You'll have to be quick." Then, turning to O'Brine and MacClintock: "We shan't need you two men any further; you might as well turn in," he said in a loud voice.

The two old soldiers nodded their heads and quickly left the library. As they were leaving, I covertly stole a glance at the window. With difficulty I repressed a gasp of horror. Mr. Middleton had aptly described that fearful, livid countenance when he had likened it to a death's-head. Were I the least inclined to the supernatural, I should certainly have thought I was gazing at an animated skull. I term it animated advisedly, for, with a malicious gleam of the wicked eyes, the face suddenly vanished.

Evidently Hand had been keeping his eye on the fearful eavesdropper.

"It didn't work!" he cried. "Quick! Everybody after that fellow!"

"Scatter!" cried Hand as he leaped to the driveway and disappeared into the gloom. I made off toward the opposite side of the house from the one my friend had started for. From then on we proceeded to play a rather dangerous game of hide-and-seek. From time to time I saw a shadowy figure moving about the grounds. In each case it turned out to be a friend, who confessed to coming as near to shooting me as had I to shooting him. It was risky business, and I did not like it.

At last I found Hand, and he told me to give up the search. We made our way round to the front of the house. On the front steps stood Mr. Middleton, leaning weakly against the portico.

"What's the trouble?" demanded Hand in alarm. "You're not hurt?"

"No—no," gasped Mr. Middleton. "It's my heart. Been bothering me lately. I have some pills that get me over these spells. Just took one, and I feel better. I'll be all right in a minute."

"Don't you want me to help you into the house?" I asked solicitously.

"No, thanks," he replied. "I'll be over it in a minute. Feel that."

He took my hand and placed it to his chest. I could feel his heart pounding as if it would burst.

"This night has been a little too much for me," he said. "What with O'Brine and MacClintock sticking guns into my back, and then this episode on top of it, I'm about ready to call it a day. By the way, Mr. Hand, did you ever see such a face as that fellow had?"

"It's a fearful sight and no mistake," replied Hand. "Before you go, Mr. Middleton, I should like to make an odd request."

Mr. Middleton turned back from his car, which he was about to enter. "All right," he said. "There's nothing unusual about your being a little odd, Mr. Hand. I must say, though, I laid it into you a trifle more than was necessary tonight. I'm sorry. But I was thoroughly enraged when I arrived here, I can tell you!"

"I can't blame you for taking exception to the way in which you were treated," said Hand. I was thankful that the darkness concealed my grin.

"I'm not so angry about it now," said Mr. Middleton. "After all, it's been quite an experience. What is your odd request?"

"There is a way in which you can be of great service to Colonel Decker," said Hand. "Unfortunately, I can't tell you what the favor is. If I did, it would spoil it. Would you be willing to come over here if we were to call you at any time in order to perform this service?"

"Why, certainly," agreed Mr. Middleton heartily. "You may call me at any time, Mr. Hand, and I promise you I will come right over."

"I can't thank you enough," Hand assured him. "It is a very unusual experiment that I am conducting, and I think that you are the very man I need to test it."

"You rouse my curiosity, sir," declared Mr. Middleton. "I am all interest. Call me at any time—any time at all. And now, gentlemen, I'll say good-night and get on home."

Mr. Middleton climbed into his car and drove away. My friend turned to me, rubbing his hands with satisfaction.

"My case is shaping up, Clark," he said. "Middleton did a lot tonight to establish my theories. I suppose you have formed the same opinion concerning that skeleton that I have. It must be Gonzalos! If Mr. Middleton recognizes the face I construct as that of his missing servant, the strongest link in my chain will be forged!"

I was about to ask him the manner in which the forging would be done, but at that moment we were joined by our four companions.

"We had our nerve wid us whin we nabbed Mr. Middleton," O'Brine was ruefully announcing as they came up to us. "Th' colonel will break us fer this sure. 'Tis lucky we'll be if me an' Hughie ain't buck privates by tomorrow night!"

"You carried out your orders admirably," said Hand. "That's all you need to worry about. The colonel told you to take your orders from me; I'll take the responsibility for them. I think, however, that we dare not continue the vigil at Mrs. Compstock's. You two men might just as well turn in—not much time left to sleep."

"I didn't see that fellow at the window," said Dick as we entered the house. "Boy, I was exercising self-control! I'd have given my right eye for one look at him. Was he as bad as Mr. Middleton said?"

"He was the most horrible sight I ever saw!" I replied.

"Well, what's to be done now?" asked Captain Bartlett.

"It is still Dick's watch," said Hand. "You other two turn in; I'll go back to work."

Before he returned to the closet, Hand accompanied the captain and me up the stairs. At the second floor we said good-night to Captain Bartlett; then Hand went to his room to replenish his cigarette-case. I followed in after him.

"More mystery than ever," I sighed.

"Nothing of the kind," he retorted. "In fact, after this latest development tonight, whatever mystery clung about the case seems to be pretty well dissipated."

"Perhaps it is to you," I pointed out, hopefully, "but as far as I'm concerned, I'm more in the dark than ever."

"Yes," he went on, ignoring the opening I had made for him to enlighten me, "Mr. Middleton's tale concerning his missing servant cleared up a lot. Mr. Middleton, I must confess, has been very helpful. He has helped me to establish another very strong point."

"What is that?"

"It is that the fellow who was looking in the library window at us tonight was lurking about this house the night Joseph Decker was killed."

"You don't mean it!"

"I do. You remember the footprints that Mr. Middleton discovered under the bush outside the den window? Well, the fellow who made them was that same fellow with the horrible face. He has lost a part of the heel of his left shoe."

I was speechless. Hand had filled his cigarette-case. He started for the door, but then he turned back to me with a smile of satisfaction.

"Oh, we are getting on, Clark," he said. "Fact of the matter is, nothing but time stands between us and the solution of the problem. I am impatient for the colonel to return tomorrow. He is necessary for the completion of my plans. I must hasten with that skull, too. As soon as I have that face satisfactorily reconstructed, I shall be ready to wind up the case."

He turned and left me. Once again I went to my room, this time to spend the rest of the night there without interruption. For an intolerable period sleep eluded me. When at last I slumbered, I found it a poor substitute for the tranquil rest I was accustomed to. I tumbled and tossed on the bed, dreaming of that horrible face I had seen at the window, whose possessor had disappeared as though snatched into the dark heavens.

14

A BAG OF IRON AND STONES

"I say, MacClintock, do you have much of this sort of weather?"

"It's been non so gude this sprring, sirr. One day gude; the next verra bad. It's the wind, sirr, shiftin' arroond all the time."

I was lazily conscious of the voices, which seemed to be far away. With a start I opened my eyes and glanced sharply at my wrist watch. To my dismay I found it was eight thirty, and I had resolved to be up and doing early. I bounded out of bed and looked out the window.

The voices I had heard discussing the weather were those of Captain Bartlett, and, of course, the colonel's chauffeur. The pair were standing on the lawn behind the house directly under my window. The complaining tones the captain had used were well merited. The weather was foul. No rain was falling, but the sky was leaden, and the atmosphere was oppressively damp. The dank smell of the swamp was heavy in the air.

I quickly dressed and looked into Hand's room. His bed had not been disturbed. I descended the stairs and found Patty and Dick at breakfast. They cheerily called for me to join them, but I excused myself for a moment. I had noticed that the door of the hall closet was tightly closed, and I wanted to see whether my friend were still at work behind it. I strode over to it and threw it open. There he sat, still bending over the bench at the back.

"Hello, Clark," he said, smiling over his shoulder at me. "Up at last, eh?"

"Yes; I overslept, hang it all! How is it coming?"

He moved aside to give me a view of his work. Although he had applied no more clay, that which had already been put on was now smoothed down. Incomplete as it was, the thing was beginning to take on a strikingly natural appearance. At once I was aware of a remarkable characteristic.

"By Jove! That fellow is an Italian!" I exclaimed.

Hand got out of his chair and moved over to where I was standing. He regarded the object on the bench critically for a moment. "I believe you can distinguish that," he said at length. "Just as the subtlety of an oil painting is indistinguishable at close range; so the characteristics of those features I've made escaped me while I was sitting right over them. Peculiar, isn't it, how racial characteristics are so pronounced, even in the unfinished form of a face such as that?"

"I'd stake a good deal on it that he is an Italian."

"I agree with you. That simplifies matters, too."

"You mean that now you are ready to let Mr. Middleton collaborate with you?"

"Not on such meager proof as this. But it solves the problem of what color eyes and hair to use. I shall complete the work on the features that I have already built up—I have not attempted to construct the lips or the nose yet, you see. If those Italic characteristics become more pronounced, I shall definitely assume that the subject was an Italian. That means a straight nose and rather full lips. It also means dark eyes and, in all probability, black hair. You see what I meant when I said we would leave those matters in the hands of the future? The future takes care of a lot of things, Clark."

He resumed his seat and went back to work.

"Seems to be taking quite a lot longer than you antici-pated," I remarked.

He laid down the small knife he was using to model the features with and turned to me. I was afraid for a minute I had offended him, but his reply reassured me.

"After you went to bed," he said, "I got back to work here. As I worked, I kept wondering what that peculiar implement could be that we found on the skeleton—that fork-like thing, you know. I had been wondering about it all evening, but what it was I could not imagine. You know, Clark, there is nothing much in the world that when brought down to the final analysis is not simple. The trouble is that when we have something which we don't under-stand, the tendency is to regard it as something exceeding-ly complex. That is what I had been doing—I confess it. Therefore, I changed my tactics and began to wonder what sort of simple object it could be. All at once it occurred to me what it was. I tell you, Clark, the solution was so simple that it nearly made me blush to think how hard I had pondered it."

"All of which fattens my inferiority complex," I said, "for I've been doing a good bit of thinking on the point, and I haven't got anywhere yet."

"You are differently situated from me. I believe I am in possession of several facts that you are not aware of. They form part of my deductions, at least. One by one the links of my hypothetical chain have proved themselves the real thing. Last night I was conscious that there were but two links unproved. My realization of what that pronged in-strument that belonged to our departed friend here really was enabled me to prove one of them. If Geering Middle-ton identifies this fellow my case is complete."

"My word, to think that you have progressed so far! How about enlightening me? As matters stand, I am al-most as much at sea as I was when we came here."

"I will, Clark, but not just yet. I am not quite ready, you see."

"Well, will you tell me what that instrument is that we found on the skeleton?"

"Of course. It was a magnet."

"A magnet!"

"Yes. It was a magnetic needle, suspended between the prongs of the fork by an axle through its center, on which it could revolve. Only the tapered end was magnetized. The untapered end was slightly heavier, of course. When the instrument was held in an upright position, the force of gravity kept the unmagnetized, heavier end down. If, however, any of the bodies possessing magnetic qualities were approached with it, the magnetized end of the slender bar would be pulled out of the vertical. Do you see?"

"Yes, I get the idea of the instrument. But what on earth did he want with it? I still don't understand that."

As Hand was about to reply, the door suddenly opened, and Dick Fairfax entered. He looked bubbling over with curiosity. "Mind if I come in?" he asked almost apologetically.

"Not at all," replied Hand heartily. "I was just explaining to Clark the significance of that pronged instrument we found on the skeleton."

"Mean to say you've found out what it is?" asked Dick excitedly.

"I'll explain it for Dick if you'd like to get back to work," I offered.

"No; this little respite will freshen me up," said Hand, proceeding to explain the thing again for Dick's benefit.

"But what the deuce did he want with it?" demanded the young man when he had been enlightened.

"That's just what I asked," I said.

"I'm assuming the thing belonged to Gonzalos," explained Hand. "We have evidence to show that he was looking for something in this house. The similarity of his actions to Buckley's is enough to indicate he was trying to discover something hidden in the walls. This instrument is further proof of it; he used it to aid him in his search. I have something else of his that he used, also. Look at this."

He pointed with his long finger to the end of his improvised bench. Dick and I crowded closer. Carefully laid out on the board were several bits of ragged, rough paper. They had been pieced together, but, aside from a few faint marks and what appeared to be hieroglyphics, I saw nothing of value on them.

"That is the paper we found on the skeleton," said Hand. "As I had hoped, the inner folds were sufficiently preserved for me to tell what the paper was."

"Well, I'm looking right at it," said Dick, "and I'll be darned if I can tell what it was!"

"I examined it carefully through a magnifying glass," said Hand. "It is the remnants of the plan of a house. From what I could make out of it, I think it is the plan of a basement, but I can't be sure of that. Suppose he had a plan of the basement of this house in his pocket, which showed not only the arrangement of the walls, but the arrangement of the plumbing as well. He would not be fooled by an iron pipe attracting his magnetic needle, you see. But if the needle inclined toward the wall where there was no pipe to attract it, he could investigate the spot to see whether it concealed what he was after."

"By thunder! That's it as sure as you're alive!" exclaimed Dick.

"But what would he be looking for that would attract a magnetic needle?" I protested. "Substances that have magnetic attraction are not usually valuable."

"That is where my hypothesis enters in," smiled Hand. "Sometimes, Clark," he added, turning back to the bench, "your manners are a trifle dubious. I distinctly heard a

very charming young lady and her stalwart fiancé invite
you to join them at breakfast. And here you are, hiding
away in a stuffy closet until they have finished!"

Dick looked at me a trifle astonished. The idiosyncra-
sies of my friend had long since ceased to astonish me. I
took Dick by the arm and guided him out of the closet.
The young man still seemed rather abashed by our abrupt
dismissal. I hastened to explain it.

"Christopher Hand is one of the most peculiar men
you ever met," I said. "Just now he is sitting in that closet
chuckling to himself at the manner in which he got rid of
us. He'll give you his reasons for it when the proper time
comes. He knows he doesn't have to explain to me; that's
one of the reasons he allows me to fuss round with him. I
hope you're not offended."

"You can't make me mad," grinned Dick. "I suppose he
has a good enough reason for keeping mum. I should be
getting back to the office, but I just can't tear myself away
from here with things in the state they are in now. I'm
going to stay right here and keep an eye on Miss Patricia
Decker's welfare until this thing is cleared up—job or no
job. I couldn't get my mind on my work now, anyhow."

"Well, I don't blame you. I don't feel safe around here
myself after seeing that cursed face in the window last
night. Gad! what a face that was! I dreamed about it, and
that headless skeleton up in the wood."

"I wish I'd seen that face. I didn't dare look at the window after Mr. Hand cautioned us. By the way, to get back
to the subject of your friend, what do you suppose he went
out for last night?"

"Oh, he went to Markstown to get the stuff to construct that face."

"No; I mean after you went to bed. He went back to
work on the skull in the closet for about an hour; then he
marched out of the house."

"I didn't know anything about that. How long was he gone?"

"I don't know. Captain Bartlett relieved me before he came back."

"That accounts for the small amount of work he's done on the skull. Did Captain Bartlett say when he got back?"

"I haven't seen the captain. When I got downstairs for breakfast, he'd gone outside. Shall we ask Mr. Hand himself about it?"

"I rather think not. If he'd wanted to, he'd have told us when we were in there. You don't want to get snubbed again, do you?"

"My gosh, no!"

Just then Captain Bartlett walked in through the front door. "Hello," he cried. "I didn't expect to see you here, Dick."

"I'm not going back to work until this thing is cleared up," declared Dick.

"I don't mean that; I thought you went with Patty," said the captain.

"What!" cried Dick. "Patty's upstairs!"

"She is not," contradicted the captain rather grimly. "She went out in her car about twenty minutes ago. I saw Pat driving, all right, when she turned out into the road. I thought you must be with her, but I guess she was alone."

Dick's face became drawn. All three of us stood there looking nervously at each other. I decided I had better do something to calm Dick's gathering fears.

"After all, it's broad daylight," I said, as reassuringly as I could.

"Yes, but I don't like it!" he cried. "By thunder! I'm going to get out the other car and have a look for her. Which way did she go?"

"She turned down toward Barkersville," replied the captain.

Dick and Captain Bartlett rushed out of the house, and I went to inform Hand. My friend rose from his work with a mutter when I told him what had happened. I followed his long, swift strides through the den and out to the rear of the house. We found Dick and Captain Bartlett at the garage climbing into the colonel's car. As Hand and I were climbing into the back seat, our departure was indefinitely postponed.

"Hello!" cried the captain. "Excitement's all over. Here's Patty."

The roadster had just turned into the drive from the road. Patty drove it back to the garage and sat looking at us through the wind-shield. She appeared a trifle guilty, as though she realized she had given us all a scare by stealing away. Dick hopped out of the car and ran over to her. Hand strode quickly back to the house.

"Phew! I'm glad she's back," said Captain Bartlett, turning to me. "I didn't realize what a tension there is around here until this happened."

"There's plenty of it!" I retorted. "There seems to be a mysterious, unseen danger about, all the time. We'll have to be more careful about Patty."

"I guess Dick will attend to that," grinned the captain as we walked over to the roadster. Patty still sat behind the wheel, and Dick leaned up against the side of the car. They seemed to have had a tiff. I imagined Dick's emotions had led him to speak rather sharply to Patty about going off and leaving him. I was about to say something to relieve the situation, but Captain Bartlett did it for me.

"Hello, Patty," he called. "Been sleuthing again?"

"Not this time," smiled Patty. "What's the matter with you all? Dick is mad at me just because I drove to Barkersville and back."

"We don't allow children out alone around here," said the captain in mock severity.

"If you call me a child again, Captain Jack, I'll—I'll—"

"I'm sorry," laughed the captain. "I should be shot."

"You're much too nice to be shot," smiled Patty.

"Thank you, fair lady," cried the captain, with an elaborate bow. "I'll take my reprieve and be off. Come on, Clark, let's leave the love-birds alone. It's going to rain pretty soon, and they'll be cooped up in the house with us all the rest of the day."

Captain Bartlett hooked his arm in mine and led me off toward the front of the house. We walked out to the road. There we stopped, as though both had become fascinated by the weird vista that stretched off into the distance before us. The Great Swamp was a sea of mist. The foot of the hillside faded into it and disappeared. The tops of the hillocks out on the swamp lifted out of the misty lake like tall mountain tops protruding above the clouds. Only the hillocks themselves had that appearance. Whereas the rose and gold of the sun transforms the tops of clouds into an enchanting fairyland, the surface of the fog that we looked down upon was dull, and dead, and gray.

"Dismal, eh?" grunted Captain Bartlett. "The swamp isn't a bad sight on a bright day, but when the weather turns out like this, it's a depressing outlook. Don't wonder Middleton got tired of looking at it."

As the captain finished speaking, I thought I heard a cry, borne to my ears on the sluggish breeze coming off the swamp.

"Did you hear that?" I demanded, almost in a whisper.

"Hear what?" asked the captain, with a puzzled glance at me.

"I thought I heard a cry out there on the swamp. Listen!"

We stood silently for a minute or two, gazing off expectantly over the dull grayish surface of the fog. At length the captain's face broke into its familiar grin. He placed his hand on my shoulder.

"You're beginning to hear things, Clark," he accused. "I reckon this business has got your nerves a little jumpy."

"No; my nerves are all right," I retorted. "Perhaps I did imagine it, though. If it was a cry, it came from afar, for it was very faint. I must have been mistaken about it. Heaven knows, nobody would venture out on that swamp while it was covered with a fog like that!"

We turned to go back to the house. O'Brine came marching down the drive with a rake on his shoulder at the correct position of right-shoulder-arms. He altered his course and walked over to us.

"Captain, sor," he began with an expression of concern on his pleasant old features, "'tis worried I am. I didn't shlape a wink th' rest o' last night!"

"Afraid of what the colonel will say, eh, Private O'Brine?"

O'Brine winced at the lowly title. "Thot's it, sor," he quickly replied. "Th' likes o' Hughie an' me shtickin' automatics in th' shmall o' Mr. Middleton's back! No sooner nor th' colonel gits home 'tis buck privates we'll be. I ain't bin in such a fix since I let th' colonel git out o' his quarters t' inspict th' rigimint wid his hind shirt-tail out."

"Don't worry, O'Brine," I said reassuringly. "Hand promised to take the responsibility, and he will."

"How did you happen to nab him?" asked the captain, with a grin. "Didn't you know who he was?"

"Sure we knew who he was, sor," cried O'Brine. "Thot's th' worst ov it! There he was in Mrs. Compstock's livin'-room pacin' up an' down like a major gineral on the war-path. 'This here's an outrage, begorra!' sez he so loud we could here him through th' winder wid no trouble at all. 'Sure an' I'll shpake t' th' colonel about it in the mornin'.' An' shpake t' him he will, you wait an' see, sor. Hughie ain't so worried—it ain't such a drop from corporal t' private. But think o' me, sor, shtill a sergeant in good shtandin'!"

"We'll see that you're protected, Sergeant," the captain promised him. "You carried out your orders to perfection. You'll get a citation for this instead of being busted."

We left the old fellow dubiously shaking his head. As we walked over to the front porch, I turned to Captain Bartlett.

"Dick told me that Hand went out after I went to bed," I told him. "He didn't come back before you relieved Dick; so he must have returned during your watch. What time was it?"

"He got back just before six o'clock. Came sneaking through the house, but I'm hanged if I knew it until he whispered right into my ear that he was back. He moves round like a ghost!"

"So I've noticed," I said, with a smile. "What did he go out for?"

"Is he ever in the habit of scavenging?" asked Captain Bartlett abruptly.

"I am telling you the absolute truth when I say he is in the habit of doing just about everything imaginable. Was he scavenging last night?"

"Apparently. When I heard him whispering into my ear in the darkness of the library, I executed one of those undignified risings from a chair that we afterwards recall with a blush. What kept me aloft I don't know, but I sailed through the air for a distance of at least ten feet. I left Mr. Hand behind me. It was just beginning to get light outside, and his figure was silhouetted by the window behind him. At first I thought it was Santa Claus."

"Santa Claus?"

"Good old St. Nick himself. But it was Mr. Hand, all right. He had on his back a bag that seemed to be weighted down by something heavy within it. I mustered what dignity I had left and asked him what he had in the bag. Now, what do you suppose he said it was?"

"I haven't the faintest idea."

"Iron and stones. Yes, sir, he said iron and stones, and with that he walked out of the library and shut himself up again in the hall closet."

"Well," I said, with a thoughtful shake of my head, "it's all beyond me. I think I'll get back and have a go at getting some breakfast, old chap. This damp chill is hard to take on an empty stomach."

We spent the morning entertaining Patty and sneaking off to see how Hand was progressing. The completion of the face went on with exasperating slowness. I therefore increased the intervals between my visits to the closet in order to get a better idea of the changes that were made.

For the first time since I had met her, Patty seemed a little pitiful. She had been overcome with sorrow for her father, but I had not got the impression that she herself was to be pitied. She had borne up bravely through all the tragedy, and it was not surprising that at last she had begun to be affected by it. Evidently I was not the only one to sense it. Dick and the captain each tried as assiduously as I did to cheer her up. We succeeded admirably, and soon Patty was even more sprightly than usual. Occasionally, however, her beautiful brown eyes would become troubled, and she would gaze sadly off into the distance. Her bright smile would be our reward for taking her thoughts away from herself.

Colonel Decker returned just before luncheon. I was greatly impressed by the tenderness and joy with which the old soldier greeted his daughter. Patty could not take her eyes off her father. Although she smiled, there was a longing almost akin to sadness in her eyes. What a blessing those two had each other!

At length the colonel became inquisitive. "Why, where is Christopher?" he asked, glancing about.

"He's off somewhere," replied Dick, glancing nervously at Patty.

"How is he getting on?" was the colonel's next query.

"He told me he had his case nearly completed," I replied. "But he's keeping very secretive about it. He does, you know. He takes no chances of making false statements. When he does tell you anything, you may be absolutely sure he knows what he's talking about."

"You might as well talk to the Sphinx now," grinned the captain.

The colonel finally allowed his daughter to go and get ready for luncheon. As soon as Patty had left us, we enlightened her father concerning the skull.

"Mr. Hand is in the hall closet—" began Dick excitedly.

"The hall closet!" exclaimed Colonel Decker.

"Yes," I affirmed. "Colonel, we found a skeleton of a man out in the wood behind this house. Hand is reconstructing the face on it."

"He's what!"

"Perhaps we had better let Hand explain it himself. Come over here to the closet, Colonel, and see what he has done."

Inside the closet Colonel Decker gazed with astonishment upon the weird, half-finished face. "What are you up to now, Christopher?" he asked.

"Hello, Colonel," said Hand, swinging round. "Have they told you about the skeleton? Well, I've taken charge of this fellow. I shall reconstruct his features, put eyes in his head, hair on his cranium, a flush to his cheek, and find out who he is."

At first Colonel Decker was astounded by Hand's grotesque idea, and then he was openly incredulous. Hand took his skepticism good-naturedly.

"As I told the others, this is nothing but an experiment," he said. "I ask only two things: keep Patty out of here, and don't tell anyone what I am doing."

"Well, all right," agreed the colonel.

"Just one more request, Colonel."

"Yes?"

"How soon can you close up the house and leave?"

"What say?" exclaimed the colonel, with a start. "Close up the house and leave?"

"Precisely."

"Now, see here, Christopher, if you—"

"You should be ready to leave by tomorrow afternoon," interrupted Hand, as though the colonel had said nothing. "Plenty of help here. I don't just know what is required to close up a house, but it shouldn't take long. MacClintock can drive you, Patty, Dick and the captain into the city tomorrow afternoon."

"And you?"

"Clark and I shall have to leave in the morning. We'll go by train. I have some very pressing matters to attend to in town."

For a moment the colonel looked coldly at my friend. Finally his stern lips melted into a smile. He reached out and patted Hand on the shoulder.

"I think you're up to something," he said. "Very well, Christopher, we'll be out of here by tomorrow afternoon."

"Tomorrow afternoon, not by tomorrow afternoon," corrected Hand. "I should say you won't be able to leave before five o'clock."

"Very well, then," complied Colonel Decker, "at the stroke of five MacClintock shall drive us away from here. How about O'Brine, and Maxwell and the cook?"

"Give Maxwell and the cook a vacation; they deserve it. Have them leave by train in the early afternoon. I may be able to use O'Brine; we'll let his case rest for the present."

Hand turned resolutely away from us, and we filed out and left him to his work. The colonel looked thoroughly mystified, but I knew he would not fail in his part.

15
A RETURN TO THE NETS

After luncheon the house-closing began in earnest. Rugs were rolled up and stored away, the furniture was shrouded in white cloths, and much of the silverware in the dining-room was packed up preparatory to its removal. I felt very much in the way. Just as I had decided to take myself out of the house, Colonel Decker approached me and took me by the arm.

"I don't like to bother Christopher," he said, "but I'd like to find out something about the way things are going. I thought perhaps you could tell me."

"I can tell you what I know about the case, Colonel," I said, "though I'm afraid I don't know what it all leads to. But let's go somewhere in private."

He took me into the den. There I told him everything that I knew. He got rather exercised over the affair with Mr. Middleton, but when I assured him that the gentleman had been pacified, to my relief, he calmed down. He took my word for it that there was no use in asking Hand for information. Like the rest of us, he resigned himself to await eventualities.

As we sat discussing the case, Maxwell came to announce that Mr. Middleton was calling. We found our visitor in the hall, hat in hand and gazing about in perplexity.

"What in the name of heaven and earth is going on, Colonel?" he asked.

"I'm closing the house, Geering," replied the colonel. "Going to take Patty away for a while. By the way, where is Patty?"

"She's upstairs, sir," replied Maxwell. "She took Mr. Richard and Captain Bartlett with her to do some things. Shall I summon her?"

"No, no, that's all right, Maxwell," replied the colonel. "By Jove, Geering, they've done for the living-room already. But we still have the den; come in and sit down."

"I can't do it," said Mr. Middleton. "I just dropped in to say good-by myself. I've been called away for a couple of days. Where are you going, Colonel? I hope you won't be gone long."

"I don't expect to be gone so long," replied the colonel. "But Patty wants to buy some clothes; she's getting married, of course. Then I think we'll take a little trip. This tragedy has been very trying for her, you know."

"I think you are very wise," said Mr. Middleton warmly. "Poor little Patty, it's too bad! But, look here, how about Mr. Hand, is he going to abandon the case?"

"I have never known him to abandon a case," I said. "He must get back to town; in fact, we are leaving in the morning. But I have no doubt that he will keep at it until he has the matter cleared up, eventually."

"It's too bad I haven't more time," complained Mr. Middleton. "I've been working on a theory—the one I told you about the other night down at the edge of the swamp. I should like to talk it over with him."

"By Jove!" I exclaimed, "Hand has something he wants to show—he wants you to help him on. Just wait until I speak to him. Don't go yet, will you?"

"Come into the den, Geering," invited the colonel. "Surely you can wait a moment to see Christopher."

"Well, all right," complied Mr. Middleton, glancing anxiously at his watch.

When they had disappeared into the den, I opened the door of the hall closet. Hand was not there. I rushed out and, finding Maxwell, asked him whether he had seen my friend. He told me Hand had left the house a short while before. Outside I found MacClintock and again inquired after Hand.

"Misterr Hand, sirr?" he said. "He got in Miss Patty's carr and drrove off."

"Where did he go?"

"He didna say, sirr."

I went disconsolately back into the house with my information.

"Afraid I can't wait," said Mr. Middleton, with a shake of his head. "I'm on my way to the train now. I'm sorry to have missed Mr. Hand. But I'll be back in a couple of days; he can get me at home."

After he had gone, I went out and talked to O'Brine. There I was listening to the sergeant recount some of his experiences, when Hand drove in. I went up to him as he got out of the car.

"Where have you been?" I demanded.

"Up to see Mrs. Compstock."

"You have! What kind of reception did you get?"

"None at all from Mrs. Compstock. She wasn't at home."

"Well, you missed Mr. Middleton."

"What do you mean?"

"He's been called away for a few days. He stopped in here on his way to the train to say good-by to the colonel."

"And to object to his treatment of last night?"

"He never mentioned it."

"Bully for him! But you say he's gone?"

"Yes. I'm afraid there's no catching him. He was in a hurry for his train when he left."

An expression of annoyance crossed Hand's face. Then he gave the old familiar shrug of his shoulders.

"Well," he said, "we'll just have to rely on someone else to identify our face. It shouldn't be hard to find someone."

As we were walking over to the house, Hand grasped me by the arm.

"The mountain is coming to Mohammed," he said gleefully. "Look, Mrs. Compstock's car is turning in the drive."

We just had time to get into the den before Mrs. Compstock was ushered in at the front. When we entered the hall, she was talking quite affably to the colonel. At sight of Hand she froze right up.

"I understand that you called upon me, sir," she said icily. "I am very sorry I was not at home, but as soon as I learned that you had come to see me, I took the liberty of looking you up. I sincerely hope that you have come to your senses."

I was quite astounded to behold the cowering, shamefaced attitude of my friend. A gleam of triumph came into Mrs. Compstock's blue eyes.

"Madam," said Hand, "I must humbly beg your pardon. I ask you to consider my position, however, since that is to blame rather than I. I was investigating a foul murder, and everything was significant. I had to hold the only cards in my possession."

"Never mind your apologies," flared Mrs. Compstock. "You have something of mine, and I want it!"

"I'm afraid I have deceived you," said Hand, sadly shaking his head. "One moment, and I will show you."

He went quickly up the stairs and out of sight. Colonel Decker turned to Mrs. Compstock, quite as abashed as Hand had been.

"I'm sorry, Clara," he said. "I found out about the surveillance you were subjected to after I got back. I assure you I would never have countenanced such a thing."

Mrs. Compstock patted the colonel on the arm. She smiled softly. Once again she was the kitten.

"Of course not, Randolph," she said softly. "That stupid Mr. Hand is to blame for the whole thing. And I don't blame him, either; rather I pity him. Let's think no more about it. He hasn't—he couldn't have prejudiced you against me, Randolph?"

"Not in the least," replied the colonel, uncomfortably. "We are just as good friends now as we ever were, Clara."

"Oh, how glad I am to hear you say that!" she cried. "It has made such a difference, your coming here to live! But—why, Randolph, what are you doing to the house?"

"Closing it, Clara. I am going to take Patty away for a while."

"You don't mean you are leaving?"

"Yes, for a little while, at least."

For a moment it was difficult to tell just what emotions took possession of Mrs. Compstock at this news. At first I thought she was pleasantly surprised, but then I thought she was filled with consternation. But she professed to be sorry.

"What a shame this all had to happen!" she sighed. "I do hope you and Patty won't be gone long. Mill Ridge will miss you, and—and I most of all."

"That is very kind of you, Clara," said the colonel with a bow.

Further conversation between them was cut short by Hand, who descended the stairs carrying my fly-box in his hand. It was the box in which he had placed the remains of Mrs. Compstock's letter. He walked right up to the woman and opened the lid.

"In this box, madam," he said, "is all that I have of your letter."

She bent over the box and glanced sharply into it. Then she raised suspicious eyes to Hand's face. He was smiling.

"Just a few charred remains," he said. "Joseph burned it, and what it set forth no one knows but yourself. Just the last line and your signature are legible. As you see, the paper is entirely burned. Now—" he put his hand into the box and pulverized the burned paper—"nothing remains of it."

"I'm glad you did that, Christopher!" exclaimed the colonel. "Now, Clara," he added, with a smile, "you are out of the case."

"And I know whom to thank for it," she cried, looking into his eyes. "And—I wish you luck, Mr. Hand."

"I'm afraid you are rather late with it," muttered my friend, quite bitterly. "Unless I can solve this mystery before tomorrow morning, it will have to go unsolved—by me, at least. It was because I am forced to return to the city tomorrow that I destroyed your letter. I didn't wish to leave you in any trepidation about it."

"Now I believe you are a gentleman, after all," cried Mrs. Compstock, laughing and giving her hand to my friend. "I am so glad this has all cleared up so nicely. And I forgive you, Mr. Hand."

"Thank you," said Hand, bowing with a tight-lipped smile. "And, as a further proof of my well-meaning, let me, on behalf of the colonel, offer you the services of Sergeant O'Brine as a guardian of your house at night. The colonel is removing all his valuables; so this house is safe. But, you know, there is a man roaming these woods."

Mrs. Compstock hesitated and pondered the offer.

"Yes, Clara, by all means take O'Brine," urged the colonel. "I'll not feel comfortable unless you do."

"That is so good of you, Randolph," she said, smiling brightly. "All right, then, I would feel easier with a man on the place. You are sure that you won't need him here?"

"Not in the least," assured the colonel. "I'll send him up this evening. I'd send MacClintock along, too, but he is going to drive us into town."

"When do you go?" she asked.

"We plan to leave tomorrow afternoon some time," replied the colonel. "Probably about five o'clock."

"I'll try to be here to see you off," she said brightly. "Well, I must be getting back. Good-by, Mr. Hand, better luck next time."

Mrs. Compstock left in high good humor. The colonel, too, seemed highly pleased.

"I'm glad that's ended," he declared. "I didn't interfere with you, Christopher, but your trying to drag her into the case was a constant source of dismay to me."

"Yes, that's ended, Colonel," said Hand. "Come, we'll give O'Brine his orders."

"There's no funny business about O'Brine's going up there, is there?" asked the colonel quickly.

"None whatever," Hand assured him. "That's why I suggested that we both go speak to him. You can hear for yourself whether I put him up to anything. I assure you that I won't."

Having nothing else to occupy me, I went with them out to the garage. O'Brine seemed quite willing to go on guard at Mrs. Compstock's. It seemed he was on friendly terms with her cook. The colonel admonished him to be on his toes to do anything the lady asked of him. Back into the house we went, and Hand immediately dived into his stuffy hall closet.

The rain the captain had prophesied did not materialize, but the day showed no disposition to improve itself. Even so, I had become tired of the house, and decided to go out for a stroll. Before leaving, I looked in upon Hand. It was my first visit since luncheon.

At last the completion of the task was in sight. The dark eyes had been set in the hollow sockets. They were wide open and staring, for he had not yet attempted to form the lids. A rather formless mass of clay stood out for the nose.

As yet no lips hid the grinning teeth. The cheeks, jowls, chin, forehead, and even the ears had been completed, and very lifelike they looked too. With a start I realized the face in that stage of completion was not unlike the one I had seen at the window in the library the night before. It gave me quite a turn.

"There's not much more to do," I observed.

"Quite a little yet," grunted Hand in reply. "Got to shape this nose—the lips, besides. Then there are the eyelids to make—delicate job, that. After that's done, the hair goes on."

"By the way," I said, "how do you know how he wore his hair? He might have parted it in the middle, on either side, or not at all."

"How do I know he had any hair on the top of his head at all? As a matter of fact, I don't think he did. We didn't see any hair out there where the skull was resting. Hair lasts for years sometimes. But the distinguishing features of a head of hair disappear under a hat, Clark. This fellow is going to wear a hat when I'm through with him."

"How'd you stick those eyes in the sockets?"

"Plaster of Paris. It's hardening now. Can't make the lids until it dries."

I left him once more and went out of the house. The fog still lay in a thick blanket over the swamp. It was quite a fascinating sight, and I decided to walk along the road to keep it in view. Sometimes the bushes completely obstructed my view of it, but for the most part I could look out over it all I wished. It gave the impression of looking out to sea. Perhaps that thought was father to the hallucination, but it seemed to me that I could see waves undulating the mist. I walked over to the side of the road. There I stopped and gazed steadily down at the fog to see whether my eyes had played me a trick. And then I suddenly lost interest in whether they had or not. Up from the impenetrable mist there came to me a man's hoarse shout of terror!

My first inclination was to rush to the rescue. I was certain someone was in dire trouble either in the swamp or at its edge. As if to warn me, my mind's eye suddenly presented me with the image of what I had come to call "the face at the window." I hesitated, but not for long. Whether someone were in peril or not, my clear duty was to investigate that mysterious cry. I drew my pistol and began cautiously to descend the hill-side.

The wisps of fog seemed to reach up for me as I made my way downward. Soon I was surrounded by the cloying moisture, and the extent of my vision was materially cut down. The bushes around me shimmered vaguely, like ghost-plants. I stopped and listened. It was well that I did, for to my right and a little below me I heard a rustle of the dead leaves that littered the ground. To my horror, the ugly head of a large snake slid out from round a bush not six feet from me. It was a copperhead. It continued right on by me, apparently not detecting my presence at all. Its passing set up a chill within me that spread throughout my entire body.

Suddenly it occurred to me that perhaps my meeting with the snake was not purely an accident. By the way it had whipped by me, it was plainly aroused. Its presence there, together with the cry I had heard, formed an unpleasant association. Keeping a wary eye on the ground, I set off in the direction the snake had come from. Before I had gone very far, my steps were arrested by the curious behavior of the trunk of a small dogwood tree. It seemed to be jerking and had assumed an elliptical course. I glanced sharply up at its branches, and my mouth dropped open. With his hands clasping the thin trunk and his legs wrapped securely around it, the figure of a man hung like a monkey from the bowed tree-top. Peering down at me

in an agony of suspense was the gleaming white face of
Gerald Furness.

"Hello!" I cried. "What have we here, a jail-bird up a tree?"

A look of reproach came into Furness's eyes, but he
made no comment.

"Hop down out of there!" I commanded. "And use your
head, Furness; this pistol happens to be loaded, and I'm a
good shot!"

"There's a snake down there," protested Furness tremu-
lously. "I nearly stepped on it! I just had time to leap into
this tree."

"The snake is gone," I said. "What are you doing
around here, anyway? I thought you'd shaken the dust of
this countryside long ago."

Furness wrapped his legs more securely around the tree
and said nothing.

"Come down," I said quietly, "or I'll put a bullet into
that part of you which, as you hang there, is nearest the
ground."

Furness quickly obeyed. He dropped down beside me,
nervously eying the pistol in my hand. Then he glanced
fearfully at the ground.

"Your snake has gone away," I said. "Don't worry about
any more of them. If we see any more, I'll shoot their eyes
out—I'm that good with a pistol. Now, then, you should
be able to find your way to the colonel's. I'll just follow to
see that you don't get lost."

With a last nervous glance at the pistol, Furness started
to make his way up the hill-side. We climbed out of the
fog and were soon on the road. Resignedly Furness turned
his steps in the direction of the house where a few days
before he had been a respected guest.

"What ever brought you back here?" I asked as I trudged
along behind him.

Furness maintained a haughty silence in spite of my efforts to pump him. I marched him into the front hall almost into the arms of Captain Bartlett. The captain, unacquainted with Furness, looked askance when he saw me covering the man with a pistol.

"Ye gods, a hold-up in broad daylight!" he exclaimed. "What are you doing with the artillery at the ready, Clark?"

"This," I said, "is Gerald Furness, come back to look over his old haunts." Then I raised my voice. "Hand," I called, "Hand, come out here and see the fish I've caught."

Everyone heard my call. The colonel, Patty, and Dick came out of the living-room, and Hand came out of the closet. Furness glanced apprehensively about and then dropped his head. Patty gave a little gasp, and her face turned deathly pale. Dick hastened to assure her that Furness's fangs, if he ever had any, had been drawn.

"Bring him into the library," commanded Hand, turning his back upon Furness. Dick took Patty back into the living-room. The rest of us escorted our prisoner into the library. Furness seemed to cower as Hand turned to him.

"Come, now, speak up!" commanded Hand roughly.

"I don't know what you mean," protested Furness weakly.

"Yes you do. I know all about you, Furness. You killed Decker!"

"No! no! I didn't, I tell you! I didn't!"

"Do you know what it means to die in the electric chair, Furness?" asked Hand grimly. "It's a pretty hard way to go out. Perhaps you can save yourself from it if you want to speak up. If not—well, it's not my funeral, you know."

"I can't! I can't!" wailed Furness. "I'd tell you everything if I could! Take me away from here! Take me to jail!"

"No; you're going to stay right here," said Hand, his steady eyes boring straight at Furness. "I think I can use you, my friend."

"I won't stay here!" screamed Furness. "I demand my rights! If I'm under arrest, you've got to take me to jail. I won't stay here!"

"Oh, yes, you will," retorted Hand, turning his back on the wretch. "We'll get a pair of handcuffs and chain you in the cellar. You'll be safe enough there tonight. In the morning perhaps you'll be ready to talk."

Furness's eyes bulged. He wet his dry lips and gulped once or twice.

Hand walked into the den and telephoned Withers. Then, after cautioning me to keep Furness covered, he went back into the hall closet. Five minutes later we heard the policeman's motor cycle stop in front of the house. Hand evidently heard it in the closet, for he came out and opened the door for Withers. They talked for a moment at the door; then they both strode into the library.

"Come on, Furness," said Hand, "we're going to put you into another cell. I don't think you'll get out of this one, either!"

Hand and Withers practically dragged Furness from the room. The rest of us followed them as they took the prisoner out through the kitchen and down the cellar stairs. Here Furness commenced to fight. He screamed, kicked, and tried to bite. Hand and Withers, inexorable, carried him over to the tool-room.

"That's the room where we found Buckley's body," I whispered to the captain as we crept up to the door and peered in. Withers was handcuffing Furness to a water-pipe. The miserable man leaned up against the wall, closed his eyes, and shuddered. Withers and Hand walked out of the tool-room, and my friend closed the door and locked it. As we walked away, there was one last despairing wail from the tool-room—then silence.

"Why don't you take him to the county jail?" I asked Hand.

"Because I think we'll need him here," was all he would say.

"By Jove! This seems rather brutal to me," said the captain. "That fellow is in mortal terror."

"Do you know why?" asked Hand as we made our way back to the hall.

"No, I must say I don't," admitted the captain.

"Well, I'm not positive yet, but I think I have a pretty fair idea," said Hand. "I'm not imprisoning him down there because I want to be cruel—that's senseless. What I'm doing to him may save some of our lives."

He went back into the closet, leaving us to ponder his last remark. I had to admit that I cared little for what he did to Furness if by doing it he brought security back to its place in the colonel's house.

16

RESURRECTION

We managed to induce Christopher Hand to come out of the closet long enough to have dinner with us. The meal started off in anything but an enjoyable manner. Everybody but the captain was preoccupied, and Patty was very nervous. It was just not possible for Captain Bartlett to allow such an atmosphere to persist. He set to work to make fun of us all, and before long we were in a lighter mood. Everybody did what he could to cheer Patty up. I regretted having brought Furness back to the house at all, for I put him down as the cause of Patty's ill-concealed uneasiness.

After dinner we all split up. Hand went back to work. The colonel escorted Patty and Dick upstairs to show them some souvenirs he had brought back with him from his native town out West. The captain and I took a turn about the grounds. Once again we stopped out by the road. The fog on the swamp shimmered whitely through the darkness. Somehow that fog seemed a bad omen. It had the appearance of the haunt of all evil.

"Christopher Hand is a pretty neat plastic surgeon," commented the captain as we returned to the house. "I inspected that face he's making just before dinner. Those features he's already completed are perfect. He should have been a sculptor."

"But he is," I said. "He's exhibited very creditably, too."

"That accounts for it, then," he said. "But I'm a good bit skeptical about the success of this idea of his. It seems impossible."

The captain left me to go up to his room, and I joined Hand in the hall closet. At last he was making rapid strides. For nearly twenty-four hours he had toiled over the thing; now the finishing touches were at hand. The nose and lips had miraculously appeared. When I entered, he was working on the eyelids.

With the blade of his knife he spread a thin coating of clay over a third of the upper surface of the glass eye. Cunningly he worked the delicate folds of the flesh. When he was satisfied with the job, he stepped back and asked my opinion of the lids.

"I don't know," I slowly replied, critically scrutinizing the region about the eyes. "Somehow they don't look quite natural."

"Of course not," he chuckled. "I haven't supplied the eyebrows yet, and the eyelids have no lashes. That is the next operation."

He selected several strands of black hair. With the scissors of his remarkable pocket-knife, he cut them into sections about three eighths of an inch in length. Then picking up the small tweezers from his little tool-kit, he commenced sticking the hairs into the clay over the upper curve of the eye-socket.

"Not too bushy and not too thick; yet not too sparse and not too thin for an Italian's eyebrows," he remarked.

The work was meticulous, but I was so fascinated by it that the eyebrow was completed in seemingly short order. When its mate had been added, we stepped back once again to inspect the result. Hand, after regarding his work thoughtfully for a moment, nodded his head and returned to his chair. The eyelashes were next. He thrust each individual hair into place with the greatest of care. The lashes in the lower lids he made much shorter than those in the upper, and he placed them farther apart. At last he was finished—or I thought he was. He laid down the tweezers and, picking up the scissors commenced to trim the eyebrows. When he had finished his clipping, he ran the tip of his index-finger lightly over the eyebrows until they were neat and trim. With that the operation was finished.

"Now," sighed Hand, "nothing left to do but put the hair on his head. That will not be so tedious as you are probably thinking it will, Clark. We'll glue that hair on. Not much care is necessary in applying the hair, because we must give him a hair-trim afterwards, anyway."

"By Jove, he was rather a handsome chap if that is really the way he looked in life," I said. "His jaw is weak, to be sure, but there is something quite dashing about him. But see here, this just occurs to me. How do you know he didn't wear a mustache?"

"I don't," replied Hand with a shrug. "His features we left to the clay, the hair and eyes we left to the future, the beard and mustache we shall leave to chance. There are a great many more men who go clean-shaven than who affect a mustache or beard. The law of averages is on our side if we leave the face unadorned."

He commenced painting the back of the head with paste. He painted a small section behind the left ear and then quickly applied the hair to it. Then he repeated the process farther over, continuing until he had the whole back of the head covered from ear to ear. Then he pasted hair to the head over the ears and slightly to the front of them. He also gave the chap a little hair in his nostrils.

"We'll just give that glue a chance to set, Clark," he said, when the job was done. "Looks rather shaggy, doesn't he? Trim him up in a minute."

For this work he had a larger pair of shears than those in the knife. He also produced a comb. The closet was turned into a tonsorial parlor. Before long our fellow had as fine a hair-cut as one could wish for.

"Well, what do you think of it, Clark?" he asked, stepping back like a barber with his shears and comb in his hands. "Look natural?"

"Well," I averred regretfully, "it doesn't look quite so natural as I hoped it would."

"Not surprising," said Hand briskly. "I haven't given him his complexion yet. We've got to put the bloom to his cheek that I mentioned."

He sat down again and grasped a cup of water resting on the bench. Then he went to work with the water-color brush.

"Dark complexion for an Italian," he said. "Good red lips, though."

At last he laid the brush down with an air of finality. He skipped to his feet and bounced back to where I was standing. Rarely had I seen him so boyishly enthusiastic. His eyes sparkled. There was a broad grin on his face, and he nudged me playfully in the ribs.

"Not bad, eh, Clark?" he chuckled. "What do you say, my boy?"

"It's one of the most remarkable things I ever saw," I replied with feeling. "If that head stood on a body, I'd say it was alive! Now what are you going to do?"

"Assuming Geering Middleton identifies him as Gonzalos, that fellow's murderer is as good as found."

"Well, I hope he identifies him, then."

"So do I, especially since it also means the condemnation of the murderer of Joseph Decker and Thomas Buckley. It will clear up another case, too—one that I thought I had failed on. But the first thing we are going to do is to try a little experiment. Here, we've got to have something to cover up that bald pate. Ah, this cap is just the thing! Suppose it belongs to the colonel, but he won't mind."

He snatched the cap off a hook and carefully placed it on the head. "Just fits!" he exclaimed delightedly. "Now then, Clark, you have your flashlight? Good. We are going to visit our prisoner below stairs. I have an idea he knew this fellow in real life. We'll give him a chance to look upon his features again. Won't prove anything if he doesn't recognize him, and quite a lot if he does.

"Now, the cellar is pitch-dark. We'll carry this head downstairs and take it into the tool-room. We'll not speak a word, and we'll show no lights. When you hear me grunt, turn your flashlight on Furness. At the same time I'll turn mine on the face. He'll be able to see the impassive face of the dead man, and we'll be able to see his face, which I hope won't be so impassive. Perhaps he'll betray himself. Come on—let's go."

Hand allowed me to precede him into the hall. He carried the head by thrusting his hand up into the cavity of the skull. He shielded the object from the others, who were at work in the living-room, by holding it in front of him as we turned our backs and marched through the dining-room.

As we descended the cellar stairs, my thoughts turned—not for the first time that evening—to Gerald Furness. It was well for him that he did not know the room that was his prison had so recently been a sepulcher. Or did he know it? At any rate, I felt like a gloomy old doomsman prowling round the subterranean torture chambers of a medieval castle. I placed my hand on my friend's shoulder. Hand's catlike instinct to get about in the dark led us to the door of the tool-room. I heard the key turn in the lock, and Hand stepped forward. As we stopped inside the door, I heard the breath of the prisoner hissing through his teeth.

I might as well have been blind for all the use my eyes were to me in that blackness. From my recollection of the room I calculated the approximate position where Furness stood before me. I directed my flashlight accordingly and waited for the signal. Then I heard Hand grunt.

My light-beam leaped forth, cutting a swath through the darkness. It showed us Furness cowering against the wall as if he had expected his death-blow from the dark. At the same instant the head seemed to illuminate itself with its own light. The glass eyes, seemingly come to life, gazed steadily at the terror-stricken man chained in the corner.

At sight of the apparition Furness's eyes narrowed. To my astonishment some of the terror left them. His lips moved over a single word. "Angelo?" he said, questioningly.

"Turn on the light, Clark," Hand briskly ordered.

I shifted my light from Furness to find the electric light bulb, which I remembered hung from the ceiling by a cord. I reached up and turned it on, flooding the room with light.

"Good God! Where's his body?" I heard Furness hoarsely exclaim. "What have you done? Is he dead?"

"Yes, indeed," said Hand, holding up the head and looking at it. "All he needs, though, is a body, and you'd never know it. Now, then, Furness, are you ready to talk? First let me tell you that if you help me, I am disposed to help you. I can do a lot for you, Furness, if you'll help me."

"I can't, I can't, I tell you!" sobbed Furness. "I'd take your offer in a minute if I could, but I tell you I can't. It would be worth my life!"

"It may be worth your life if you don't," said Hand grimly.

Furness groaned. "I dare not help you, and I dare not help myself!" he said miserably.

"I think I know what's holding your tongue," said Hand. "Perhaps you will be in a better position to speak very shortly. For the present you can help me, I think, without putting yourself in danger. If you will, I promise you I will remember it."

"What is it?" asked Furness suspiciously.

"You seemed to recognize this fellow," said Hand, indicating the head. "You spoke a name, Angelo, when you saw it."

Furness gazed fixedly at the face. "I don't know whether I recognize it or not," he said at length. "I thought I did at first, and it still looks like—like a man I once knew."

"Does it look very much like him?"

"There's a resemblance. It isn't his face, but there's something about it that almost makes me think it is."

"This face is made of clay," explained Hand. "I constructed it on a skull which I found. Furness, I think that skull is your friend Angelo's. I want you to help me make these features more exactly as Angelo's were. If you do, as I said before, I'll help you."

The prisoner thought the proposal over carefully. Finally he raised his eyes to Hand. "All right," he agreed. "I know you, Mr. Hand—I know you better than you think I do. If you say you'll do something for me if I do something for you, I know you mean it. What do you want me to do?"

"What do you suggest my doing to alter this face correctly?"

"Well, in the first place, you made him too good-looking. He had a perpetual sneer on his lips. His mouth was drawn upward—let's see—on the right side. It was due to a cut he once got on his face, I guess. The scar of it extended from his mouth right across his cheek to his eye."

"Clark, go up to the closet," ordered Hand briskly. "Get the clay and the paint material. We'll alter this face right here."

When I returned with the material, he had taken a box into the tool-room. It stood on end, and on top of it rested the head. Under Furness's directions he was remodeling the mouth. With the blade of his knife he fashioned the scar on the right cheek.

Furness seemed to be getting into the spirit of the thing. He got quite excited giving Hand directions. Finally he agreed the mouth and scar were exact duplicates of those possessed by his friend Angelo.

"Let me see," he mused, "that nose isn't right. I think it had a crook in it. Can you bend the center of it over to the left a little?"

Hand's fingers got busy with the nose. He altered it until it suited Furness's critical eye. Then Furness became pensive once more. He thoughtfully pulled his lip as he gazed at the face.

"I have it!" he suddenly exclaimed. "He's too wide awake. His eyelids drooped more than you have them there—about half open."

Once again I was sent upstairs to the closet, this time to get the tweezers. In order to droop the eyelids, Hand had to withdraw the eyelashes and then set them in again. Finally that job was completed.

"Anything else?" inquired Hand, straightening from the task.

"He's a dead ringer for Angelo," declared Furness, with more truth than perhaps he thought.

"How about the hair?" asked Hand.

"He was a young chap—no more than thirty, but Angelo was bald."

When Hand removed the cap, Furness's eyes popped open in astonishment. Angelo was bald!

"Do you think he's too fat or too thin?" asked Hand.

"I'd say he's about right," replied Furness. "I swear, Mr. Hand, Angelo's spirit must have stood beside you when you made that face!"

"Maybe," said Hand with a smile, "but I noticed his bones were small. That gave me the idea that nature didn't intend him to be fat. Now, we've practically ruined our paint job. I'll just have to touch him up again. How is that complexion I gave him?"

"I think he was a little darker if anything," said Furness. "The shade you have him now is all right, though."

Hand busied himself with the paint-brush until he had repaired the damage wrought by altering the features. Then he turned to Furness. "We'll have to go, Furness," he said. "Should you rather have the light on or off?"

"Don't leave me alone here any more!" pleaded Furness with a return of his terror. "I can't stand it! Something may happen to me—something you know nothing about!"

"I think I do know something about it," disagreed Hand. "You'll have to stay here for a while, at least. It may not be long. How about the light?"

"Turn it off," said Furness in a hoarse whisper.

I felt rather heartless going off and leaving the poor fellow like that. I followed Hand, however, who led me quickly upstairs. As we entered the dining-room, I saw that the others were walking out into the hall. Hand dodged off into the shadows of the dining-room, motioning for me to go out to the hall.

"Going to bed?" I asked as I stepped out of the dining-room.

"It's nearly eleven," said Colonel Decker. "How long are you fellows going to keep at it? Say, I want to see that—I want to talk to you before I turn in. Patty, aren't you going to kiss me good-night?" he demanded of his daughter, who had started up the stairs.

Patty turned with a bright smile. She came down two or three steps and kissed her father.

"Good-night, dear," she said, patting him affectionately on the shoulder. "Come right to bed now, you need rest."

No sooner had Patty disappeared when Hand came out of the dining-room carrying the head. The others were astonished when they saw it. Hand explained the help he had received from Furness; whereupon the captain suggested that we let the man go as a reward. As usual, nobody took him seriously.

I had been elected to take the first watch in the library again. We said good-night to the others, and they went off to bed.

"Now then, Clark," said Hand briskly when we were alone, "we've got more work to do. Go get a suit of your pyjamas, your bedroom slippers, and your bathrobe. While you're there, bring the blankets off your bed and your pillow. Hurry up."

As usual, I was left in complete darkness concerning my mission. Neither was it explained how I was going to sleep with no blankets and no pillow. When I returned with the incongruous assortment, Hand was in the library. The head rested on the seat of a chair. My friend was pacing up and down with the very stick in his hands that I had been struck down with on the Ridge Road.

"Ah, there you are!" he exclaimed. "Just button that pyjama coat up around the pillow. I'll attend to the trousers first, and then fix up the sleeves of the coat when you're through with that."

While I buttoned the pillow up in the pyjama coat, he stuffed the trousers with the blankets. He did it rather carefully so that the stuffed appearance was as little noticeable as possible. When he had finished, he tied the trousers to the lower part of the pillow, joining the upper and lower parts of the dummy.

"What shall we stuff the sleeves with?" he mused when that was done. "Your shirts! Of course! You always carry a bale of them with you. Go get them."

My shirts were sacrificed. He set the dummy in a chair, which he moved into a far corner of the room from the door.

"That's it; just the place," he affirmed, glancing round the room. "Hold him, Clark, while I put your bathrobe on him."

I held the dummy as Hand carefully stuffed it into my bathrobe. When this was done, he carefully put it back into its sitting posture in the chair. He folded the arms so that the extremities where the hands should have been were hidden from view. Then he placed the slippers at the end of the trouser legs. The figure was rather startling, sitting there very lifelike, but with no head.

And then the bludgeon that had laid me out on the Ridge Road was brought into requisition once more in that strange affair. Hand stuck the smaller end into the neck of the dummy. The heavier end protruded eight or ten inches above the collar of the pyjamas. It provided a ludicrous head-piece for our fellow.

But then Hand picked up the head of Angelo. He placed it on the stick in the same manner as one would put an inverted bucket on a pole. It bobbed up and down for a moment with a disquieting motion.

"I selected your pyjamas, Clark," he said, fumbling at the neck of the dummy, "because they have ornate, turn-over collars. We can turn them up like this, you see, and conceal the fact that this fellow has nothing but a stick for a neck."

I was speechless. Even though I knew it to be so, I could scarcely believe that the figure sitting in the chair did not live. The face suddenly appeared menacing, vengeful. The glassy eyes stared accusingly at me, as if demanding retribution. I shook myself as if to cast off an evil spell.

"There he is," said Hand, "just as he was the last night of his life."

"I'm not superstitious," I said, as stoutly as I could, "but I'm hanged if I can stand here and look at that thing!"

Hand was pondering. Suddenly he snapped his fingers.

"I have it!" he exclaimed. "Did you notice how that head bobbed on the stick? Go get me that bachelor's sewing-kit of yours."

When I returned with it, he selected a spool of black thread. He had brought the paste in from the hall closet. With it he stuck one end of the thread to the inside of the skull, near the base at the back. He unwound the thread until he was able to set the spool on the floor behind the chair. Then he quickly left the room.

He returned a moment later with a large folding screen under his arm. This, an ornate Japanese affair, had stood in a corner of the hall. He unfolded it and set it up before the dummy, completely obscuring it from view. Now he took another spool of thread from my sewing-kit. This he tied to an upper protrusion on the screen. He also set that spool on the floor, at the base of the screen.

"Now," he sighed, "everything is ready. Through your fortunate capture of Furness, Mr. Middleton's absence has not embarrassed us. When Dick relieves you, tell him to stay away from this screen. Have him tell the same to Captain Bartlett. And now, Clark, I am going to bed."

"The window!" I gasped, suddenly thinking of the face I had seen through it the night before. Then I saw that Hand had drawn the heavy velvet curtain over it.

"No, Clark," he said, with a smile, "we alone have seen this fellow come to life."

17

SETTING THE TRAP

In spite of my doubts about it the evening before, I slept well that night. I found, when I went to bed after being relieved by Dick, that Hand had foraged for me. From somewhere he had supplied me with a pair of blankets and a pillow.

We rose quite late. Even so, I should have slept longer had Hand not roused me. He stood beside the bed, smiling down at me.

"Better get up, Clark," he said. "We'll have to hurry as it is to catch the ten-forty train from Barkersville."

We were the last to have breakfast in the now cheerless dining-room. Colonel Decker hung about, trying to pry some information from my friend. All he got was another instruction.

"Get hold of Withers," ordered Hand. "Furness is still locked up downstairs. Better get him some food. Then have Withers pack him off to the county penitentiary. You'll stay at the Colton while you're in the city, of course. You may look for me any time, Colonel. Ha, there is MacClin-tock coming round. Come on, Clark; we'll just have time to catch that train."

Everybody stood on the steps and called good-by to us. MacClintock made good time to Barkersville. As we were getting out at the station, Hand leaned forward and spoke to the driver.

"You have everything straight, MacClintock?"

"Yes, sirr."

"Your orders are most important."

"I'll carry them oot, sirr."

"Good-by, then, MacClintock. Never mind; we'll carry the bags."

We entered the station, and Hand marched up to the ticket window. He purchased two one-way fares to New York. The ticket agent, a sharp-faced old fellow, eyed us over his spectacles as we went out to the platform. There we were the cynosures of four or five chaps, typical of those always to be found around a country railroad station at train time.

We had not long to wait for the train. I had thought that once we got started, Hand would open up to me. Instead he buried his chin in his hand, rested his elbow on the windowsill, and stared blankly at the passing scenery. I contented myself with trying to puzzle out what lay in store for me.

The train stopped at Basking Valley and Mine Hill. Still Hand did not budge. At length it whistled and slowed down for the next station. Hand tapped me on the shoulder.

"Come on, Clark," he said, rising from the seat.

"Aren't we—"

"We'll have to hurry; these trains don't stop for long."

We got our bags and scrambled off, alighting before the train had come to a full stop. Then I noticed that Hand, whom I had followed, had got off the wrong side. Before us, at the side of the track, was some sort of dilapidated mill, quite evidently in disuse. On the other side of the train, all but its roof obscured by it, was the station. I quickly followed Hand, who had scurried into the old mill.

My friend picked his way over the gaping holes in the floor to the other side, where much of the wall had collapsed outward. There he leaped to the ground, and I followed suit. A small stream ran alongside the mill. This we precariously crossed on the tumbled rocks of a broken dam. On the other side we plunged into thick bushes. The train was just pulling out of the station.

"I should like to know," I said, catching up with Hand, "where on earth we are going."

"Back to Mill Ridge," he grinned.

"Are we going to walk?"

"No, indeed," he replied, and then plunged on into the bushes.

After a while we came out upon a lane. A short way on stood an automobile, a small, enclosed delivery car. On the front seat sat a bored individual, one whom I recognized on sight. It was Blanchard, the janitor of our rooming-house. This was not the first time that Hand had found him useful during an investigation. He was smoking a pipe, which he now removed from his mouth while he peered at us. Then he replaced it and sat sucking meditatively on it as we approached him.

"Well, Blanchard," said Hand, "right on the dot."

"I been cruisin' around this state all mornin', wastin' time," replied Blanchard. "I got over to Newark early, but they had this thing already waitin' for me to take out. You got a pull with that guy, all right. I decided I might as well take a drive. But say, this here engine's got one gosh awful knock into it."

"It would seem that it goes, and that's all that's necessary," responded Hand. "Get in, Clark."

I started to climb up beside Blanchard, but Hand stopped me.

"Not there; get in the back."

"In the back!"

Stanley Hart Page

"Yes, both of us. Our return to Mill Ridge is going to be very privately accomplished. Start your motor, Blanchard. I'll tell you where to go."

I have had more comfortable rides than the one back to Mill Ridge. We sat on our bags and bounced and jounced over the rough roads. Hand's knowledge of those back roads was nothing short of astounding.

"I didn't know you were familiar with this country," I said.

"I wasn't, either, a short time ago," he replied. "When I went into New York the other day, I had myself driven back. Before I dismissed the car, I had the driver cover these roads pretty thoroughly. When you are after somebody, it's not a bad idea to know the lay of the land."

There was a little square hole in the front of our compartment. Hand kept looking through it, keeping tabs on where we were going. But I had utterly no idea where we were proceeding. Finally, however, he gave the order for Blanchard to stop.

There was even something unusual about the way this order was carried out. The motor spluttered and died while the car was still in gear. Blanchard guided it over to the side of the road and stopped.

"How was that?" he inquired over his shoulder.

"Good," commended Hand. "Now get out and fuss with it. Look around sharply, Blanchard. See, if you can, whether anyone is in the bushes."

Hand kept looking through the little square hole. Finally he left it and went briskly to the rear of the compartment.

"All right, Clark," he muttered. "Quick, now, across the road and into the bushes."

He leaped down and scurried across the road. In a trice both of us were out of sight in thick bushes. We could still hear Blanchard fussing around the motor.

For a moment I could not place myself; then my surroundings took on a more familiar look. Still, all of New
Jersey, or at least that part of it, looks pretty much alike
when you get yourself into its bushes. Hand, crouched
over, was making his way toward a particularly heavy
clump. I followed him into it and, guided by his example,
squatted down on my haunches.

"Where are we?" I whispered.

Hand extended his arm and pointed ahead with his
index-finger.

"There is Mrs. Compstock's mail-box," he said.

"Mail-box?"

"Yes, the stump where she put that note, you remember."

"Ah, then we are on the hill-side down the lane from
the colonel's."

"Yes, and before you ask, I'll tell you what we are going
to do. We are going to wait, Clark, and we are going to
wait as quietly as we know how. Not a sound, and keep a
bridle on your inquisitive nature, my boy. We may be here
for some time."

Suddenly Blanchard started the delivery truck. A moment later he drove off. The day was just as damp as the
one preceding it. Already I felt a little chilly. I could smell
the fog on the swamp below us, and the skies above were
gray and cheerless. It was not the first time I had lain in
ambush, but I could see that it was going to be one of the
worst. At last I risked a whisper.

"Do you think there's another note in the stump?"

"No; I know there isn't. I felt in it as we passed it."

That information had to do me. I supposed that we
were waiting for Mrs. Compstock to visit the stump again,
to place in it another of her unintelligible notes.

We had arrived at the thicket shortly before twelve.
Even though my breakfast had been late, as time wore on,

I imagine I acquired that lean and hungry look that Shakespeare wrote of. My friend, catching my eye, smiled and thrust his hand into his coat pocket. When he withdrew it, he held an enticing-looking package. Unwrapping it, he handed me a husky meat sandwich. After I had devoured it, he handed me another. Then he wrapped the package up and replaced it in his pocket. He took nothing, although there remained two more sandwiches. I divined from that that our wait had only begun, even though it was past three o'clock.

Several cars went by during the afternoon. But later, when I was wondering whether the outcome of my crouching on the damp ground would be pneumonia or rheumatism, I heard another, coming from the direction of the colonel's house. As it passed above us, its horn sounded two short blasts. Hand looked at the watch on his wrist. I glanced at it and saw that it was ten minutes after five.

"There they go," breathed Hand. "That was MacClintock; he didn't forget to toot. So far our watch has been uneventful, Clark, but we may see something now."

But we did not. The daylight faded and quickly left altogether. Even so, there we continued to sit. I thought bitterly of the long, uncomfortable hours that we had wasted. And then I heard another car approaching from the direction of the Ridge Road. Again I felt my pulse beat with excitement, as I had at the approach of every car. But I expected the machine to go right by, as the others had, leaving me more disheartened than ever. Soon I could see its lights filtering faintly through the underbrush.

Then, nearly above us, it stopped!

I scarcely breathed. Straining my ears to catch every sound, I was soon aware that someone had alighted. A moment later we could hear the bushes being parted, and someone making his way through them. Whoever it was did not linger very long. In the space of three minutes the car drove off. Not until the last faint sounds it made had died away did Hand stir. Then he was off silently and swiftly, signaling me with the familiar pressure of his fingers to follow him.

Holding my hand on his shoulder as a guide, I followed Hand. Somehow, in the blackness, he found the stump. He felt around it; then I heard him sigh with satisfaction.

"Stand up close to me, Clark," he whispered. "That's it, spread your coat out."

He used a faint little electric torch. Glancing down, I saw that he was directing it on a note in the same handwriting as the first. It was a short note, and although I was looking at it from the wrong direction, I could read it. This is what it said:

"It seems all fog will clear. If you begin I will search for you immediately."

"Quick, Clark," said Hand, "hold this light."

Holding the note on the flat of his cigarette-case, he took out a pencil and commenced to add to it. As he worked, I saw that he was exactly imitating the hand that had already written on the paper. Although I knew him to be a good forger, I was amazed at his cleverness under those circumstances. I was equally amazed at what he wrote. It was this:

"I will look for you first. Don't go in some other library."

He quickly folded it, at the same time ordering me to extinguish the light. Vaguely I could see him replace the note in the stump; then he whispered again.

"Up to the road, Clark," he said. "No noise, but be quick about it."

Up on the road he hesitated, but then he struck out in the direction of the colonel's house.

"I'd like to see whether the tracks of Mrs. Compstock's car are fresh in that dust," he said. "But I dare not show a light."

"What do we do now?" I asked, using the same low tone of voice as he had.

"I think my trap is set, Clark," he replied. "Now we must go watch over it and, if we get the chance, spring it!"

18

DENOUEMENT

There is something about Christopher Hand that he cannot conceal from me. That is a certain air of excitement when he is bringing a case to a close. Although his features do not alter in the slightest, and his actions remain as cool and steady as ever, an air of tension seems to emanate from him. I could feel it as I walked in the darkness by his side.

Hand turned in before we came to the colonel's drive. Under the overhanging boughs of the trees, we skirted the lawn to the back. We approached the dark hulk of the garage and moved along its side. Before advancing round to the back of the garage, Hand stopped and gave a low whistle. To my astonishment, it was answered from behind the garage. Immediately we went round the corner.

"Christopher!"

Although the voice was low-pitched, I recognized it as Colonel Decker's. Several vague forms moved in the darkness before us.

"Yes," replied Hand, "I see that MacClintock has carried out his orders admirably. Patty and Dick went on to New York?"

"They did," replied the colonel. "In my car. Captain Bartlett and I returned in a machine that MacClintock hired in Summit. This is the first time," he added, with some asperity, "that I have ever been called upon to take orders from MacClintock, but that is what I've been doing ever since we left the house to drive to New York!"

"'Tis not my fault, sirr," broke in MacClintock's voice. "I was carrying oot ma orrderrs that Misterr Hand—"

"Sorry, Colonel," interrupted Hand, speaking cautiously, "but I wanted you to act perfectly naturally; I didn't dare let you in on too much. Mrs. Compstock was there to see you off, I hope."

"Yes, she was."

"That worked out well, then. Fortune has smiled on us in another way, besides. I haven't time to tell you about that now."

"You never tell us anything," grumbled the colonel.

"I'll tell you everything very soon, I think," responded Hand. "Did you hide that car all right, MacClintock?"

"I did, sirr. I left it in the abandoned rroad I was telling ye aboot at the top of the rridge. Then I brought the colonel and the captain doon thrrough the woods."

"That's good. How long have you been here?"

"Since just after dark!" snorted the colonel.

"Is Withers here?" asked Hand.

"Yes," replied the voice of the policeman. "I come up in here just as soon as it got dark."

"All right, then," said Hand, "I guess we're ready. We are going into the house through the den, but we are going to sneak it. No lights and no noise, but go swiftly. All right, let's go."

The night was so dark that caution was really unnecessary. But we did move across the velvety lawn without a sound. We gathered in a dark knot at the door of the den while Hand unlocked it with a key the colonel passed to him. Then we filed silently inside and stood in the darkness of the den as Hand relocked the door.

"Now," said Hand swiftly, "three of us are going into the library, and the three others are going to be stationed in the living-room. Withers, you and the captain and MacClintock go into the living-room. Hide behind the chairs. Don't move; not even if the house is broken into, which is what I expect to happen. If we have any intruders, I think they will go right into the library. I think they are going to get a surprise in there. If they do, you'll hear it. That is the time for you to close in on them. I know MacClintock and Withers are armed; are you, Captain?"

"I have my service automatic," replied Captain Bartlett.

"Good," said Hand. "Come on, Colonel, you and Clark and I are going into the library. Quiet, now, everybody!"

The other three drifted away into the gloom of the hall. The colonel and I followed cautiously after Hand into the library. My friend took us each by the arm and led us over to the side by the window. I felt myself stumbling into a large leather couch that stood there.

"Get behind that couch," ordered Hand. "Stay out of sight until I switch on the lights overhead. Remember, don't stir until I switch on the overhead lights!"

The colonel and I situated ourselves kneeling behind the couch. We could just hear Hand moving about the room. Once or twice I heard a sort of clinking noise, like two pieces of metal hitting together. After a while everything was silent.

The luminous dial of my wrist watch informed me that an hour had passed since we had entered the library. I was getting cramped. The colonel, whose bones were older than mine, shifted his position.

How he got into the room I could not say, but a man's voice, low and harsh, broke the stillness of the library. The voice spoke with a sibilant, slurring pronunciation that made the blood tingle in my veins. Now I could not even hear the colonel breathing.

"This here's the library, ain't it, Pete?" it said. "Come on, let's have a light. Easy, now."

An electric torch was snapped on. It shifted quickly about.

"All right," said the voice, "let's get goin' wit' the crowbars. You two guys work on the walls. Me, I'm gonna have a crack at the floor. Far's I know that ain't been tried yet."

"How about lights?" asked a guttural, growling voice.

"Yeah," said another voice, "s'pose the lights is off?"

"Use yer own lights," growled the first fellow. "The house lights is off, like as not. Clara knows her onions, but just the same I ain't takin' no chances. Come on, get to work!"

"Hello, Granley," said a new voice abruptly.

Although I could see no part of the room except the corner where I crouched, I could tell that consternation had laid hold of the house-breakers. One of them dropped something heavy on the rug, and we could hear their quick movements as they swung about to face the newcomer. The new voice was harsh and metallic.

"The chief!" I heard one of them breathe.

"Still at it, eh?" went on the latest voice. "You fellows are fools, every one of you! You're not only wasting your time, but you're running a risky game, besides. Why don't you go out and find Zechalli and do us all some good?"

"Stow it, chief," said the slurring voice. "We think you croaked Zechalli. I know damned well you croaked Joe Decker, and you give it to Muth, too, I'll bet a pretty penny. I know you croaked Joe, because I seen ya do it! I was—"

"Shut up!" snarled the chief. "Get out of here, all three of you. Use your head, will you, Granley?"

Evidently the three men were afraid of the chief. For a full minute there was silence.

"Well, how about it, Granley?" snapped the chief.

"All right," was the muttered reply. "All right for now, chief. But somethin' better show up soon, I'm tellin' ya. I still think them jools is here, an' if—"

"You do, do you?" rasped the chief. "You always did think wrong, Granley. You let me do the thinking. Zechalli has the jewels. Now clear out! I've never deceived you yet, and I tell you Zechalli has the jewels."

All at once there was a terrific crash in the library. I was so startled by it that I bobbed my head up above the couch. The men in the room had all directed their lights over toward the corner whence the sound had come.

The screen had fallen down, revealing the dummy of Angelo sitting in its chair!

Hand, I knew, had pulled the screen over with the thread he had attached to it the night before. But I did not think of that then. In the lap of the dummy lay a heap of flashing, scintillating gems!

"The jools!" gasped one of the men, with almost a sob. "The jools, an' Zechalli had 'em!"

"Put out the lights!" screamed one of them. "Put out the lights, I tell you!"

One of the lights snapped out, and then the other two. But the weird figure in the chair remained as brilliantly illuminated as though it shed its own grotesque light. But I traced the light to its source. It came from behind a portiére beside where I knelt behind the couch. Hand was flashing his own torch on the dummy.

As I glanced back at the dummy, my heart missed a stroke. The weird head was nodding—damningly, accusingly. The eyes in the strong light-beam flashed angrily, and the shadows played on the clay features grotesquely.

A dry, rasping sob came to my ears.

"No! no!" someone shrieked. "I didn't kill you. Stop nodding at me! Oh, my God!"

The shrieking voice moved across the library toward the dummy. A pair of white, clawing outstretched hands came into the light-beam. The arms followed them, slowly, staggeringly. And then, his cheeks and lips turned to putty, stark terror gleaming from his bulging eyes, and his mouth sagging open, the light fell on the face of Geering Middleton!

Why had I not recognized that voice before? It had been too cold and rasping, unlike the polite, well-modulated voice Middleton had used in our company. Then, too, Middleton had been furthest from my thoughts.

His voice was disguised now, also, as he advanced upon that fearful apparition in the chair, disguised by a terror that was strangling the life out of his body.

"You're dead!" he gasped in a tortured voice. "Curse you, Angelo, don't look at me with—"

Middleton lurched toward the chair. Then he halted, swayed on his feet, and fumbled foolishly at his breast. Then, with a hoarse, ravaged shriek, he sprawled in a heap on the floor.

Then the overhead lights flooded the room with brilliance. The three men over by the door were standing in tense, odd attitudes of awe. One I recognized instantly—the face of the window! He was the only one who had his wits about him. He turned and whipped out the door.

The other two stood gazing dumbly, first at the dummy and then at the shapeless heap on the floor that was Geering Middleton. They allowed us to frisk them without offering to struggle. One of them winced when I touched his arm. I felt a bandage under his coat.

"Did you get shot on a rainy night up on the Ridge Road?" I asked him.

He grunted and shook his head in the affirmative. The captain had been right, I had winged my man.

"Here's the only bird that flew out our way," I suddenly heard the captain say. "He's the one with the ugly map. MacClintock—Corporal MacClintock got him."

"You don't mean Corporal MacClintock, Captain," corrected the colonel. "You mean Sergeant MacClintock."

The old Scotsman looked as if he could have fallen on the colonel's neck and kissed him. Instead he thrust out his chest and looked terrifically proud and happy. He, with Withers and the captain, was herding the man with the fearful face back into the library.

Withers's quick eye took in the huddled form over by the seated dummy. He strode over and rolled Middleton over on his back. When the man's face came into view, the policeman fell back a step, his eyes popping. Then he knelt quickly beside the body and placed his hand over the heart. When he looked up, his face was a puzzle.

"He's dead!" he said in a solemn voice.

"Fortunate for him," remarked Hand.

"Yes, fortunate for him," repeated the colonel slowly. "I can't understand it, but he must have been the man. You heard, Withers?"

"Yes, I heard," replied Withers, looking down at the dead face of Middleton, still distorted with the terror that had killed him.

"He was the man, Colonel," said Hand. "Yes, there lies the murderer of your brother, the murderer of that fellow sitting there, of Thomas Buckley, and heaven only knows how many more!"

19

THE CASE

After his astonishment at finding that the dead man was
Middleton had passed, Withers's official attention was
fixed on the jewels reposing in the lap of the dummy. I
was already gazing at them in wonder. There were daz-
zling tiaras and diadems, ablaze with diamonds, rubies,
sapphires, and other immense gems. There were ropes of
pearls, necklaces, jeweled decorations, and a heap of priceless rings. In the center of the flashing heap lay a black
rod about three feet long, a sort of knob on one end of it
encrusted with a fortune in diamonds.

Withers blinked and opened his mouth once or twice
before he found his voice.

"Gee whiz!" he exclaimed. "What are those?"

"The crown jewels of the former principality of Schweizburg," announced Hand sententiously. "These thugs
shot up a New York art gallery where they were on display
for sale and got away with them. I've searched for them
many months. Thought I'd failed. Peculiar, isn't it?"

Next Withers stretched out his hand toward the head
of the weird dummy. His fingers seemed to pick something
out of the air. Then that awe-inspiring head once more
commenced its terrifying nodding. I knew what Withers
held. It was the black thread Hand had attached to the

skull, and with it he had made Angelo accuse his own murderer!

Suddenly Colonel Decker swung purposefully about to face Hand.

"Well, Christopher?" he asked, significantly.

Hand spoke to the fellow with the hideous face.

"Are you Granley?" he asked, and the man, crestfallen, nodded his head. "I thought so. You know more of the murder we're interested in than these other two fellows. You witnessed it."

"Yeah?" mumbled Granley.

"You were standing under the window in the den."

"What makes ya think so?"

"Your footprints were there. They were the same as those you left when you stood under the library window the other night. You've lost part of the heel of your left shoe, my friend. I can prove you were present at, or about the time the murder was committed, you see. If you want to escape being accused of it, you'd better help me prove Middleton guilty."

Granley shifted his feet; then he glanced sharply at Hand. "I guess yer right," he grunted. "I'm ready to string my yarn, if yer ready to listen to it."

"All right, Granley, you'll get your chance to string your yarn, but not in your own way. I'm going to tell you what I know, first. It will be an added inducement to tell the truth, I assure you.

"In the first place, Colonel," began Hand, turning to face his old friend, "I want to apologize for having kept you in the dark so long. This case was an extremely delicate one. I dared not take a chance with it. A thoughtless word or a suspicious glance would have warned Middleton of his danger. I had to keep my opinions to myself—I had no choice.

"I suspected Geering Middleton from the first day I worked on the case. My suspicions were directed to him for two reasons. Neither reason, I must confess, was very strong. The first was Middleton's brand of cigars. He was smoking one, you remember, when he showed us Granley's footprints under the lilac bush. He dropped it when he tripped on the step at the back door. I retrieved it. It was the same brand as the one we found in the ash-tray along with Joseph's. It had been smoked in the same manner, too—hardly any teeth-marks on it. But the brand is not an unusual one, and many men smoke cigars without chewing them.

"Middleton's showing us the footprints threw me off the track. It was a bold move, but Middleton was a bold man. He had to be!

"That was the first reason that I mention. The second was this: Later that day my attention was again called to Middleton. I purloined a blotter at Mrs. Compstock's house. It had been used but once—to blot a check. Of course the writing was reversed on the blotter. When I reflected it in a mirror, I saw the signature was Middleton's. The check had been made out to cash and was for one thousand dollars. Clara Compstock cashed it Saturday in Markstown—I found that out later."

"They worked together, then!" said the colonel heavily.

"It seems so," replied Hand. "Now, I soon became convinced that something of the greatest value lay hidden in this house. I was sure Buckley had lost his life because he was looking for it. I felt sure Joseph's death was a result of the same sort of activity. I was more convinced of it after my investigations in New York. I took Buckley's finger-prints when we got him out of the wall in the tool-room. The New York police have his finger-prints, too. His right name is Muth, but he has a hundred aliases.

Joseph said he had been a waiter in a London hotel, but I
don't think so, Colonel. The two of them were in league—
looking for something in this house. Their search led them
to their deaths."

"That was merely hypothesis," objected the colonel.

"Precisely," admitted Hand. "And the hypothesis called
for a guardian of the treasure, or whatever it was they were
looking for. It also designated that person the murderer.
Once again my thoughts turned to Geering Middleton. He
was a former owner of the house. Perhaps he left something hidden in it. I decided to look him up.

"I knew, of course, Middleton had been one of the most
successful high-class jewelers in New York. I also knew
that the business which he sold when he retired collapsed
soon after. I enlisted the aid of the New York police. We
discovered that several expensive stones purchased at Middleton's could not be traced beyond that establishment.
The trail was well covered—that preliminary investigation
only uncovered fragmentary evidence. But we did gather
enough to convince us that Middleton had a rather mysterious source from which he stocked his store. My hypoth-
eses progressed. I pictured Middleton acquiring precious
stones unlawfully, cutting them, resetting them, and selling them from among his stock at attractive prices. Perhaps he had made a regular business of it. Perhaps he had
his own robber gang to keep his store supplied. If such
were the case, it's no wonder the new owners went under
so quickly. The store couldn't operate honestly."

"Still nothing but hypothesis," pointed out the colonel.

"Not altogether," protested Hand. "I have been in touch
with the New York police since then. They have absolutely
determined that several stones purchased at Middleton's
had been stolen beforehand. Three of them were taken in
hold-ups. How many more there are we don't know. The
New York police had gathered so much evidence that they

were ready to act against Middleton. I persuaded the commissioner to hold off until we had cleared up this murder mystery."

"I begin to think," said Colonel Decker slowly, "that you are of the opinion Joseph was a member of this robber gang you speak of."

"I am," said Hand firmly. "When I got back here from New York, Captain Bartlett and Clark had practically sewed up the case by finding that skeleton. What other opinion was there except that the fellow had lost his life in the same way that Joseph and Buckley lost theirs? Evidently the search for hidden treasure went on here before Middleton left."

"What in blazes would he sell the house to me for if he had that treasure buried in it?" demanded the colonel.

"I'll admit that was a stumbling-block," said Hand. "You can't hope to solve crime though, unless you have imagination. Believe me, I rejected many possibilities before I selected the final one. The whole thing had the appearance of a gang split up—every man for himself, almost. I decided that Middleton had brought a fortune in loot out here and hid it in his house. Probably he had double-crossed the gang. He retired from business and, like as not, from leadership of the gang. They got on to him, Gonzalos was put into the house to watch Middleton."

"Yer a little off the track there," broke in Granley. "We knew he had the stuff out here. It was the last big haul he engineered. He told us we'd have to stow the stuff till the bulls got through lookin' for it. We put Zechalli—that's Gonzalos—in here to look out for our interests, d'ye see? Go on, fella, if ya get astray, I'll steer ya back."

"Gonzalos," continued Hand, "undoubtedly decided to double-cross the whole gang. I think he intended to find the treasure and get away with it himself. He went about his search in an intelligent way. The scepter among these jewels, centuries old, is an iron staff encrusted with precious stones. In Schweizburg iron is symbolic of valor. Several of these decorations are iron, also. Gonzalos devised a magnetic detector that would lead him to his prize. With it he got too close to the treasure and, as a consequence, lost his life. Middleton threw the body into an almost inaccessible spot in the wood. But, as we have seen, Gonzalos dead was a far more deadly enemy to his slayer than he ever was alive. Middleton found himself compelled to explain Gonzalos's disappearance to the gang. He hit upon a clever ruse. Don't you think he might have told the gang Gonzalos actually did find the jewels and had disappeared with them? I must admit I can't just understand Middleton's subsequent actions. The only plausible hypothesis was that he left the jewels right here. That has now been proved correct. But why he didn't move the jewels to a safer place I don't understand. Instead he hired a detective to protect him from the gang."

"Yer off the track again," said Granley in his horrid, slurring speech. "He didn't hire no detective. The detective was Pete, one of me two pals, this one right here. Middleton didn't hire him; he took him in whether he liked it or not. Pete kep' his eye on things to see that the chief didn't move nothin'. The rest of us went off lookin' for Zechalli—or Gonzalos, if ya like that better. Pete's a sun-of-a-gun. He kep' his eyes open—the chief knew better than to fool with him!"

"That explains it," said Hand, with satisfaction. "Middleton's gory ruse didn't work so perfectly as he had hoped. He still had the gang on his neck. He maneuvered to throw them further off the track. Rather clever scheme, too. He proceeded to build a new house and moved into it. You get the impression he intended to give—no further interest in the old house. The gang would take the cue and leave Middleton alone, at last assured that Gonzalos was the man to seek. Someone in that gang had a head on his shoulders. He saw through the scheme."

"It was Joe Decker," growled the gangster. "How ya found this all out, fella, is two jumps beyond me."

"A process of reasoning," said Hand shortly. "I suspected it was Joseph. Middleton, no doubt, intended to sell this place to some innocent person. He could let the treasure lie safely in the walls, unsuspected and secure, until he felt it safe to retrieve it. By a lucky chance Joseph was able to call his bluff. You were looking for a house, Colonel. Joseph arranged for you to buy this one. Middleton, of course, could only have betrayed himself by refusing to sell it to you. His strategy was turned on himself. His position was more precarious than ever.

"You moved into the house, Colonel. Joseph came to live with you. He induced you to engage Buckley, another member of the gang. Together they searched for the treasure. They didn't know about Gonzalos's little magnetic needle—he had taken the secret of it with him. At length Joseph and Buckley got to tampering with the cellar walls. Middleton, no doubt, was keeping secret track of their movements. He probably spied upon them at night. Buckley got too close to the treasure. He disappeared. I am quite certain Middleton placed his body in the receptacle that had contained the treasure. Middleton took the jewels away—probably the first chance he had had to do it."

"How about Furness?" I demanded.

"I think Furness was an emissary from Granley," explained Hand. "No doubt Granley had become suspicious of Joseph and Buckley. It is easy to think that the pair had decided to appropriate the treasure for themselves. Gangsters are forever suspicious of one another. Such faithlessness and intrigue are always present in their affairs. Without them they would be practically invincible. Heaven knows what secret plottings lay behind this. But the case had narrowed down. Dr. Metz was eliminated. We had Middleton, Furness, and Clara Compstock."

"What about—was she involved in this?" asked the colonel, almost timidly.

"She was," replied Hand. "Joseph, Furness, and Clara Compstock were all members of the gang. Gangdom throws peculiar people together—fancy Joseph and Clara Compstock operating together! They were, however, on a rather higher plane than these chaps we have captured tonight. The New York police have established that those three helped dispose of the stolen goods. They traveled about the country as trustworthy, accredited representatives of the famous house of Middleton's in New York. I have kept in touch with the New York police, you see.

"Now, Clara Compstock and Furness were differently situated. Furness was opposed to Middleton and terrified by him. Mrs. Compstock, on the other hand, was conferring with him and receiving money from him. She was riding two horses, for she was playing along with the gang, too. I'm coming to that. At any rate, Mrs. Compstock and Furness were neither of the type to have committed the murders. Middleton was by far the most likely, all things considered.

"Joseph was left in a quandary the day after Buckley disappeared. He must have had two lines of thought: either that Buckley had found the treasure and departed with it, or that Middleton had killed Buckley and, likewise, departed with the treasure. He meant to find out what he could. He couldn't find Buckley, but he could find Middleton. Therefore he forced Middleton to make an appointment with him in the den that night. What prompted Joseph to shoot I don't know. Middleton's bullet-proof vest saved him from the first shot. There was no second shot, because Middleton picked up the dagger and buried it in Joseph's heart."

"How are you going to prove that?" asked Captain Bartlett.

"By Granley," replied Hand, "and, I hope, by the bullet-
proof vest."

The captain dropped to his knees beside Middleton's
still body. He ran his hands over the torso.

"He's wearing it!" he cried, looking up at Hand.

"I thought he would be," replied my friend, dropping
down beside the captain. "He needed its protection, since
he was out to meet his precious gang of thugs. It's just
possible that we can find the mark of Joseph's bullet."

He quickly unbuttoned Middleton's vest. Under the
shirt was revealed a brown garment. It was of steel mail,
covered with canvas. This we could see, because the canvas
on the left side was torn and pierced, and the steel links
beneath it were bent and twisted.

"There it is," breathed the captain.

"The last link in my chain," said Hand simply.

"Say," said Granley, who seemed not to be interested
in this last episode, "would ya mind tellin' me where ya
found them sparklers?"

"Not at all," grinned Hand, rising to his feet. "I have
a small magnet among the articles that I carry round with
me. With it I fashioned a detector somewhat like the one
we found on the skeleton. According to my theory, Middleton had taken the treasure out of this house. I hoped he
had taken it to his new house, and I was not disappointed.
I broke into his house. With my detector I found the treasure buried in his cellar. I had the advantage of his hurried
disposal of it. It was easier to find than it was when it was
buried here.

"But I told you, Colonel, that I had some further information concerning Mrs. Compstock. It is this. Clark
and I, by a lucky circumstance, stumbled upon the lady
sending messages to the gang. She put them into an old

stump down the road, where, I have no doubt, they were called for by Granley or one of his men. I made a copy of the first one we found. Here it is. I'll read it:

"'We are positive now, but they and you are to be in the same old funny little house. If we don't see you, look for us. Yet don't think I do not want this thing to happen. You see it, don't you?'

"Code, of course," went on Hand. "Pretty simple code, too. I fathomed it on my second try. As an experiment, I tried reading only every other word. Of course, it made no sense. But then I tried reading only every third word. Immediately it became clear. It is:

"'Positive they are in old house. Don't look yet. I want to see you.'

"I took it to mean that Mrs. Compstock was positive the jewels were in Middleton's old house. She was also warning the gang not to risk searching for them yet, and asking one of them, Granley, no doubt, to confer with her.

"After finding that message I felt pretty sure I could control matters to suit myself. Therefore, when I was ready, I asked you to close up the house, Colonel, and move out. That, you see, created a sufficient reason for Mrs. Compstock to remove her objection to Granley's searching the house at once. I have no doubt that she left a note for him yesterday afternoon, right after she learned that you were leaving, telling him that probably he would be able to break into the house tonight. At any rate, she left another, right after you left this afternoon, telling him the coast was clear. I got that one, too. It was:

"'It seems all fog will clear. If you begin, I will search for you immediately.'

"Reading every third word, that one went:

"'All clear. Begin search immediately.'

"To this I added:

"'I will look for you first. Don't go in some other library.'

"When decoded, that supplement reads:

"'Look first in library.'

"Then I put the note back into the stump. Now you see why I felt confident that they would go straight to the library after breaking into the house."

"The man's a genius," sang out Captain Bartlett.

"Just the same, I nearly bungled the whole affair," said Hand. "It's just a wonder that Middleton didn't see us prowling round this house tonight. He must have arrived after we did, thank fortune!"

"By gad!" exclaimed the colonel, suddenly. "What was Middleton doing here, anyway? He said yesterday he was going away for a few days."

"I imagine he altered his plans when he heard you were going, Colonel," smiled Hand. "I banked on his being present when your house was broken into. You may be sure that it was no altruistic motive that brought him here to protect your property. To say that it made him nervous to have these men about would be to put it mildly. He knew that if they tore your house to pieces, it would cause a commotion, and he was afraid of what it might lead to. He was vitally interested in driving them away from here. But now, Granley, what have you to tell me? I think you witnessed Decker's murder."

"Right again," said Granley. "I was here, seein' what I could find out for m'self. I seen the light was on, and I got up behind that bush by the winder. Joe Decker and some other guy is havin' a long powwow. Joe wants dope—he never could get along without it—and the other guy wants money. Joe ain't got neither. He finally kids the other guy into givin' him some snow, promisin' to pay for it later. When the peddler's gone, who pops in but Furness? He's

my man—yer right. He tells Joe he thinks he bumped
Muth off and got the sparklers. Joe says that's a lot o'
bunk, that the chief must be the guy. Furness don't believe
him and gets next to him with some phony business they
was wrapped up in over in England once before. Joe gets
sore as blazes. He shows Furness just how he can send him
up the river and kicks him out.

"Well, Furness ain't hardly out of the room than I no-
tices somebody standin' out on the lawn, lookin' at the
winder. He walks up to the door, and I seen it was the
chief—Middleton. He's a bad actor, or he was—bump ya
off in a second! He walks in on Joe, and the two of 'em
gets their heads together. I tries to hear what they're sayin', but they're talkin' so low I can't get it."

"Were they smoking cigars?" asked Hand.

"Yeah. The chief lights one up. Joe was smokin' one,
and he lights up another. Well, they was at it for quite a
while. Finally Joe hops up and paces back and forth, angry
like. At last the chief gets up, grins at Joe, and starts for
the door. Holy Moses! I seen Joe Decker put his hand in
the pocket of his bathrobe and shoot right through the
pocket at the chief. Middleton gets a jolt, but the bullet
don't seem to hurt him. He grabs a knife, and before I
knows it, he sinks it into Joe's chest right up to the hilt!
Joe goes down, and the chief leans over him. I wish ya
could of seen his face! He takes the end of Joe's bathrobe
and wipes off the handle of the knife. Think of havin' the
presence of mind! Then he ducks out quick. I was afraid to
move for a while, but finally I made tracks. That's about
all I can tell ya."

"All right, Granley," said Hand. "If you testify in court
like that, it will help you. Withers, I'll leave you to get
these men to the county penitentiary. Furness is already
there. I'll leave the colonel, Captain Bartlett, and Mac-
Clintock to help you guard these fellows. There is only

one other member of the gang unaccounted for. Clark, you and I will pay a last call on Mrs. Compstock."

I know the reader is wondering what became of Clara Compstock. I know just as well that I cannot tell him. When Hand and I arrived at her house that night, we found O'Brine and the cook having a tête-à-tête in the kitchen about Ireland. There was no one else in the house. It was Hand's opinion, and it still is, that the lady betook herself to a safe place to await the outcome of Granley's expedition to the colonel's house. Hearing no subsequent word from him, and seeing later in the papers of his arrest, she probably disappeared as quietly as possible. I always take Hand's word for everything; so I suppose that is what happened. The colonel, at least, heaved a sigh of relief. After all, it would have been hard for him to testify against her.

Colonel Decker's old house in Mill Ridge has stood unoccupied since the night Middleton ended his miserable life in it. The colonel bought an expensive place on Long Island, where he lives with his daughter and son-in-law. He offered me the privilege of fishing on his Mill Ridge property. Not long ago I availed myself of it.

I took a taxi from Barkersville—the same we had encountered in Mrs. Compstock's lane. As we drove down the road to the colonel's property, I looked out over the swamp. The hillocks were floating on a sea of fog, just as they were on that last day. We turned into the weed-grown drive. A feeling of uneasiness stole over me as I looked up at the house—lonely, deserted, a dismal monument to the tragedies it had witnessed. I looked back at the grim lake of fog that hid the Great Swamp.

As the driver brought the car to a stop at the front porch, I leaned forward and touched him on the shoulder.

"You can start right up again," I said. "I've changed my mind—I'm going back."

NOVEMBER JOE

DETECTIVE OF THE WOODS

H. HESKETH-PRICHARD

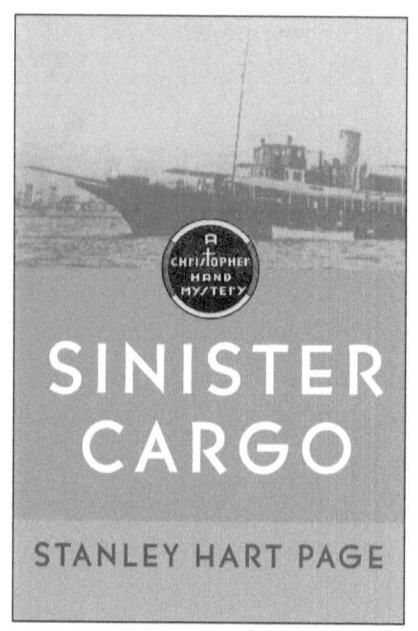

SINISTER CARGO

STANLEY HART PAGE

FOOL'S GOLD

STANLEY HART PAGE

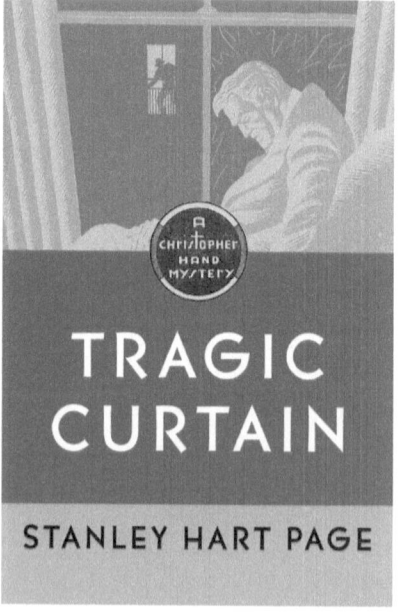

TRAGIC CURTAIN

STANLEY HART PAGE

COACHWHIP PUBLICATIONS

COACHWHIPBOOKS.COM

FEAR OF FEAR

FLORENCE RYERSON
COLIN CLEMENTS

MURDER IN THE FAMILY

NICE PEOPLE MURDER

Mary Hastings Bradley

3 DETECTIVES
FEMMES AUDACIEUSES
MERWIN · SOMERVILLE · FOOTNER

THE 5.18 MYSTERY

J. Jefferson Farjeon

COACHWHIP PUBLICATIONS

COACHWHIPBOOKS.COM

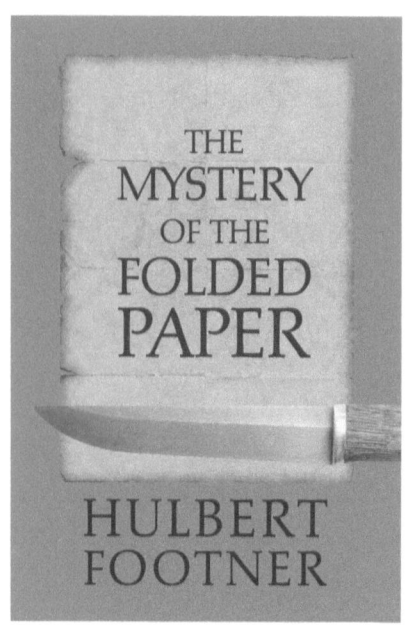

THE
MYSTERY
OF THE
FOLDED
PAPER

HULBERT
FOOTNER

The
Hollow Tree
Mystery

MADELON ST. DENIS

VIRGINIA RATH

FERRYMAN,
TAKE HIM ACROSS!

No Face to
Murder
EDITH HOWIE

COACHWHIP PUBLICATIONS

COACHWHIPBOOKS.COM

THE QUINNY HITE
MYSTERIES
CHINESE RED · HERE LIES THE BODY

RICHARD BURKE

I'll Hate Myself in the Morning

Murder on the Left Bank

Elliot Paul

MURDER'S COMING

GRAVE WITHOUT GRASS

BY
DONALD CLOUGH CAMERON

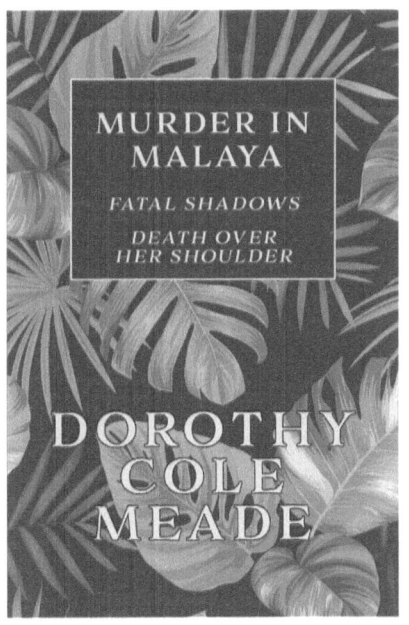

MURDER IN
MALAYA

FATAL SHADOWS

DEATH OVER
HER SHOULDER

DOROTHY
COLE
MEADE

COACHWHIP PUBLICATIONS

COACHWHIPBOOKS.COM

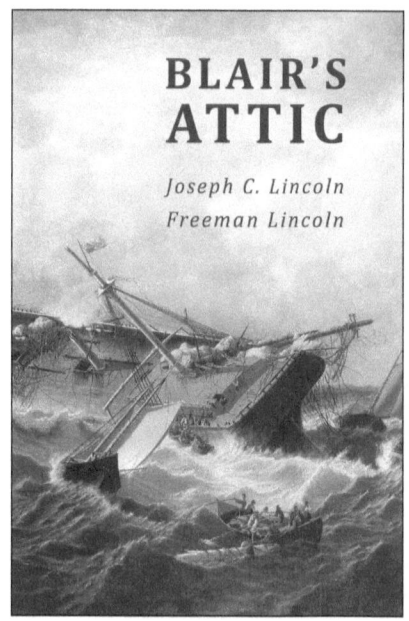

COACHWHIP PUBLICATIONS

COACHWHIPBOOKS.COM

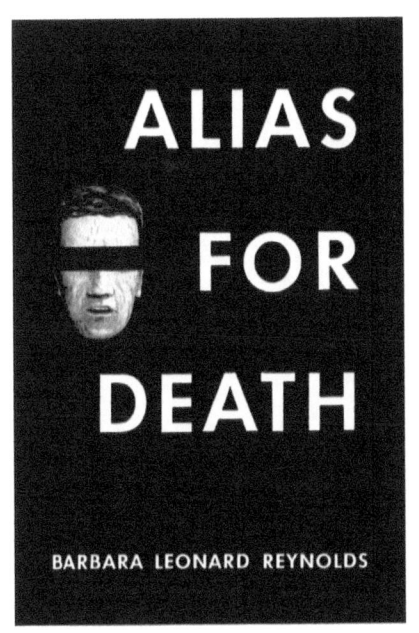

ALIAS FOR DEATH

BARBARA LEONARD REYNOLDS

THERE IS NO RETURN
THE ADELAIDE ADAMS MYSTERIES
ANITA BLACKMON

Jack Dolph

MURDER MAKES THE MARE GO

FEAR CAME FIRST

VERA KELSEY

COACHWHIP PUBLICATIONS
COACHWHIPBOOKS.COM

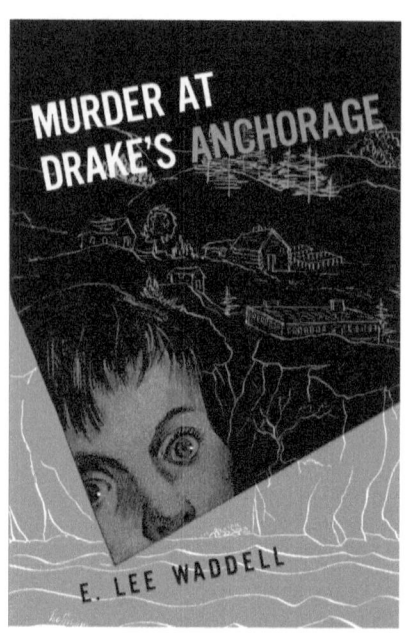

MURDER AT DRAKE'S ANCHORAGE

E. LEE WADDELL

MURDER AT THE KENTUCKY DERBY

CHARLES PARMER

MURDER ENDS THE SONG

ALFRED MEYERS

3 DETECTIVES
MURDER ON THE RAILS
WHITECHURCH • THORNE • TORGERSON

COACHWHIP PUBLICATIONS
COACHWHIPBOOKS.COM

THE FIRES AT FITCH'S FOLLY

KENNETH WHIPPLE

DRESSED TO KILL

Emma Lou Fetta

GRIMM DEATH

THE GROUSE MOOR MURDER

JOHN FERGUSON

COACHWHIP PUBLICATIONS

COACHWHIPBOOKS.COM